THE EDEN STORIES

The Late, Great Planet Jupiter

TERRY TOLER

The Late, Great Planet Jupiter

Published by: BeHoldings Publishing

Copyright @2020, BeHoldings, LLC
Terrytoler.com
All Rights Reserved

Unless otherwise noted, all Scripture quotations are taken from Holy Bible, New Living Translation, copyright © 1996, 2004, 2015 by Tyndale House Foundation. Used by permission of Tyndale House Publishers, Inc., Carol Stream, Illinois 60188. All rights reserved.

Cover and interior designs: BeHoldings Publishing
Editor: Jeanne Leach

For information, address support@terrytoler.com.

Our books can be purchased in bulk for promotional, educational and business use. Please contact your bookseller or the BeHoldings Publishing Sales department at: sales@terrytoler.com.

For booking information email: booking@terrytoler.com
First U.S. Edition: January 2021
Printed in the United States of America
ISBN 978-1-7352243-4-3

OTHER BOOKS BY TERRY TOLER

Fiction

The Longest Day
The Reformation of Mars
The Great Wall of Ven-Us
Saturn: The Eden Experiment
The Late, Great Planet Jupiter
Save The Girls
The Ingenue
The Blue Rose
Saving Sara
Save The Queen
No Girl Left Behind
The Launch
Body Count
Mercury Protocols

Non-Fiction

How to Make More Than a Million Dollars
The Heart Attacked
Seven Years of Promise
Mission Possible
Marriage Made in Heaven
21 Days to Physical Healing
21 Days to Spiritual Fitness
21 Days to Divine Health
21 Days to a Great Marriage
21 Days to Financial Freedom
21 Days to Sharing Your Faith
21 Days to Mission Possible
7 Days to Emotional Freedom
Uncommon Finances
Uncommon Marriage
Uncommon Health
Suddenly Free
Feeling Free

For more information on these books and other resources visit TerryToler.com.

Rapturo: "to seize upon by force; to snatch up."

THE
LATE, GREAT PLANET
JUPITER

1

Red Spot, Jupiter
September 12, 2061

There were too many people on Jupiter. Then there weren't.

Jack Wolf, Vice Prescom of the Jupiter Order of States, sat at the desk of his predecessor, Prescom Andrew Bartlett, in his oval-shaped office in Red Spot, the modern day capital of Jupiter, staring at the cover of the assessment report sitting on the desk in front of him. Prescom was short for Presidential Commander.

He'd opened it a few minutes before, read the first line, and then unceremoniously slammed it shut.

Estimated number of people missing: 19 billion.

Nineteen billion people vanished into thin air. Poof. Like a puff of smoke in the wind. Including Prescom Andrew Bartlett. Jack and Andrew sat in that very office the day before, when at exactly 3:30 p.m., Prescom Bartlett suddenly disappeared. Only his clothes were left behind in the chair where he was sitting. A few seconds later, the power went off.

They were discussing, ironically, of all things, the overpopulation of the planet. Jupiter was two and half times larger than all the other planets in the solar system combined. With more than eighty-billion people, keeping up with the basic needs of a population that size had become almost unmanageable.

The daily food needs alone for that many people were astronomical. The average Jupiterian ate 1,885 pounds of food annually. Multiply that by eighty-billion people, and Jack wondered why he ever agreed to be Andrew's running mate in the last election. They'd run on a platform of solving the world's problems. Their first year of ruling Jupiter hadn't lived up to expectations. The meeting the day before had been unproductive. No good solutions were offered.

I guess we don't need as much food now.

Vice Prescom Wolf couldn't even manage the slightest grin for his own joke.

He looked back down at the report. No need to open it. The rest was obvious. Plane crashes. A commercial airmobile crashed into the Red Spot World Tower, a hundred and twenty-story sky riser, just blocks from their location. Over ten thousand were dead from that event alone. Millions of mobile crashes caused more deaths than had been counted and untold injuries. Hospitals, schools, businesses, and entire cities were without power. Looting, rioting, and panic filled the streets. Chaos. A run on the banks. Suicides. People were jumping from buildings and bridges.

Again, helping the food supply problem.

A slight rap on the door told him the Cabinet was ready for him in the conference room.

He took a deep breath. Drastic times called for decisive leadership, Bartlett always said. Andrew Bartlett was that type of Prescom. Not lacking in leadership abilities. His main problem was his charisma. He had a lot of it. People believed in him. What was wrong with that? When he over promised and under delivered, which he often did, he somehow convinced everyone things were going to be okay.

Wolf knew then, just as he knew now, things were not going to be okay. Life as they knew it had changed forever. He resented Bartlett. He disappeared and left him to clean up the mess.

If that was even possible.

* * *

"Where do we start?" Vice Prescom Wolf asked the twelve men and two women members of Bartlett's leadership cabinet. All of them were sitting around a large, red, solid-wood conference table with large, red, high-back chairs. A screen for audio visuals was at one end on the wall, but nothing was set up. There would be no presentations. The only reason they had lights and communications was because this was the Red House—the Prescom's personal residence along with his working offices. A powerful generator was providing much-needed electricity to the building so they could run the world. Or at least try to.

"Do we start with the estimated nineteen-billion people who are missing or the ten billion who are dead?" Wade Wilson, the Staff Chief for Vice Prescom Wolf asked.

"We start with the ten billion dead," Greg Jennings, the man over the Department of Interior replied immediately. "The nineteen billion are missing. Nothing we can do for them now."

"I disagree," J.B Hader, the head of the Department of Commerce retorted sharply. "The nineteen billion have left a huge deficiency in personnel. We're missing teachers, doctors, plumbers, scientists, engineers, architects, men and women who run the basic services of Jupiter. A third of all garbage men are missing for goodness sakes."

Jack Wolf found it strange that not one of the Cabinet members was missing. In fact, the preliminary report said that less than five percent of the government officials were part of the missing. A phenomenon he would think about at another time since an argument was about to break out among the cabinet members.

"Bodies are rotting in the streets!" someone shouted.

"I don't have enough policemen to maintain control!" another one bellowed a little louder than the other.

"Disease is going to start spreading very quickly. Another ten billion will die if we don't do anything," Greg Jennings said.

"Soon, people won't have enough food or clean water," the Director of the Department of Human Services spoke up for the first time.

"Gasoline supplies are shut off," Commerce Director Hader said, throwing his hands into the air.

"We need communications. All the lines are down and jammed." The Director of Infrastructure was over communications and transportation and put her concerns on the table.

"A third of my armed forces are gone. I can't guarantee I can protect the world from any rogue forces. I need fuel to power my tanks, planes, and ships. I need..." The Secretary of Defense David Nelson made sure he wasn't left out, and his deep booming voice was drowning out the others.

"The farmers need the fuel to power their machines to harvest their crops," the Secretary of Agriculture said during a slight lull in the hostilities.

"We need the fuel to get electricity back in the cities, so people have power in their houses," Hader retorted.

Everyone began talking over each other again.

"I need workers. Less than a dozen people out of a thousand showed up for work today," Hader added.

"If they don't have food, it doesn't matter how many people you have!"

"We need drugs and medicines," Susan Bates said. "Hospitals are running out. They need blood. The hospitals are without power. Nursing homes are running out of supplies. People are dying because their machines are off from no electricity." Susan Bates was in charge of the Federal drug regulations and distribution.

"Let them die! We need to focus all our resources on the living. We have to prioritize what we do have and make hard decisions."

Wolf wasn't sure who said it. Totally inappropriate whoever it was.

"My parents are in a nursing home! They'll die soon without medicine. I can't believe you'd be so cold," the Staff Chief Wilson said angrily.

"Well, my parents are missing. I don't even know where they are," Rhonda shouted.

"My son is missing," someone said. "My son was the pilot of a plane that went down. I have no idea what happened to him."

Wolf kept trying to speak over the fray but with no success. Tensions were boiling over. He had to do something quickly or the meeting would spiral completely out of control.

He put his fingers to his lips and let out a loud whistle that reverberated through the room.

"People!" Wolf said strongly. "Let's work the problem. Fighting among ourselves isn't going to help. We've all lost someone. I'm sorry about that. But every one of us has a job to do. The people are counting on us. That's why you were given this job. We have to pull together. Let's take things one at a time."

Hader started to speak again but Wolf stared him down.

"You're not even the Prescom," someone near the other end of the conference table said. That started another argument among themselves. The noise started as a low din and then erupted into a shouting match.

This time Staff Chief Wilson got everyone's attention, not with a whistle but with a loud, high-pitched scream, "Shut up!

Once he got their attention, he said, "The first order of business should be the swearing in of Vice Prescom Wolf as Prescom. Article twenty to the Founder's Document says that if the Prescom is incapacitated then the Vice Prescom will assume his duties temporarily. The Cabinet can declare that the Prescom is permanently incapacitated, and then Vice Prescom Wolf can become Prescom. It takes a two-thirds vote of the cabinet to find the Prescom is permanently incapacitated."

"How do we know he's not coming back?" someone asked.

"We don't know," another agreed.

"The country needs leadership. They need to see Vice Prescom Wolf become Prescom, so they have one person to rally around," Staff Chief Wilson argued.

"I agree," several around the room voiced.

"We should wait. Andrew may come back," Brock Benson said. He was Andrew's lifelong friend.

Another argument broke out as several resorted to name-calling. A fist fight might ensue if it wasn't stopped soon. Two men stood and faced each other with their fists balled.

"Gentlemen," Wolf said in a strong and authoritative voice to the two men. "Andrew is clearly incapacitated, and I've already assumed his duties temporarily. I think we should wait to vote to make it permanent until we see if he does come back. Let's give it three days and then discuss it again. We have bigger problems than that to worry about. For now, I'll assume his duties and authority but not his title."

A calm finally settled on the room. The two men sat back down, and the entire room let out a collective sigh.

"Let's take things one at a time," Wolf said. "Personally, I think we don't worry about the twenty-nine billion people who are not with us. We need to focus on those who are still alive. We have to get resources to them."

"What about the dead?" Jennings said.

"Let's discuss that," Wolf replied. "Have all the cities gather their dead and bring them to one location just outside the city limits. Take a picture of each person. If they have an ID on them, then take the picture with the ID. That way we can identify them later."

"What do we do with the bodies?" Jennings asked.

"Burn them," Vice Prescom Wolf said.

Several started to object, but he raised his hand to tamp them down. "Greg is right," the Vice Prescom said emphatically. "If we don't get rid of the bodies, we'll have a plague on our hands. There's no way the coroners and funeral homes can process that many people. I hate to do it, but it's the best solution to the problem."

For four hours, they methodically addressed each issue of each person in the room.

"Gasoline shortages."

"Let's tap into the strategic reserves."

"How much food is in the supply chain?"

"Ten days' worth."

"Get power and communications restored."

"Airplanes should remain grounded for a couple more days."

"Impose a curfew. Only essential personnel should be out on the streets after dark. Encourage everyone to remain in their homes if possible. Keep the streets clear for emergency vehicles."

Wolf was proud of the people in the room. They were trying their best to come up with solutions. When they couldn't, the matter was tabled for discussion at another time. By the end of the meeting, a skeleton plan had been developed, and everyone had their instructions on what to do.

They had a long road ahead of them, and he had to somehow get the people in the room to work as a team. They were all selected for their abilities. It took a certain ego to ascend to their level of success. Wolf would have to learn how to harness that ability and energy into overcoming almost insurmountable problems. Today had been a good start in that direction.

Until... they were brought back to a stark reality.

"All children under eight are missing," Aria Decker said soberly.

A somber pall went over the room.

"Are you sure?" Wolf asked.

"Those are the reports."

"Are there any theories about what happened to them? To all of the missing..." Wolf asked.

Brock Benson was head of the Worldwide Intelligence Agency, known as the WIA and oversaw the collection of information and data. Most of the people in the room instinctively turned to him.

"Obviously, we don't know for sure, but we're developing some preliminary theories," he said, thumbing through some papers sitting on the table in front of him.

"What are some of the theories?" Wolf asked. "We all realize it's speculation. We won't hold you to any one of them."

"One theory is that aliens snatched them. As you know, there have been a lot of UFO sightings and activity recently. People have gone missing before. Some people claim they were abducted and brought back to Jupiter. Mostly we have discounted those accounts. But we're going back and revisiting them."

Wolf waved his hand dismissively. "There have always been rumors about aliens and UFOs. I've seen everything that's classified, and there's no evidence of life on other planets. No evidence there's ever been life in our solar system. I don't think that's a very plausible theory."

"Another is some kind of solar burst."

"We haven't seen any unusual solar or cosmic activity," Neil Burlington said. He was the head of Science and Research. "If such activity occurred, we would've detected it."

"Another theory is a sudden loss in gravity and only certain people were affected and were suddenly propelled into the atmosphere where they burned up," Brock said.

"Why did it affect some and not others?" Wolf asked.

Brock just shrugged his shoulders.

"Wouldn't we have seen them go into the air?" Rhonda asked. "My personal driver is one of the ones missing. He was driving me home. He just disappeared. One second, he was there, the next he was gone. Fortunately, the mobile was stopped at a light, and I was able to get it stopped before we hit anyone. If it was a sudden loss of gravity, how did he go through the ceiling of the mobile?"

"Like I said, it's just a theory. I didn't say it was a good one," Brock retorted.

"Anything else?" Wolf asked.

"That's all we've got so far."

"Okay. Keep working on it."

Aria Decker raised her hand to speak. Aria was the newest member of the cabinet. The head of Diplomatic Relations. A new position Prescom Bartlett had established three months ago. One of her main responsibilities was interacting with the various religious groups on the planet.

"I have a theory," she said after Wolf called on her.

"What do you think happened?" he asked.

"The Seizure."

2

When Danielle "Danni" Howell opened the door to her house, her mom was standing there with her hand on her hip and a not-very-happy look on her face.

"Where have you been, young lady?" Mom said.

"I was at school," Danni answered dismissively, even though fear was rising inside her. She hadn't been at school. Or at least not after first period.

"You weren't at school. Where were you?" her mom said accusingly.

Her mom obviously knew something. Maybe not everything but enough to know she wasn't at school. *How did she know?* From experience, Danni knew that every time she did something wrong, she always got caught. Somehow her parents always knew what she was doing as if they had a spy camera following her around, watching her every move.

"I was with some friends," Danni said as she walked out of the room in a huff and down the hall into her bedroom. A room she shared with her twelve-year-old sister Avery, who must have followed their mom down the hall because she came in the bedroom right after her with a wide grin on her face, obviously delighting in her older sister's latest troubles.

"The school called and said you left after first period," her mom retorted.

"It's Senior Skip Day."

"You're not a senior! You're only a sophomore."

Danni sat down on her bed with one leg crossed under the other. Her fear had turned to anger.

"I'm sixteen. I never get to do anything." She decided to play the victim. Sometimes it worked on her mom. Never on her dad.

"Wait until you have three kids. Then you'll know what it feels like to never do anything. With your brother's ball practice and your sister's music lessons, school, church, laundry, cooking, cleaning up after you, I don't have a minute for myself. Would it hurt you to help around the house sometimes?"

Danni wasn't the only one who knew how to play the victim. Her mom was much more experienced than she was. Now she felt guilty. She actually didn't help around the house much. Mostly, she stayed in her room on her caller or computer. The last few months she'd become more and more withdrawn from her family. The school counselor said she might be depressed.

Danni shrugged her shoulders. "At least my room is clean," Danni said. That's all she could think of. She had no good comeback.

"That's because I cleaned it," Avery said, making a face at Danni from behind their mom's back.

"Shut up," Danni said.

"We don't use that language in this house," her mother said in an exasperated tone. "Now, where were you? And don't lie to me."

"We went to the mall and hung out."

"And?... You weren't at the mall all day. Where did you go?"

"We went to Liz's house." Liz was her best friend. Both her parents worked, so they had the house to themselves. Along with a couple boys who came over. Not much happened. Liz and the boys opened her parent's liquor cabinet and drank some, but she didn't. Her parents would kill her, she told them. Not literally, but they could make her wish she was dead. Sometimes she already wished she were.

"Were there any boys there?" her mom said sharply.

"Yes, Mom. There were lots of boys there. We had a big party. Got drunk. Are you satisfied? Is that what you want to hear? Your good

11

little girl let you down one more time. I'm sorry I'm not perfect like Avery."

Avery sat in the background, smiling smugly. The twelve-year old was the seemingly perfect child who never did anything wrong. Danni had always heard that the younger sister always struggled to live up to the feats of the older. In their family, it was the other way around. Avery got straight A's. Was pageant beautiful. Loved church, which was the main thing as far as her parents were concerned. Avery sang in the choir and on the worship team. She loved the youth group. Danni only went to church because they made her.

Danni felt so much hostility. She'd felt the pressure to be perfect since she was a little girl since her dad was pastor of the Red Spot Christian Church. For as long as she could remember, she was always being judged. She had to dress right, say all the right things, and know all the answers to the Bible quizzes. Always be on her best behavior. When she did something wrong, which was often, she was punished more severely than the other kids.

"Avery, go out there," her mom said, but Avery didn't leave right away. "Now!" she insisted. "And close the door," she added.

When Avery was gone, her mom said sweetly, "Honey, I don't expect you to be perfect. I just want what's best for you. You don't know it now, but when you're older you'll appreciate it."

"Yes, you do expect me to be perfect!" Danni shouted, surprising herself with the level of pent up frustration that was coming out. She'd always held it in and never really said how she felt. The words started spewing out like a geyser hurdling water from underground into the sky.

"Nothing I ever do is good enough for you." Tears welled up in Danni's eyes. "So, I skipped school. Once! So did a lot of kids. I get good grades. I have to be home by nine o'clock every night. Even Friday night. All my friends can stay out till midnight. Do you know how embarrassing it is to tell them I have to leave and go home just as everyone's getting there? The kids make fun of me. They call me 'goody two shoes.'"

"It's for your own good. Your dad and I love you. There's a lot of bad things that can happen to you at midnight."

"You don't trust me!"

"No, we don't," her mom said, raising her voice. "You have to earn our trust. Skipping school and lying about it isn't making me feel better about trusting you." She let out an exasperated sigh. A look of what seemed like regret crossed her Mom's face. She probably wished she hadn't said it quite like that.

The tension was building in the room.

"I'm going to ask you again," her mom said. "Were there any boys at Liz's house?"

"No!"

"I don't believe you."

"Why am I not surprised?"

"Give me your caller."

"Why?"

"You're grounded."

"I didn't do anything."

"For a week. Maybe longer. We'll see when your dad comes home."

"The school dance is Saturday!"

"You should've thought about that before you skipped school. Where's your caller?" Her mom started going through her backpack.

"Mom! Get out of my stuff."

"It's not your stuff. It's my stuff. I bought it for you." Her mom had her caller in her hand. It was ringing. She powered it off.

"Mom! I'm sorry. I won't skip school again." Danni was crying now. Tears were flowing down her face. She was madder than she'd ever been at her mom. This wasn't fair. She did skip school and there were boys there.

I made out with one of them. She wanted to shout the words at her mom.

Anything to hurt her like she was hurting. Nothing more than that happened. Now, she wished it had. But... she didn't even like the guy. He was a senior. She was afraid of him. Was it him or her parents she was really afraid of?

"Stay in your room until your dad gets home. He's not going to be very happy."

"I hate my life! I hate all of you! I'll just stay in my room until I die!" she shouted as her mom walked out and slammed the door. Danni threw a pillow against the door, then curled up in the bed, sobbing.

Ten minutes later, the power in the house went off.

3

The Same Day, 3:07 p.m.

Ruth Williams was trying to get her six-week-old daughter, Katherine, to stop crying. She'd tried everything. Changed her diaper, fed her, rocked her, stood holding her, walked around the house with her. Bounced her up and down. Nothing was working.

Ruth was exhausted. She hadn't slept through the night in six weeks. Before that, nine months of pregnancy had taken its toll. She had to be hospitalized for the last two weeks from complications. The doctors wouldn't let her out of bed for risk of potentially losing the baby. Her life also was in danger for a while they'd said. After eighteen hours of labor, Kate came into the world. Nothing has been the same since.

Her caller rang. Her husband Jake was calling.

"Hi honey," she said. "How's work going?"

"It's going well. How's Kate?"

Kate, as they called her, had quieted down giving Ruth a welcomed respite from the screaming. Her ears were still ringing. "She's good. Loud as ever. I can't believe lungs that small can produce such a loud scream."

"Are you okay?"

"Katherine has been a handful," Ruth said with a sigh. "I don't know what I'm doing wrong. She won't stop crying." A pang of guilt sliced through her like a knife. Her mother had six kids—four in diapers at one time—and somehow, she had managed. She came and visited for two weeks after Kate was born and was a big help. But she lived five-hundred miles away and now was no help other than the occasional moral encouragement.

"When are you going to be home?" Ruth asked, dreading the answer.

"I have to work late tonight."

"Again? That's the third night in a row. I could really use your help. We miss you."

"It's only temporary. I'm in training. As soon as that's over, things will settle down. I'm sorry. I miss you too." Jake had recently started a new job as regional sales manager for a food and beverage supply company. The job paid more jupes but required longer hours. He took it for the medical benefits. Almost all of the delivery was paid for by the insurance company. A godsend, considering all the complications had created an astronomical hospital bill.

"Kate's growing up and you're missing it."

Jake chuckled. "She's only six weeks old. I think I have time before she's grown."

"It's really hard," Ruth said, choking back the tears, her voice cracking as she said it.

"Do you want me to call my mother? She can come over."

"No!" Ruth said abruptly. "I can handle it."

Jake's mother, Naomi, lived nearby and was helpful, but that only made Ruth feel guiltier. Naomi had the magic touch. All she had to do was pick Kate up, and she'd stop crying.

"She won't mind," Jake said.

"I said I can handle it," Ruth said sharply.

"OK. Call her if you need her. I'm sorry about dinner. I'll be home as soon as I can. Love you."

"Love you," Ruth answered back half-heartedly as Kate started crying again.

A few minutes later, the caller rang again.

Naomi.

"Hello, sweety. How's my baby girl?"

She's my baby girl, Ruth wanted to say, but she didn't want to be rude.

"We've had a rough day," Ruth said honestly as more guilt came over her.

She loved Naomi, and her mother-in-law meant well. She didn't try to make Ruth feel inadequate even though she did. Naomi had the perfect home. The perfect marriage. The perfect husband. And had raised the perfect son.

That was true. Ruth adored Jake. She couldn't have asked for a better husband. Whatever Naomi did in raising him, she should be commended. Jake was as perfect as his mother. A fact that made her feel even more inadequate. She wasn't the perfect wife. As much as she tried, she never felt like the house was clean enough, the food cooked well enough, her body sexy enough. Especially after the pregnancy. She had twenty unwanted pounds that wouldn't go away.

And what happened to her hips? Kate had pushed them out wider than they were before. Naomi was thin and perfectly curved. How did she do it? Ruth had asked her once, and Naomi replied, "Good genes and walking five miles a day."

How could Ruth walk five miles a day? She barely had the energy to get out of bed in the morning.

"I'm coming over to help you," Naomi said, interrupting her thoughts. Jake had obviously called her.

"It's not necessary. I've got it under control." Kate was screaming at the top of her lungs now in her crib in the other room. Ruth had put her there when the caller rang so Naomi wouldn't hear her crying. Kate was so loud Naomi could still hear her through the caller.

"Oh, my poor baby. I can hear her crying. She wants her Nana. I'll be right there." Naomi hung up before Ruth could protest further. If she were honest, she was glad she was coming over. She could use the break.

Ruth walked back in the room and picked Kate up and checked her diaper again. It was clean.

"What's wrong, baby?" she said as she paced the floor, bouncing Kate up and down.

She tried everything. Pacifier. A bottle. Kate just spit it up. She wasn't hungry. A friend told her that if you've checked everything and nothing was wrong, then just lay your child in the bed and let them cry. It won't hurt them.

"You don't want her to learn that you'll pick her up when she cries," she had said.

"I feel so bad when she's crying."

"That's what she wants you to feel."

"She's six-weeks old. I don't think she's smart enough to think that yet."

"Trust me. You're spoiling her."

"I don't think I can do it. It breaks my heart to hear her crying all alone in her room."

Ruth had tried it a few nights and couldn't do it for longer than ten minutes. She had a soft heart. As soon as Kate cried, she had to pick her up. But even that wasn't working.

Maybe I should try it again.

She laid Kate back down in the bed and swaddled her in a blanket. The baby monitor was on the table, and she checked to make sure it was on. The other end was in her bedroom. She went to her own bedroom and laid down. Kate was still screaming.

Ruth started crying. Slowly at first and then deeper sobs. After ten minutes or so, Kate fell asleep, and so did she.

The power flickered on and off and then went off completely waking her. It took a few seconds to get her bearings. An eerie silence filled the room. Kate wasn't crying.

She fell asleep. Finally.

How long was I asleep? She looked at her watch.

Only ten minutes.

The nap was short, but Ruth felt a little better. With Kate asleep, she'd use this time to get dinner ready for her and Naomi, who'd be arriving soon. More pressure. Ruth wasn't a good cook. Naomi could be a gourmet chef at a restaurant if she wanted. Jake never seemed to care that she couldn't cook like his mother, but Ruth was determined to get better.

Then she realized she couldn't cook with the power off.

Her parents had always told her not to open the refrigerator door when the power went out. That would let the cold air escape. If she kept it closed, it would stay cold longer until the power came back on. The power going out was unusual. So many people lived on Jupiter that the power company often performed rolling blackouts to conserve energy. Especially during the hottest months of the year when people used their air conditioners. However, the rich and powerful lived in Red Spot, so they made sure the power was almost always on.

Fall had come to Red Spot along with milder temperatures. This power outage was probably just routine maintenance. She walked back in the bedroom to lie back down.

Her mother had always told her to sleep while her baby was sleeping.

She felt restless.

I should check on her.

She's fine.

A sense of satisfaction came over her. She really did love her life. Jake was a wonderful husband. Kate was a beautiful baby. Her mother always said she should thank God for all her blessings. When her sister had tragically died in a mobile wreck when they were young, Ruth decided she didn't believe in God. Jake did and went to church every Sunday. He attended Red Spot Christian Church. She went with him a couple of times. Now that she had a baby, she should go more often.

Unable to fall asleep, she got back up and went into the kitchen. The power was still off. She checked her caller to make sure it was fully charged. *No signal.* That was strange. No power and no caller service had never happened as long as she could remember.

Some sirens blared at a distance. Several.

Must be a fire or something.

A feeling of dread suddenly came over her. Unlike anything she'd ever felt before.

Kate.

She dropped her caller on the counter and walked quickly into Kate's room. Her mouth flew open in astonishment.

Kate was gone! The only thing in the crib were the swaddling clothes.

4

Carter Hall sat in a chair in his living room, downing his second glass of strong drink. It would take at least two more before the pain would start to go away. Well... not go away, just buried deep enough to where he wouldn't feel it. Like a drowning man. He read where a drowning person gets an overwhelming sense of calm after the panic goes away and at that exact moment right before death overcomes him. That's what he felt like.

He was drowning in grief. The only difference was the drowning man was put out of his misery within a couple of minutes. His grief continued, day after day, night after night. Tomorrow, he would wake up from his drunken stupor, and the pain would start all over again. He'd put up with it until around three and then start the ritual all over again.

Carter stared at the blank vision screen. The power had gone out, and the shows he usually pretended to watch had disappeared into a sea of black. Not that he cared. Vision was boring. But it helped pass the time. He had no job and nothing to distract him from his misery. Soap operas, game shows, and reruns helped him make it to three o'clock without going completely insane.

He never let himself drink before three. The self-control allowed him to convince himself he wasn't an alcoholic. He got up and walked over to the kitchen to pour another drink. Another attempt at self-control. He didn't keep the bottle of liquor next to him in the living room. In order to drink, he had to make himself work for it.

"This one's for Taylor," he said as he raised the glass to toast his soon-to-be ex-wife. Seven years they'd been married. She cheated on him four times... that he knew of. He kept taking her back after she begged for forgiveness and promised never to be unfaithful again. The last time was four months ago. He'd finally had the courage to kick her out. She moved in with the last guy until he beat her up and then kicked her out on the streets. The last he heard; she was working as a prostitute on Sixth street in downtown Red Spot. About seven blocks from their condo.

A loud explosion startled him out of his slight buzz. The ground shook, and the glasses in his cabinet rattled so loud it sounded like they might break.

What was that?

He ran outside and onto the street, realizing once he got there that he had no shoes on. A large black pillar of smoke filled the sky to the north. Coming from downtown, where the skyscrapers were. A former firefighter, his first instinct was to run toward the smoke. He'd done that four months ago and had gotten fired when he ran into a burning house to save an eighty-seven-year-old man. The Chief ordered him to stay out of the house until they could get the fire on the roof under control. He disobeyed the order and was suspended, then fired, pending an appeal. The fact he saved the man was no consolation to his boss, even if it was to him.

Taylor?

Why was she the first thing he thought of? She worked in that direction. He ran back inside and put on his running shoes. He used to run five to ten miles a day. He bolted out of the house and down the street. On foot would get him there faster than in his mobile. A number of mobiles were strewn along the street. Some had crashed, others were vacant and in strange positions resting on lawns, or up against the curb or a parked mobile. One was smashed into a house, resting in one of the front rooms.

Strange? What's happening?

The scene unfolding didn't make sense to him. What did the wrecked mobiles have to do with the explosion? Two were in the middle of the street, mangled, having obviously crashed into each other. He stopped to look inside. No one was there. Clothes were laying on the front and back seat of one, in the front seat of the other.

Where were the people who were driving the mobiles, and why weren't they wearing their clothes?

He quickened his pace. At first, he saw people milling around, almost in a daze. Then he saw a throng of people, running his way. Panicked looks were on their faces. All ages were running as fast as they could toward him. Many looked like they hadn't run a block in years. Yet, they were sprinting toward him. Survival was a very powerful instinct.

Carter shouted at one, a middle-aged man, overweight and balding, running his way, "What happened?"

"People are missing," he said, but continued running before Carter could ask anything further. That answer didn't make sense. Missing? What did that mean?

The throng got thicker and so did the smoke. A number of people had black soot on their faces. Several had injuries and were bleeding as they ran frantically from the direction he was heading. They'd probably been hit by falling debris, he concluded.

He stopped to help a woman who fell on the pavement. She had twisted her ankle. He helped her to the side, out of the street as a firemobile barreled by. She grabbed Carter's arm as he started to run toward the chaos from where she'd come.

"Don't go that way. It's too dangerous. Save yourself."

"I'm a firefighter," he said. "I know CPR. Do you know what happened?"

"An airmobile hit the tower."

The tower was the largest office building in Red Spot. A skyscraper that spanned more than a hundred and twenty floors.

"A commercial airmobile?" Carter asked the woman.

"Yes," she said. Her hands shook uncontrollably. He helped her to her feet, and she hobbled away as he processed the information.

A commercial airmobile hitting a skyscraper could bring down the whole building. The diesel fuel would ignite the structure with the power of a bomb going off. He wondered if it was terrorism or an accident. How could an airmobile hit the tower by accident? It was a clear day. The sun was shining. Any pilot could see the tower from miles away. Unless the pilot was somehow disabled.

Carter came to a cross street where he needed to make a decision. Right took him to the tower, two blocks over. There, he could enter the building and help whoever he could. Left was the red-light district of Red Spot. The place he'd last seen Taylor. In one of the windows. It had nearly broken his heart.

He stood staring down the street, to the right, at the tower, assessing the situation. The wind had shifted and was blowing the thick black billows of smoke the other direction. The fire was two thirds of the way up the building. He could see the point of impact. Mangled metal and broken glass had fallen all the way past where he was standing. The airmobile wasn't visible. It must've gone into the building. He could see people trapped above the floors of impact. Saving them would be nearly impossible.

He saw a figure out of the corner of his eye falling from the building. Someone had jumped. Arms and legs were flailing as the man fell rapidly to the street below. Carter looked away right before the man hit the ground. That helped him make his decision. Nothing he could do for those people. It wasn't his job anymore anyway.

He turned the other direction and began running. Sprinting even faster this time. His pulse raced and his lungs burned. From the smoke, but also from being out of shape. He hadn't run this hard in several months. The effects of the alcohol were completely gone. The adrenaline had overwhelmed his senses to the point he wasn't even thinking clearly.

Would Taylor even want to see him? If he could even find her. He turned onto her block and ran past her window, not realizing it until he was near the end of the block. He turned back around and went by each window until he found the one where she'd been. None of the girls were in the windows.

He burst through the doors and up the stairs. At the top, he found a reception area with two doors. A woman was at the desk, trying frantically to make a call.

"I'm looking for Taylor," Carter said.

The woman pointed at the closed door. Carter tried to open it, but it was locked. One shove of the shoulder knocked it open. He heard several women scream. He ran toward the noise. The girls were huddled in the back room.

"Carter?" he heard Taylor say.

He turned toward the sound of his name but couldn't see where the sound had come from. When she called his name again, he finally realized she was standing behind another man.

"You're coming with me," Carter said strongly.

"No, she's not," the man standing in front of her said. "I own her. She belongs to me."

"Taylor," Carter said with authority. "Step out from behind the man and get your things. You're coming home."

Taylor tried to move, but the man put his arm up to block her.

Carter took two steps toward him.

The man pulled out a knife and swung it at him in one motion.

Carter reacted with lightning speed. He stepped inside the wild swing and brought the palm of his right hand under the man's nose, crushing it with such force the man fell to the ground in a heap.

"Let's go," Carter said, taking Taylor by the hand, ignoring the other girls who were stunned. Carter and Taylor ran down the steps and onto the street. Just as they did, the ground began to shake violently. They stopped and stared back at the tower where more floors were engulfed with flames. Suddenly, the top began to collapse on the building. He wanted to run but couldn't make his legs move. He could only stare as each floor descended onto the one below.

It sounded like a freight train rumbling on the tracks. They could hear the screams over the sirens and alarms still blaring. As a black pillar of smoke began to rise from the ashes of the building and headed their way, they started running the other direction. Carter looked back. The entire building was gone. Now there was nothing more than a large plume of smoke rolling down the street like an avalanche devouring all the light in its path.

He gripped Taylor's hand tighter. They ducked into an entryway of a building just off the street. The door was locked. There was no time to break it open. They were suddenly engulfed in the large plume of smoke. Everything was dark grey. They struggled to breathe. He pulled Taylor closer to him and covered her mouth and nose with his shirt. He turned his head away from the smoke, gasping for breath.

When the dust cleared enough to see at least a few feet in front of them, he took her hand, and they started running again.

"Where are we going?" she said.

"Home. We're going home. You'll be safe with me."

5

3:46 p.m.

"Naomi must have Kate," Ruth said aloud, trying to calm her fast beating heart.

How long was I asleep?

She stood in Kate's room, staring at the crib. Kate's clothes and blanket were laying there. Why would Naomi change her clothes? Why didn't she hear her come in?

"Naomi?" she called out as she walked out of her daughter's room. No response. She called out her name again. Then a third time, but there was no answer. Ruth was shouting by the third try.

A quick walk through the entire house confirmed that Naomi was not there, and there was no sign of Kate. Sheer panic gripped her as she suddenly had trouble catching her breath. She tried to calm herself down. The only explanation was Naomi had gotten to the house, came inside, and took Kate somewhere outside.

The back porch.

The back door was locked. Naomi couldn't have gone out that door and then locked it from the inside. Ruth opened it anyway and stepped on the back deck, scanning the backyard.

"Naomi! Kate!" She shouted their names several times.

Ruth walked back inside, closed the door, and walked quickly to the front window and looked out. Naomi's mobile wasn't there. Her thoughts were processing as fast as a calculator, trying to keep herself from thinking the worst.

She must've taken Kate for a drive to get her to quit crying.

That sometimes worked.

But how did the front door get locked? She unlocked it and looked outside, walking all the way out to the street. Sirens were still blaring in the distance. The power was off through the entire block. No one was milling around. She looked both directions and didn't see Naomi or Kate anywhere.

She ran back inside, tears were now streaming down her face. This time, she almost ran through the house, looking in every closet, every nook and cranny. Under the beds. Behind every closed door including all the kitchen cabinets and pantry.

Where is my baby?

Anger and fear were welling up inside along with the tears. If Naomi did take Kate, she shouldn't have done so without telling her. She grabbed her caller off the counter. The signal bar was still not registering any power. She tried calling Jake, but it didn't go through.

A message came on the caller saying, "All circuits are busy now. Try your call later."

Naomi's number was in recent calls, so she hit the contact, and it dialed Naomi's number, but the same message resounded through her caller.

A door slammed shut. Outside, coming from the driveway. Ruth raced to the front door and opened it. Naomi was walking up the sidewalk toward her with nothing in her arms but her purse.

Ruth was nearly hysterical.

"Do you have Kate?"

"Why would I have her? I just got here."

"Oh my God! My baby is missing!"

Naomi ran past Ruth and into the house and into Kate's room.

"Where is she?"

"I don't know. I thought she was with you. I laid down for a few minutes. I didn't think I fell asleep. Maybe I did." Ruth rubbed her hand against the top of her head. Then rubbed her eyes. Fidgeted. Then wrung her hands. "When I woke up, she was gone."

"This isn't making sense. Calm down and start over. From the beginning."

Ruth was choking from the tears so she could barely get the words out. "I don't know where Kate is. I put her to bed. Now she's gone. Her clothes are still here." Ruth picked up her clothes and waved them in the air.

"Someone must've taken her," Naomi said. "Who would do that?"

"The front and back doors were both locked."

They checked the windows. All were locked from the inside with no signs of any forced entry.

"Did you check the garage door?"

"Yes. I checked the garage and the garage door."

"Were they locked?"

"We never lock the inside door from the garage, but the door leading outside to the backyard from the garage was locked."

"Let's look again."

They walked quickly to the garage. The door to the garage from the house was unlocked and the door leading out of the garage to the backyard was locked, just like Ruth said. Ruth's mobile was still there, where it usually was. The space in the garage for Jake's mobile was empty with no sign he was there."

"Jake must've taken her," Naomi said.

"He's at work."

"He probably came home early. He pulled into the garage and took her for a drive."

Ruth tried to calm herself as she thought of that possibility.

"That must be it," she finally said. "He didn't want to wake me because he knows I haven't been getting much sleep."

Ruth took a deep breath and wiped the tears off her face. She threw her arms around Naomi and clutched her neck. Naomi was shaking and Ruth could feel her heart beating against her chest. Her outer demeanor was calm, but she was clearly unnerved by it all.

"I've never been so scared in my life," Ruth said. "That has to be it, right? It's the only explanation. Jake has her."

"It's okay, honey. It's understandable."

"What's with all the sirens?" Ruth asked.

"I heard on the radio that a plane hit the Tower," Naomi said. "Traffic was a nightmare. That's why it took me so long to get here. I had to take the back roads. People were panicking. Some people just left their mobiles in the middle of the road."

"I bet Jake is stuck in all that traffic," Ruth said as she took another deep breath. She was starting to feel better. "He probably took Kate for a ride. She's been crying nonstop all afternoon. Sometimes a ride in the mobile will get her to settle down. I'm going to kill him for not leaving me a note."

Naomi laughed and so did Ruth, relieving some tension. Her heart was still racing. It might not slow much until Jake got back to the house with Kate.

"Let's get you something to drink," Naomi said. "You go sit down."

Ruth did, but not before looking out the window. An ambulance raced by as she did, its siren blaring and the driver seemingly unconcerned about his speed considering he was in a residential neighborhood.

Naomi handed her a soda, and the ice-cold liquid was soothing to her parched throat which was now sore from screaming out Kate's name over and over again. Ruth couldn't sit still. She stood and looked out the window again. Then walked over to her caller. Then took a sip of her drink and repeated the process every few minutes.

"I can't get a call to go through," Ruth said. "And we've been without power for over an hour now."

"My caller doesn't work either," Naomi said, pulling it out of her purse and shaking it as if that would get a signal.

"I don't understand what an airmobile hitting the Tower has to do with us not having power all the way out here," Ruth said. They lived several miles from downtown.

"It might just be the rolling blackouts. Or it may be related to the tower being hit."

"That's horrible that an airmobile hit the Tower. Are there any people dead?" Ruth asked.

They both jumped as they heard another mobile door slam. Ruth bolted out of the chair and ran to the window and looked out. Her husband's secretary, Jasmine, was walking up the sidewalk to the front door. Ruth opened it before she got there. Fear and panic pulsed through her veins again.

Jasmine walked through the opened door and into the living room, touching Kate's hand with hers when she walked by.

"Jasmine, this is Naomi," Ruth said. "She's Jake's mother. This is Jasmine, Jake's assistant."

Naomi didn't bother with any formalities. She just stared at Jasmine like she was wondering why she was there instead of her son.

"I don't know how to tell you this," Jasmine said, her voice cracking as she spoke.

"Jake's dead?" Ruth said more as a statement of fact than a question.

"I don't know..." She said it, stammering over her words.

"What is it? Was Jake at the Tower?" Ruth was suddenly certain Jake must've been at the Tower on a business meeting.

Where was Kate then?

"No... We were at work. Jake was in his office."

"When was this?"

"Around 3:30."

"Jake was in his office..." Ruth said, in a manner urging her to get to the point.

"Then he wasn't," Jasmine said. Her eyes were glassy, almost as if she was in shock or at least not thinking clearly.

"Did Jake leave to come home?"

Please say yes.

"He never left the office."

"You said he wasn't in his office. Which is it?"

"I don't know."

"Jasmine," Ruth said with frustration in her voice. "You're not making sense."

"My office is right by Jake's. You know. You've been there," she said, pointing to Ruth.

"His office is all glass. I can see him, and he can see me. He can see outside."

"Jasmine, where is Jake?"

"He disappeared."

"We don't know what you mean," Naomi said strongly.

"I was looking in his office, then I looked down to type something and then I looked up and he was gone."

"Where did he go?"

"That's what I'm trying to say. Jake was gone, but his clothes were there."

"What?"

"His clothes were laying on the chair right where he was sitting."

Just like Kate.

6

5:34 p.m.

Danni was still mad at her mother.

Because of that, she holed up in her room and wasn't going to come out until her mother came and made her leave for mid-week church, which she would certainly do shortly. Surprisingly, Avery had not been in to gloat. Even her seven-year old brother, Todd, hadn't come into her room to annoy her. The whole house was quiet.

That's weird.

Not that she could necessarily hear what was going on in the other rooms. The door was still closed, and the headphones to her music player were blasting rock songs in her ears. Too loud as far as her mother was concerned, as she often said, but just like Danni liked it. Slipping them off, she listened for sounds coming from the house. Normally, she could hear plates and silverware clanging as dinner was being prepared. The activities of the house usually emitted a familiar sound.

Nothing.

By now, Avery should've been in the bathroom, blow-drying, spending at least thirty minutes on her hair with Danni yelling at her to hurry so she could get ready.

None of that was happening. She looked at the clock on her wall.

5:34

They usually left for church at 5:30.

They didn't even tell me about dinner.

Her mom must be really angry. Danni suddenly felt a twinge of guilt. She had said some horrible things to her.

She deserved it! I don't deserve to be grounded.

When her dad got home after church, the grounding would probably be extended for another week. He was worse than her mom.

Danni took off the headphones, got up out of bed, and put her ear to the door, listening. Not hearing anything, she cracked the door slightly and looked down the hall. No sign of anyone.

She eased out of her room and walked slowly down the hall and into the main living room. The sun was setting at the back of the house and casting rays of sunshine through the sliding glass door leading to the back yard, illuminating the room.

No one was there.

They went to church without me.

Danni felt two emotions. Relief and almost exuberance that she didn't have to go to Wednesday night church and hurt that her entire family was giving her the cold shoulder and ate dinner and left for church without even saying goodbye.

She walked into the kitchen and found no evidence they had eaten dinner at home. Even worse. They must've gone out to eat, maybe round pie. They knew it was her favorite. Anger was starting to boil up in her again.

Why do I care?

What's this?

Before she had a chance to fully answer her own question, she found the clothes Avery was wearing on the floor of the kitchen in a heap. Danni picked them up and held them up to her chest almost feeling like she was doing something wrong. Avery was very particular about her things. She would never leave them lying on the floor. Not even in the closet they shared. They had a running feud about that very issue. Danni often threw her clothes on the floor. Avery always hung or folded hers up neatly and complained incessantly about having to step over Danni's clothes.

Before she knew it, Danni had instinctively folded Avery's clothes for her and sat them on the counter. She walked slowly back down the hall to her brother's bedroom. The door was closed, so she knocked quietly. An eerie feeling came over her and caused her to act strangely. She never knocked. Another running feud in their household. Danni often barged into her brother's room, unannounced, to his vehement objections.

Hearing no response, she cracked the door slightly and peered in. Seeing nothing and no one, she opened it wide. Clearly, Todd had been there recently. Like Avery, he kept his room perfectly neat. Not because of his own personal obsession like his sister, but because his parents made him. Todd was a people pleaser. He'd do anything for the approval of their parents.

As she started to close the door, out of the corner of her eye, she saw a tee shirt, a pair of pants and underwear sitting on the floor next to the chair at his computer. Socks and shoes were next to them. Strewn in no orderly manner. More like they just suddenly fell there. After inspecting them, she came to the same conclusion. Something strange was going on in the house.

She called out Todd's name, even though she knew he wasn't there. Then she called out for Avery and went back into her room and looked in the closet and the bathroom. Clearly, Avery hadn't been in the bathroom recently. Going to church without thirty minutes to an hour of primping in the bathroom was not an option for Avery.

Was church cancelled, and they all went out to eat without her?

The master bedroom was on the other side of the house. The door stood open, and Danni called out for her mother. Getting no answer, she almost tiptoed in, scared at what she might find. In the same fashion, the clothes her mother had been wearing were in a heap on the floor in the bathroom in front of the mirror.

Several used tissues were on the bathroom counter and one was on the floor on top of the clothes. Danni picked one up that was still slightly wet. Had her mom been crying?

A wave of guilt rose up in her. She said some horrible things to her.

"She deserved it!" Danni said again, this time out loud but immediately regretting it.

No, she didn't. No mother deserves to be told by her daughter that she hates her. That was mean and cruel. As mad as Danni had been, and as much trouble as she often got in, she wasn't mean, and wasn't a cruel person. She'd apologize when her mom got home from church.

Her thoughts were interrupted by a knock on the door. Danni jumped. She walked cautiously out of the bedroom, into the living room, and to the front door where another louder rap startled her, even though she expected another knock. Looking out the peephole, standing at the door, was the last person Danni expected to see.

Old Lady Pinkerton.

The crazy lady from church.

She was a rich widow who her dad called his thorn in the flesh. A reference to a verse in the Bible. One of the apostles who was constantly annoyed by someone or something. Mrs. Pinkerton tried to run the church with her jupes and influence. Dad wasn't easily controlled but learned to tolerate her. Now she was standing at her door. She almost decided not to answer it, but curiosity got the best of her.

She cracked the door slightly.

Mrs. Pinkerton had a weak smile on her face, almost a smirk, when she said, "Why am I not surprised that you weren't taken?"

"My parents aren't here," Danni said, unsure what Mrs. Pinkerton meant by that comment.

"I know."

She was holding clothes in her arms. They looked like her dad's clothes, but she couldn't be sure.

"Why aren't you at church?" Danni asked.

"May I come in?"

"I guess." Danni opened the door wide, and Mrs. Pinkerton walked right in and kept going into the living room where she sat the clothes down on a table beside a chair and then sat down in the chair. She looked the same as she always looked, antique. Like the highest end antiquity in a pawn shop. Sickly thin, blueish color hair, wire rim glasses, and a flower-color dress that came well below her knees, and black shoes with low heels.

"Come sit down, honey," the crazy lady said. "I have something to tell you."

"I'll just stand," Danni retorted. Old Lady Pinkerton might run things at the church, but she wasn't going to tell her what to do in her own home.

"Are your brother or sister here?" Mrs. Pinkerton asked, looking inquisitively over her glasses.

"No. They're with mom at church."

The crazy lady just shook her head and let out a slight sound that sounded like a tsk. She rocked the chair back and forth with a steady effort. She looked at Danni in what could only be interpreted as disapprovingly. A familiar look because she'd seen it many times from her parents.

"Your parents aren't coming home," she said. "Neither are your brother or sister."

An overwhelming feeling came over her that a sixteen-year old girl could never describe fully. Maybe fear, or grief, or dread. Why was this lady acting so smug and almost secretive?

"Just tell me what happened to my parents," Danni said. "Where are Todd and Avery?"

She said it in a confrontive tone and walked over and stood in front of the chair standing over Mrs. Pinkerton.

"Stop rocking!" She grabbed the arms of the chair and stopped it. "Where are my parents?"

"Do you remember that sermon your dad preached a couple weeks ago? About the seizure?"

Danni shook her head no, even though she vaguely remembered it. Mostly her mind was elsewhere during the sermons. Even then, she knew what the seizure was. She'd heard her dad preach on it many times. He may have even written a book about it.

"Are you telling me my parents were seized?"

Mrs. Pinkerton started rocking again. "That's what I'm saying."

"Then why are you still here?"

A sad look came over Lady Pinkerton's face. Her shoulders sagged, and her entire body language changed as she drooped in the chair. Her lip started quivering. Tears welled up in her eyes. She looked up in the air toward the ceiling.

"I don't know," she said weakly as her voice trailed off.

The realization of what was happening suddenly hit Danni like a steamroller.

"Why am I still here?" Danni said, unable to fight back her own tears, suddenly realizing she was sixteen-years old and all alone.

7

"How could Jake just vanish into thin air?" Ruth asked Naomi, feeling stunned at the news.

Jake's secretary had just left after informing them that Jake was sitting in his office one minute and the next minute was gone. Not even a minute, actually. Just a few seconds. His secretary had looked down, typed something, looked up, and he was gone. The only thing left of him were his clothes.

"Were you and Jake having any troubles?" Naomi asked.

"What?" Ruth said with a glare. "No. What do you mean by that?" she said angrily.

"I mean... Could he have staged his disappearance? Could Jake have come home and taken Kate and is hiding from you for some reason?" She said it hesitantly but with a hint of accusation in it.

"Naomi! You know me better than that. And you know your son. Why would he leave me without telling anyone? And take the baby. He doesn't know how to take care of a baby. I've done everything since we brought Kate home."

"I'm sorry for asking, but that's what I mean. Were the two of you fighting? I know having a newborn can put a real strain on a marriage."

"Why would he leave without telling you then?" Ruth suddenly stood from the couch she was sitting on. "Was he mad at you too? I don't think so... Wait a minute. Do you know something? Do you know where Jake is?"

"No. No. No. I don't know anything. I'm just trying to wrap my brain around what has happened. Why would Jake be missing?

Where's Kate? Nothing makes sense. I wasn't accusing you of any-thing."

Naomi pulled out her caller again and tossed it back into her purse. "Still no signal."

After an awkward silence, Naomi said, "I'm going to go back to my house. Maybe Jake's there. I would call Carl, but I can't get a sig-nal. My caller is still not working." Carl was Naomi's husband of forty-nine years.

"I'm going with you," Ruth said emphatically.

"You should stay here in case Jake comes home."

"No. I'm coming with you. You know something you're not telling me."

"I don't know anything. I swear. Remember how surprised I was when I got here, and Kate was gone. If I knew something, why would I even come over?"

"Well I'm coming too. No way I'm staying here alone in this house. Something weird is going on. I hope to God, Jake and Kate are at your house."

"If Jake did take Kate, Carl will know it," Naomi said.

Ruth grabbed her purse and scribbled Jake a note.

Gone to your parents. Will be right back. I hope you're okay. I don't un-derstand what's happening. I don't know where Kate is. I hope you have her. Ruth. Call me! I'm scared.

The drive took about twenty minutes. All the traffic lights were out, and mobiles were trying to navigate the chaos. Crashed mobiles littered the road but most had been pushed to the side. They turned on the radio, but the coverage was related to the airmobile crashing into the Tower. According to reports, the building was no longer part of the skyline. It had fallen to the ground. All one hundred and twenty-two floors. They couldn't even begin to estimate the number of dead.

They turned it off when they started talking about the number of people missing.

"Sounds like a lot of people from the Tower are unaccounted for," Naomi said. "I feel bad for the people in that building when the airmobile hit."

"It must've been horrible," Ruth said, although she had her own tragedy unfolding. Thinking about other people's pain and loss wasn't even possible at that moment. She'd give anything to hear Kate screaming in her ears. Anything to feel Jake's arms around her or hear his voice. She checked her caller and still had no signal bars.

Maybe Naomi was right. Jake was leaving her and took the baby. She had been awfully moody and short with him lately. It seemed normal, considering how difficult the pregnancy had been. Why would he leave without saying something? Why would he take the baby? Considering the alternatives, she actually hoped he had. At least she'd know they were alive. Even then, if Naomi was in on it, she vowed to never speak to her again.

They traveled most of the distance without speaking. They pulled into the driveway and opened the garage. Jake's mobile wasn't out front. Carl's was in its spot. Ruth bolted out of the mobile and into the house, the first one through the back door.

"Jake!" she called out his name knowing he wasn't there, but frantically calling his name anyway.

Their house had power. The vision set was on, blaring in the living room. Ruth assumed Carl was in there watching it, so she called out, "Carl, do you know where Jake is?" No one responded.

Carl wasn't in the living room. Or in the kitchen. Or anywhere downstairs. Naomi rushed upstairs to their bedroom. Ruth was right behind her. Carl wasn't there.

"Where is he?" Ruth said as she started crying again. "Where is everybody?"

Naomi rushed back downstairs. Ruth followed her. She opened the back door and called out his name. "Carl, answer me. Are you here?"

No response and no sign of him.

"At least we have power," Naomi said. "The vision is on. He was watching it."

The channel had a large banner across the bottom that read Special Report. Reporters were talking about the Tower. Naomi and Ruth stood in the kitchen.

"I don't understand where Carl is," Naomi said.

"Maybe Carl staged a disappearance along with Jake," Ruth said sarcastically.

Naomi glared at her but didn't respond to the obvious jab.

"What do we do now?" Naomi said.

"I'm going back to the house," Ruth answered. "They have to be there soon. Jake came by, picked up Kate, and then came and got Carl, and they went somewhere. I don't for the life of me know where or why he'd do that without telling anyone."

"Carl always keeps that vision set so damn loud," Naomi said as she walked around the couch looking for the remote to turn down the sound.

Something caused her to stop in her tracks.

"What is it?" Ruth said, seeing the abrupt look of shock come over Naomi's face as she put her hand over her mouth and pointed at the chair.

"Naomi what's wrong?"

Naomi burst into tears and collapsed to the floor on her knees. Ruth walked cautiously from the kitchen around the couch and put her hand to her mouth as well as she couldn't believe what she was seeing.

Carl's clothes were on the chair. His shoes and socks were on the floor.

Ruth put her arm around Naomi's shoulder, and they both allowed their bodies to sag down. Doubled over. Sobbing uncontrollably. Naomi had both hands over her eyes. Ruth rocked back and forth, wailing in agony.

"We have to find out what's going on," Ruth said between sobs.

Before, they weren't paying attention to the vision even though it was so loud they could barely hear themselves talk. Ruth turned and faced it as she heard someone mention people missing. Not the missing from the Tower, but people missing all across Jupiter. Naomi choked back her sobs and turned and faced the vision set as well.

"Tens of thousands of people have been reported missing," the news anchorman said. A live feed from a camera across the bay from where the Tower stood was in the background. Smoke was coming from the ashes. Emergency personnel were at the scene trying to tend to the wounded. A headline said search and rescue operations were underway. But they were talking about something else.

"Maybe billions are missing," the anchorman said. "We have no way of knowing."

Ruth looked at Naomi and said, "People are missing. Why?"

"We are getting reports of missing children," the co-anchor, a woman added.

"Apparently, all children under the age of seven or eight are gone. No one knows where they are. All that's left of them are their clothes."

Their clothes.

Kate really was missing. Like millions of other kids.

"What is happening to our babies?" Ruth said, the sobs returning.

"Where's Carl? Where's Jake? Why did they disappear without their clothes?" Naomi was talking hysterically.

"This is unfolding into the greatest tragedy in the history of Jupiter," the anchorman said. "Millions are missing and presumed dead. I don't want to speculate, but the death toll could be in the tens of millions, maybe even the billions. If every child under eight is dead, that would be over two billion children. That is unimaginable."

"What do we do?" Ruth said as she helped Naomi to her feet.

"I have no idea," Naomi answered. "At least we know it's not just us. It's happening everywhere. We also know that we can't just go looking for them. Something has happened. Something supernatural. Something beyond our control."

"I want to go home," Ruth said. "In case they come back. Maybe they just disappeared temporarily."

"I'll drive you. You shouldn't be alone."

They turned off the vision and all the lights and got back in the mobile, both too stunned to talk.

Until finally Naomi said, "I'm sorry I said that about Jake leaving you. I know he's madly in love with you. I was just trying to figure out the truth."

"I keep thinking I'm going to wake up, and it's all a dream," Ruth said, letting out a long sigh.

"If those reports on the vision are true, things are going to get worse before they get better."

"Will you stay with me?" Ruth asked gently. "I don't think I can stand to be alone."

"Of course, honey. We're in this together."

Ruth heard a ping on her caller. She got it out of her purse and fumbled with it at first from excitement. She had a signal! And a voice mail message. From Jake. She put it on speaker.

"Hi honey. I'm sorry I have to work late tonight. I'll try to call later. Love you."

She looked at the time of the call. 1:43 p.m. Before he went missing.

"I don't know how things could get any worse!" she said as the excitement turned back to anguish.

8

Dr. Matthew King was the head of Obstetrics at the Mount Zion Community Hospital in Red Spot. The largest and most respected facility on Jupiter, the hospital delivered more than three hundred babies a day and had as many a thousand newborns in the facility under their care at any one time.

He sat at his desk finishing some last-minute paperwork before he could go home, having just completed a long ten-hour shift. The lights flickered slightly and then the power went off. He looked up at the lights which came on five seconds later as the backup generator roared into action providing the essential electricity needed until the power was restored from the utility company.

The rolling blackouts had become a nuisance for a large organization such as his that relied on the constant supply of power to keep the babies in their care alive. Especially those who had to be connected to a machine to sustain their lives.

He was just about to slip his white doctor's coat off and hang it in his closet and head home when an urgent voice came over the intercom calling his name.

"Dr. King, come to delivery, stat."

Stat meant there was some kind of emergency. Probably a woman having difficulty in labor. A few seconds later another voice called his name with the same level of urgency.

"Dr. King, you're wanted in the ER, stat."

Followed by a third alarming message that reverberated through the whole hospital.

"Dr. King, Nursery, stat. I repeat stat."

What the heck?

He bolted out of his office and down the hall and saw several people running frantically in all directions. Where should he go first? He had three urgent calls requiring his services.

Delivery.

He'd go there first. His job was first and foremost to deliver babies. There were many capable physicians in the ER and dozens of capable nurses in the nursery. Whatever was going on there would have to wait.

The back way to the delivery area was one floor down and through two large double doors with large red letters that read 'Authorized Personnel Only.' He was met by a nurse who said to follow her.

He tried to match her pace. She was almost running to delivery room 103. When women came in, they were given a room and stayed there through their entire labor and delivery.

A woman lay on the bed, sobbing. Three nurses and a doctor were standing around. He didn't hear a baby crying. There must've been a complication because the baby was not in the room, and she was clearly no longer in labor. The woman stopped crying when he walked in.

"Where's my baby?" she said in a demanding voice as if he would know.

"What's the problem?" Dr. King asked Royce Johnson, a young but capable physician. He was clearly shaken by something.

"Let's step into the hall," he said.

Dr. King followed him out of the room into a long hallway with rooms lining each side. He noticed a lot more activity than usual.

"I was delivering Mrs. Smith's baby," Dr. Johnson said. "She was ten centimeters dilated. Then..."

"Then what?"

"I saw the baby's head. The power went off. When it came back on... He was breathing heavily like he'd just finished a hard workout at the gym.

"Take a deep breath, Royce, and take your time. Tell me what happened."

"When it came back on, the baby was gone. I could no longer see the head. It disappeared."

"I don't understand."

"The labor stopped, and the baby was gone."

He was rocking back and forth on his feet and then pacing around in a small circle. Dr. King grabbed him by the shoulders to stop him from fidgeting. "Did you deliver her baby or is it still in her womb?"

"No."

"You're not making sense."

"Nothing makes sense. I'm freaking out."

A voice on the intercom said, "Dr. King, you must come to the nursery, stat."

A few seconds later, "Dr. King, you are needed in the ER, hurry."

"I don't know what you're trying to tell me," Dr. King said. "I have to go. Is your patient stable?"

"Yes."

"Then this can wait. Go in there and take care of your patients. The mother and the baby need you to be calm. I'll be right back."

As he was walking away, several nurses tried to get his attention. He looked over at the board. They had more than a hundred women in labor in rooms. It was going to be a busy night. One nurse was insistent he come in the room, but he couldn't. He had emergencies happening all over the hospital.

They paged him again.

"I'm coming," he said in a frustrating voice.

Where should he go first? He decided on the ER. He stood at the elevators waiting to go down to the main floor where the ER was located, but it was taking too much time, so he took the stairs and ran down the four floors, getting there in almost no time. He went to the main area where women were processed in. Pregnant women were instructed to come in through the main lobby unless it was an emergency, then they were processed through the ER. His experience had been that a lot of women came to the emergency room anyway. The lobby had a larger number of women in it than usual.

"What's going on?" he said to his head nurse, Janice.

"We're not sure. We have more than a dozen ladies here who say they were pregnant but lost the baby."

"What's the emergency? Why do you need me? We have normal procedures for that. Just follow them."

"You don't understand. These women were pregnant, and then the babies disappeared from their wombs."

"Dr. Johnson in delivery said the same thing. Maybe these women weren't pregnant."

"These women are all our patients. We have sonograms. They were pregnant... Now they're not."

"Dr. King, you are wanted in delivery, stat," the voice echoed through the hall.

"Dr. King, come to the nursery, now." That voice was Dr. Sellers. Head surgeon.

Why was he in the nursery?

"Are any of your women in critical condition?" Dr. King asked.

"No. They're all perfectly normal and healthy. Except for being emotionally distraught."

"I don't know what's going on. But they need me in the nursery."

"What do I tell the ladies happened to their babies?"

"Don't tell them anything yet. Just make sure they're stable. Do the normal procedures for a miscarriage. If they were pregnant, we need to scrape the uterine lining and get everything out of them."

He heard a commotion out in the lobby. Dr. King opened the door slightly. The ER was filling up. It looked like there were more than a hundred ladies standing in line demanding to be seen. Just a minute before there were only a dozen or so. Most were crying, some were hysterical.

What is going on?

He took the stairs again up to the nursery. He could hear screaming and wailing before he even went through the doors and into the nursery area. After delivery, the babies were brought to this area and treated. The mothers were given their own rooms. They had over a two- thousand-room capacity in this area, and the nursery could hold at least that many babies.

Most were kept in the main nursery area. Large paned windows allowed the friends and family to view the babies from the hallway. Dr. King walked quickly past that area and then came to a complete stop.

The nursery was empty!

The baby beds were there, but there were no babies. Just clothes and blankets. The nurses were congregated in a corner. Standing like zombies. Stunned. Not moving at all. No sense of urgency to do anything.

Just down the hall, Dr. King looked through the windowpane where they kept the babies born prematurely and the most seriously ill babies who needed to be on machines. The room was empty as well, except for a few nurses standing on the side. Some of the machines were still on, but the wires were dangling off the beds.

Around the hall, a number of patients were in the hall, screaming at the nurses and doctors. Dr. Sellers was talking to several of the ladies, clearly trying to calm them. When he saw Dr. King, he immediately left them and walked rapidly toward him with the most serious scowl on his face. The hallway was long, so it took a few seconds to get to him.

In the meantime, Dr. King was paged two more times.

I know. I'm doing the best I can.

What the hell is going on?

"Dr. Sellers, what's going on in our hospital? All hell has broken loose."

"The babies are missing," he said in a matter-of-fact tone which didn't match the words. He was above all else a professional who'd seen just about everything you could see in a hospital.

"What do you mean by missing?"

"They're gone. More than a thousand babies are gone!"

"That's impossible."

"It's not impossible, because it happened. I saw it with my own eyes. I was on the floor seeing patients. I walked by the nursery and there were a thousand babies, some sleeping, some screaming their lungs off. Everything was normal. Now there are none. I wouldn't believe it either, if I hadn't seen it."

"Did any alarms go off?"

The babies were fitted with a bracelet. If any child was taken off of the floor with the bracelet on his or her wrist, the alarm would sound. There was no way for someone to steal a baby. If the alarm went off the entire hospital was notified and went on lockdown. Stealing more than a thousand was impossible.

"No alarms went off," he replied. "The alarms are in the baby's beds. Perfectly intact. They haven't been cut or anything. And even the babies in the private rooms disappeared. We also have about three hundred moms missing and some of my nurses and doctors."

"Some of our staff are missing?" Dr. King asked. "And all the babies on the entire floor?"

"Yes. I'm telling you, every baby on the floor is gone. And so are three hundred or more moms."

"Dr. King, you're wanted in the ER," the voice on the intercom said. "Hurry! It's your wife."

A wave of panic came over Dr. King. His wife was eight months pregnant.

"I've got to go. I don't know what to tell you. Just manage the situation until we can figure it out."

He rushed downstairs, taking them two at a time. When he got to the ER, a nurse met him and told him his wife was in room 47. He burst through the doors where Olivia was in the bed in a hospital gown, a stoic look was on her face. As if she was in shock. A nurse was in the room but wasn't caring for her. Olivia didn't appear to be in any distress. Her stomach wasn't enlarged. She looked like she did before she was pregnant with what would be their first child.

He walked to her side and felt her stomach. The gown flattened. Her belly had returned to its normal size except for the stretching. There was definitely no baby inside of her. Did she already have it without him? He looked around the room. There was no baby and no sign of a delivery.

"What happened, honey?" he said lovingly, but with deep concern.

"I was driving, and my water broke." She was remarkably calm. "All over the floor of the mobile. I felt it."

"Felt what, babe?"

"I felt the baby leave my stomach."

"Where did he go?" They were having a boy. Joshua. He couldn't believe the words coming out of his mouth. Where could it go?

She didn't answer, only shrugged her shoulders as tears welled up in her eyes. What could she say? One minute she was pregnant, the next minute she wasn't. The same thing happened in the delivery room. Even the babies who had been delivered were gone from the nursery.

All he knew to do was take her in his arms. While he was profoundly aware of the grief he and his wife were about to go through, his thoughts suddenly turned to his hospital as he heard his name paged again.

He knew that in a matter of minutes, maybe a couple of hours, the hospital would be overrun with tens of thousands of women who were pregnant and under their care but had now lost their babies. How would they process and care for them all? It would be a nightmare. They'd need every available employee right away.

How would they deal with the emotional fallout? How would he deal with it? His wife would be devastated. So would he, but he could not let his mind go there. He had a job to do. The ramifications alone of a thousand newborn missing in the nursery was beyond comprehension. What would they say to the mothers? How would they explain it?

He kissed his wife on the forehead and said to the nurse, "Take good care of her for me."

He looked his wife in the eye and said, "As soon as they finish with you, go home. I'll be there as soon as I can. I don't know what happened. I'm so sorry. But I've got to go. You're not the only one. Every baby is missing."

9

"Are you ready to change your life?" Tom Collins shouted at the top of his lungs to a throng of more than fifty-thousand people who'd gathered in a large convention center to hear Jupiter's most popular life coach proclaim a brand of spiritual enlightenment through personal transformation.

"Say this after me: I love myself," he implored his adoring followers.

The multitude enthusiastically shouted the words as the atmosphere was building in intensity.

"Say it again," Tom encouraged them. At over six-foot five, Tom was a commanding figure with a strong, powerful, and authoritative voice.

"Say 'I am powerful.'"

It went up almost like a chorus.

"Again!" Tom said, jumping up and down on the stage.

The crowd did the same, jumping up and down with their hands in the air, mimicking what he was doing. They'd do almost anything he said. Known as Jupiter's Pastor, Tom Collins had sold more than a billion books. His most famous was called *Unleashing the Power of the Universe Within*. His show, Dr. Tom was syndicated on more than four thousand, four hundred vision stations around the world and more than a hundred thousand radio stations. He preferred Dr. Tom to Reverend Tom even though his doctorate was purchased through an on-line university more than twenty years ago. Having Doctor before his name made him feel more significant than Reverend.

"Say 'I believe!'" he shouted it at the top of his lungs, which was unnecessary since the soundmen were instructed to keep turning up the volume. The sound was almost deafening.

"Say it again."

"And again."

As the devotees neared hysteria, he put his arms up to quiet them. A hush fell across the huge auditorium. Tom knew how to work the crowd. Emotional manipulation was an art form he'd become an expert at.

"Do you believe in a higher power?" he asked in a quieter tone. "I know I do."

"Yes," a resounding cheer went through the crowd.

"Whoever you call God today, whoever you pray to, it's there that you will find your inner power," Tom said with believability. "You have to focus your mind to find that power within you. Your inner self is screaming inside to be set free. Can you hear it?" Tom held his hand to his ear, cupping it like he was listening to something.

"There you'll find the ability to do the impossible. There is the will to overcome your fears and live your dreams. God doesn't want you to be mediocre. He wants you to be successful."

The crowd erupted in applause and sustained it for nearly a minute.

"The highest state of consciousness is when you realize that you are love," he said in a quieter tone. "When you love yourself, then you can unleash your power to the world. Do you love yourself today?"

Tom noticed a pretty young blonde girl on the front row, wearing a bright red pants suit, smiling at him. He made a mental note to tell his assistant to bring her to his room after the session was over. Something easier now that his divorce was final. He didn't have to go to as much trouble to hide it. The girl seemed to like what he was saying about love, so he kept it up.

"Love opens the door to understanding. It's the offspring of spirituality that produces oneness with the universe and with the creator. Love is when your soul connects with another." He looked right at her when he said it. He flashed her a smile which she seemed to return.

Based on their response, the crowd was enjoying what he was saying about love as well.

"Spiritual love is like extending your hand," Tom continued, holding out his rather large right hand in front of him. "Everyone raise your hands high in the air," he implored.

The crowd dutifully did what he said.

"Reach for that power in the universe. Bring it into your own heart and soul. Bring the love from everyone in this room into your body. Give your love to those who are near you. Say it out loud, 'I love you, Jupiter.' Say it again. 'I love you, Jupiter.'"

"Repeat it over and over again."

It sounded almost like a chant.

"Are you satisfied with your mediocre life?"

"No."

"Do you want something more out of life?"

"Yes."

"Then do something different. If you always do what you've always done, you'll always get what you've always gotten."

The applause was less than before. The crowd was losing some of its energy.

Tom saw himself on the big screen and straightened his hair which normally stayed in place even with the jumping around. He was smartly dressed in a blue suit jacket, black slacks, and a solid white polo shirt. No tie. His hair was perfectly styled and dyed jet black, his nails manicured. Plastic surgeons had sculpted his face, so his near perfect features were that much more enhanced. Even though fifty-one years old, his forehead and face were wrinkle-free from the monthly injections of a poison that tightened the skin and eliminated the wrinkles. Makeup covered any other perceived flaws. He was pleased with what he saw on the big screen.

"Do you believe in me?" he said as music started in the background, perfectly timed. He had done this performance a hundred times and had perfected it with the help of focus groups who helped him develop every word for maximum timing and effect.

"If you believe in me, then do the works that I do," he said as he told them to sit down.

The people settled back in their seats.

"Give and it shall be given unto you," Tom continued. "Giving is the currency of the universe."

On cue, more than a hundred volunteers made their way to the front with plastic buckets.

"The more you give, the more you will get. Do you want a new house?" he asked.

"Yes."

"Then give."

"Do you want a brand new mobile?"

The crowd cheered wildly again.

"You have to give something to get something."

"Do you want a new job? A new wife? A new husband? A new life?"

"Yes."

"I can't hear you."

They said yes much louder.

"We're going to give you a chance to give, right now. The ushers are going to pass an offering bucket. Dig deep. Give all you can. The more you give, the more you'll receive."

Tom always took an offering at his events, even though each participant paid more than a thousand jupes to attend. Jupes was the currency of Jupiter. Some paid as much as ten thousand jupes to meet with him backstage and have their picture taken with him.

A private meeting costs a hundred thousand jupes. One event generated over almost a hundred million jupes in revenue with registration, product sales. and the offering. Tax free. Jupiter exempted non-profit organizations from having to pay taxes.

An investigative reporter did a special on Tom, exposing what they called 'abuses.' Admittedly, Tom had twelve houses, ninety-seven mobiles, a yacht, and a three-hundred-million-dollar private airmobile—all kept in the nonprofit's name, so he didn't have to pay personal taxes.

He'd defended the expenditures. "I've sold more books than any other man alive," he said in the interview. "I'm the CEO of a billion-dollar organization, with thousands of employees. I make less than I deserve, considering how successful I am at making the organization jupes."

Having to answer those charges infuriated Tom. The reporter edited the interview to make him look bad and took some of his words out of context. He'd seen a drop in attendance and in financial support and book sales. It had taken him a couple years to recover back to the level he was at before the interview.

Tom believed he was doing a great service to the world, and no one should question his motives. He was doing God's work, he argued vehemently. His dad always told Tom growing up, that God had a plan for his life, and he had a calling and should use it for God's Kingdom. Tom rebelled against his father who, in his mind, was nothing more than a humble pastor of a church of a couple hundred people with a poverty mindset. Tom broke out of that thinking shortly after college and left his father and mother behind, only talking to them a couple times a year. Early on in his success, he sent them jupes. They sent it back.

Tom exited the stage as the offering started and went back to his dressing room. Waiting for him was a young, pretty woman—a college intern—holding in her hand a bottle of water and a power bar. He patted her on the head and told her she looked pretty. His right-hand man who'd been with him for more than twenty years was already in the room and Tom acknowledged him with a wave.

The lights flickered then went out altogether. He instinctively looked up. They came right back on.

Tom was just about to tell his associate about the pretty girl on the front row when someone burst into his dressing room without knocking.

"Hey!" Tom said. "Don't you knock?"

"You've got to see this," the man said, ignoring the comment.

Tom rushed out of the dressing room with his assistant and the intern right behind him. He walked the short distance to the stage and came around the curtains. People were filing out of the room in the back. The ushers were still at the front holding the offering buckets. They'd only gotten to the first row.

"Where's everyone going?"

Tom wondered if there had been a fire alarm or some kind of bomb threat that spooked everyone. His next thought was the offering.

"Why couldn't this have happened ten minutes from now, after we took the offering?" he said to his assistant.

His mouth suddenly gaped open.

On the front row, was a red pantsuit. Laying on the chair and the floor. He had to take a second look. Tom blinked his eyes twice and then rubbed them. The clothes the pretty blonde was wearing were laying on the floor.

His eyes quickly went to the back, but he didn't see her. He noticed clothes strewn in the chairs throughout the convention center.

He rushed down to the floor where his ushers had congregated.

"What happened?" Tom said.

"We started taking up the offering," one of the men started speaking. "The lights went out. When they came back on, half of the people were gone!"

"Gone?"

"All that was left of them were their clothes." He picked up some-one's clothes from the chair on the front row and waved them in the air.

"Everybody else panicked. They started screaming and ran for the door."

Tom looked through the buckets. They were all empty. They hadn't even made it to the first row.

"What happened to all the people?" the assistant asked.

Tom knew immediately.

My parents. They're gone.

The realization hit him like a ton of logs had just fallen on top of him.

And I wasn't taken.

10

"Pastor Howell, I'd like to have a word with you," Mrs. Pinkerton said as she walked through the opened door into his office at the Red Spot Christian Church.

A slight look of annoyance formed on his face and was not lost on her. She'd felt for a while that animosity was building between them. Their running feud started the moment he was hired. He was the wrong man for the job in her opinion. When the church voted to call him as their pastor two years before, the vote had been 84-1. She was the lone dissenter. The only one with the foresight to see he was trouble.

"I'm kind of busy right now," Lindsey Howell answered. "I'm preparing for Bible study tonight." He had his Bible and several other books lying open on his desk.

"This will only take a minute," she said as she pulled out a list. A former teacher, Mrs. Pinkerton was meticulous in details. More of a self-proclaimed visionary, organization was not Pastor Howell's best skill, one of her criticisms of him, which she voiced to others as often as she could.

She thought she perceived a scowl come across his face. That behavior was totally unacceptable. Her family started the church more than eighty years ago. She'd been its most prominent member for more than forty years and gave the most jupes, by far. The church couldn't even keep the doors opened if it weren't for her. For some reason, he never gave her the respect she deserved.

Pastor Howell shrugged. "What is it this time?" he said in a tone that didn't match the sarcasm of the words.

Whether he meant for them to be or not, the words were biting and only raised the anger in her. She prided herself on always maintaining self-control and decorum. It would take all of her good nature to keep her tongue bridled. Pastor Howell could bring out the worst in her if she let him. She was determined not to.

At least once a month, her concerns had been brought to him, kindly and respectfully. Every time he'd ignored them, much to her displeasure. Mrs. Pinkerton was determined to keep bringing them up until he saw things her way or until she gained enough support to have him removed from his position. Right now, she had virtually no support. It would take time for people to come around to her way of thinking.

"The first thing," she said as she adjusted her glasses and scanned her notes. "It's about your daughter."

"Avery?"

"No. Avery is a doll. The older one. I don't remember her name. The troublemaker."

"Danni," he answered, not responding to her troublemaker comment.

She had said it to get a rise out of him. It hadn't worked.

"What about Danni?" he asked.

"Danni. That's right... I have some concerns about Danni. About her attitude."

Pastor Howell chuckled. "I have my own concerns about her attitude sometimes," he said, obviously trying to make a joke. "She's sixteen-years old. I think most teenagers get an attitude every once in a while."

"I didn't," Mrs. Pinkerton retorted. "My parents would've never let me act that way."

Pastor Howell started to respond, but she dismissed it with a wave and continued before he could say anything.

"I've noticed Danni has resorted to wearing denim pants on Sunday morning. I thought we agreed that she could wear them to youth group on Wednesday night, but on Sunday morning, she should be dressed appropriately, like a lady." Mrs. Pinkerton was speaking in a very prim and proper voice for effect. She had on a dress, even in the afternoon, midweek. She always dressed modestly in public.

"We never agreed to anything," the Pastor retorted. "I agreed that a top she wore one Sunday wasn't appropriate. I discussed it with her, and she hasn't worn that shirt since. I don't see anything wrong with kids wearing denim pants to church. All the kids do it."

"But she's the pastor's daughter. Don't you think she should set an example for the others?"

His jaw clenched. He was dressed casually as well. An open-collared shirt, short sleeves. Highly inappropriate, in her mind, for a minister of the gospel who would be leading a Bible study in only a few hours.

"I've noticed that you don't wear a tie-on Sunday morning anymore. Is that something we should expect from you going forward?" she asked.

"I think that having a more casual appearance makes people feel more comfortable. My goal is to reach the lost. Slacks and a polo shirt give us more of a family atmosphere on Sunday morning. Most congregants don't wear ties anymore, so I want them to feel like I can relate to them."

"I think when a preacher stands up in front of the congregation to bring God's Word, he should always wear a tie."

"Jesus never wore a tie," Pastor Howell retorted.

"So, you're comparing yourself to Jesus now?"

"That's not what I meant. I just mean that he was a man of the people. He spent time in the home of tax collectors and prostitutes. He didn't try to put on a superior air in front of them. He was just himself. I feel more comfortable not wearing a tie. I think the content of my sermon is the most important thing."

"About the content," she said. "I'm glad you brought that up. You're wrong about the seizure being before the tribulation. The tribulation comes first. Then the seizure."

The pastor had just finished a series about the end times. It was all she could do to bite her tongue as he preached what she considered heresy.

"I believe the seizure will be before the tribulation," he argued. "Can't we just agree to disagree?" he said, trying to strike a more conciliatory tone.

"Not when it comes to God's Word," she said angrily. "I'm not going to sit back and let you preach false doctrines."

"I think honest people can disagree. I don't see how it's heresy just because we have a difference of opinion about something. We don't know the answer to a lot of things in the Bible. They are mysteries. We won't know about the seizure until it happens."

"If you would read your Bible," she said angrily, "you would see the error of your ways. The Bible clearly teaches that the seizure comes after the tribulation. I have a list of verses for you to read that will prove my point." She sat the list in front of him.

"I do read my Bib..." he stopped himself in mid sentence. "I know all the verses. I wrote a book about the seizure. Look. The main thing for me is this. Whenever the seizure happens, Mrs. Pinkerton, I just hope to be in it."

She let out a slight chuckle, letting the tension ease some.

"I hope you are too," she said halfway under her breath. Then she added, "I don't think it'll happen in my lifetime. I'm getting old."

"I think we should always be looking for Jesus to come back," he said encouragingly. "It could happen at any time. There are many signs pointing to it."

"Well... We know it won't be now. The tribulation hasn't come yet."

He didn't respond.

"Was there anything else you wanted to talk to me about?" he said.

"I know I mentioned this before, but why does it have to be so cold in the church?"

"So, I can make sure everyone stays awake," he said laughing.

She wasn't amused. Her house was kept at eighty degrees in the winter and the same in the summer. She couldn't stand to be cold. Probably because her thin, wiry frame didn't have an ounce of fat on it and contributed to her cold nature.

"Actually, the lights are so hot on stage, I'm sweltering if the air isn't turned down some. Believe it or not, we have people who complain that it's not cold enough. Can't you just wear a thicker sweater?"

"Why do we need all those lights? I feel like I'm going to a bar when I come to church. The music is too loud. Lights flashing everywhere. I think it gives people the wrong idea."

"We're trying to be more contemporary on purpose. It reaches more people."

"Reaching more people is not necessarily a good thing."

"I disagree. Our church is bigger than it's ever been. We're baptizing more people than ever before. We're getting young people to come. They're the lifeblood of the church. Without the young people, the church will eventually die if all we have is older folks. No offense intended," he added.

"About your daughter, Danni, what are you going to do about her?"

"Nothing, Mrs. Pinkerton," Pastor Howell said sharply. "I'm just glad she's coming to church. I don't want to alienate her further. She's at an impressionable age. Too many preacher's kids fall away from the church after they leave home. I don't want that to happen to Danni. She's too good a kid. If I come down on her too hard, she'll rebel. She's already struggling to find herself."

Mrs. Pinkerton let out a big sigh.

The lights in his office flickered. She looked up at them. When she looked back down, Pastor Howell was gone.

Vanished into thin air. She jumped out of her seat and leaned over the desk, looking across the other side.

Pastor Howell's clothes were still there, but he was gone.

She let out another sigh. Emotionless, she walked around the desk and picked up his clothes and folded them neatly.

She paused, thinking, and then finally said out loud, "I guess I was wrong about the seizure after all."

11

Pastor Lindsey Howell sat in his office at the Red Spot Christian Church, talking with Mrs. Pinkerton about his daughter Danni when he suddenly heard a loud shout. So loud it startled him. Right after the shout, he heard the sound of a blaring trumpet. Everything after that was just a blur.

In the twinkling of an eye, he was changed. His old body was gone, and he had a new spiritual body. Suddenly, he was being propelled upward at a high rate of speed. Through the roof of the church and into the air, he was speeding like a rocket toward the clouds. Out of the corner of his eye, he could see tens of thousands of people traveling in the air with him, all flying with purpose, all headed in the same direction, with no control over their bodies.

Mrs. Pinkerton wasn't flying with him, but his wife was and so was their son, Todd, and daughter Avery. The kids had wide grins on their faces and were barreling through the air like they'd been shot out of a cannon. The clouds opened up, and Jesus appeared wearing a white robe. Everyone came to a sudden stop and were set down on solid ground. The multitudes began to gather around Jesus.

All at once, the entire throng fell to their knees and cried out proclaiming, "Jesus Christ is Lord to the glory of God the Father!"

A tremendous overwhelming joy flooded Lindsey at the realization that he was with Jesus. All fear immediately left him, and he felt no more pain, and the frustration from his conversation with Mrs. Pinkerton was a distant memory, even though it had happened only seconds before.

"Absent the body, present with the Lord," Lindsey said to himself out loud, remembering a Bible verse he knew well and was now experiencing firsthand. He took a moment to acclimate himself to his surroundings.

Behind where Jesus stood were gates leading into heaven. There wasn't one pearly gate; there were twelve. They were large, majestic gates, and each was adorned with jewels that reflected the light, which was the glory of God that permeated every square inch of the heavenlies.

"You will now receive your vested garment," Jesus said.

Each person was suddenly clothed in a white robe. The garments were radiant and exceedingly white. No launderer on Jupiter could've possibly whitened them to that extent.

"Receive the salve," Jesus shouted.

A salve was put on their eyes so they could now spiritually see all the mysteries of the heavenlies.

They were then led through the gates and into heaven. At a distance were twenty-four thrones around one large throne. Twenty-four elders sat on the thrones in white robes with golden crowns on their heads. Around were a great multitude of which no one could count. From every nation and tribe and people and tongues, they were standing before the throne and before the Lamb who was radiantly clothed in white.

One thing Lindsey immediately noticed was that Jesus was everywhere at once. He was with them, but also at the throne. He was seated at the right hand of the Father and yet Jesus was right next to him. The Bible verse where Jesus said he would never leave us or forsake us took on new meaning for him.

Looking at the thrones, the Ancient of Days took his seat. His vesture was like white snow, and the hair of his head was like wool. His throne was ablaze with flames, and its wheels were like a burning fire. Lindsey knew the Ancient of Days was Jesus as well.

"Rest a little longer," Jesus said to them. "Until your fellow servants and their brethren who are to be killed and those who will die are completed also."

Lindsey understood what he meant. People were still on Jupiter. The worst was still to come for those who were left behind. Those who were in heaven were to wait until all things were accomplished on Jupiter and the fate of those who remained was decided.

Shortly thereafter, they were shown to their mansions where everyone prepared for the marriage supper of the Lamb.

* * *

"Lindsey, what do you think is going to happen to Danni?" Nancy, my wife on Jupiter asked me. We were sitting in my mansion enjoying the time together while waiting for the commencement of the marriage supper of the Lamb, which was to take place in heaven sometime between the seizure and the second coming of Christ. During the time when Jupiter faced the great tribulation.

Even though there was no marriage in heaven, Nancy and I had a special bond, having been one flesh on Jupiter. Avery and Todd were out in the heavenlies, playing somewhere and having a great time, I was sure.

"I don't know, honey," I responded soberly. "It will be up to her whether she accepts or rejects Christ. There is still hope, though."

A loud resounding harp rang throughout the heavenlies. When that happened, everyone stopped what they were doing and immediately started rejoicing. The sound meant someone on Jupiter was saved. The Bible was right when it said there was joy in all of heaven and in the presence of God's angels when one person repents. With over fifty billion people still on the planet, and with the shock of the loss of so many people to death and to the seizure, some were turning to God. Most, it seemed, had turned their hearts cold.

We looked with anticipation each time we heard the harp, to see if our beloved daughter Danni was the one who came to repentance. So far, she hadn't.

"Was heaven like what you expected?" Nancy asked me.

"Better than I could've ever imagined," I responded.

"Oh, I know," she said. "Me too. Words can't even describe it. I knew it would be amazing, but it's beyond what I could even comprehend on Jupiter."

"The most valuable thing on Jupiter was gold," I said. "It's just dust on our feet."

Every street was lined with gold in heaven.

"Remember how our kids kept getting in trouble for tracking dust into the house?" Nancy said with a large grin. "Now, I get on them for tracking gold into my mansion!"

We both laughed heartily. There was a lot of laughing in heaven. A lot of rejoicing. Non-stop.

As if on cue, the harp sounded, and we raised our hands and began rejoicing with the others. Excited for the souls that had been saved, but wishing Danni was one of them.

We were fully aware of what was happening on Jupiter, even though there was nothing we could do about it. While there was no sorrow, pain, or tears, we felt the sense of loss, not having Danni with us. On Jupiter, I didn't know if the people in heaven knew what was happening on the planet. It was a mystery. Now I knew the answer.

In fact, I knew most of the mysteries of the universe. They would not all be unveiled until the final judgment, but they mirrored what was described in the Bible. We were all given new spiritual bodies after the seizure like the Bible said. The verses said that we wouldn't all sleep but would all be changed. It said our new bodies would be like Christ's glorious body. And they were incorruptible, powerful, spiritual, and eternal. Things were starting to make sense.

We were also given a new language. Even the babies and children who were seized were given new bodies and could now talk. Those with physical infirmities on earth didn't have them in their new bodies and were just like the rest of us.

Like our spirit on Jupiter was confined to our physical bodies, our spirits were what was transported from Jupiter into heaven and were now confined to a spiritual body. One without any of the sufferings of the flesh, without the emotions of fear, anxiety, and anger that plagued us on Jupiter.

We were glorified together. Along with saints from other planets. What a wonderful feeling.

"I didn't know there was life on other planets," I said.

"That's amazing, right," Nancy responded. "It makes sense. While we were on Jupiter, we could see the other planets. It was foolish to think we were the only ones with life."

We learned that every planet once sustained life or would someday. God put an Adam and an Eve and a Garden of Eden on each planet along with a tree of the knowledge of good and evil. Every Adam and Eve eventually ate of the fruit and brought sin and death to their planet. Jesus came to each to provide a sacrifice for their sins and to provide a way to heaven.

"They all eventually destroyed themselves," I added. "Venus is just a hot hell now. The surface is over nine hundred degrees. It was once a thriving planet, then an unbeliever shot a missile into the atmosphere and caused a great flood."

"Look at Saturn and its beautiful rings," Nancy said. "They let the Nohelim's destroy them. How stupid was that?'

"Very!"

"I hear earth is going to have life soon."

"I heard the same thing."

"I hope they don't destroy themselves as well."

"Let's go look at it."

We flew off together into the heavenlies until we arrived just outside earth's atmosphere.

"Wow!" Nancy said. "Look how beautiful."

Earth had form, and darkness was no longer on the face of the deep. It had everything it needed to sustain life, but God hadn't yet created man on the planet. Earth was magnificent and looked like it would be a wonderful place to live. It wasn't as big as Jupiter, but every bit as majestic.

"It seems like the pattern is for Adam and Eve to eat the fruit and bring sin to the world," I said. "Man, then starts doing evil, and Jesus comes to die for man's sins. You would think that Jesus would be all man needs. Instead, most people reject him. Every planet does the same thing. They all have the Bible. I don't know why they don't just believe it. Things would be so much better."

"They can just look at creation and know there is a God," Nancy said.

"They are without excuse."

"Let's go check on Danni," Nancy said. "I'll race you!"

We flew off the other direction back to where we came until we arrived at Jupiter.

"I let you win!" I said jokingly.

Truthfully, she could've easily beat me if she wanted to. We both stopped in our tracks to admire Jupiter from our vantage point.

"Look at the red spots," I said.

"They're beautiful."

That's where the wealthiest people on Jupiter lived. The real estate was in great demand because of the beautiful landscape, with vast colors and views of the water with the mountains as a backdrop.

"I wonder how many people from the Red Spots were seized," Nancy asked.

"I don't know. Jesus said it's hard for a rich man to enter into heaven."

We came to the portal that looked into our house. We couldn't believe what we were seeing as our mouths flew open in amazement.

"Look at that," I said. "I can't believe it."

"Mrs. Pinkerton has moved into our house," Nancy said. "She's living there with Danni."

"I wouldn't believe it, if I hadn't seen it with my own eyes," I said, wondering what it all meant.

PART TWO

How will they hear without a preacher?

12

Danni tossed and turned in bed, unable to sleep, when suddenly, she felt her body begin to rise into the air. Propelled upward with such speed, in less than a moment she was standing before Jesus, just outside of heaven.

She cried out to him, "Have mercy on me, Lord!"

But he said to her, "Depart from me. You are cursed. I send you into the eternal fire, prepared for the devils and angels."

Danni could see heaven behind Jesus. The pearly gates were at the entrance. Behind them were the thrones, beautiful streets of gold, and mansions lining the roads. Her mother and father, and Todd and Avery were standing just inside the gates, watching. She wanted to go to them but couldn't. A force was preventing her. They had a sad look on their faces.

"But Lord, I did many things in your name," Danni said to him. "I was baptized in the church. My dad was the pastor. I memorized many Bible verses." By that point, she was pleading with him.

"I never knew you," he said lovingly, but strongly. "Be gone!"

She felt her body suddenly being propelled backward. Instinctively, she reached out her hand toward her parents, but they were too far away to help her. She went across a great chasm and into a fiery lake where she could see millions of people engulfed by the flames, even though their bodies weren't being consumed like they'd be in a normal fire.

The fire started licking at her skin, and she was in immediate torment. Her mouth was parched with thirst. Her sister, Avery, was standing just outside hell. A man stood next to her. Danni reached out her hand again, extending it as far as she could, trying to touch her, but Avery was too far away. Danni tried running toward her, but her legs were like irons shackled to the ground. The harder she tried to run, the more she sunk into the fire, as if she was running in quicksand.

"Avery, have pity on me," Danni cried out. "Can you dip your finger in water and cool my tongue, because I am in agony in this fire?"

The man next to her said, "Remember that in your lifetime you received many good things. More than your sister, Avery. Now she is comforted here in heaven, and you are in agony."

"Then I beg you to let her go back to Jupiter and tell those who are left. Let her warn them, so that they will not also come to this place of torment."

"You had your chance. You should've told them while you were there."

"I didn't know. I didn't know. How could I know?" She kept saying the words over and over again until her throat became so parched, she could no longer speak.

* * *

Danni let out a huge scream and bolted straight up in her bed. She looked at her arms and hands. The dream seemed so real. She could feel the fire burning her arms. Her throat was parched just like it had been in the dream. Her whole body shook. She was terrified.

Mrs. Pinkerton rushed into her bedroom, not bothering to even knock. Within a second, she was sitting on the bed next to Danni. Tears streamed down Danni's face. Mrs. Pinkerton took her in her arms and held her close. Danni couldn't speak.

"It's okay, honey. I'm here. It was just a dream." Mrs. Pinkerton stroked her hair and wiped the tears from her eyes with her hands.

"Do you want to talk about it?" Mrs. Pinkerton said.

Danni shook her head. She could feel the fear ravaging her body.

"I'm so thirsty," Danni said.

"I'm going to get you a drink."

Mrs. Pinkerton left the room, and walked toward the kitchen. Danni followed her. Once there, she drank the water down like she hadn't had anything to drink in days. Like she just spent several days in the desert. The actual symptoms she felt in the dream, which were now etched into her memory, were manifesting in her physical body.

"This is why I didn't want you to be alone," Mrs. Pinkerton said.

Mrs. Pinkerton had insisted on staying the night. Danni argued with her even to the point of being rude. "This is my house," she said, but Mrs. Pinkerton wouldn't listen. How could she make her leave?

"I'm so glad you're here," Danni said sincerely, choking out the words. Suddenly, she was happy she was there.

"Do you want to go back to bed?" Mrs. Pinkerton asked.

Danni shook her head violently. "I can't sleep. I'm afraid that if I close my eyes again, I might have the same dream."

"I understand."

Mrs. Pinkerton took her hand and led her into the living room where they sat down on the couch. Neither one of them said anything for several minutes. Danni regained her composure enough to sit up and create some distance between her and Mrs. Pinkerton. While she was glad the lady was there, she still didn't fully trust her.

"I can't believe my parents are gone," Danni finally said. "What am I going to do?"

Mrs. Pinkerton just shrugged her shoulders. "You just have to keep on living. God is giving you a second chance at life."

"I don't even want it. Not if my mom's not here."

"You're a young woman. You have your whole life ahead of you."

Tears were flowing down Danni's cheeks again as she put her head in her hands.

"I said some horrible things to my mom... Before she died. They were so hateful. I don't know how I can live with myself. Those were our last words."

"We all have regrets. Did you know that I have a daughter?"

"No," Danni said with surprise.

"She was just a little older than you, the last time I saw her... That was almost twenty years ago," she said as her voice trailed off.

"You haven't talked to her?" Dannie asked. "Why not?"

"She's called a few times and sent me a few cards. At Christmas. On my birthday."

"Why don't you call her?"

"I don't think she'd want to talk to me. I said some very hateful things to her too. Things I didn't mean. But there's no way to take them back now. I don't even know if she's still on Jupiter. She probably isn't."

Mrs. Pinkerton put her hand to her face and wiped away her own tears.

"That's what I mean about living your life with regrets," Mrs. Pinkerton added. "I'm an old woman. There's nothing I can do about them now. You're still young. You have time to make things right."

"How do I do that? I don't even know where to start." Danni lifted her feet off the floor and pulled her legs close to her chest with her arms around them.

"You can make your parents proud of you."

"Why would they be proud? I'm the one left behind. God didn't even want me in heaven."

Mrs. Pinkerton let out a nervous chuckle.

"I guess he didn't want me either. What do you say we make some breakfast?"

* * *

About a half hour later, they finished eating pancakes with syrup and whip cream on top.

"Mom never let us put whipped cream on our pancakes at breakfast. She always said breakfast was the most important meal of the day." Danni said it, mimicking her mom's voice. Not in a disrespect-ful way, just in a humorous one.

Mrs. Pinkerton noticed a slight smile. The first she'd seen from the girl. But the worried look returned almost immediately.

"What am I supposed to do?" Danni said.

"About what?" Mrs. Pinkerton asked as she finished cleaning the last dish. They were still in the kitchen, and Danni was leaning against the counter across from the sink.

"I'm a kid," Danni continued. "I don't have any jupes. I'm all alone. How am I going to pay the mortgage on the house? Where will I go?"

"Do you know where your parents kept the bankbook?"

"'I think so."

Danni walked out of the kitchen, across the living room, and to her parent's bedroom. They had a little desk in the corner. In the top right-side drawer was a bankbook. She grabbed it and took it back in the kitchen.

"What is the balance?" Mrs. Pinkerton asked.

Danni handed it to her as Mrs. Pinkerton walked over and sat down at the kitchen table. She opened it, took one look, and let out a sigh. "Fifteen jupes," she said.

Mrs. Pinkerton suddenly felt deep regret. When Danni's father was hired, she had insisted that his salary be lowered to just above a living wage. "A preacher should be a servant of God and not be do-ing it for the jupes," she argued.

Pastor Howell had complained vehemently that it wasn't enough with a wife and three kids. He took the job anyway because he felt God leading him to the church. He believed God would provide. The church voted him two raises against her objections, but she sud-denly realized it still wasn't enough.

When Nancy, Danni's mom, started selling a product out of her home part-time, Mrs. Pinkerton vehemently objected to that as well. "A pastor's wife should take care of the kids and work at the church," she argued strongly. Eventually, the church put Nancy on a small stipend and gave him a housing allowance which he said helped. But it obviously wasn't enough, considering how little he had in his account. They were barely scraping by.

"Don't worry about it right now, honey," she said. "Your father has some pay coming. And some vacation pay. I'll make sure you get those."

"What about college? Where will I live? They'll make me move. I love our house."

"You don't worry about a thing. I'll make sure you're taken care of. I'm a very rich woman. I'll take care of your college."

"Why would you do that for me?"

"Let's just say I owe it to your father."

She thought about her own daughter. This might be an opportunity for her to redeem herself in God's eyes. He was obviously not pleased with her. That's why she was left behind. Maybe she could make a difference even if it was too late for her.

"What's going to happen to the church?" Danni asked.

"I don't know,' Mrs. Pinkerton said. "But that's a good question. What does happen to a church after the seizure?" She let out a nervous laugh.

"What's so funny?" Danni asked.

"It's not funny," Mrs. Pinkerton said as her tone got more serious. "I mean... How do you hire a pastor? Everybody who's left is obviously not a Christian. The church can't have a pastor who's not a Christian."

"Will anyone even show up for church on Sunday?"

"I expect they will. I would think some people will be there who are curious. Some will come because they are desperate for answers. Some because they want to make things right with God if it's possible. The former members like me who were not taken—they'll be too embarrassed to show their faces. I have a feeling Sunday morning is going to be very interesting."

"Without a pastor, the church will eventually have to close its doors," Danni said.

"We can't. My family started that church. I can't let it die."

"I don't know how you can help it. Me and you might be the only two members left for all we know," Danni said. "How can you run a church like that?"

"I'll think of something," Mrs. Pinkerton said. The wheels were already turning as an idea was formulating in her mind.

13

Carter and his estranged wife, Taylor, had watched in horror as the Tower in downtown Red Spot crashed to the ground, sending a large plume of smoke and debris their direction as they were now trying to run away from it. They ducked into an entryway of a building on a side street and had been sheltered somewhat but were now running again after the dust and smoke had cleared enough to where they could see where they were going.

They sprinted together toward his house seven blocks away. His lungs burned from the toxic chemicals in the smoke, and his eyes were watering as his face was covered in soot and grime from the remnants of what was left of the once-majestic building that dominated the skyline of Red Spot.

The building collapse was almost impossible to believe. He had no idea what happened other than reports that an airmobile crashed into it. At this point, his only concern was to get his wife to the safety of their home.

They came to their street, and Taylor matched him step for step. Like old times when they used to run together. Back when they were a happy couple. Back before she cheated on him four times. Before she left him to become a prostitute and cheated on him countless times with God knows how many men. Thoughts he was trying to put out of his mind after he recklessly threw caution to the wind and bolted into the brothel and got her out of the hell-hole of a life she'd made for herself, beating up her pimp in the process.

Once through the front door of their home, Carter and Taylor stood in the hallway, hands on their knees, bent over, gasping for air. Taylor was covered in soot as well. Her face was black as if it was painted on, to the point she'd be unrecognizable if he didn't know it was her.

"That was crazy," she said, between gulps of air.

Carter struggled to catch his breath enough to respond.

"I heard that an airmobile crashed into the Tower," she continued, not as out of breath as he was.

"It looked like a war zone. I've never seen anything like it," he responded, which was saying a lot considering he was a Strategic Commander of special operations for the armed forces of Jupiter and had led many missions of combat into some very dangerous settings. He knew firsthand what a war zone looked like.

He walked into the kitchen, opened the refrigerator, and got out two bottles of water. Taylor followed him. He gave her one and downed the other in one gulp. Carter stuck his head under the faucet and turned it on, letting the water wash away some of the soot and grime on his face. The cold water felt good inside and out.

"We need to get out of these clothes," Taylor said. "Before we get soot all over the furniture." They had already tracked it inside on the floors.

"You can use our bathroom," Carter said. "There's still no power, so you go first. There's probably just enough hot water for one shower."

"You should take it," she said.

"No. You go ahead. A cold shower will feel good. I've taken many cold showers out in the jungles and on the base. I'm used to it."

She just nodded and said, "OK. Thanks."

He went into the laundry room and stripped off his clothes. The house was a modest two bedroom with two and a half bathrooms. The second bedroom was meant to be a kid's room eventually, but since they never had kids, it became Taylor's craft room.

Carter got into the shower off the room and turned the water on, all the way to the cold side so he wouldn't take any hot water from Taylor.

The cold water was a jolt to his already frayed system. After he became acclimated to it, the chilled water brought a cleansing to his body and soul. He felt alive again. Just having Taylor in the house, even for just a few minutes, had invigorated him. Saving her from her pimp or whoever that scumbag was had given him a new purpose. Like when he was saving the world from terrorists and drug dealers and all-around bad guys. He felt like a man again instead of a drunk wasting his life away on a couch, pining away for a woman, a lost love.

He wondered if he would lose her again. It didn't matter at that moment. She was there, and safe in their home. Could he forgive her? Could he take her back? Was the betrayal too great? He decided he wasn't going to think about it.

The realization he came to as he scrubbed his body so hard with the soap it almost hurt, was that he had made a choice between Taylor and the Tower. He chose Taylor. If he had it to do over again, he'd do the same thing, a hundred out of a hundred times. Had she been in the Tower he would have run in there after her and would have perished along with all the other souls. He'd have been fine with it.

She was the love of his life. There would never be anyone who would capture his heart like she had. That fact came into clear focus for him. That's why he drank. To mask the pain of losing her. Maybe after her shower, she'd leave, and he'd lose her again. She might stick around and use him until the dust settles and the chaos in the street subsides and then take off. He might wake up one morning, and there'd be a note on the counter. Like the last time. He might take her back, and she might cheat on him again.

Whatever. Whatever happens, happens.

Carter got out of the shower and found a pair of underwear, shorts, shirt, and socks that were in the laundry, washed but not folded. After donning them, he walked into the living room where he picked up the glass still half full of strong drink, picked it up and carried it back to the kitchen where the bottle was still on the counter. He took them both, held them over the sink, and poured them down the drain.

In the refrigerator were two six packs of canned beer. He opened each one and within seconds they were gone. The smell of alcohol was so strong it permeated the entire room. The kitchen pantry had a case of hard liquor. Each bottle was opened in ritualistic fashion, and he ceremoniously emptied them into the sink. Satisfied, he took the bottles and cans and stuffed them into a couple garbage bags and took them outside and dumped them into the trash can.

Back inside, he turned on the water and sent the final remnants of the substances he'd used to dull the pain of the loss of Taylor off the sides of the sink, out of the house, and out of his life forever.

Today was a defining moment in his life. The day he decided to live again.

* * *

Taylor came out of the bedroom dressed in shorts and a T-shirt. Her shoulder-length, sandy blonde hair was still wet and hanging like strings from her head. A pained look was on her face. Carter didn't know if it was guilt, shame maybe, or just from being over-powered by the obvious smell of alcohol that still hung over the room. If it was the alcohol, she didn't say anything.

"You kept all my stuff," she said softly.

"Yeah... Well."

"I mean..." Taylor was choking back tears. "Everything is the same as when I left. My toothbrush is still right there beside yours. All my makeup and jewelry. Clothes."

They had a fairly good-sized master closet. Taylor's clothes and shoes took up two thirds of it. Carter had his stuff crammed into a small corner. He never changed it or moved any of her things. Except her shoes by the door. He wanted his only three pairs to be close to the door for easy access. The only things of hers that he'd moved. Her brand of shampoo was still in the shower.

"All your stuff is still in the craft room. I didn't touch any of it," Carter said.

"Why did you keep my things?"

"I thought you might want them. I didn't want to throw them away. You never came back for them."

"I know. I was too ashamed. I figured you hated me," she said, turning her head away.

"I did. For a while." Carter was a big, strong, tough man with steely eyes and a rough exterior, and he was doing everything in his power to keep her from seeing him cry. It wasn't working as tears were escaping out of the prison of his eyes and rolling down his face. The best he could do was turn away like she'd done, with his back to her so she couldn't see him roughly wipe them away.

"I'm sorry..." Taylor said sweetly coming up from behind and putting her hand on his shoulders, kissing him on the shoulder blade through the shirt.

Her touch sent goosebumps down his arms with a jolt as strong as the icy, cold water in the shower. He'd dreamed of her back in his house. He'd longed to hear her voice again. To feel her touch. He didn't turn around but just put his hand to his eyes. Taylor backed away, clearly not sure what to do or what was appropriate.

"Do you want me to leave?" she asked.

Carter laughed, breaking the tension.

"What's so funny?"

"Why do you think I saved your ass?" he said.

"Honestly, I don't know. I can't imagine why you'd ever want to see me again." Taylor was obviously racked with guilt. Understandably.

"Truthfully," he said, turning back to face her, "when that airmobile hit the Tower, I went to help the people in the Tower. It's who I am. It's in my DNA. But all I could think about was you. Where you were? Were you safe? I didn't care about anything else but finding you and bringing you home."

"How did you know where I was?"

"I saw you down there one day."

"I didn't think you knew." The pained looked on her face became even more evident with each word he spoke.

"Yeah. Well. I did. But all I could think about was getting you home, to where you'd be safe. Where I could protect you."

"That's so sweet. You shouldn't have, though. I don't deserve it. Those people in the Tower did deserve it... Deserve you."

Carter shrugged his shoulders.

"It's always been you," he said. "I don't know why. You make me so mad sometimes." He balled his fist and tensed his shoulders and his jaw as he said it. "But..." his voice trailed off.

"It's getting dark," Taylor said, cutting him off in mid sentence, saving him from the awkwardness of having to express his emotions. "Where are the matches and candles?"

"The usual place."

"I should've known. The house doesn't look any different than the day I... Never mind. I'll get them."

Carter was a survivalist. He'd seen so much war and hardship, when he came back and returned to civilian life, he was obsessed with stockpiling food, supplies, weapons, and ammunition. He built a saferoom in the house with a large steel door and locks that were almost impenetrable. Inside, were enough supplies to last for two years. He wondered if they might need them for a few days at least, with all of the chaos he'd seen downtown.

Within a minute, Taylor returned with several candles, flashlights, and matches in her hands. She lit a candle on the kitchen counter, illuminating the room and casting eerie shadows across it. She abruptly turned around and walked into the kitchen pantry. When she emerged, in her hands were three power bars.

"Are you hungry?" she asked. "I made dinner." She said it as she waved the bars in the air.

"You shouldn't have gone to so much trouble," Carter said, letting a smile come on his face.

"It's the least I could do since you saved my ass," Taylor said playfully.

"Should we bring out the fine china?" he asked with a wide grin.

"I don't think we ever had any fine china," she said, laughing.

For three hours they sat in the living room, joking, laughing, and avoiding any hurtful topics. It felt like old times to him. At least some of the better old times.

Finally, as it was getting late, a somber, hurt look came over Taylor's face as her eyes narrowed. Tears were welling up in her eyes again. She was fidgeting with her hands.

"I really am sorry," she said meekly.

"I know." Carter couldn't look at her when he said it.

"Will you ever be able to forgive me?"

"I already have. I did a long time ago."

"It'll never happen again. I swear."

"Then don't ever bring it up again," he said roughly.

She started to speak, but he stopped her. "I think we should go to church," he said.

Her eyes widened in surprise. "Okay... Do you have one in mind?"

"The one a few blocks from here. Red Spot Christian Church. I want to go this Sunday."

"That sounds good. I think that's good. I'll go with you."

Carter stood from the chair and walked over to the couch where she was sitting and extended his hand. She put her hand in his, and he lifted her up from the couch.

"It's late. Let's go to bed."

He kept his hand in hers, and she put her other hand on his arm as they walked back to the bedroom but first stopped in the kitchen and picked up the candle to take with them.

"I'm glad you are home," he said before they went into the bedroom together.

14

"I just want to die," Ruth said to Naomi as she lay on her bed in a fetal position, sobbing uncontrollably.

A few hours before, Ruth had discovered her newborn baby, Kate, missing from her crib. The only thing left of her were the swaddling clothes she'd been wrapped in. Shortly after, she learned her husband, Jake, was missing from work. He disappeared out of his office, and the only thing left behind were his clothes. Those same clothes were now laying on the bed. She clutched the shirt Jake had worn to work that day and held it tightly to her chest. The shirt was now wet from her tears.

Every attempt Ruth made to reach her parents and sister were in vain. She was assuming the worst. They were likely gone as well. Everyone who was important to her was missing, except for Naomi, her mother-in-law.

Naomi, Jake's mother, was trying her best to comfort Ruth but she was also dealing with her own loss. Her husband, Carl, was missing along with her son. Yet she was the one trying to be strong for Ruth. She had expressed concern for Ruth's mental well-being several times. Ruth had said more than once that life was no longer worth living without her husband and daughter. Naomi had insisted on coming back to the house with Ruth, saying she was afraid to leave her alone, and was not sure what she might do to herself.

Life as they both knew it would never be the same.

"They were my whole life. What am I going to do?" Ruth said between sobs.

"I know, honey," Naomi said gently. "It's hard. We'll get through it together." She sat next to Ruth on the edge of the bed and stroked her hair and back, trying her best to comfort her.

"Where did they go?" Ruth cried out.

"Let's listen to the news reports. Maybe they'll have more information."

Ruth had found a battery-powered audio, and they listened to it for more than an hour until they couldn't stand it anymore. The reports said more than a billion people might be missing. Millions... maybe billions... more were dead. An airmobile had hit the Tower and knocked it completely to the ground. An unimaginable tragedy was unfolding that affected the entire world. Naomi had no idea what to think happened, and Ruth had many understandable questions.

Ruth turned the audio back on. The audio station was linked to the local vision network reporting live on the situation from downtown. The scenes they were describing were horrific.

"I am speaking from Market Street, just two blocks from where the Tower stood," said the voice on the audio. A correspondent for the vision station was near the site of where the airmobile hit the Tower causing it to collapse.

"This is as close as we can get to it," he continued. "As you can see, the entire Tower is gone." Apparently, the vision station was showing live pictures. They didn't have power at Ruth's house, so they could only picture what was happening.

"A hundred and twenty floors have disintegrated. The loss of life is staggering. Authorities are still calling it a search and rescue but from the looks of it, it will most likely just be a recovery effort. It's unlikely that anyone could have survived that carnage. Some officials are telling me it's also unlikely they can even identify the remains. The diesel fuel from the airmobile powered the fire and caused the steel girders on the building to get so hot they collapsed in on themselves, causing the whole structure to implode."

"Do we know why the airmobile flew into the Tower?" the anchorman asked.

"We are getting reports that thousands of airmobiles have crashed. About 42,000 were in the air at the time of the incident.

About a third were piloted by individuals who suddenly vanished into thin air. Or at least that's what we presume because the airmobiles slowly descended into a crash. We think it was by chance that this one happened to crash into the building where so many people were working. That's all we know from here."

"Thank you, Eric. We'll be back with you at a later time. The Governor of Red Spots has issued a statement," another voice—a woman—said. Probably a co-anchor. "We urge all residents to stay calm," she said, probably reading from a prepared statement. "We cannot estimate how much damage has been done or the extent of it, but it has been a catastrophic event. The public is advised to stay in your homes. Leave the roads clear for emergency workers. Do not, I repeat, do not attempt to go to the hospitals unless it is a life or death matter. They are overrun with people. Please stay in your homes."

"It sounds really bad," Ruth said.

The audio was distracting Ruth from her pain, at least for the moment. Her tears had stopped.

"It's a huge disaster," Naomi said. "I can't believe this is happening."

"Initial reports estimate that as many as ten-to-twenty-billion people around the world are missing," the anchorwoman continued.

Ruth gasped.

"That's impossible," Naomi said. "How could so many people be missing?"

"Reports are," the anchorwoman continued, "that every child under the age of seven or eight is missing. Newborns were snatched from their mother's wombs. Children were taken out of their mother's arms. It's unfathomable what has happened. More than a billion children are missing and presumed dead. Do we have any more reports on what might have caused it?"

The anchorman responded, "Officials are refusing to speculate. However, we have heard reports that it may have been caused by aliens."

"Aliens!" Ruth let out a scream.

Naomi nodded as her mouth flew open. "The thought of my grandbaby being abducted and in the hands of an alien is unimaginable." Naomi grabbed Ruth's hand and squeezed it as she said it. "What could alien creatures want with babies?" Ruth shuddered at the thought.

"I don't think it's aliens," Naomi said, trying to dismiss the theory. "We would see them, or their spacecraft."

The reporters talked for several minutes about the possibilities of aliens snatching the children and what they might be doing with them, upsetting Ruth even more.

Naomi reached to turn the audio back off just as the anchorman said, "We want to go to a guest. Dr. Tom Collins. The motivational self-help guru is on the line. Dr. Tom, can you hear me?"

"Yes. I'm here," a deep and authoritative voice came across the audio.

"I've been told in my ear that you have a theory as to what happened. Why do you think all those people are missing?"

"I don't think it's a theory," Dr. Tom said. "I think it's a fact. The Seizure occurred today."

"What is the Seizure?" the anchorman asked.

"It is a Christian belief that comes from the Bible and the teachings of Jesus. The Christian denominations believe and have taught for centuries that Jesus would come back for every believer and that they would be taken from Jupiter into heaven."

Ruth was sitting up in the bed, listening intently. Her eyes were affixed on the audio.

"That seems as far-fetched as alien invasions," the anchorwoman said.

"It may sound far-fetched, but it's the most logical explanation. I don't know this for a fact, but I would guess that most people who were taken today were very active in a church and professed to be Christian."

"That's right!" Ruth said. "Jake went to church every Sunday. He was always trying to get me to go."

"Carl didn't go every Sunday," Naomi added. "But he did profess to be a Christian." Carl was Naomi's husband who Ruth and Naomi found missing from her home. The only thing left of him was his clothes laying in the chair in front of the vision set.

"My parents are missing," Dr. Tom said. "My dad is a pastor of a church. He has believed in Christ his whole adult life, and he preached that one day the seizure would come. I believe that's what's happened to him and all the others. God took them."

"Are they coming back?" the anchorwoman asked.

"Yes. Those who were taken will come back in seven years. After the tribulation."

Ruth started bouncing up and down with excitement. "Did you hear that? They're coming back."

"He said it wouldn't be for seven years," Naomi retorted. As disturbing as that news was, it might be what could keep Ruth from taking her own life. So, they took it as good news.

"Shh. Let's listen," Ruth said, her entire mood having changed. "I want to hear what he's saying."

"Thank you, Dr. Tom for the information. It's an interesting theory. One that we will be, no doubt, hearing a lot about over the next few days. Let's go back to our reporter downtown at the Tower. Eric, how many people were believed to be in the Tower?"

"I have been told that 13,000 people work in the Tower on any given day, not including visitors. The death toll may be as much as..."

Ruth turned off the audio angrily. Her face was crunched into a deep scowl.

"Why would God take my baby from me?" she said to Naomi with disdain in her voice.

"We don't know that he did. The reports said it could've been aliens."

Ruth glared at Naomi.

"I refuse to believe aliens took my baby," Ruth said emphatically. "The thought of it... Imagining my baby being raised by aliens... or worse. That's ridiculous. My mind can't go there. If I have to believe anything, I would rather believe Jake and Kate are in heaven."

"There's no way to know. Where did Jake go to church?"

"Red Spot Christian Church. It's just down the road from here."

"I wonder if they would know."

Ruth's eyes suddenly widened. "That's a great idea!"

"What is?"

"I'm going to go down to that church and demand answers. I want to know why God took my baby, and I'm going to demand he give her back to me. This isn't fair."

"They may not know," Naomi countered. "Or they may not even be there. Aren't they all taken? Didn't he say everyone who was a Christian went to heaven?"

"I don't know," Ruth said, the excitement gone from her voice and her face.

"Maybe I shouldn't have said that," Naomi quickly reversed the course of the conversation. What Ruth needed right now was hope.

"We can go down there if you want," Naomi said. "I'll go with you. Maybe someone there will have some answers."

"I have to do something. I can't just sit around and do nothing. If Jake and Kate aren't coming back, I want to go be with them. I just want to die."

"You can't say that Ruth. You don't mean it."

"I do mean it. I want to die and go be with them."

"How do you know that you'll be with them? Carl said that if you die without Jesus you don't go to heaven."

Ruth started rubbing her eyes roughly.

"I hate these Christians. That's why I never went to church. It's not fair. Why would Jake leave me? I'm a good person. I can't believe he'd rather be in heaven than with me. I know Kate would rather be with me. She had her whole life ahead of her. Now it's just taken from her." Ruth started crying again. "That's why I have to go to the church," Ruth said, choking back the tears. "I'm going to demand answers. Do you agree?"

"I suppose... I mean. Of course, I'll go with you. I want answers too."

Ruth turned the audio back on.

"We have just received word that Prescom Andrew Bartlett is one of the ones missing," they heard a voice on the audio say.

Ruth's mouth flew open again.

Naomi's did as well, as both seemed shocked by what they were hearing.

Prescom Bartlett was beloved by many, including the two of them.

"Vice Prescom Jack Wolf has temporarily assumed his duties. He will be addressing the world shortly."

"The Prescom is dead," Naomi said as they both stared at each other in disbelief. "I didn't think this tragedy could get any worse."

She was wrong.

15

"If we don't do something soon, we're going to have a riot on our hands," Dr. Matthew King, head of Obstetrics at Red Spot Community Hospital for Obstetrics, said to his leadership staff gathered in his office. While he had said it facetiously, he wasn't completely void of concern about the remote possibility of that very thing happening.

"How many babies are missing?" Dr. King asked.

"Nine hundred and sixty-seven," Dr. Sellers, his head surgeon, said. He was looking at a piece of paper compiled by his team at the request of Dr. King. "We're also missing two hundred and forty moms, along with forty-three nurses, and seven doctors."

"How many women were in labor when everything happened?" Dr. King asked.

Dr. Sellers turned the page over and said, "Two hundred and forty-three. Some of them disappeared as well. About a third of them."

"And how many pregnant women do we have in the emergency room right now who have lost their babies?"

"The last count was over five thousand. We don't have an exact number. That's been increasing by about a thousand an hour but is slowing down. The line stretches outside the door, as you can imagine."

The hospital only had approximately two thousand rooms. There's no way they could handle that many patients.

"All right," Dr. King said after taking a deep breath. "Here's what we're going to do."

Everyone was looking at him with deep concern, yet no one had offered any suggestions when asked. The ladies who'd already delivered babies over the last couple days were demanding answers which, of course, no one had. A pregnant woman's emotions were generally unstable and heightened after pregnancy and delivery anyway, with fluctuations in hormones. Coupled with the sudden unexplained disappearance of their babies, and they were on the verge of a total collective meltdown.

"Send all the Moms home who've already delivered their babies," Dr. King said matter-of-factly and with no emotion.

"All of them?" Maggie, his chief nurse asked with surprise in her voice.

"Yes," he replied.

"What about the ones who had C-sections?" Dr. Sellers asked.

"Send them home as well. Let them recuperate at home. We need the rooms. Unless they're life threatening or can't walk out of here on their own."

"What do we tell them happened to their newborns?" Maggie asked.

"I don't know..." Dr. King said, trying to think of a good explanation the women and their families would accept. He realized nothing he could say could bring their babies back or make the situation better for them. His job was to bring them to full term, deliver the child, and take care of both of them and then send them home. There were no children to take care of. There was nothing he could do for them.

"Tell them it was an act of God," he finally decided. "Tell them to watch the news. Every baby in the entire world is missing. It's not our fault. The Governor said everyone should stay off the streets. So, they need to go home. Right away. And stay there. If they have a life-threatening situation, then they can come back. Otherwise, they need to leave so we can take care of the most serious cases."

"You're going to have a lot of unhappy moms," Maggie said.

"There's nothing we can do about it. My baby is gone as well," Dr. King said angrily. "Tell them that. Tell them the head doctor's wife was eight months pregnant and they lost their baby. So, we know what they're going through. It's not like we wanted this to happen or caused it."

"How do we tell them? Individually or all at once?" Dr. Sellers asked.

"All at once. Make an announcement over the intercom. Let's get them out of here as quickly as possible. I know it's callous. But it's the best we can do under the circumstances."

Satisfied with that solution, Dr. King turned his attention to the emergency room. How could they possibly treat more than five thousand women? The emotional pain of those pregnant mothers must be just as great, if not greater. He couldn't imagine what it would be like to carry a baby however many months, then have it snatched out of the womb in the blink of an eye, with no reasonable explanation.

An emotional trauma his own wife was going through at that very moment. Alone. He needed to get home to her as soon as possible, but he had a responsibility to the hospital, the staff, and to their patients.

Treating five thousand women was not possible with their limited staff. And more were coming. He made a difficult decision.

"Janice," Dr. King said, turning his attention to Janice Burkett, head nurse in the Emergency Room. "Lock the doors. Put a sign out front saying we're full and can't take any more patients."

"We're an emergency room," Janice said. "We're supposed to be open twenty-four seven."

Dr. King appreciated her response. His staff was professional, and care of the patients was their primary concern. But Dr. King learned early on in his professional career that they can't save everyone. If they tried to, they wouldn't be able to help the ones they could save.

"It can't be helped," he retorted, certain he was doing the right thing. "We're out of room. They'll have to go to another facility."

"There's no other facility they can go to," Janice said. "The hospital emergency rooms are all overrun with patients. People are dying in the streets."

He was searching for an answer. "Do we have enough antibiotics for five thousand patients?"

"Yes, Dr. King."

"For ten thousand?"

"Maybe. Barely," Janice answered.

"How many patients can we treat with antibiotics before we run out?" Dr. King asked.

"We have at least a couple of weeks in stock for a thousand patients."

"That's the dilemma," Dr. King said soberly. "Do we treat five thousand patients for one week or ten thousand patients one time? What do you think, Dr. Sellers?"

"The main thing we need to prevent is infection," Dr. Sellers said. "We obviously can't save the babies. While traumatic, the woman's health is not life threatening. Unless she gets an infection, which could happen if we don't get everything out of her uterus. I know where you're going with that question. If we give every lady one day's worth, will it stave off an infection?"

Everyone waited for an answer.

"Hard to say," he said, answering his own question. "Some women will not get an infection. Others will. The problem is that we don't know which ones will and which ones won't. My opinion is that if you give one day's supply to everyone, you're wasting it. Better to give a full week to less people and hope we get some drugs later to treat the women who do get an infection. It's a hard decision. It's like we're playing God."

"The other thing to consider," Janice said, "is that we have no idea when we're going to get any more drugs. What about patients next week? And the week after. It may be awhile before our supplier gets any in stock, considering what's happening around the world."

"I don't think that matters," Dr. King said. "Think about it. There are no pregnant ladies left on Jupiter. It will be at least nine months before we have another delivery in this hospital. And I'm not sure anyone is going to be eager to get pregnant after what happened this time. I have no idea what this is going to mean for our business moving forward. We'll have to worry about that later."

"So, what do you want me to do?" Janice asked.

Dr. King rubbed his eyes roughly. This was why he was the head of Obstetrics. To make hard decisions. He never in his wildest dreams anticipated this one.

"Lock the doors," he finally said. "Distribute one week's supply of antibiotics to the women already inside the facility until you run out. First come, first serve. Then send them home. Those outside will just have to go somewhere else."

"What do you want my doctors to do?" Dr. Sellers asked.

"Janice, if you come across someone who you think is seriously ill, then take them back to a room. Dr. Sellers and his doctors will examine them and treat them accordingly. Even then, if possible, send them home. If it's life threatening, then let's do what we can. That's all we can do."

The team scattered to follow the instructions. Dr. King walked behind his desk and slumped in his chair giving himself a minute to catch his breath and slow his heartbeat. The minute turned into five minutes as he felt overwhelmed. He looked at the paperwork piled on his desk that had taken so much of his attention that day. He hated paperwork with a passion. Treating patients was his first love. Now, the paperwork didn't matter. He might never get to it. He had much bigger worries.

The intercom suddenly blared into action, carrying his message to the patients.

"Ladies and family members. Please gather your things. The hospital is closing. In an orderly fashion, please exit the hospital. We deeply regret what has happened to your babies. It is beyond our control. It was an act of God. But you need to go home. Thank you."

When the message started, Dr. King leaned forward in his chair and looked up at the ceiling, listening carefully to the message. After it was over, he slumped back in his chair and put his hands to his face, giving himself a few more minutes to grieve the loss of his own son.

Seven minutes later, a fire alarm went off, sending a high-pitched siren blaring in his office and throughout the hospital.

16

The fire alarm shook Dr. Matthew King out of the momentary reflection on the loss of his son.

What's going on?

The intercom erupted.

"Dr. King, come to the nursery, stat!"

Another urgent message followed.

"Dr. King, come to ER, stat!"

I can't be at both places. I'm just one man.

Dr. Sellers burst into his office. Out of breath. A look of panic was on his face.

"What's going on?" Dr. King said.

"There's a riot on the nursery wing," he said between gasps for air. "Women are refusing to leave without their babies. Our doctors and nurses insisted. There was a physical altercation between one of the husbands and one of my doctors. It spun out of control and started a massive fight. It's utter chaos. They're looting the nursery. Destroying equipment. Turning over beds. Someone set fire to the baby cribs in the nursery. We put it out, but then they started dragging mattresses into the hall and setting those on fire. I pulled the alarm."

"That's ridiculous!"

An urgent call came over the intercom again.

"Dr. King, nursery, stat."

"How bad is the fire? Do we need to evacuate the entire hospital?" Dr. King asked.

The voice on the intercom answered his question.

"We have fire in the nursery! Someone has set fire to the cribs and is dragging mattresses and beds into the hall and setting them on fire. Everyone exit the building, now!" The urgency in her voice told them it was a dire situation.

Dr. King pulled out his caller and tried to dial the emergency police response. All he got was a fast-busy signal.

"The police will be of no help," Dr. King said with resignation. "They're overrun as it is with everything that happened at the Tower. We're on our own. Go back to the nursery. See if you can calm the situation. If not, just get your people out of there to safety. I'm going to the ER."

They both ran out of his office. Dr. King headed to the elevators until he realized they were on lockdown because of the fire alarm. The constant blare of the siren was deafening. The red lights on the walls were flashing, sending strobes of light up and down the hallway.

He took the stairs and ran the four flights down, taking the steps two at a time. He heard screaming in the ER. Two of his nurses were huddled at the bottom of the stairs just inside the door. They stopped him from running out into the main emergency room area.

"What happened?" Dr. King said.

"We locked the main doors. We were distributing antibiotics to the women like we were told to do and then sending them home. Somebody on the outside threw a rock through the window. More rocks were thrown. Then they broke down the doors. The people outside saw us distributing the medications. People were fighting over them. I've never seen anything like it. They were practically killing each for a box of pills."

Dr. King peered out from behind the door. Bodies were laying on the floor. Blood was everywhere. Some of his nurses were huddled behind the desk. Crouched down. A terrified look on their faces. One was laying on the floor, bleeding and moaning. She appeared to be badly hurt.

Suddenly, the sprinkler system came on, spraying the room with water as smoke started filling the stairway and the main lobby. They had no choice but to exit the stairway or they would be overcome with smoke. Fortunately, a lot of people left the ER when the fight started. Others grabbed the medicine and ran for the door. The ER room was almost empty. Shards of glass were everywhere. The room was drenched from the water.

They started caring for the wounded. Several were dead, crushed by the stampede of people. Others were severely injured. The fire alarm finally turned off. Dr. King could still hear the sound ringing in his ears for several minutes. He presumed that the sprinkler system put out the fire.

He instructed his staff to do what they could for the injured.

"Carry them back to rooms if they can be saved. If they're dead, just leave them where they lie."

He bolted back up the stairs, ignoring the smoke.

When he came to the nursery floor, he saw the same type of scene in the hallway and rooms. Injured were everywhere, including some of his staff. The doctors and nurses who weren't injured were caring for the wounded. The conditions were not ideal. A haze of smoke still lingered over the room. People were doubled over, coughing. Everyone was soaked. Puddles of water were on the floor. The entire area looked to be ransacked. Mattresses were smoldering in the hallway.

Dr. Sellers was one of the ones injured with a gash on his head, but he was still caring for the wounded. Like the ER, the floor was mostly empty. Everyone had left in a panic, except the injured and his staff who'd dutifully stayed to care for the injured.

Dr. King started barking instructions.

"If you have patients who are serious, take them to the ER. If they're dead... Just leave them. If they can walk out of here and their injuries are not life threatening, do what you can, and then send them home."

He left the scene and went back down to the ER. He saw a woman writhing on the floor. As he bent down to check her, he put his hand behind her to lift her up but cut his hand on broken glass laying under her. He winced in pain. A nurse saw what happened and found some gauze and tape and wrapped his hand tightly to stop the bleeding.

Ignoring the pain, he carried the woman back to a room and sat her in a bed. He then went from room to room, checking on the patients. He gave the nurses and doctors of the ER the same instructions as the nursery personnel.

"If the patient's injuries are not life threatening, treat them, and send them home."

"I don't have a ride," one lady said. "I don't have a husband. I'm single, and my brother is missing. I don't know how to get home."

He started to tell her to call a mobile for hire but realized there wouldn't be one. He couldn't put her out in the streets.

"I'll figure something out," he said.

***

Dr. King arrived at his house at 3:30 in the morning after dropping the single lady off at her apartment. He was exhausted. His hand was aching from the gash that required fourteen stitches to close. Dr. Sellers had stitched it up for him without anything to numb the pain. All the medicine had been looted from the ER as well as the nursery. He treated Dr. Sellers's gash on his head, which he was able to close with butterfly stitches which didn't need numbing. They had somehow been able to joke about how lucky Dr. Sellers was compared to him.

Olivia, his wife, was awake, lying in their bed. Her eyes were red from crying. He rushed to her side and took her in his arms. She wouldn't let go of him for several minutes.

He told her everything that had happened at the hospital, leaving out the goriest details. Twelve people were dead, including one of his doctors. All they knew to do was put the bodies in body bags and store them in the freezer until authorities could come and get them.

"What happened to your hand, Matthew?" she asked with alarm in her voice.

"I cut it on some broken glass. It needed stitches, but I'll be fine." He looked her in the eyes. "How are you feeling?"

"Horrible. It's hard."

"I understand. I don't know what's happening. Every pregnant woman in our hospital lost her son or daughter. They just disappeared."

"What did you tell them about what happened to their babies?" Olivia asked.

"That it was an act of God and wasn't our fault," Matthew said.

"Was it?"

"Was it, what?"

"Was it an act of God?"

"I don't know, honey. I guess."

"I think we should find out."

"How?"

"I heard someone say that it was the seizure."

"What's the seizure?"

"I don't know," Olivia said. "Dr. Tom Collins was interviewed, and he said God took everyone to heaven."

"I don't really believe in God."

"Don't you want to know what happened to our baby?"

"Of course. But can we ever really know? Our son's gone. I don't know how to find out what happened to him."

"I've been thinking about it. I want to go to church and see if we can find some answers."

"I don't think you should get your hopes up," Matthew said.

"I want to go to church. I have to know."

"OK. We'll go to church."

"Promise."

"I promise. Now I'm taking a shower and then... I'm going to bed. I'm exhausted."

17

Sept. 13, 2061

Prescom Jack Wolf knew his words were about to drop a bomb-shell on the entire cabinet meeting. "I think we should reopen the stock market," the Prescom—formerly, the Vice Prescom—said.

The fourteen people in the room had made it official when they determined that Andrew Bartlett, the former Prescom, was incapac-itated, after he disappeared along with twenty billion other people earlier in the week. Wolf was sworn in with little fanfare and was in his second day on the job, trying to manage the global catastrophe now his problem to solve.

As expected, the cabinet members erupted, objecting strongly. Especially J. B. Hader, the Director of Commerce. "With all due re-spect," he said, "that will throw the entire world into a depression," Hader said.

"A depression is inevitable," Wolf said. "There's no way to avoid it. The sooner we let it happen, the sooner we get out of it. What we have to figure out is how to limit the damage, especially for us."

Every person in the room was extremely wealthy, along with their friends and business associates who had helped Bartlett get elected.

"By the way, all the power is back on to the areas we discussed," Royce Johnson said. "The Red Spots area is at a hundred percent power. So are all the wealthy areas of Jupiter. We'll start on the rest soon." Royce was in charge of infrastructure such as roads, utilities, and various modes of transportation. The urgency was to get power on to the more affluent areas and to businesses first. Then focus on the other, less affluent regions of Jupiter.

Transportation was also a priority. Businesses thrived on travel and communication. Airmobiles were still grounded. The priority was to get them back in the air as soon as possible. That was taking longer than track cars, buses, and clearing the roads to through traffic. Caller service was still down in most areas, but a priority.

"That's good," Wolf said without much enthusiasm. He was more concerned about the financial impact of the crisis which was the focus of the meeting.

"The stock market will go down by eighty percent within hours," Hader argued. "That will destroy all of our portfolios."

Others were agreeing with him, openly showing how upset they were at the suggestion to open the stock market.

"We are the ones who'll take the biggest hit," Hader added.

"Shouldn't we be thinking about what's in the best interest of everyone?" Aria Decker, the Director of Diplomatic Relations said. "Not just the people in this room."

"It's not just us. It's all the rich people on Jupiter. The wealthy are the ones who pay the bills," Hader retorted. "We start the businesses and take the risks. These people wouldn't have jobs without the business owners. If we take care of them, then that'll benefit everyone."

Several voiced their agreement, and Aria didn't say anything further. All eyes in the room turned back toward Wolf.

The Prescom took a deep breath and paused before speaking. "The stock market will go down, whenever we open it. Today. Tomorrow. Next week. Next month. How long are we going to keep it closed? We have to open it sometime. We need to open the banks as well."

All the banks on Jupiter were closed. The people were allowed to take a maximum of fifteen jupes a day out of the cash machines. Banks were closed because of a concern of a run on them. They only kept ten percent cash reserves as required by law. Woefully insufficient, a normal bank would run out of jupes in a matter of hours.

Most of the people in the room owned a bank so they were able to protect some of their cash.

"That would be economic suicide," Greg Jennings, the Director of the Treasury said. "Are you trying to destroy our entire economic system?"

The whole room erupted again. The concern was that if they opened the banks and there was a run, then the bank would run out of jupes. Everyone in the room could lose all or most of their fortunes because bank deposits were only insured up to $100,000 per account.

Wolf knew this conversation wouldn't go well which was why he had a plan before he brought it up. As the cabinet members began shouting over each other, he raised his hand to quiet the din.

"I've thought about it," Wolf said slowly. "The problem is going to be much worse than we think. The people missing have mortgages, mobiles, and mobile payments, credit card debt, student loans, and business loans. They obviously have no way to pay those back. The banks and financial institutions cannot sustain those levels of losses."

Wolf figured most in the room hadn't thought that far ahead.

"We will suddenly have a glut of empty houses," Jennings, in his role as Director of Treasury must have considered this. "There will be foreclosures. Repossessions. The legal system will be overwhelmed. The banks will only be able to sell the assets at pennies on the dollar if they can sell them at all. A lot of our banks hold those loans. The government backs them."

"The treasury can print more jupes," Brock Benson the Director of Intelligence said even though this wasn't his area of expertise.

"Then our currency will be worthless," Jennings said, knowing the ramifications of flooding the planet with excess cash.

"We have to protect our own wealth, first and foremost," Wolf said to the agreement of those in the room as most nodded.

"How do you propose we do that?" Hader asked.

"We seize the assets of the people who are missing," Wolf answered immediately.

The room suddenly grew quiet as the idea began to sink in, and all eyes were suddenly deeply fixed on Prescom Wolf, waiting for his next words.

"We start with their bank accounts. Then their houses," Wolf added.

Aria as she let out a loud gasp. "Can you legally do that?" she asked.

"I've declared a national emergency," Wolf said. "We can do anything we decide to do."

"Those people left Jupiter without making a provision to pay their debts," Hader said, obviously liking the suggestion. "From what I can tell, very few of the rich are missing. It's mostly the poor and middle class. They left the world on their own volition. It's not fair that we should be left with all their debts."

On Jupiter, five percent of the population held fifty percent of the total wealth. The people in the room accounted for approximately twenty percent of the total wealth on Jupiter.

"I agree," Jennings said. "I don't think our wealth should be jeopardized because a minority of poor people decided to leave the planet without saying anything to anyone."

"And it would work, right?" Prescom Wolf asked.

"It wouldn't solve all the problems," Hader replied. "This twenty percent of the population who are missing, represent a huge part of the spending power of Jupiter. Businesses are going to have to replace those sales somewhere. There will be less demand for products. In the short-term anyway."

"That will lead to a global depression," Jennings said.

"We can't avoid that fact," Wolf retorted. "We just have to keep it from destroying our government. If it gets too bad, there'll be a revolution, and we'll lose our power."

"Not to mention our own wealth," Hader said. "Anything we do has to preserve as much of our assets as possible."

"Here's what I would propose," Wolf said. "Let's freeze the bank accounts of those who are missing. Seize their checking and savings accounts and their retirement accounts. Even take their social security and their houses, mobiles, furniture, anything of value. Roll that jupes into an account that the government holds. Then let's make low interest loans to the banks. Long term loans. Say thirty years. That will help the banks with liquidity and will cover their cash reserves. That will at least let them reopen. Currency is about confidence. We have to restore confidence."

A murmur went through the room as excitement was building.

"What do we do with the jupes once it's in the government accounts?" Hader asked.

"We reimburse ourselves for our losses," Wolf said.

Another, stronger murmur went through the room. Aria spoke up over the din.

"What about their heirs?" Aria asked strongly. She was the newest cabinet member, holding a position responsible for interacting with religious groups. This was not her expertise, and Wolf wished she'd stay out of the conversation.

"What about them?" Hader asked.

"Aren't they entitled to the assets of the missing?" she asked.

"No," Hader responded emphatically. "That's what we're saying. Those people left on their own. They didn't pay off their homes or debts before they left. They're deadbeats as far as I'm concerned. We're just foreclosing on their assets to pay off their debts."

"Sounds like you're foreclosing on their assets to pay off *your* debts," Aria said brusquely. "That's wrong."

"You impudent fool!" Hader said. "You will not speak to me that way or accuse me of doing something illegal."

Prescom Wolf raised his hand again to quiet the argument. "Aria's right. It would be illegal. That's why I propose we vote to suspend the Constitution."

The entire room exploded with a collective gasp.

"Hear me out before you speak," Wolf said. "We have a worldwide emergency. A democratic society will not survive in this chaos. I suggest we establish a new world order with the authority centralized within this room. Whatever decisions are made in this room are law. It's for the people's best interest."

"Let's vote on it," Staff Chief Wilson said. "All in favor, raise your hand."

Everyone's hand went up except for Aria's.

"The motion carries," Wilson said.

"If I may speak freely, Mr. Prescom," Aria said, raising her hand to be heard.

"Go ahead," he said tersely, sharing Hader's offense at Aria's words.

"From what I can tell, the people who are missing were all Christians."

"I never liked them," Hader remarked.

Wolf held up his hand to silence him. "Let her speak," Wolf said. "What difference does that make?" Wolf knew how much power and wealth her dad had and didn't want to offend her.

"A big difference. These Christians were good and decent people. They were the ones who held families together and helped the poor and needy and fed and took in the homeless. Even though they weren't a majority, they did a lot of good in the world. I think we're underestimating what's going to happen to the moral fabric of our society now that they're gone. You can see it already in this room. You're talking about stealing their property to line your own pockets."

Hader glared at Aria. "What are you accusing us of?" he said angrily.

"I'm not accusing you of anything. You condemn yourself by your own actions and words."

"I don't understand what you mean," Wolf said.

"These Christians were the only things holding back evil in this world," Aria said soberly. "Now that they're gone, evil will be set free on the world. I've been reading about it. God restrained evil on Jupiter for the sake of the Christians. They're gone now. I'm afraid God is no longer going to hold back evil. From what I've read, we have seven years. That's how long it will take for us to destroy ourselves with our evil."

"That's ridiculous," Wolf said as Hader and others agreed and started mocking Aria. He waved his hand again to silence them.

"I don't think so," Aria said.

"What are we supposed to do about it?" Wolf said.

"That's the thing," Aria continued. "I don't think there's a thing you can do about it. Evil is about to be unleashed on Jupiter. I'm warning you. You think you have trouble now; you haven't seen anything yet."

"God help us all," Hader said mockingly.

"I think it's too late for God to help us," Aria said.

* * *

After the meeting was over, Aria walked back to her office, stunned. Bringing up the issue at the cabinet meeting hadn't been her intention. It's just that she had to speak up. What they were doing was wrong and infuriating. That Hader guy made her so mad. All of them. Just callously stealing people's hard-earned jupes and assets to protect their own interests. That's why she knew the cabinet couldn't be trusted to do the right thing. She didn't even know what the right thing was or if she could make a difference.

But she was determined to try. Aria wasn't one of the wealthy ones in the room, but her parents were. Bartlett had given her the position as a favor to her dad who was one of the ten wealthiest men on Jupiter. Aria was an idealist, more concerned about the welfare of mankind than the fortune which would someday be hers. She wondered if she'd ever get a chance to spend it.

On her desk was a book written by Reverend Lindsey Howell called *The Late, Great Planet Jupiter*. A fascinating read, it chronicled what would happen in the end times. In the first chapter of the book, Howell predicted a seizure of the church. He said billions of people would suddenly go missing without any notice. He was right; she was certain of it.

She researched him and found that he pastored a church there in Red Spot, not far from where she lived. No one picked up at the church when she tried to call; it just went to a message machine. The website said that the church would be meeting this Sunday, at ten o'clock. She was going to go there and see if he was among the missing. See if she could find some answers.

Now she had an even greater concern. Pastor Howell mentioned a second thing in his book. He said that after the seizure, a centralized government would be formed. It would be called the New World Order. The book was written twenty years ago. Howell was obviously somehow able to look into the future and see what was going to happen. The cabinet had just voted to establish a new world order government on Jupiter.

She'd only read the first two chapters, and both had already come to pass. She couldn't wait to read the next chapters to see what's going to happen next. First, she had to get to the church and meet this Pastor Howell.

This Sunday. Ten O'clock. I'm going to Red Spot Christian Church.

18

"You're dead," Danni said to Mrs. Pinkerton.

"I'm not dead yet," she said back to her.

"Yes, you are, Mrs. P." Danni had started affectionately calling her that.

"I had an ace!" Danni added strongly.

"You had the Ace of Clubs. The Ace of Spades is the only thing that can kill my king."

"Darn," she said, quickly putting her hand over her mouth. "Oh... I'm sorry," Danni quickly corrected herself. "I'm not allowed to use that word."

Mrs. P. didn't say anything. She had said much worse over the years.

"I guess it doesn't matter. I'm not allowed to play cards either," Danni said chuckling nervously.

Mrs. Pinkerton felt a twinge of guilt. She had taught Danni how to play a card game called War. Something her parents wouldn't have approved of. Cards was one of the vices Mrs. Pinkerton allowed herself. Once a week, she and three other ladies from the church played cards at her house. Those three ladies were gone. They vanished with the rest of them. Now, she was teaching those games to Danni. She didn't see anything wrong with it.

She suddenly wondered if maybe she had been too hard on Pastor Howell, Danni's father. It was easy to be judgmental toward him and overlook her own shortcomings, not that she considered playing cards all that bad. Maybe Dannie wearing denim pants to church wasn't such a bad thing either. Or the pastor not wearing a tie.

With each passing day, she was learning that Danni was really a good kid. For the first time in a couple days, Danni was actually smiling and having fun. The cards were taking her mind off her troubles, at least temporarily.

"I guess I'm corrupting you," Mrs. P. said. "Anyway. If you draw an Ace of Spades on the next card, then I'll be dead, and you'll win the game."

Danni's eyes widened in anticipation as Mrs. Pinkerton slowly drew the next card.

The Ace of Spades!

The odds of that card being drawn weren't very good. Mrs. Pinkerton wondered if God had arranged that to try and lift the girl's spirits.

Danni bolted out of her chair. "Yes!" she said. They had played four games, and this was the first she won. She was so excited she danced around with her hands in the air. "I can't believe I finally won one."

"You did. You won fair and square."

"Let's play again."

"It's getting late. What time are you supposed to go to bed?"

"Ten o'clock."

The clock was about to strike midnight.

"We should go to bed."

Danni suddenly got quiet. The excitement completely drained from her face.

"I don't have school," she said. Mrs. Pinkerton knew school had been cancelled for the fall. They'd only had another two weeks left anyway, and the officials decided to start the fall vacation early.

"I'm tired," Mrs. Pinkerton said with a yawn. "I'm not used to staying up this late. I'm going to bed. We can play more tomorrow."

Mrs. Pinkerton stood, kissed Danni on the forehead, and went into the guest room. She settled in the bed and fell right to sleep.

A few hours later, she was awakened by a noise in the living room. At first, she thought she'd imagined it and turned over to go back to sleep. Then she heard it again. She sat up in bed and noticed a light coming through the slight crack under her door. A robe was at the end of the bed and she slipped it on. As she was about to open the door, she heard the noise again, louder this time.

With the door cracked slightly, she could see a shadow of a figure coming out of the kitchen and walking into the living room. She called out, "Danni? Are you awake?"

"Sorry, Mrs. P.," she heard the quiet voice say. "Did I wake you?"

Mrs. Pinkerton opened the door and walked out into the living room. Danni was sitting on the couch with a drink of water in her hand, still wearing the same clothes she had on when Mrs. Pinkerton had gone to bed. She looked at the clock, and the time was two o'clock in the morning.

"Is something wrong?" Mrs. Pinkerton asked.

"I couldn't sleep."

She closed her robe and walked over to sit next to Danni on the couch.

"How come?" she asked, immediately knowing how dumb the question sounded. The girl had just lost her parents and siblings. Who wouldn't have trouble sleeping? Rather than letting her answer, she tried to be reassuring.

"I understand why you can't sleep. Do you want to talk about it?"

Danni shook her head and sat down the drink and then shrunk into a ball, pulling her legs closer to her on the couch and resting her head on her knees.

"I'm afraid," Danni finally said meekly.

"What are you afraid of?" Mrs. Pinkerton asked. "I'm here with you."

"I'm afraid to close my eyes. What if I have that dream again?"

Danni woke up screaming the night before, waking Mrs. Pinkerton. She had rushed into Danni's bedroom to find her in a cold sweat, shaking, obviously distraught from the nightmare. Mrs. Pinkerton hadn't realized it had affected Danni to such an extent that the girl was terrified to go to sleep.

"Tell me about your dream."

"No! I can't. It was horrible."

"It will help to talk about it. To get it out."

Tears formed in Danni's eyes. She quickly wiped them away, probably not wanting Mrs. Pinkerton to see them.

"You don't have to talk about it if you don't want to. I understand. I'll just sit here with you."

"I don't want to keep you from sleeping."

"It's okay. You're more important than sleep. I can sleep when I'm dead," Mrs. Pinkerton said with a slight laugh, although Danni didn't respond to the joke.

I wish there were something I could say.

It had been years since she dealt with a teenage girl. She barely remembered what it was like. Really, she'd probably never been this close to her own daughter. She couldn't remember a time when she and her daughter shared this intimate a moment. The best thing was to not say anything, she decided. Danni would open up when she wanted. It didn't take very long.

"I dreamed I died. I was in hell."

"Oh, honey."

"My parents were there. So was Avery. And Todd. They were in heaven looking at me."

Danni changed positions on the couch. Mrs. Pinkerton thought about leaning in closer but decided against it. Danni was finally opening up. This was good. She just needed to listen.

"I asked Jesus to have mercy on me. But he didn't," she said angrily. "He said I was cursed and doomed to hell. Then he threw me in the fire."

"You don't have to tell me, if it's too hard."

"No, I want to." Danni had a faraway look in her eyes as she continued.

"Hell was horrible. The flames were burning my arms, and my face, and my hands. It seemed so real. Avery was standing just outside of hell. I reached for her." The last words barely came out above a whisper as she was choking back the tears

As tears started running down Danni's face, Mrs. Pinkerton moved closer. She put her hand on the girl's shoulder and comforted her as her shoulders slumped further and her head was buried in her knees.

"But I couldn't reach her," Danni said with renewed resolve, sitting up a little straighter. "I asked for some water. I said something like, 'Avery, dip your finger in water and put it on my tongue.' But she didn't move. Jesus said that Avery was in heaven, and that I had to live in agony for an eternity. That she couldn't help me anymore."

Anger lurked behind every word. Mrs. Pinkerton couldn't tell if Danni was angry at her sister, or God... or herself.

"What happened next?" Mrs. Pinkerton asked, mesmerized by the intensity by which Danni was relating the dream. Danni knew every detail. Mrs. Pinkerton was beginning to believe this might've been more than a dream. Maybe God was trying to tell Danni something.

"I said to Jesus, 'Let Avery go back to Jupiter and tell everyone and warn them, so they don't come to this place of torment.'"

Danni roughly wiped away the tears again.

"What did Jesus say?" Mrs. Pinkerton said in a gentle voice.

"He said it was too late," Danni said as her words turned into sobs. "He said I should have warned them when I was on Jupiter. I said, 'How could I have known?' I didn't know." She buried her head back in her knees as she pulled them closer to her clearly in anguish.

"Was that it?" Mrs. Pinkerton asked after giving her nearly a minute to compose herself.

"That's when I woke up."

"That may not really be a bad dream," Mrs. Pinkerton said.

"It was horrible!"

Mrs. Pinkerton reached over to Danni, took her chin, and lifted it up while turning it toward her.

"The Bible says that in the last days, young men will dream dreams and young girls will prophesy. Clearly, we're in the last days. What if God was giving you that dream? As a prophecy, as a warning?"

"I don't understand."

"Honey. You're not dead yet. You're very much alive. It's not too late for you. You're not in hell. Do you remember what Jesus said to you?"

Danni looked into the distance, thinking.

"He said that I should've warned the people on Jupiter. When I was back there."

"Yes! What did you say to Jesus?"

"I said that I didn't know. How could I know?"

"You do know, now. Don't you?"

"Know what?"

"You know the truth. You've seen hell. You've seen how horrible it is to be separated from God. You need to tell the people of Jupiter what you saw. You need to warn them. It's not too late. You didn't have a dream."

"I didn't?"

"No. You had a prophecy. Just like the Bible said would happen in the last days."

"Why would God give me a prophecy? I'm a nobody."

"You don't have to be a nobody. Your dad's gone. Somebody has to carry on his legacy. The people of Jupiter need to know what you saw in that dream. They need to know what it's like to die and be without Jesus. You're the one to tell them."

"I wouldn't know where to begin."

"Sure, you do. You know the Bible better than anybody left on this planet. You've heard your dad preach a thousand sermons. Besides, God will give you the words."

"Do you mean at church?"

"That's exactly what I mean! You should take your dad's place."

"I could never get up and speak before other people."

"You can and you will. I'm sure of it. God has called you to something special. Jupiter needs you."

"I can't."

Mrs. Pinkerton took both hands and put them on Danni's shoulders and turned her toward her and looked her straight in the eye.

"You can do this. God is calling you to do it. You are one of the young girls the Bible prophesied about in the last days."

"I'm sixteen years old."

"Go look up the verse. It says that maidservants will prophesy. You don't have to be anything special for God to use you. In fact, that's who he loves to use. The person we least expect him to use."

"I don't know."

"I can't sleep now," Mrs. Pinkerton said with urgency in her voice. "I'm so excited, I could spit!"

She stood from the couch and began pacing the room.

"You could spit?" Danni said, laughing. "What are you talking about?"

"I'm as excited as a pig on slop!"

"Stop it!" Danni giggled. "You're cracking me up."

"Those are just some old sayings my parents used to say."

"You're funny."

Finally, she said to Danni. "You'd better get some sleep. Can you go to sleep? Don't worry about the dream. You won't have it again. God gave it to you for a reason."

Danni nodded her head in understanding and stood up from the couch, the life having returned to her face.

"We have a lot to do between now and Sunday," Mrs. Pinkerton said.

Danni looked at her with her eyes wide and her mouth agape. Mrs. Pinkerton stared back, actually feeling alive herself for the first time in years. Maybe God was going to finally use her. She gave Danni a hug and sent her off to bed.

I love this girl. She thought to herself. *I love this girl!*

19

Sept. 14, 4:30 a.m.

Danni felt like she was doing something wrong.

Sitting in her father's desk chair in his study was something she never would've done when he was alive. Why was she so nervous? He was gone. Seized. Not coming back for seven years, if she remembered her Bible prophecies correctly. Until then, she was on her own. The house was hers to run, and the sooner she took charge of the situation the better.

Even with growing confidence, she opened the middle drawer to his desk slowly, as if he would suddenly appear and yell at her. Surprisingly, it was mostly empty. A few writing instruments and scant office supplies were all she found. She remembered he did most of his studying at the church office.

The top drawer to the left, where she'd found the checkbook, had a few more things in it—mostly miscellaneous papers and an unopened sugar bar. That made her chuckle. Her mom wouldn't approve, which was probably why it was hidden in his desk. The other drawers were sparse as well.

One thing did catch her eye. A small piece of paper with three numbers written on it. She held it carefully in her hand and stared at the numbers, trying to make sense of them.

7, 25, 3.

Nothing came to mind. No one's birthday or anniversary. She leaned back in the chair unsure what to do next. While deep in thought, Danni heard a noise in the other room that caused her to jump.

Mrs. Pinkerton.

She held her breath and sat completely still, trying not to make a sound, hoping she wouldn't come in the room. As much as she appreciated what Mrs. Pinkerton had done for her, it was like her parents were still there, hovering over her, telling her what to do. An argument had broken out between them the day before. Danni wanted to go outside and explore the damage in the neighborhood and see if any of her friends were still on Jupiter. Especially Liz, her best friend. She was fairly certain Liz was taken, but the caller service was sporadic, and she hadn't heard from her, so she didn't know for sure.

Liz only lived a few blocks away. Danni was dying to go to her house and check things out. Mrs. Pinkerton had forbidden it. The news was reporting gangs of young thugs going from house to house, looting the vacant homes and robbing the occupants at gunpoint. Danni resented the overreach, even if Mrs. Pinkerton was right. Why did the old lady think she was her boss, or worse, her parent? No one made Mrs. Pinkerton her guardian, and she had no right to tell her what she could and couldn't do.

Danni thought she was old enough to take care of herself but didn't have the courage to stand up to her. Truthfully, she did need Mrs. Pinkerton's help. Mrs. P. was going to pay the mortgage. Danni also knew her food supply would run out soon. According to the news reports, the grocery store shelves were bare. The jupes in the checkbook was only $15.00 and wouldn't buy much of anything. Mrs. Pinkerton had offered to help, and Danni was putting up with the intrusion until she could think of another solution.

That didn't mean she didn't value her time alone. It gave her some sense of independence. When her parents were alive, the dead of night was when she found the most solace. Same now. Being cooped up in that house alone with Mrs. P. every day was wearing on her nerves. She had to get out of the house and soon.

Now Mrs. Pinkerton was about to interrupt the only time she had to herself. Danni winced when she heard a light tap on the door.

At least she knocked. This time.

"Come in." Danni didn't know what else to say.

Mrs. Pinkerton opened the door slightly and stuck her head in. "What are you doing?" she asked, seemingly more out of curiosity than accusingly.

"I don't know," Danni replied.

"Did you have another bad dream?"

"No. But I couldn't sleep. I thought I should look through my dad's stuff and see if I could find anything."

Mrs. Pinkerton paused as if she was waiting for Danni to tell her what she had found.

"Did you find anything?" she finally asked.

"Nothing, really." Danni waved the small piece of yellow paper with the three numbers on it. "I did find this," she said before catching herself. She had decided to find out what the numbers meant on her own before Mrs. P. found out. As far as she was concerned, it was none of Mrs. Pinkerton's business.

Too late.

She walked into the room and took the paper from Danni's hand. She wasn't wearing her reading glasses, so she held it out from her body, extending her arm at a distance, alternating between squinting and moving the paper back and forth trying to bring it into focus.

"Any idea what those numbers mean?" she asked.

Danni just shrugged.

"They look like a combination," Mrs. Pinkerton said. "To a lock. Did your dad have a safe?"

Danni glanced at the closet door, trying not to be obvious, but Mrs. Pinkerton saw her because she turned and looked in that same direction.

"He has a safe in his closet," Danni responded reluctantly.

"Let's see if this is the combination to it," Mrs. Pinkerton said as she walked to the closet and opened the door.

Danni's mouth flew open in surprise at the nerve of the woman. What right did she have to look in her dad's safe? Danni bolted from her chair as Mrs. Pinkerton searched for a light switch. Danni found it and turned it on, trying to think of a way to get Mrs. Pinkerton to not go through her dad's stuff without seeming rude or ungrateful.

It was a delicate dance she found herself doing.

"There's the safe," Mrs. Pinkerton said as light flooded the room. "I was right. It's a combination safe. It's huge. I wonder what's in it."

The closet was a medium-sized walk in. The safe was black, free standing, and on four legs. Danni had never been in the closet, but she did remember seeing the safe when they moved in. The solid piece of furniture was about four feet tall and two feet wide. White engravings were etched in a decorative design, creating a border around the sides. In the center was a combination lock with a silver lever handle about four inches below it.

With a flick of the wrist, Mrs. Pinkerton spun the lock in a clockwise direction. It made a fast, clicking sound, as it made several revolutions before stopping.

"This is a fancy safe," she commented, clearly excited, like she was about to discover a hidden treasure.

Danni thought she was just being nosy. Like she was at church. Always wanting to know the latest dirt on everyone else so she could gossip and tell it to others. Danni wanted to yell at her and tell her that what was in the safe was none of her business and that she should get out of the house. But she couldn't find the courage.

Before she could say anything, Mrs. Pinkerton turned the knob, slowly, methodically. To the right, stopping on seven. Back to the left, to twenty-five. Right again, stopping on three. She took a deep breath, looked at Danni, and then pulled on the lever.

Nothing happened.

"That's strange," she said. "I would've bet my house these numbers were to this safe."

In a way, Danni was relieved. She was convinced those numbers were to the safe as well and figured Mrs. P. had gotten the numbers wrong since she didn't have her reading glasses.

"Oh well," Danni said. "You tried." She took the paper from Mrs. Pinkerton's hand and walked back out of the closet, flicking off the light switch as she passed it. Thankfully, Mrs. Pinkerton followed her without trying a second time to open the safe.

"You should get some sleep, Danni," she said.

"I'm going to stay up a little while longer. I can't sleep." Danni walked over to the bookshelf on the far-right corner of the room. She pulled out the book her dad had written. *The Late, Great Planet Jupiter.* "I want to read some of this. Reading makes me sleepy."

"Okay, sweetie. Tomorrow we'll see if we can find out what those numbers are for. Goodnight." Mrs. Pinkerton let out a big yawn as she walked out of the room, leaving the door open.

Satisfied Mrs. Pinkerton was safely in her room, Danni went back into the closet. She got on her knees in front of the safe so her eyes were even with the lock and she could see the numbers clearly. She spun the lock the way Mrs. Pinkerton had and then carefully entered the combination. It still didn't open. Something wasn't right. She was certain the numbers were for the safe.

The thought occurred to her to try the numbers in reverse order. 3, 25, 7.

It still didn't open.

Think Danni. The numbers had some familiarity to them.

Her eyes suddenly brightened. Her mother's birthday was 4-8-26. Excitement rose inside her. She carefully tried those numbers. When she got to 26, she stopped and took a deep breath. One pull on the lever and it gave way, opening. A smile formed as she thought about how clever her dad was. He must've known a robber might find the combination and the safe. They would never think to change the numbers by one to match her mom's birthday.

The first thing she saw were two guns. A handgun and a small rifle. She had already assumed her daddy's guns were in the safe. A quick inspection confirmed they were both loaded. Her dad had taught her at an early age how to handle both guns. She wasn't proficient but knew how to load, unload, turn the safety on and off, aim and fire them. These might come in handy if looters tried to rob her house, Danni decided.

At the bottom right of the safe was a box of papers. Danni started looking through them. They were the type of things you'd expect to find in a safe. Birth certificates. Wedding certificate. Important papers for the house. Her dad's ministerial credentials. Before Danni could study them more closely, Mrs. Pinkerton's voice erupted behind her.

"I see you got the safe open," she said.

"Yeah. I figured it out," Danni said, trying to catch her breath and slow her heartbeat which was suddenly racing.

Mrs. Pinkerton had a caller in her hand. Danni's.

"You got a message," she said.

Danni bolted to a standing position.

"A message?" she said. "Who was it?"

"Liz."

"Why do you have my caller and why are you reading my messages?" Danni said, sharply snatching the caller from her hand.

"I heard it make a sound," Mrs. Pinkerton retorted. "From my room. You left it on the kitchen counter." Danni walked past her and out of the closet but not before giving her a nasty glare.

Are you still here? The message read.

Liz was alive! Danni immediately had mixed emotions. Regret for her friend but joy that she had someone left behind to go through things with.

Yes. I'm here. Danni typed in the words hurriedly, rushing out of the office and into the living room. The caller buzzed. Danni stopped in her tracks and just stared at the message with her mouth agape.

Please help me. Hurry.

20

When the message from Liz came across Danni's caller, it hit her like a lightning bolt suddenly flashing from the sky with no warning. She'd given up hope that her best friend Liz wasn't seized. Now, the message was clear. Liz was in some kind of trouble.

Please help me. Hurry.

Danni read the words on the screen over and over again. She gave the caller to Mrs. Pinkerton who stared at it for several seconds.

"What does it mean?" Danni asked.

"I don't know."

"It means Liz is alive and in trouble."

"Maybe."

"I have to go over there."

Danni took the caller back from Mrs. Pinkerton and started responding to Liz's message. *Where are you? What's wrong?* When she finished typing the message, she walked swiftly to her room and began changing her clothes. Mrs. Pinkerton followed her.

"You can't go out," Mrs. Pinkerton said. "It's five o'clock in the morning. It's still dark out."

"I have to. My friend needs me."

"There's a curfew. Sundown to sunup. If you go out, you'll get arrested."

"She doesn't live far from here. I'll go the back way through the yards. No one will see me."

"What are you going to do when you get there? You have no idea what kind of trouble she's in. You don't even know if the message is from her. It might be a trap."

"That's a chance I'll have to take."

Mrs. Pinkerton raised the intensity in her voice. "You heard the police reports. There are gangs going from house to house robbing people at gunpoint. You can't go out. It's not safe."

Danni matched her intensity. "I'm going. I'll be careful." She sat on the edge of her bed and put on her shoes. She went back to her closet and took out a light coat. The night air on Jupiter could be chilly in September.

"You're not going," Mrs. Pinkerton said with authority.

"You can't tell me what to do," Danni said dismissively.

"I just did. I will not let you go."

"How are you going to stop me?"

"You're just as stubborn as your father."

"Don't you talk about my father! He couldn't stand you." The words were coming out of Danni before she could stop them. "Never say anything bad about my dad ever again. You made his life miserable. You're the one who's a stubborn old fool." Danni's voice was shaking as she said it. Anger was raging inside of her. Years of pent up frustration were suddenly surfacing like a volcano ready to erupt.

"That's not what I meant..." Mrs. Pinkerton lowered her voice. "Listen to reason," she said. "You don't even know that the message was from Liz. If it was, who knows what kind of trouble she's in. And what are you going to do about it? You're a kid."

Danni ignored the comment and bolted from the room.

Mrs. Pinkerton followed her.

She went back into her dad's office and grabbed the unwrapped bar from the drawer and stuck it in her coat pocket. She was suddenly hungry and needed strength. She'd barely eaten anything since the seizure happened and had hardly slept.

Mrs. Pinkerton seemed tired as well and was having a hard time keeping up with Danni as she went from room to room gathering what she wanted to take with her. She went back into her dad's office and into the closet with the safe. She considered taking a gun.

"No, Danni. You don't want to do that!" Mrs. Pinkerton said with alarm in her voice.

Danni decided she was right and walked out of the closet, brushing her shoulder roughly against Mrs. Pinkerton as she walked quickly to the back door and opened it. It would lead through the neighbor's backyard and give her the most direct and safest route to Liz's house. She'd only have to cross the street twice.

"Danni!" Mrs. Pinkerton shouted as Danni started to leave. "I forbid you to go."

Danni turned back to face her, rage boiling inside. "You forbid me!" she shouted. "Who do you think you are? You're not my mother. I don't even want you here."

"You need me here," Mrs. Pinkerton retorted. "What are you going to do for jupes and food? How are you going to pay the mortgage?"

The words sent Danni over the edge of restraint. "Get out of my house!" Danni shouted at the top of her lungs. "When I get back, I want you gone. This is *my* house. I don't want you here."

"You ungrateful, impudent brat! You can't talk to me like that," Mrs. Pinkerton said the words with vitriol for effect.

"I just did. Get the hell out of my house. Now!"

"Don't swear at me, you godless little girl. No wonder you weren't taken."

Danni started to respond. She wanted to say, "You weren't taken either," but stopped herself. The words hurt like a knife stabbing her heart. Danni couldn't deal with that pain right now. She needed to focus on helping Liz. Instead, she just said in a softer but resolved voice, "You heard me. Get out of my house," and then was out the door.

"Danni! Don't go. I'm sorry."

Those were the last words Danni heard as she jumped over the back fence and into the neighbor's yard. She blinked back the tears, trying to focus as she darted through the adjacent yard and down a back alley to the next street over. She stayed along the fence line in the shadows, careful not to be seen. When she came to the street, she hid behind the mobile in the driveway and looked both ways.

The streets were empty except for the strewn mobiles and debris littering the yards and streets. Several of the houses had obviously been looted. She heard sirens and what sounded like gunshots at a distance. Her heart was racing like a bullet track car, and her breathing was shallow and rapid.

Satisfied no one was coming, she sprinted across the street, toward the house across from her and the safety of the shadows. A good hundred feet, time suddenly slowed down as she couldn't span the distance fast enough. Ninety feet. Eighty feet. Eventually fifty feet. Danni was fast but she felt like she was running in place. Twenty feet. Ten feet. Finally, she made it to the other side and pressed her back against the side of the house and looked back furtively to see if anyone had seen her.

Trying to catch her breath, she pulled out her caller. No response from Liz to her message. She dialed her number. No service. Liz's house was only a few blocks away. She started running toward it. Through the maze of houses. Some that looked empty.

A noise stopped her in her tracks.

A whimper. Quiet at first. Then louder. She looked around to get her bearings. The sound was coming from the backyard of the house next door to where she was standing.

Bruno.

Danni slipped through the back gate and into the familiar yard. The house was owned by the McFee family. Members of her dad's church. Danni had babysat their kids. They had a dog named Bruno. A Mastiff, Bruno was a large dog. Muscular with thick, stocky legs and wide neck and shoulders. He was highly protective of the kids and Danni. Downright mean to a stranger. An imposing figure if you didn't know him. Danni was praying he would recognize her voice and not attack her in the dark.

Bruno began barking loudly when Danni opened the gate. So loud, she was concerned he would attract attention to her.

"Bruno! Be quiet. It's me. Danni."

The barking turned to an excited yelp. Danni's eyes had adjusted to the darkness, and she could see that Bruno was chained to his doghouse just off the back deck. She hadn't even thought about animals who were left behind. Bruno was chained because he once dug under the fence at night and got out. It took several hours of searching to find him.

He'd obviously been there for four days with no food and no water. Danni was torn. She needed to get to Liz's house, but Bruno was clearly not in good shape. Danni got to him in seconds. He could hardly control his excitement. She sat down beside him trying to calm him. He almost knocked her over while jumping on her and trying to lick her face.

"I'm sorry, boy. I forgot about you. Your family is gone, aren't they? I know. So is mine." She stroked his head as he laid it on her lap, settling down a little. Danni pulled out the bar and quickly unwrapped it and fed it to Bruno who almost swallowed it whole. She found his bowl and filled it up with water from the outside faucet. He gulped it down in large slurps. She filled it two more times before he finally stopped.

"I've got to go."

Bruno started whimpering again as if he knew what she was saying.

"I'll be back, though. I'll come and get you."

Bruno started to bark as Danni stood to leave. She sat back down and looked around trying to quiet him.

"Bruno! You have to be quiet. I promise. I'll come back for you. Stay right here."

She started to leave. A ding on her caller startled her. Danni pulled it out of her back pocket. Liz had responded to her message.

Someone's in my house. I'm hiding in the upstairs closet.

I'm on my way, Danni hurriedly typed.

Adrenaline started racing through her body again.

I wish I had the gun. I need a weapon.

She paused. Mrs. Pinkerton was right. What was she going to do? How could she help Liz? There were people in Liz's house. They might have guns. The layout of Liz's house started scrolling through her mind. She pictured the downstairs and the stairwell and the hallway to Liz's bedroom. She knew the closet well. They'd played in it many times as kids.

A thought came into her mind. She unhooked Bruno's chain from the stake in the ground but kept him attached to it at his collar. The excitement returned to him as he started jumping around. The bar had given him new energy. Maybe it was just the interaction with a person.

"Settle down, big guy. Do you remember Liz? She needs our help."

Bruno acted as if he knew what she was saying as he settled down and sat next to her.

Bruno is better than any weapon. He'll scare the living daylights out of whoever is there.

"Let's go," Danni said to Bruno as he obediently walked next to her.

They slipped out of the yard and crossed the street. Danni barely looked. Bruno had given her a new resolve.

Seven minutes later, they arrived at Liz's house.

21

From her vantage point from across the street behind some hedges, Danni had a clear view of the front doorway and driveway and saw two men at Liz's house. A medium-sized white van was parked in the driveway. The front of the van faced out toward the street, probably for a quick getaway. The two men were loading things from the house into the van, clearly looting the house.

Men. Not young thugs or gang members. Middle aged men, slightly overweight, but strong and obviously resolved to take everything of value from the house. From the looks of it, the van was about full. Danni surmised that when the van was full, the men would leave to unload it and then come back. That would be a perfect opportunity to get Liz out of the house.

I'm here, she messaged Liz. *There are two men with a van. Downstairs. Let's wait until the men leave. Then you can get out.*

The difficulty with that plan was the anger on the edge of erupting inside Danni again. Like it had with Mrs. Pinkerton. Every time Danni saw the men come out of the house with something that belonged to Liz and her family, the flames of rage were fanned. Bruno must have sensed it too because he growled every time he saw the men. Fortunately, he didn't bark and give away their position, but Danni didn't know how much longer she could keep him quiet.

She was beginning to wonder if she made a mistake bringing the dog. The men didn't appear to be armed. The prudent thing to do was let them finish the job. While Bruno could take them down there was no reason to initiate a confrontation. If he barked, that might not be possible.

And there was something inside Danni that wasn't going to let the men drive away with all of Liz's worldly possessions her parents had worked hard for. As bad as things were, Liz would need those things. Danni's dad had always said if she was being robbed to let the attacker take everything. It wasn't worth risking her life over things.

At that moment, she wasn't so sure. Maybe she was emboldened by finding the strength to tell Mrs. Pinkerton off. For the first time in her life, she stood up for herself. Also, for the first time, she didn't feel guilty about her harsh words. Mrs. Pinkerton deserved them. Danni was realizing she needed to grow up and fast. The weak, little, depressed girl wouldn't survive long in these conditions, and she was determined to survive. That's why she was at Liz's house. She had to take some risks and show everyone she could do this. Even if there was no one left to see her do it, she'd do it for herself.

Her thoughts were interrupted by the two men arguing just inside the front door. While they were distracted, she used the opportunity to cross the road without being seen to look inside the van. She slipped open the driver side door while imploring Bruno to keep quiet. The keys were in the ignition. Before she had time to think about it, she took them out and stuck them in her pocket.

She felt a smile come across her face. Liz's possessions were not going anywhere. But neither were the men. She thought about putting the keys back in the ignition but couldn't make herself. At that point, she should have left and gone back to her hiding place, but a large, black bag in the front seat caught her eye and raised her curiosity. Danni made sure she had a good grip on Bruno's chain with her right hand, reached across the van with her left, grabbed the black bag, and pulled it across the console to the driver's side seat.

She unzipped the top. Inside were jupes. Lots of it. And jewelry. The expensive kind. Danni assumed not all of it came from Liz's house. Her parents weren't that rich. These men had obviously looted a lot of houses and stolen from a lot of people. The rage inside her was overwhelming her better judgment. She wanted a confrontation with these men.

Her breath quickened. Her pulse began racing. She knew she didn't have much time to think through the situation. Seconds probably. The sound of the men arguing had subsided. She second guessed herself. Hesitated. There wasn't time for the argument to play out in her head. So, she just grabbed the bag, pulled it out of the van, and inched away not bothering to close the door which might draw attention to herself.

Too late.

One of the men came out of the house just as Danni emerged from the other side of the van to cross the street. He let out a yell. More of a shriek. "Stop! Right there! Don't move!"

Danni kept moving. But slowly. Circling to her left. To where she was facing him. When the man saw Bruno, fear flashed across his face, and he quit walking toward her.

"Drop that bag," he said roughly.

"This is my friend's house," Danni replied back just as strongly. "These are her things. You have no right to them."

"It's every man for himself. The house is vacant. That bag belongs to me. Drop it." The man started walking toward her again.

"Don't come near me," Danni said with urgency. Bruno began barking loudly, startling the man so much that he took two steps backward. Danni could barely hold Bruno back. He was in front of her now, straining to get away. The man looked petrified.

She considered her options. They could turn and run with the bag and disappear, but she wasn't leaving there without Liz. The bag wasn't the most important thing. Maybe she could use it as a bargaining chip to get away. She also had the key to the van. They didn't know that. They weren't going anywhere anytime soon. Liz wasn't getting out of there without a confrontation.

A figure flashed across an upstairs window. Liz must have heard the commotion. Danni could see her peeking out the window from behind the curtain. The other man heard the commotion as well because he came running out of the house. Danni signaled with her eyes for Liz to come downstairs and go out of the house, although there was no way to know if Liz knew what she meant. Hopefully she would go out the back door.

The second man stopped next to his partner. From the look on his face, he didn't seem as scared of the dog. He was meaner looking. More hardened. Like a criminal. His eyes were darting back and forth as he was obviously trying to think of a plan. Danni sensed he would hurt them if he had the chance.

At that moment, Liz appeared at the front door. "Run! Run!" Danni screamed out to Liz. The men looked confused at first, not sure who Danni was yelling at. The men were between Liz and Danni's position. She didn't run. Her eyes were glazed like she was frozen in fear. The mean man started toward her. Danni screamed. Liz's eyes widened in fear. He was within a few feet of her when he reached out his arms to grab her.

Liz surged forward and to his left as she brushed just under his raised arms, leaving him grasping at air. He didn't react fast enough, clearly surprised by her quick and evasive movement. His hand did manage to grab her shirt as she passed by, but she pulled away, the shirt ripping as his grip failed.

Liz ran past the second man and came and stood behind Bruno who was going berserk. Barking, and pulling on the chain with all his strength. Danni could feel the chain cutting into her hand as she frantically tried to hold him back. They needed to run, but Danni's feet were grounded in place.

"Bruno! Bruno!" Danni shouted. Finally getting his attention. "Sit!" she commanded. Danni's arm ached from the strain of holding him. Liz grabbed the chain and held on to it as well.

Bruno sat, surprising Danni. However, he was tense, ready to spring into action at the first aggressive movement by the men.

The two looters were obviously considering their next move. "Drop the bag. We don't want to hurt you," the first man said.

"I can't do that," Danni retorted. "This jupes doesn't belong to you."

"Kid. I'll hurt you," the mean man said. The one with the shifty eyes. She saw the rage in him building. The veins of his neck were pulsating, his jaw was clenched as were his fists. When Danni didn't obey his commands, he reached into his back pocket and pulled out a knife. That caused Bruno to tense and then stand to his feet.

The man hesitated.

Danni started backing up slowly. She pulled on Bruno's chain and ordered him to follow them. Between Liz and her, they were able to get Bruno to back up as well, but it was like a tug-of-war on the playground. Bruno was ready for a fight. One he would win, although Danni wasn't sure since the man had a knife. That changed things.

For a moment, Danni thought about setting the bag on the ground and leaving. The men would surely let them go. Then she realized that they needed that jupe. They had nothing. With Mrs. Pinkerton gone, Danni had no way to support her and Liz. This bag was a lifeline. Maybe from God. Maybe not. Who knows? It seemed to Danni like God had abandoned her. Either way, she had to fend for herself. There was no way she was leaving there without that bag.

They kept backing up. The men matched their steps. Getting closer because they were moving forward, and their steps were bigger.

"Don't come after us," Danni said angrily. "I'll let the dog loose, and he'll rip you apart." The man raised his knife further in a menacing manner. His look had turned evil. He seemed like someone who had killed before and wouldn't hesitate to do it again.

"Get ready to run," Danni said to Liz. "Through the yards. Back to my house." Their eyes made contact. Liz nodded. Danni tightened her grip on Bruno's chain, wrapping it around her hand several times while Liz released her grip.

"Are you ready?" Danni asked. Liz's eyes told the answer. "Then go! Now."

Liz turned and began running. The men reacted, but Bruno made them hesitate. It was all Danni needed. She jerked on the chain, making eye contact with Bruno and shouting instructions to him. As she turned, he did too and began running with her as she darted into the darkness to the side of the house. She heard the footsteps of the men on the pavement as they followed them.

Liz slowed as Danni couldn't run as fast with Bruno at her side and the bag in her hand. Liz screamed, telling Danni the men were gaining on her.

Danni didn't dare to risk looking back. Her pace quickened as Bruno started matching her steps making it easier for them to run together. She sprinted across the next street over and took a quick glimpse behind her. Enough to see that the men were still following. Further back but coming faster now that she was no longer in the dark and they could see where she was going.

The streetlights had given away her location. Liz was purposely holding back, letting Danni and Bruno catch up to her.

When they caught up to Liz, Danni led them in a different direction, afraid to lead them to her house. They could get there before the men, but did she have enough time to get one of the guns?

That was a chance she had to take as she altered their direction and began running back toward her house which was just a few blocks over. They could barricade inside. Get the gun. Defend themselves. Bruno would hold them off.

Could she kill a man? *If I have to.*

They were still coming. Closer. Gaining ground.

So close, she could hear their heavy breathing and the obscenities they were throwing her way. Danni's lungs were burning. The beating of her heart pounded in her ears. Her house was their only chance. They had to make it. They weren't far, now.

Liz looked back and let out a scream and started running faster.

Danni got off the grass and onto the street. She could run faster on the pavement. Bruno, even in his weakened state from not eating for four days, was matching her step for step. His powerful strides were giving her strength, almost carrying them.

They rounded a corner. Liz was just ahead. Danni stopped and turned to face the men.

They stopped. Were suddenly bent over, gasping for air. Clearly out of shape.

Danni considered her options. Maybe she didn't have to lead them to her house. Even if she fended them off now, with a gun, they would come back. There was too much jupe in the bag.

Just as quickly as they stopped, they started running again. Faster. Danni stumbled backward, slightly losing her footing from the sudden movement.

They shouted at her. More obscenities and threats.

Danni turned and began running. Her muscles didn't respond as quickly. They were screaming at her, begging her to stop. The men were almost on them. Danni let out a yelp. Weak. Not able to muster enough air to let out a loud scream.

They were almost to her house. A figure up ahead emerged from the shadows.

Suddenly a loud noise pierced the night. A gunshot. Danni instinctively ducked. Bruno stopped in his tracks. Liz fell to the ground ahead of them.

The figure was holding a rifle.

Mrs. Pinkerton.

Her dad's rifle. Calmly, confidently, Mrs. Pinkerton fired a second shot. Over everyone's heads. Liz stood back up. Danni turned around and looked behind her.

The men were running the other direction.

22

"They'll be back," Mrs. Pinkerton said calmly but soberly, speaking of the two looters she scared off with Danni's father's rifle.

She sat in the rocking chair in the living room, that same rifle resting in her lap. Danni stood at the window, nervously looking out from behind the curtains for any sign of the two men who had looted Liz's house. Bruno, the neighbor's huge Masstiv dog, was laying on the couch, his head contently snuzzled on Liz's lap, clearly satisfied from the large bowl of food he'd scarfed down in a matter of seconds.

The sun would be coming up shortly. None of them slept much that night, but everyone was wide awake, on high alert, wondering when the men would come back looking for them.

Danni knew better than the others that the men would be back for reasons she hadn't yet told them.

"Yeah," Danni said, nodding her head, agreeing with Mrs. Pinkerton while pointing at the black bag sitting on the dining room table filled with jupe and jewels. "Especially with what's in that bag."

Liz looked that way. Mrs. Pinkerton kept rocking with a distant look on her face.

Danni immediately regretted mentioning the bag. Did she want to tell Mrs. Pinkerton what was in it? A twinge of guilt sent a sharp pain through her chest. Her lungs already hurt from the sprint from Liz's house and the adrenaline still flowed through her veins from the confrontation with the men and the danger they were still in.

Now that things had calmed down, she regretted the harsh words she'd spoken to Mrs. Pinkerton earlier that night. Especially since the lady had just saved her life.

That didn't mean she didn't have a right to her privacy. And the right to decide her own future and fate and what happened inside her own house. She readied an argument in her mind should Mrs. Pinkerton try to exert her authority again. She'd just be nicer about it.

The room was silent for a good minute. Still no reaction from Mrs. Pinkerton about the bag, which surprised Danni. She expected her to ask about its contents in her usual nosy manner. Mrs. Pinkerton's bags were packed and sitting next to the garage door. She'd obviously intended to leave as Danni had rudely insisted.

Thank God she didn't leave.

"I'm so glad you came along when you did," Liz said, which was exactly what Danni was thinking.

"What happened at the house?" Danni asked. "Where are your parents? Were they seized?"

"I don't know what you mean, by 'seized,'" Liz said. "My parents were on vacation. They were on an airmobile flying home. I think it went down. Although I'm not sure. No one knows what happened to them. They are presumed dead. I guess they are." Her voice trailed off as she said it.

Danni explained to her about the seizure. Liz didn't think they were seized. Her family wasn't active in any church. Liz doubted they were Christians who would've been taken to heaven with the others.

"I tried to call you a thousand times," Liz said to Danni. "There was no service."

"You should've come to my house."

"I was afraid to leave the house. I heard about all the looting and the people missing. Turns out I wasn't even safe in my own home."

Liz seemed like she needed to talk. Open up. She'd been through a severe trauma and had been alone at her house for days with no contact with anyone. At least Danni had Mrs. Pinkerton. Except... she tried to throw her out of the house. How stupid was that? She would've been all alone as well. As Danni thought, Liz kept talking after a short pause.

"I was sleeping, and I heard a window break downstairs," Liz continued. "I looked out and saw the white van and knew immediately they were there to loot our house. I'd seen the van at other houses in the neighborhood. I was so scared."

"You must've been terrified. You poor girl," Mrs. Pinkerton said sincerely.

"I hid in my closet. Fortunately, they stayed downstairs and never saw me. I could see them loading the van from the upstairs window. It made me mad to see them taking all our stuff, but I couldn't stop them. I guess they're taking the rest of it right now." Her voice cracked as she said it.

The van.

Danni took the van key's out of her pocket and waved them in the air. "They won't be taking anything without these."

"What are those?" Mrs. Pinkerton asked.

"Keys to the white van over at Liz's house."

"Why do you have them?" Liz asked.

"I stole them," Danni said, grinning. "Along with the bag. The keys were in the ignition, and the bag was on the front seat. So, I took them." Danni said it hesitantly as if she'd done something wrong. She wanted to say it confidently, like it was the normal and right thing to do, which she was convinced it was.

"That was dangerous," Liz said. "They could have killed you."

Mrs. Pinkerton was silent, staring off into the ceiling, rocking back and forth, showing no emotion. Danni didn't know if she was mad at her or had realized she was out of line and was keeping her mouth shut because she should. Liz's stuff was none of her business either.

Danni shrugged her shoulders while she pulled the curtains back and looked out again. No sign of the men. It was just a matter of time. "I couldn't let them take your things," she finally said.

Mrs. Pinkerton stopped rocking. Bruno stuck his head up from Liz's lap. "Come on girls. Let's go."

"Where are we going?" Danni asked.

"To get that van."

* * *

Mrs. Pinkerton was in the driver's seat of her mobile. Danni and Liz were in the backseat with Bruno who they were afraid would tear the house apart if he hadn't been allowed to come. Mrs. Pinkerton had the rifle in her lap. They were parked a block from Liz's house with a good view of the two men who were obviously frantically searching for the keys.

The men looked through the van. Then went into the house for several minutes. Now, they were searching through the yard and in the bushes. Mrs. Pinkerton had a sly grin on her face, obviously amused by the men's efforts which she knew would be in vain.

The three waited patiently, hoping the men would leave. Maybe they'd leave to get another set of keys.

After a few minutes, Mrs. Pinkerton seemed to lose patience. "Are you ready?" she asked. The plan had already been explained to them while they were waiting.

"I'm ready," Danni replied nervously but resolutely.

Liz just sat there holding onto Bruno with a glazed, petrified look on her face.

Mrs. Pinkerton inched the mobile forward, slowly. The men were distracted by the search for the keys and didn't notice as she pulled up in front of the house, the driver's side door facing the house. Her window was down. She called out to the men.

"Nice to see you again," Mrs. Pinkerton said jokingly.

The men looked up, and a flash of recognition came across their faces. The mean one started toward the car.

Bruno bolted from Liz's lap in the back seat and had his face in the window, barking loudly at the man. If the window hadn't been up, he would've jumped out of the mobile and attacked them. Liz tried to hold him back.

"I wouldn't do that if I were you," Mrs. Pinkerton said as she stuck the barrel of the rifle out the window and pointed it at him while at the same time motioning for Danni to get out of the mobile.

Danni jumped out of the back seat and ran to the van. She had the ignition key already between her fingers and was relieved when the van started right away. The men let out a yell and started running toward her, but it was too late. Danni put the van into drive and sped off down the street with the men running after her.

"Nice doing business with you," Mrs. Pinkerton said laughingly as she passed to the right of the men who were standing in the middle of the road. They glared at her, shook their fists, and hurled obscenities at her. Mrs. Pinkerton stopped the vehicle and got out, still brandishing the rifle.

She pointed it at them and said, "If I see either of you in this neighborhood again, I won't hesitate to use this gun. Next time, I won't aim above your heads. If you know what I mean."

She got back in the mobile, gunned the engine, and squealed the tires as she sped off.

* * *

Danni slowed down on the next block and pulled over to the side of the road to wait for Mrs. Pinkerton to come around the curve. She heard the tires squeal and saw the large four-door sedan round the curve like a sports mobile. Mrs. Pinkerton had a wide grin on her face. Danni settled in behind her.

Mrs. Pinkerton had suggested they hide the van at her house. The men would obviously come looking for it on Danni's street. While the men didn't know which house they lived in, they might search the street until they found them. There was no good place to hide the large white van.

Danni didn't object nor resent the suggestion, perfectly content to let Mrs. Pinkerton take charge of the situation.

She'd been too hard on Mrs. Pinkerton. The well-meaning lady, while annoying, was just trying to help Danni. In her own way. Mrs. Pinkerton was controlling and manipulative, but she was also generous, loving, and kind. Like her dad. Ironic that Mrs. Pinkerton and her dad were so alike.

Danni took one hand off the steering wheel and wiped a tear from her eye. The thought of her dad missing, gone from her life, sent a pang of emotion through her. She missed him. Several emotions were surging inside of her. Guilt. Hurt. Grief. A sense of loss. For years, she pushed her dad away and kept him at arm's length. Never let him get to know her, nor did she get to know him. Not really. At that moment, Danni determined she wouldn't do the same thing to Mrs. Pinkerton.

The drive took about ten minutes. Mrs. Pinkerton had taken the back way, staying off the main thoroughfares to keep from running into any law enforcement. The neighborhood was in the older part of town. The trees were tall and majestic, having been planted years ago with time to develop and become fully grown. The houses got bigger as they went deeper into the maze of streets. At one time, it must've been the nicest neighborhood in Red Spot, Danni decided.

In the back of the development was a large iron gate, with a decorative P on it. Danni couldn't see the house from that vantage point. A high, stone wall ran from the gate in both directions as far as the eye could see. This must be Mrs. Pinkerton's house.

Danni's mouth formed a "Wow," which she let out quietly to herself as they drove through the gate and onto a long driveway that led to the estate that dominated the landscape in the distance. Older but stately, sprawling was the best way to describe it. Large columns lined the front. Massive windows ran up the sides and were arched. Gaudy. Gloomy, a teenager might think who didn't appreciate anything old. Just like Mrs. Pinkerton, Danni thought, which was ironic since the smallest woman she'd ever seen lived in the biggest house Danni had ever seen.

They pulled around to the back of the house where another large building sat with garage doors one after another lining the front. Danni counted eight of them.

One opened and Mrs. Pinkerton drove into it, coming to a stop deep inside. She got out of the mobile and motioned for Danni to follow her in and park behind her. That one bay had enough room for four or five mobiles. Once inside, Danni saw at least a dozen mobiles of various shapes and sizes in the other stalls. All fancy. Expensive.

Danni knew Mrs. Pinkerton had jupe, but she had no idea how much. The intrigue deepened. Who was this lady? How did she have so much jupe? Why did she drive an old four-door airmobile when she had all these expensive ones sitting in her garage?

And why would she sleep in the guest room at Danni's house, when she had this huge mansion and could live the life of luxury? For that matter, where did she learn to shoot a rifle?

I don't know. None of this makes sense.

But she was determined to find out.

23

Saturday, September 15
9:30 a.m.

The grocery store was out of the three things Mrs. Pinkerton and Danni went in to get. Sodas, dog food, and paper rolls.

"Why would they be out of paper rolls?" Danni asked with exasperation, staring at an entire roll of shelves completely empty.

"Look over there," Mrs. Pinkerton said.

Danni turned her gaze in the direction she was pointing. A heavy-set woman with very tight legging pants was waddling toward the register with a cart piled high with paper rolls.

"She looks like she needs them more than I do," Danni said sarcastically, causing Mrs. Pinkerton to laugh out loud. More like a snort than a laugh.

"What are we going to do?" Danni asked in a half-joking, half serious tone. "We're almost out of paper rolls."

"I have twelve restrooms in my house. I'm sure there are one or two rolls in each. That'll last us for a while. I'm a very small woman. I don't need much."

The way she said it caused Danni to burst out in giggles. The tension of the night was starting to ease as was the memory of the sharp words they'd had with each other the night before. Words Danni had come to regret.

"I'm more concerned about the dog food," Mrs. Pinkerton said. "Bruno will eat us out of house and home."

"He liked that meat I fed him. Let's go look for some more." Bruno was told to stay in the vehicle with Liz against his strong and vocal objections. Mrs. Pinkerton's mouth flew open when they reached the meat aisle. The display cases were completely empty.

"This is not good," she said. "People are obviously hoarding food and supplies."

"What are we going to do?" Danni asked.

"Let's go to the frozen section. There may be some things left over there. Although, I doubt it."

The frozen cases were mostly empty as well. The meat was completely gone as were most vegetables. Danni opened the case and took out one of the few packages left.

"Brussels Sprouts. Eww... I'm not eating that."

"You will if you get hungry enough," Mrs. Pinkerton said in a motherly kind of way. Danni ignored it. Her dad always said that old people were set in their ways. Mrs. Pinkerton had certain characteristics and faults Danni would just have to learn to accept.

"This is worse than I thought," Mrs. Pinkerton continued. "I figured there would be food shortages, but I didn't think it would be this soon. Follow me."

Mrs. Pinkerton began going from aisle to aisle, filling the cart with whatever dry goods she could find. Cereal. Rice. Canned beans. Peanut butter. Chips. Along with perishables like toothpaste, soap, and shampoo of which there was still a supply. She found some cans of tuna fish, and cat food.

"I don't think Bruno's going to want to eat cat food," Danni said as she contorted her face into a frown at the thought of eating tuna fish.

"Like I said. We'll all eat anything if we're hungry enough. Including Bruno. Besides, I have a cat at the house."

When the cart was full, Mrs. Pinkerton said they had enough and should leave some for others, so they went to the checkout counter.

"I'll pay for this," Danni said proudly. She pulled out a wad of jupes she'd taken out of the bag and brought with her for this very purpose.

"Where did you get that kind of jupe?" Mrs. Pinkerton asked as her eyes widened.

Danni leaned in and whispered, "From the bag. It's full of jupes."

"How much?"

"Several hundred thousand jupes," Danni said while looking around to see if someone was listening to their conversation even though no one was around but the clerk.

"Oh, my word!" Mrs. Pinkerton said with surprise.

"I know. Those men must've robbed a bank or something. The bag also has a bunch of jewelry in it."

Mrs. Pinkerton abruptly ended the conversation as the clerk started scanning the items, obviously not wanting her to hear them.

"We'll talk about the bag later," Mrs. Pinkerton said, and Danni nodded in agreement.

"Seven hundred forty-five jupes," the clerk blurted out after she had scanned the last item.

"What?" Mrs. Pinkerton shrieked. "There's not a hundred jupes worth of groceries in this cart. Maybe one twenty-five."

The clerk just shrugged.

"This is price gouging," Mrs. Pinkerton said roughly. "Don't you have any decency. How are people supposed to feed their families? Most people don't have that kind of jupe."

The store had clearly jacked up the prices and was taking advantage of the difficult jupes. Not enough to pay for it all.

"We're going to have to put some things back," Danni said as the clerk glared at her.

"Don't worry," Mrs. Pinkerton said. "Put your jupes away." She opened her purse roughly to let the clerk know she wasn't at all happy. She pulled out seven one-hundred-dollar bills along with some smaller bills until she had the full amount covered.

Mrs. Pinkerton walked out of the store in a huff. Still clearly agitated. They loaded the supplies into the trunk of the mobile and sped off.

"This situation is dire," Mrs. Pinkerton said. Danni and Liz were in the back seat, trying to calm Bruno who was overly excited about Danni's return.

"We'll be okay," Danni said. "There's a lot of jupes in that bag."

"Honey, in three weeks, that jupe isn't going to be worth the paper it's printed on."

"What do you mean?"

"Inflation," Mrs. Pinkerton answered.

"What's that?" Danni asked.

"It's when prices go up," Liz answered. "My teacher in school talked about it not that long ago."

"Supply and demand," Mrs. Pinkerton said. "There's a run on food. There'll be a run on the banks. People will be trying to get their cash out. As food and supplies run out, the stores will keep raising the prices. Eventually, there will be rioting in the streets as people are starving."

"The government will have to do something," Danni said.

"That's what I'm afraid of," Mrs. Pinkerton said, her voice trailing off as she said it.

All of her dad's sermons on the new world order, the anti-Christ, the mark of the beast, and the great tribulation started flooding Danni's mind. She suddenly knew exactly what Mrs. Pinkerton was afraid of.

*　*　*

Mrs. Pinkerton didn't drive straight to Danni's house. Instead, she drove to Liz's house first. Satisfied that the two men weren't around, she gave Danni and Liz instructions. "Go get everything out of the house you think we might need. Food. Supplies. Paper rolls. Nothing big. Liz I'm sorry. But leave everything you don't absolutely need. Just get a few clothes and things you can't live without. I'll stay out here and watch for any trouble."

Liz and Danni made several trips. The trunk was full, so they started loading things into the back seat.

"Show me how to get to Bruno's house," Mrs. Pinkerton said when they were finished.

Danni gave her directions. They arrived in no time since it was only a couple blocks away. Mrs. Pinkerton shut off the mobile, got out, and walked around to the back yard. Liz and Danni and Bruno followed. Bruno became beside himself as they walked into the backyard and his familiar confines. He broke out of Danni's grasp and ran to the back door.

Locked. As they expected.

Mrs. Pinkerton reached into her pocket and pulled out a credit card. She jimmied the door until it suddenly opened, much to Danni's surprise. How did she know how to do that?

As soon as the door opened, Bruno bolted into the house, almost knocking Mrs. Pinkerton over. He ran from room to room, barking wildly. Obviously searching for his family. It made tears come to Danni's eyes as Bruno kept desperately searching but not finding anyone. He eventually jumped on the couch, laid down on his belly, and started whimpering.

Mrs. Pinkerton ignored him. They had more important things to concern themselves with.

"See if you can find his dog food," Mrs. Pinkerton said. "And a leash. His bed. Whatever dog supplies you can find. I'll start gathering up the food."

They went through the house only taking the essentials. It seemed strange being in their house, taking their stuff. They obviously didn't need it. They were in a better place. Still, it felt like a violation.

Danni had in her hand some jewelry that looked valuable. "Should we take these?"

"Better us than the looters," Mrs. Pinkerton responded. "It won't do us much good, but I'd hate to see it in the hands of a bunch of savages like those two men. Maybe we can do some good with them."

Danni felt like those savages. She knew they were doing the right thing, but it felt wrong. Never in her life had she stolen anything.

Liz must've sensed what Danni was feeling. Maybe feeling it too, because she said, "I think the McFee's would want us to have these things. You know. For what we're doing for Bruno."

Those words made Danni feel better. That made sense. They would need jupes and resources to take care of him. It was only a matter of time until looters ransacked the house. Danni suddenly understood what Mrs. Pinkerton meant. She didn't need the jupes from the jewels. She had plenty of jupe. The items were being taken for safekeeping. Maybe they'd be sold later and given to the poor. The church. Traded for needed supplies. Mrs. Pinkerton wasn't doing this for her own gain. Neither was Danni. They were doing the right thing, considering the circumstances.

They found two large bags of dog food which was the most important thing they found, although Danni wasn't sure how long that would last. At least it was something and was food Bruno was used to. They also found several paper rolls. Danni suddenly felt the urge to hoard it. She suddenly realized how the large woman in the store felt, even as irrational as it was.

When they arrived back at Danni's house, they pulled into the garage so Mrs. Pinkerton's mobile wouldn't be on the street. No reason to go to all that trouble only to have the mobile looted in a matter of minutes.

Mrs. Pinkerton's bags were still by the garage door. Danni picked them up and carried them into the guest room. Mrs. Pinkerton followed her in.

"What are you doing, Danni?" she asked.

Danni walked over and gave Mrs. Pinkerton a hug, obviously surprising her and catching her off guard because she didn't immediately return the embrace. Danni held on for several awkward seconds until Mrs. Pinkerton finally reciprocated.

"I'm really sorry about what I said," Danni muttered softly. She'd had those feelings for a while and wanted to say the words; she had just never found the right time. Or the courage. Now that they were home, she had to say them before Mrs. Pinkerton left.

"I don't want you to leave," Danni implored.

"Honey, we're all going to have to leave," Mrs. Pinkerton said soberly, taking Danni's hand and leading her back into the living room where Liz was standing. "It's not safe here."

"Where are we going?"

"To my house. You too, Liz."

"I don't want to leave my house," Danni retorted strongly but not too strong as to offend her.

"I know," Mrs. Pinkerton answered. "But those men are going to come back. You've got their jupes and their van. They'll come back with weapons. If they don't, somebody else will. Right Liz? You know what I'm saying. Also..."

"What?" Danni asked.

Mrs. Pinkerton hesitated.

"What is it?"

"I heard on the news that the new Prescom has ordered that all houses owned by people who were seized immediately become the property of the new government they're forming."

"They can't do that!" Danni said.

"They can and they will. It's only a matter of time until they take this house and all the possessions."

"They wouldn't throw me out on the streets."

"You would become a ward of the new government. I don't know what would become of you. I'm not going to let that happen. We have to get you out of here. You too, Liz. They'll take your house as well. What's left of it."

Liz nodded. "She's right, Danni. The government can do anything they want."

"You'll be safe at my house," Mrs. Pinkerton said. "I have plenty of paper rolls!"

Danni let out a nervous laugh. Mrs. Pinkerton held out her arms and they all circled into a group hug.

"Go get your things," she said, patting them on the back. "Get all the food and supplies you can find. Let's load up all the vehicles. We'll drive them over to my house. I've got plenty of room in the garage."

For four hours, they went through the house getting anything they could find that might be useful and they didn't want to fall into the hands of looters or the government. Tears were rolling down Danni's cheeks as she packed up her room, wondering if she'd ever be back there again. She started to take some of Avery and Todd's things, but she knew she had to leave them. Her heart was wrenching as she turned out the light and closed the door to their rooms.

How her life could turn upside in a moment. A few short days ago, she was safe, secure... a few problems, but they all seemed so insignificant now. What she would give to go back to a few days ago. When she was grounded. She'd give anything if her mom was there to punish her.

Regret suddenly came over her like a flood. How could she live with those last words she had so hatefully spoken to her mom? She'd replayed them in her head every day since all this happened. Mrs. Pinkerton shouted something, jolting her back into reality.

The mobiles were loaded.

Danni emerged from her room with tears flowing down her cheeks. It was all she could do to hold back the sobs. Mrs. Pinkerton tried to console her as they stood in the kitchen. She took her in her arms and said things were going to be okay.

"There's one more thing you need to get," Mrs. Pinkerton said softly, still holding her.

"What's that?" Danni said, pulling away from the embrace and rubbing the tears away from her eyes.

"Your dad's book. You know. The one on the seizure."

"Okay." Danni went into the office and found *The Late, Great Planet Jupiter*, by Lindsey Howell sitting on the desk right where she'd left it. She carried it back into the kitchen and handed it to Mrs. Pinkerton.

"Why do I need the book?"

"Because you're going to teach on it tomorrow morning at church."

24

Pastor Lindsey Howell's Mansion, Heaven
Date and Time Unknown

There is a synchronicity between heaven and Jupiter, I have discovered. Events unfold at the same time even though heaven has no time. Jupiter has seconds, minutes, hours, days, years, decades, and centuries. Many different increments of time are measured on Jupiter. Heaven has no time denominations, and yet we have a sense of time as it's happening on Jupiter even though we aren't bound by it.

There is a Bible verse that says that with the Lord, a day is like a thousand years, and a thousand years are like a day. I always thought that to mean one day in heaven was like a thousand years on Jupiter. I've come to realize it's the other way around. Seemingly a thousand years pass by in heaven, and we come to find that only a day has passed on Jupiter. We experience so much in heaven in one day that we never could've on Jupiter.

We also have a better understanding of what happened and is happening on the planet. Spiritual eyes, they are called here. There's a song we used to sing that had a line that said, "The things on Jupiter will grow strangely dim." That's not entirely true. Until Jupiter passes away, we are intimately aware of what's happening to our loved ones. We see things so much clearer now. We're collectively rooting for them. Encouraging them. Praying for them. Joining Jesus and agreeing with him as he is interceding on their behalf. Especially with this upcoming difficult time they will face when the tribulation comes upon them, as we are aware, and I wrote about in my book.

That's why we are all gathered in my mansion today. The loved ones of the people on Jupiter who are going to the Red Spot Christian church today have all assembled in my mansion. It's Sunday morning.

Mrs. Pinkerton has just opened the doors to the church. Danni's pacing back and forth, nervously. Her best friend Liz is trying to calm her down. A few people are sitting in the pews of the church. Not many.

"I can't do this," we hear Danni say to Mrs. Pinkerton who wants her to use my book and explain the seizure to everyone who attends services this morning.

"You can do this," she says encouragingly. "You'll be fine. Just picture your dad looking down on you. He would be so proud."

I was proud. Hopeful. Maybe this would be the day Danni would be saved and secure her place in eternity with us. We were all hopeful. All of the relatives.

We went around the room of my mansion and everyone introduced themselves.

"I'm Nancy. Pastor Lindsey's wife on Jupiter," she said as she smiled at me. There's no marriage in heaven, but her smile still warms my insides in the same way it did on Jupiter. Maybe not the same way. Even more exhilarating, as is everything in heaven.

"These are our kids," Nancy said.

"I'm Todd," he said with a wave.

"I'm Avery. Danni's little sister." She was twelve.

Everyone in the room said a friendly hello to them.

"We have some other kids here today," I said.

"I'm Kate," a beautiful girl sitting across the room said. Her face was childlike. Her manner was soft, sweet. "I was only six weeks old when I was seized. That's my mom, Ruth." She pointed to a young woman sitting in a pew on Jupiter, halfway back on the right side. Clutching tissues. Crying. "That's my nana, sitting next to her. Naomi."

Naomi had her arm around Ruth, consoling her as she had been doing for days since the seizure.

Even though Kate was a baby on Jupiter, she had a new spiritual body, fully developed in heaven while maintaining those childlike qualities. She had spiritual eyes just as mature as the rest of us.

"I'm her dad, Jake Williams," a man sitting next to her spoke up and said. Ruth is my wife. Naomi is my mother. Ruth's mother-in-law."

"I'm Carl. Naomi's husband." Carl and Jake clasped arms. They looked alike, I thought to myself. You could tell they were related, even in their heavenly bodies.

"I'm Joshua," a quiet, unassuming voice said from the back of the room. It only took a couple more sentences for his personality to shine through. "I guess I'm the youngest one in the room. I was taken before I was born. I guess I have the fewest number of sins of everyone in the room."

The room roared with laughter. He said it with such a wide grin, his manner endearing, his excited look of anticipation as funny as the joke itself. There's a lot of humor and fun in heaven. We laugh all the time.

"We have another pastor in the room," I said. "Randy Collins. Introduce yourself and your wife."

"I'm Randy. This was my wife on Jupiter, Cindy. Tom Collins is our son. Our other children are here in heaven and might be along shortly."

"Hi Cindy," I said. The room echoed the greeting.

She waved to the group with a broad and inviting smile.

A group of two older couples were sitting together. They were Carter and Taylor's grandparents.

"We've been praying for those kids all their lives," one of them said. Carter is the firefighter married to Taylor, the prostitute. Their story reminded me of the man in the Bible who took back his wife even though she was a harlot. It was a beautiful story of redemption.

It seemed like another redemptive story was unfolding before us. Carter had taken Taylor back with open arms and had forgiven her. It was his suggestion that they come to church.

"They just arrived," Carter's grandfather said. Everyone looked through the portal and saw the young couple make their way through the doors and down to the fourth row. They sat behind Danni and Mrs. Pinkerton who were now sitting on the front row.

The rest of the relatives arrived shortly thereafter along with a few people not represented in my mansion. Nancy and I were committed to interceding for them and agreeing together for everyone in the room, not just our daughter who we loved with all of our hearts.

Mrs. Pinkerton stood to speak. "Thank you all for coming today in what is a very difficult time for everyone."

Mrs. Pinkerton seemed different to me. Humbler. The sharp, judgmental demeanor I knew was gone.

"My family started this church eighty years ago. For forty years, I've never missed a Sunday, and these doors have always been opened. I wanted to make sure they were open for you today."

Okay... Still the same old Mrs. Pinkerton. Maybe she has changed. Hard to say. If she has, then not completely. I had to give her grace. Something that was easy for us to do now that we have experienced it firsthand in heaven. We all stood before the judgment seat and were declared righteous by God through Christ even as all of our sins flashed before our eyes and were removed from us completely. Mrs. Pinkerton just needed the Lord. A heartfelt change. I would pray for her.

After a few more minutes she introduced Danni. My daughter stood from the pew and walked to the podium. I saw her knees wobble. Her hands were shaking. She was gripping my book, so much so that she had a hard time opening it. I saw her try to take a deep breath. It reminded me of my first sermon. I was petrified as well.

"The missing people were seized," Danni said, meekly at first. She looked out over the crowd. A couple dozen people were spread out in different parts of the sanctuary. None were recognizable at first glance. It seemed like they were all new people.

"Can you speak up?" a man shouted from the audience. He wasn't someone with a family member in my mansion.

"Jesus said this would happen," Danni said, her voice trembling.

"What happened?" the man said angrily. "Where are all the people? Where's my wife?"

"They were seized." Danni began flipping through the book. She looked over at Mrs. Pinkerton who smiled reassuringly. It didn't help. How could anyone explain what had happened to his wife in a way that would make him feel better?

"What do you mean, 'seized'? Who took them?"

Danni didn't know how to answer him. Finally, she said, "God took them."

"Why would God take my baby?" Ruth asked. Kate sat up on the edge of her seat in heaven. Ruth was her mother. Kate was the baby taken from her crib in the seizure. The only thing left behind were the swaddling clothes. Ruth was traumatized and still not over it. At the church obviously to find answers.

"I don't know," Danni said, honestly.

"Get somebody up here who does know," the man said roughly. "I didn't come here to listen to some kid who doesn't know what the hell she's talking about."

Mrs. Pinkerton stood to her feet and faced the man. "Don't you swear in God's house. This girl is doing the best she can to answer your questions. Her dad was the pastor here. He was a good man. He wrote a book about the seizure. Danni knows all about it. She's just nervous. Shut up and give her a chance to explain."

The man didn't answer. He got up and left.

Mrs. Pinkerton's brusque manner and confrontive tone didn't surprise me. I was surprised when she said she thought I was a good man. I didn't expect that. Maybe there was hope for her after all.

"Go ahead, Danni," Mrs. Pinkerton said. "You're doing fine. Don't listen to them."

Another man entered through the doors and sat on the back pew. A man who looked familiar to Danni. She thought maybe she'd seen him on vision.

Pastor Randy Collins caught my eye. His son Tom was the man who had just entered the church. Tom was an accomplished motivational speaker who was used to speaking in front of thousands of people. Maybe he could help Danni if she continued to struggle. I could sympathize with Randy and Cindy. They had a child who hadn't been saved as well. A prodigal, so to speak, like our girl. Maybe Tom and Danni will meet after the service.

Not really a service, I realized. You can't have a service when none of the leaders or participants have the Holy Spirit living in them. It was becoming more of a question and answer session than an actual church service.

"Like I was saying," Danni continued, "Jesus said that there would be a seizure. A 'rapture' as some call it. That's where all the Christians on Jupiter are taken from the planet up to heaven—all at the same time."

Danni was speaking with more confidence now.

"My dad wrote about it in this book." Danni raised the book in the air. "Only those who were actually saved were seized. All of us are here because we were never really saved."

"Why were little children taken? And babies?" someone asked in a sincere tone.

"Because they hadn't reached the age of accountability," Danni answered. "They didn't know better. Like your baby." Danni looked at Ruth as she said it. "She was too young to make a decision about Jesus. So, she was automatically saved and went to heaven."

"Good answer," I said. Nancy looked at me and nodded in agreement. "That's just how I would've said it." Randy Collins nodded in agreement as well.

Dr. Matthew King stood to his feet. His son Joshua was taken from his wife's womb along with thousands of his patient's babies. "I've never really believed in God," he said. "I guess that's why I'm still here. I'm a scientist. A doctor. I believe what I can see. But I saw babies disappear right in front of my eyes. With no reasonable explanation. You may be young, but what you're saying makes sense to me, as far fetched as it sounds."

"But why would a loving God take a baby away from her mother?" Ruth said, tearfully.

"I'm sorry," Danni said.

"Because he is a loving God," I answered even though those on Jupiter couldn't hear me. Being in heaven, I know how loving God really is. He doesn't want anyone to perish. Not babies. Not adults, Not kids. Not grandparents. No one. But the tribulation is coming. The loving thing to do was to remove all the Christians so they wouldn't have to suffer unnecessarily. Especially the babies. It wouldn't be fair to them. No child should have to go through what these people would soon face.

"Your baby is in heaven, if that makes you feel any better," Danni said. "Your baby is with God."

"Will we ever see them again?" Ruth asked.

"Is it too late for us to be saved?" Taylor asked. "I've done a lot of bad things in my life. That's why I'm here. Is it too late for me?" Her husband Carter grasped her hand and squeezed it. Tears were forming in her eyes.

"We've all done bad things," Naomi said. "That's why we're still here. Thank you, Danni, for explaining it to us."

I wished the questions would stop for a moment. This is a perfect opportunity for Danni to share the gospel and tell them how to be saved. It wasn't too late for them. Danni knew how to be saved, even if she didn't accept him as savior before the seizure when she had the opportunity.

Everyone there had the opportunity at one time or another. I learned once I got to heaven that the Holy Spirit moved in everyone's heart at least one time to give them the opportunity to be saved. They had rejected it. Now might be another opportunity if they give Danni the chance to explain salvation to them.

"It's not too late to be saved," Danni said.

"Good girl!" I shouted before I had a chance to stop myself.

Danni started to speak. A noise erupted in the back.

Thunderous noise. Footsteps. The back doors to the sanctuary burst open.

Armed government guards appeared. Their guns were drawn.

25

"What is the meaning of this?" Mrs. Pinkerton said as she rushed to the center of the sanctuary to confront the armed soldiers who had entered the church.

"Don't come any closer," one of the men shouted, his automatic rifle in its most ready position, aimed right at her head not more than three feet away.

She was unmoved. "This is a house of worship. You are defiling it."

"Who is in charge here?" the man said, ignoring her vitriol.

"I am," Mrs. Pinkerton said.

Danni was still standing behind the podium; a spirit of fear had momentarily come upon her. She overcame it as she left the podium and stood next to Mrs. Pinkerton and faced the man. "I'm in charge too," Danni said.

"Then you're under arrest. Both of you."

"On what charge?" Danni asked calmly.

The man lowered his weapon and reached into his pocket. The other soldiers aimed their weapons at the other people in the church. One kept his weapon firmly affixed on Mrs. Pinkerton and Danni.

The soldier took out a piece of paper from his pocket. "This is an executive order issued by the Prescom of the Jupiter States, Jack Wolf. It says that it's unlawful for you to meet."

Mrs. Pinkerton took the paper from the soldier's hand and began reading it out loud.

"On September 12, 2061, the Prescom, upon finding that a disaster has occurred, and further disaster is imminent, thus declaring the entire planet of Jupiter under a state of global emergency. Among other things, I do hereby temporarily prohibit mass gatherings defined as any planned or spontaneous, public or private event or convening that will bring together or are likely to bring together more than ten people in a confined or enclosed space at the same time, including funerals and religious functions."

Mrs. Pinkerton peered over her glasses. "This order is unconstitutional. We have the freedom to assemble and the freedom of religion."

"Not anymore," the soldier said roughly. "Read the next line."

"Any violators are subject to fine or indefinite confinement," Mrs. Pinkerton said.

"You're both under arrest," the soldier said rudely.

"This is an outrage," Mrs. Pinkerton shouted as the man grabbed her arm.

A woman suddenly stood from the other side of the sanctuary. Someone Danni didn't know but had noticed during her talk. She had something in her hand.

"Stay right there," the soldier instructed. The woman ignored the instruction.

"Release that woman," the lady said with authority. She walked briskly toward the soldier. He released Mrs. Pinkerton's arm but turned the rifle on the woman and followed her steps until she stopped in front of him.

Danni and Mrs. Pinkerton slowly moved to the side of the aisle to give her room to approach the soldier.

The lady flashed what was in her hand in front of the soldier's face. Danni had no idea what it was but was concerned that the woman might escalate things further. The soldiers seemed on edge and would fire their weapons if sufficiently provoked.

"My name is Aria Decker. I'm the Director of Diplomatic Relations. I'm part of the Prescom's cabinet." She smiled at Danni as she said it.

"There are more than ten people here," the soldier said. "They've violated the order."

"I know," Aria replied. "But it's okay. I'm in charge of enforcing this order. I'm here on behalf of the Prescom. I'm authorizing these people to meet. Look around. There's barely more than ten people here. Anyway, I'm saying they can meet. If you'd like, I can get the Prescom on the caller."

"That won't be necessary," the soldier said, sheepishly. "I hope you know I was just doing my job."

"I do know that, and I appreciate it. In the future, you don't need to barge into churches with your guns raised, threatening to arrest people. These people are hurting. They're just searching for answers. Just start by giving them a warning. You don't have to arrest anyone."

"Yes, Ma'am," he said, backing away as the other men lowered their weapons. "You have a good day."

Mrs. Pinkerton glared at the man as he turned to leave the church. Danni let out a big sigh of relief.

Aria put her hand on Danni's shoulder and said sweetly, "You can continue. Sorry for the interruption."

* * *

Heaven

The entire heavenly throng in my mansion let out their own collective sigh even though we all knew the soldiers were coming. We just didn't know how it would end. I thought that perhaps the enemy had timed the intrusion to prevent my daughter from presenting the gospel to the group there.

Anticipation was building among us. In heaven and in the church, I could tell. We could see the Holy Spirit arriving at the church about to make his first appearance. The Bible says that where two or more are gathered, he's in their midst. But that only applies to Christians. No one in that church is saved or has the Holy Spirit living in them. It appears as if he's there to draw the men and women to him. Or at least that's what I hope is happening.

The entire heavenly room prayed that each person attending church that day would respond to the call. This might be their last chance. Some or all of them might not survive the tribulation.

Aria and Mrs. Pinkerton returned to their seats. Danni took her place behind the podium. I was proud of how she had the courage to confront the soldier and tell him she was in charge. I always knew she had it in her but had never seen such confidence and boldness. It became apparent that it was real as she began speaking with more confidence.

"I want to read a Bible verse that might shed some light on what has happened," Danni began.

Everyone in the church sat up and was listening intently. Except for Dr. Tom. He was sitting in the back, with his leg crossed, his right arm extended across the back of the pew. A sly grin was on his face.

We all noticed it in the heavenlies.

Tom's father must have noticed as well because he said, "Tom knows these verses like the back of his hand. He even believes them to be true."

I nodded, understanding what he meant. Danni was the same way. She'd heard me preach thousands of times. "Tom believes in Jesus," his father said. "But that's obviously not enough to be saved."

We all got quiet as Danni began reading.

"But I do not want you to be ignorant, brethren, concerning those who have fallen asleep, lest you sorrow as others who have no hope. For if we believe that Jesus died and rose again, even so God will bring with him those who sleep in Jesus."

Danni paused to let the words sink in.

I beamed in admiration.

Danni pointed to the woman who had spoken earlier. "What's your name?" Danni asked.

"My name is Ruth."

Ruth was the mother whose baby was taken from her crib.

"What was your baby's name?" Danni asked.

"Kate."

"This verse tells us that Kate is with Jesus."

In the heavenly mansion, Kate sat in her chair with a huge smile on her face. Jesus is with us. We are never apart from him.

Back on Jupiter, Ruth smiled weakly, clearly trying to draw hope from Danni's words.

Danni continued. "Let me read the rest of the verse. 'For this we say to you by the word of the Lord that we who are alive and remain until the coming of the Lord will by no means precede those who are asleep.'"

"Is that talking about us?" the man on the second row asked.

"What is your name, sir?" Danni asked.

"I'm Carter Hall, and this is my wife, Taylor." He smiled sweetly at his wife sitting beside him.

I knew him. Their grandparents were there in my mansion with us. They were watching the portal to the church intently. I knew their whole story. How he had saved her after the airmobile hit the tower. And how they were now trying hard to save their marriage.

"No. He's not talking about us," Danni said soberly to the man. "He's talking about those who were taken. Those who were Christian. The rest of the verse says, 'For the Lord himself will descend from heaven with a shout, with the voice of an archangel, and with the trumpet of God. And the dead in Christ will rise first.' That's what happened on Tuesday."

"I didn't hear a shout or a trumpet," Dr. King said. He was the director of Obstetrics at the hospital where all the babies disappeared along with his own son Joshua who was with me in the room.

"I didn't either," others echoed all across the sanctuary of the church.

I heard it, I wanted to tell them. We all did. It was glorious. I was sitting in my office talking to Mrs. Pinkerton when I heard the shout and then the trumpet and the next thing I knew, I was flying in the air and suddenly in heaven in the presence of Jesus. It was so amazing. I'm glad I was alive in the generation that got to experience it.

"Only those who were seized heard it," Danni said, interrupting my thoughts. "But this tells us that they all went to heaven to be with Jesus."

"It's the only logical explanation," Dr. King replied. "How else could all these people just disappear?"

"I heard they were taken by aliens," Carter said.

"That's nonsense," Mrs. Pinkerton chimed in roughly. "They were seized."

Danni wanted to keep the tone more positive. She could tell her words were sinking in. The people were clearly searching for answers. For the first time in her life, these words were coming to life, and she was understanding them.

Danni read the rest of the verse. "Then we who are alive and remain shall be caught up together with them in the clouds to meet the Lord in the air."

A collective gasp went through the church.

"That's what happened," Danni said. "They all met Jesus in the air."

"Wow!" one person said. "That must've been amazing."

"In the twinkling of an eye, the Bible says, they were all changed." Danni closed my book that she had been reading from, and her look turned more solemn.

"That's what happened to all of our loved ones," Danni said with tears filling her eyes. "My dad and mom. My brother and sister. They were all taken. I miss them desperately. I'd give anything to have them back. Really, I'd give anything to be with them."

The tears were noticeably running down her cheek now. She didn't bother to push them away. Others were feeling the same sense of sadness as several began noticeably crying. Some were sobbing, weeping intensely.

There is no crying in heaven, but I understood what they were feeling. The Bible verse had new meaning to me as well, just from a different perspective. I could understand both how they felt and how we felt. For us, we were with Jesus in heaven. There is no more pain and no more suffering. No more tears and no more sadness. I want that for them so badly. I want it for Danni. For Ruth. Carter. Taylor. Dr. King. Mrs. Pinkerton. All of them.

The people on Jupiter wanted it badly as well.

* * *

"Will we ever see them again?" Taylor asked Danni.

"Can I see my baby?" Ruth asked. "I heard someone on vision say that we will see them again in seven years."

"That was probably me," Dr. Tom said as he stood from his seat and walked to the front and stood next to Danni. She moved aside to let him have the podium.

The room grew eerily silent.

"Will we see our loved ones again? It depends," he said slowly. "After the seizure is seven years of tribulation. Suffering, unlike the world has ever seen. At the end of the seven years, those who were taken will come back and reign on Jupiter with Christ for one thousand years."

"Including my baby?" Ruth asked.

"I think so," Dr. Tom said.

"I can wait seven years."

"The problem is that most people won't survive the tribulation," Dr. Tom explained. "Without God's help, we'll all die."

"Is that true, Danni?" Dr. King asked.

"Yes," she said. "Most of Jupiter and everyone on it will be destroyed. There are coming plagues, earthquakes, and persecution unlike the world has ever known."

"There will be an elect who will survive," Tom said, with sincere optimism coming from his voice. "Those people will live to reign with Christ for the thousand years. But only those who accept Christ as their Savior during those seven years."

"I want to do that," Taylor said.

"Me too," Ruth echoed.

A murmur went through the entire sanctuary.

"How do we do that?" Carter asked.

"You confess Jesus as Lord, and you believe in him, and you will be saved," Danni said. She had heard her dad deliver the invitation to salvation a thousand times.

"I believe," Taylor said.

"It's more than just belief," Dr. Tom said soberly. "I've believed in God and Jesus all my life. I don't remember a moment when I didn't believe. But I wasn't taken. I got off track. I believed other things that weren't true. You have to believe it in here." He pointed to his heart. His huge hand patted his chest several times. "Only those who truly believe and make Jesus Lord of their life are saved."

"I want to believe. I just don't know how," Ruth said, tearfully. "I want to see my baby and husband again, so bad."

Sensing an opportunity, Danni said, "Everyone, bow your heads." "If you want to be saved, say this prayer after me. If you really believe it, you will be saved."

"Dear Jesus," Danni said.

The people in the room repeated her words.

"I ask you into my heart, right now, to be my Lord and Savior..."

Every person in the room said the prayer.

26

Heaven

Every relative in my heavenly mansion is watching the proceedings intently. Their spiritual eyes affixed to their relatives. Expectation and hope filled the room.

When a person is saved on Jupiter, all heaven rejoices. A herald appears, and a picture of the person is flashed across the sky. The entire throng of witnesses erupt in applause and cheering. We all stared at the sky with tremendous anticipation.

The first picture appeared. Taylor Hall. The prostitute who her husband had saved. Her grandparents squealed with delight. Carter, her husband's picture appeared next as the room erupted in applause, and thanks to God permeated the room. God had not only saved their marriage; he had now saved their souls for an eternity.

Dr. King and his wife Olivia were next. Joshua, their son, stood to his feet with his hands in the air, praising Jesus and shouting Hallelujahs. Even though he was seized from the womb and never knew them on the earth, he knew them in heaven, and now he would spend an eternity with his parents.

Pastor Randy and Cindy were on the edge of their seats, faith exuding through every fiber of their spiritual being. I could see the pride in their eyes as their son Tom had a part in sharing the gospel with the people, testifying to his own shortcoming in not truly believing in his heart. When his picture appeared in the sky, they flew into each other's arms. They danced around with all their might, their arms clenched together, huge smiles of joy on their faces. We all rejoiced with them.

"Yes!" I heard Kate say in her soft, childlike voice. I'd looked away from the sky momentarily to watch Randy and Cindy rejoice their son's salvation and hadn't seen Ruth's picture flash across the sky. Ruth would be reunited with her baby soon. And her husband Jake and father-in-law Carl. They would all be reunited someday.

Naomi's picture appeared next. The reunion would be glorious.

Aria Decker was saved. The government cabinet official who had rebutted the soldier's efforts to shut down the assembly. I was so thankful she'd been there. Certainly, God's providence led her there today, for that moment and time. Not only for her benefit, but for everyone who had attended.

A short pause in the pictures. Then a shout from the heralds. Trumpets. Loud cymbals were playing as Danni's picture appeared. Nancy, Todd, and Avery erupted in adulation. I just slumped back in my chair. My girl was saved. All I had wanted for all my children was for them to know Jesus. Now they all did. I would see her again.

The heralds left. They were done.

Mrs. Pinkerton.

What about her? Her face hadn't appeared in the sky. I saw her lips moving as she said the prayer with the others.

Yet, she was the only one in the room who wasn't saved.

PART THREE

For there will be greater anguish than at any time since the world began. And it will never be so great again.

27

September 11, 2062
One Year After the Seizure

Things were going well on Jupiter; then they got even better.

Prescom Jack Wolf had proven to be a more effective leader than anyone thought possible considering the difficult circumstances forced upon him when the previous Prescom disappeared along with nineteen billion other people, throwing the solar system's largest planet into chaos.

D-Day as he called it, although no one knew why. Disappearance Day, some speculated. Devastation Day maybe. Death Day as some families called it. Those who'd been hit particularly hard by it.

Dictator Day to the most cynical. Wolf's power grab was a large part of the reason for his Prescomial success. He formed a new government called the New World Order, which firmly established him as the Dictator and his cabinet the most powerful and elite governing body the planet had ever known. The cabinet members deserved a lot of credit as well, if only for the simple fact that they carried out his every command competently and with little questioning.

Aria Decker somehow maintained her position as Director of Diplomatic Relations and her influence with the Prescom increased to the point that she sat right next to him at every cabinet meeting. Favor from God, she believed. For such a time as this.

Prescom Wolf knew nothing of her born again experience at Red Spot Christian Church nearly a year before. Not that she kept it secret from him, but he had little interest in her personal religious beliefs, except to the extent that Aria could use her influence to keep the religions in line. As long as they didn't publicly criticize him or the New World Order, the churches were free to meet without interference from the government.

All restrictions were removed for the churches, allowing them to meet freely, and Aria had the authority to manage them as she saw fit. Her resolve was to give them every opportunity to grow and prosper and spread the gospel, which they were effectively doing in record numbers.

Red Spot Christian Church in one year had more than fifty satellite campuses and more than two-hundred-thousand people who attended the campuses each Sunday morning. More than twenty million watched the services on-line. The world-wide church didn't have the numbers they had before D-Day, but the Lord was adding to their numbers daily.

Aria had many more ideas and plans to implement. Her thoughts were interrupted as Prescom Wolf entered the Cabinet room and took his place beside her.

"As you are aware," Prescom Wolf began, "today marks the one-year anniversary since D-Day. The celebrations are scheduled to begin at 1:00, so we'll make this meeting shorter than normal."

Aria wasn't sure why they were called celebrations. The planning started as a memorial tribute to those who disappeared and lost their lives and quickly evolved into a day honoring Prescom Wolf. There would be a parade and fireworks, and most people were given the day off from work so they could attend or watch it on vision. While some criticized the Prescom for his pomposity, most were looking forward to the festivities and were appreciative of what the Prescom had done to revive Jupiter.

"Wade. Are the details for the unveiling of the Grand Monument finalized?" the Prescom asked Wade Wilson, his staff chief.

"They are sir. The sculptor finished his work last night. Just in time. I told him thirty years in prison awaited him if he didn't," Wade said with a laugh which the room joined almost as if on cue.

"Excellent!" the Prescom said.

The Grand Monument of Red Spot Hill had been in the works for six months. The twelve massive statues of Prescom Wolf were interspersed among the main square, with the Prescom in various poses. The estimated costs of the entire display were more than ten million jupes. Paid for out of the treasury. A small cost of the entire project, considering the celebration cost more than fifty million jupes when taking into consideration security, fireworks, the parade, viewing areas, and the evening balls that were being held throughout the city in the Prescom's honor.

"How are we coming with the new currency?" Prescom Wolf asked, changing the subject. A question for Greg Jennings, the Head of Treasury to answer.

"Very good, sir," he replied.

Aria knew that most department heads answered every question in the affirmative, even if things weren't going well. No one wanted to experience the wrath of Prescom Wolf. He demanded perfection of all of them including himself.

"The new denominations have been determined and the images picked out," he said. Prescom Wolf's image was going to be on all the new currency. Greg's idea but one the Prescom eagerly embraced. The new bills would be called Junipers.

"A microchip has been designed." Greg held out a small, computer chip, barely the size of a grain of rice. "The chip will be implanted in each person. It'll have all their data on it. Name. Birthdate. Government ID number. Banking and credit card information. No one will be able to buy and sell without this chip."

"When will it be ready for implementation?" the Prescom asked.

"That will take several months, maybe a year," Greg answered.

"You have three months," Wolf said.

Greg started to raise what appeared to be an objection, but Wolf had moved on to the next question which was for J. B. Hader, Director of Commerce.

"J. B., do you have any ideas on how we can get the stock market even higher?" Right after D-day the stock market lost nearly sixty percent of its value, devastating the portfolios of the rich, especially those sitting in that room. Due to decisive action from Prescom Wolf, the stock market was now at record highs. The men and the women in the room had seen their net worth increase by ten times in the last year. Some of them considered D-Day the best thing that ever happened on Jupiter.

"I've suggested to Greg that the treasurer infuse more liquidity into the stock market and that he lower interest rates, but he has resisted," J.B. said. Aria saw Greg glare at J.B. He glared back.

"Why is that Greg?" the Prescom asked.

"I'm worried about inflation," he answered.

"Inflation only hurts the poor," J.B. argued. "Basic goods cost them more. Inflation can help the rich if managed properly. It gives us a greater return on our savings and investments. We can charge the middle-class higher interest rates on their home loans, mobile loans, and credit card debt. We see record spending from the lower and middle class. The more we extend and make credit available to them, the better it helps the stock market. We need liquidity to make that happen."

"Inflation might help us, but destroying the economy won't help us," Greg countered.

"With all due respect, D-Day destroyed the economy, yet we're doing better now than ever before." His hands were animated as he said it.

Greg opened his mouth to say something, but Prescom Wolf spoke before he could get the words out.

"No one wants to destroy the economy," he said. "But I want growth. The economy is growing at eighteen percent. I want that number up to twenty-five. Make it happen. Both of you."

"Sir. There is already a great disparity between the upper class and the lower class," Aria said. "It's growing every month. Inflation will make it worse. People will see their paychecks increase, but the costs of their basic needs increase at a greater rate. Ultimately, they will be worse off."

"A rising tide lifts all boats," Prescom Wolf said. "The rich provide the jobs. The more jupes we make, the better off the poor are."

"If that were only true," Aria said. "It seems like the rich get richer and the poor get poorer."

"Survival of the fittest," Hader said. "It is the law of the universe."

"We cannot forget the poor and less fortunate and leave them behind. They need to participate in this economic boom," Aria said more strongly.

"Which is your job!" Prescom Wolf interjected. "One in which you're doing very well, I might add."

"Thank you, sir," Aria said knowing Prescom Wolf had just signaled to her to shut up. He didn't want to hear anymore from her.

"Besides, that's what the churches are for," Prescom Wolf added. "They can feed the poor and take in the homeless. That's why I let them exist."

The churches are to spread the gospel of Jesus Christ, Aria wanted to say but thought better of it. Instead she said boldly, "Then increase my budget with some of that liquidity from the treasury. I can put it to good use through the churches. That will make you look even better in the eyes of the people, Mr. Prescom."

"He looks pretty good already," Wade Wilson, the staff chief said with a sarcastic chuckle. "His approval ratings are through the roof."

"Aria is right," Wolf said. "We have an election in two years. One we need to win. My approval rating is high now, but that can change on a dime. Circumstances are fluid. The economy is doing well now, but we never know when another disaster is looming. Add ten percent to Aria's budget. She can use that to buy more influence with the pastors. No one influences the masses like the clergy."

Ten percent. Some of the other cabinet members spend more than that on their personal travel budget each year. *Oh well. Ten percent is better than no percent.*

"I think we're done here," Wolf said. "I have to get fitted for my suit for the ceremony at one. Good work everyone. I'll see you in a few hours."

Everyone stood to leave. Rather than immediately leaving, Prescom Wolf turned to Aria and said, "Can I see you in my office before you go?"

"Of course."

I wonder what he wants.

*** *

Aria had only been in the Global Office twice since Prescom Wolf took over. Wolf was more protective of his privacy than previous administrations. If he was meeting with her there, alone, then it must be important.

The office had been completely remodeled at great expense. Lavish carpeting and drapes accented the large red mahogany desk, made from rare wood from a province in the west. A large portrait of Prescom Wolf dominated one wall; another wall was filled with books. Wolf was an avid reader. Aria wondered when he had the time. Wolf was a workaholic. Word was that he only slept four hours a night. The rest of the time he was working. Studying. Planning. Scheming in her mind. Plotting his next move.

He was as hard working as he was shrewd. He didn't have the charisma or the integrity of the previous Prescom who was seized, but his instincts were usually spot on. To his credit, the poor had benefited from his leadership. He had expanded distribution. Basic services were now available to the masses. Even the poor had callers, refrigerators, mobiles, and vision sets. All provided at low costs. Most were rich compared to the poor of a year ago even if the disparity and gap between the poor and rich had grown as well.

Prescom Wolf burst into the room with his usual flare and vibrancy. He always moved with a sense of urgency. Whatever, he wanted to talk to her about, she was sure he would get right to the point.

"Aria."

"Yes. Sir."

"Do you know the identity of the two witnesses?" he asked. The last question she expected from him.

Aria swallowed hard. *Did he notice? She* did know their identities.

"No, sir. I don't," she said trying to maintain eye contact.

"Find out for me. Okay?"

"I will, sir."

"That's all I had," he said, as he stood and held out his hand.

Aria shook it.

Why does he want to know? This can't be good.

I must warn them.

28

Two months later
Mrs. Pinkerton's Estate
3:00 a.m.

Danni and Bruno, who was sleeping at her feet, were suddenly startled awake from a deep sleep. For the past year, she'd been living at Mrs. Pinkerton's estate. Her parent's house had been seized by the government and sold. Aria said it was to line the pockets of the politicians. The government took the homes of all heads of the household who'd been seized. Millions were left homeless.

Danni rubbed her eyes roughly and shook her head from side to side, even though she was wide awake. This had happened several times before. For the past year, God had been speaking to her in dreams, telling her events before they happened. Mrs. Pinkerton said they were prophecies and fulfillment of Scripture. Some of them were frightening. All were vivid. In color. She'd heard a Bible teacher on vision say that if a dream was in color, it was from God.

Eerily, just about everything she dreamed came to pass. She threw the blankets aside and rushed over to the desk in her spacious suite. Liz was asleep in the room next door. On the desk lay a note-book and writing instrument. Fumbling with the light, Danni closed her eyes, picturing the dream in her mind, making sure she remembered every detail.

Not that it was necessary. She never forgot a dream. They were etched into her soul. She journaled them anyway.

Danni started writing. When she was finished, she went back to bed.

* * *

"Did you sleep well?" Mrs. Pinkerton asked Danni in the morning when they sat down to have a cup of coffee together on the back patio before breakfast. They'd settled into a routine. They'd have coffee together, then breakfast. and then Danni would go to Dr. Tom's estate where they recorded their morning radio show together.

The morning was beautiful, the weather perfect. The patio looked out over one hundred expansive acres of trees, rolling hills, and a large, majestic mountain in the distance. When the sun shone on the side of the mountain at just the right angle, they could see red spots. That's where the city and mountain got its name.

"I had another dream," Danni said.

Mrs. Pinkerton stared off into the distance, her coffee cup up to her lips, her hands firmly clasped around the edges. She was blowing on the cup just above the rim, to get the beverage to cool. Or maybe a nervous habit. Mrs. Pinkerton was sitting in her rocking chair, slowly pushing it back and forth with her foot. She seemed her happiest when she was in a rocking chair. She had at least one in every room of the massive house.

"You were in my dream," Danni said.

"Really. I hope it was a good dream."

"I don't think you should go on your trip."

Mrs. Pinkerton stopped rocking.

"I've been looking forward to this trip for months. Years really. Before William died." William was her husband who'd been dead for fifteen years.

"So has Naomi. You know that. She'd be heartbroken if we didn't go."

Mrs. Pinkerton and Naomi were going on a cruise. To the Anih C Province on the far side of Jupiter. They were leaving in the morning and would be gone for three weeks. Mrs. Pinkerton was right. The two ladies had been flittering around the house for days like a couple of giddy teenagers, picking out clothes together, trying things on, shopping for things they didn't have, and making all the necessary preparations.

Danni hated even bringing it up. "I know," she said. "It's only a matter of time before the Tribulation starts. I don't want you to be on some cruise ship, miles away, when it does."

Mrs. Pinkerton waved her hand dismissively. They'd had many conversations about this topic. Things were going so well on Jupiter, Mrs. Pinkerton questioned whether the Tribulation was really going to happen. "Maybe we're misinterpreting the Bible," she'd said.

Danni was convinced the Bible was right, and the events would start unfolding soon. This was the calm before the storm.

"It was Naomi's idea," Mrs. Pinkerton said. "Her... She and Carl were supposed to go on this cruise this year. My grammar is getting bad in my old age. Anyway. I don't want to disappoint her just because you have a feeling."

Danni ignored the dig.

Naomi was also a widow. Not technically a widow, since her husband Carl was seized, still alive in heaven as Naomi believed by faith, as did Danni. Mrs. Pinkerton was beginning to question the whole seizure and had doubts about whether there was even a heaven. Naomi thought this cruise would be a good time for them to be alone. Maybe she could talk to her about it.

Mrs. Pinkerton and Naomi had become best friends. Almost inseparable. Naomi's house had been taken from the government nine months before. Mrs. Pinkerton insisted she move in with her as well. She shared a two-bedroom suite with her daughter-in-law Ruth, her son Jake's wife, whose house was also seized.

Sharing a love for cards, Naomi and Mrs. Pinkerton would stay up late at night, playing for hours. Naomi always slept late the next morning when they did. Mrs. Pinkerton rose at the crack of dawn regardless of when she went to sleep.

Ruth rarely slept, it seemed. She still couldn't get over the loss of her husband and her baby, Kate, who was seized from her crib. The memory of Kate missing, and the ensuing panic still haunted her. Everyone tried to comfort her and encouraged her to trust God. She would see them again someday.

Ruth admitted that she had her good days and bad days.

Danni was looking forward to some alone time with her. If she were honest, she was really looking forward to a three-week break from Mrs. Pinkerton.

"Anyway. The trip is already paid for," Mrs. Pinkerton retorted, breaking Danni's train of thought.

"I have a bad feeling about it," Danni finally said after nearly a minute of silence.

"We'll be fine."

"I guess."

Danni wasn't so sure.

* * *

Danni was in awe every time she drove up to Dr. Tom Collins's estate.

The house on two-hundred-plus acres was four times larger than Mrs. Pinkerton's. It consisted of eighty thousand square feet of living space, three swimming pools—two outside and one inside—six tennis courts, a garage that held nearly a hundred mobiles, and a small airport complete with a helipad, landing strip, and two airmobiles, including a commercial jet that could carry up to two-hundred people.

And a recording studio.

One of the wings of the house contained a fully equipped vision and radio studio where Dr. Tom recorded his videos and audio materials and produced his radio show, *Ask Dr. Tom*, which aired on more than forty-four-hundred radio stations. His popularity had never been higher. Since the Seizure, Tom was often called upon by the networks to bring motivation and optimism to the masses. Since being saved that Sunday morning at Red Spot Christian Church, his message had changed, and now he said there was a power behind the words that wasn't there before.

A new program, started a little over three months ago, had grown to syndication on more than five-thousand stations. Wildly popular, *The Two Witnesses*, was a thirty-minute show dealing with end times prophecy. The show wasn't designed to make jupes or have advertisers.

When Tom had suggested Danni co-host it with her, she wasn't sure she could do it. Turns out she was a natural behind the mike. The chemistry between them was unmistakable. Danni sometimes felt some romantic sparks as well, but always tamped them down.

The program wasn't without risk. They had valid concern the government would try to shut it down. Therefore, tremendous precautions had been taken to protect their identities.

A sophisticated internet connection that couldn't be traced distributed their program, encrypted it, and with only the stations having the code to play it. The software itself cost more than a hundred-thousand jupes and was created by some of the best internet minds. Each person worked on one section so no one saw the final product.

The biggest problem was the topics often concerned the New World Order and Tom and Danni's uncompromised condemnation of it. The Prescom wanted the program shut down and the two witnesses arrested.

"Leave the two witnesses alone," Aria had urged the Prescom. "Let them go. If their purpose or endeavor is of human origin, it'll fail. If it's from God, you won't be able to stop them. You may even find yourself fighting against God."

At this urging, the Prescom had yielded to Aria. Mostly because he felt like the only way to find them was to let it air. Let them slip up and make a mistake. He had his best minds working on tracking the connection. So far, he hadn't succeeded. Aria warned Danni and Tom that it was only a matter of time until the Prescom found them.

Danni didn't care. She was prepared to be martyred for Christ. So was Tom. Danni wanted to stand in the middle of the square in front of all the gaudy Prescomial statues and proclaim the gospel to the multitudes there. With boldness, like the Apostles of Jesus did centuries before.

But Tom had convinced her that she would be arrested immediately. What good would that do? Right now, she was having so much success with the radio program, he argued that they shouldn't jeopardize it unnecessarily. Danni had reluctantly relented.

She walked into the studio at 8:45 in the morning. Right on time as she always was. Funny that when her parents were alive, they could barely get her out of bed to make it to school on time. Now that she had a purpose in life, a calling, she couldn't get out of bed soon enough to get to the studio and record their next program.

She wondered if maybe it was because she couldn't wait to see Tom. Her heart warmed every time she saw him.

He smiled when she walked in, sending a tingly feeling through her. He was busy setting up the microphones and preparing the recording. They never discussed the topic beforehand. They decided that was part of the success. The show was spontaneous, Spirit led, and neither knew what might come of the other's mouths. More often than not, it was something hilarious.

Today's topic took a serious turn from the very beginning. Perhaps it was because of Danni's dream and prophecy which she intended to reveal at the end of the program.

"Do not be deceived," Danni said into the microphone. "These great times will not last."

"Can you explain to our listeners what's coming?" Dr. Tom asked. "Prescom Wolf says our best days are ahead of us. What do you say?" They never used each other's names.

"There will be a shaking unlike anything we've ever seen before. It's time for the children of God to make preparations," Danni said with authority.

"What are you doing to protect yourself?" he asked, even though he already knew the answer. Carter Hall, who was saved at the first church meeting after the Seizure, was in charge of rounding up supplies which were being stored at Mrs. Pinkerton's and Dr. Tom's estates in specially constructed bunkers. Carter was a survivalist and was perfect for the task and had volunteered enthusiastically.

"Along with trusting in God, I'm being prudent and wise as an ant who stores up food for the winter," Danni said.

"How much food are you storing?"

"Three and half years' worth is what the Lord has told me."

"What do you say to those who are skeptical? You look outside and the sun is shining. The birds are singing. The stock market is at an all-time high. It's hard to believe that things are going to get that bad. They were bad after the Seizure and we bounced back. Why couldn't we do that again? I know the answer. But some of our listeners don't."

"Faith is the substance of what is hoped for, the evidence of things not seen. It's a matter of faith." Danni could feel the power of God behind her words. Sometimes she couldn't even believe they were coming from her. Others felt the same way. Tom was twenty years older and often commented that she was wise beyond her years.

"The Tribulation is prophesied in the Bible," Danni explained. "You can read Jesus's own words. He prophesied the Seizure. He said it would be followed by seven years of tribulation. Such as the world has never seen. Unimaginable suffering. Prescom Wolf won't be in power in less than two years. An anti-Christ will rise to power. He will reign for three-and-a-half years until he will be destroyed when Christ comes again."

"You really believe this is going to happen?"

"I'm certain of it."

"I am too. Mark our words," Dr. Tom said.

For twenty more minutes, they discussed the topic. The time flew by as they skillfully complemented each other, building on each other's words. A good program. One that would help a lot of people.

Nearing the end, Tom said, "Let me read a verse from the Bible. These are Jesus's words, 'For there will be greater anguish than at any time since the world began. And it will never be so great again.'"

Danni shuddered.

Not because she was afraid of the coming events, but because of her concern for the world. She had grown to love the people of Jupiter. In some ways, she had become their pastor. She and Tom. They co-pastored Red Spot Christian Church. With the favor of God, the church was growing beyond what they ever imagined possible. The radio show was the most listened to program in the history of Jupiter.

They'd come so far. The movement started with less than a dozen people, one Sunday morning, the week after the Seizure. Those people there that day had become the church elders. Carter, his wife, Taylor. Ruth and Naomi. Dr. King and his wife, Olivia. Mrs. Pinkerton. Liz. Dr. Tom. Aria was asked to be an elder but declined given her position in the Prescom's cabinet. Better to remain at arm's length, so she could act almost like a spy on their behalf with no formal ties to the church.

Her job was to be a liaison between the government and the church, so it was natural for her to have a lot of interaction with them. The irony wasn't lost on all of them. God had clearly saved her and put her in that position for a purpose. Similar to the biblical story where a young boy was sold into slavery by his brothers and earned the king's favor and became the ruler of his house. Just so he could store up grain for his family for the coming famine.

"Do you have any final words before we end our program?" Tom said to Danni, shaking her out of her deep thoughts.

Danni took a deep breath. "I had a dream this morning." She paused. Her hands were shaking.

Tom stared at her intently, obviously taken in by the seriousness of her tone.

"I see a plague coming on the world," Danni said. "Red Spot will be shaken like it has never been before. The New World Order will be brought to its knees. The plague will ravage the world. Businesses will be shuttered. Multitudes won't be allowed out of their houses."

Danni stopped for effect.

"Is that all?" Tom said.

"No. God showed me that a third of the people will die."

29

Global Laboratory for Virology and Infectious Diseases (GLOVID)
Anih C Province
One year, two months after the Seizure

It had been five days and neither monkey was showing any symptoms.

Yuan Woo, the Assistant Director of GLOVID, sat in his office studying the tests results from the latest blood work on the two monkeys recently injected with a strain of Flu-us, a super virus Dr. Woo had created in his lab.

As the foremost virologist on Jupiter, Dr. Woo had degrees in Immunology, Epidemiology, Micro-Biology, and Virology. For the past two years, his primary job had been to create new viruses in his lab and study the possible effects on humans. The project had been funded after a strain of flu killed nearly twenty million people ten years ago before it ran its course and died out. So far, it hadn't resurfaced in humans.

Another, more deadly strain, killed more than fifty million people nearly a hundred years ago. It originated from bats. The scientific community was constantly worried it could resurface and cause a global pandemic.

Cells of both of those strains were kept on ice in the GLOVID laboratory for research. Two years before, Dr. Woo had gotten the idea to combine the two strains. He asked his staff what would happen if a bat bit a pig and infected it with a strain of virus genetically compatible with the pig virus. Could it transmit to humans by eating the pigs? While the possibility seemed remote, his job was to consider every potential threat to the destruction of mankind. The staff had begun experiments right away.

After significant research, Dr. Woo concluded in his report to the Global Health Organization (GHO) that the "recombinant merging of the two virus strains was unlikely." The report further read, "The cellular structures, genetic codes, the mode of transmissions, infectivity, and overall efficacy were so different between the two that the possibility of the two viruses creating a super flu-us were .000015 percent."

His work was halted until he found a new strain of virus had formed in cave bats in a remote region of Jupiter, discovered under the most unusual circumstances. A peasant pig farmer found a number of his animals dead one morning. Rather than destroy them, he sold them in the local market.

Several villagers died from eating the infected pigs. Dr. Woo was called in to investigate. Autopsies were performed on the dead villagers. What Dr. Woo saw horrified him. The flu-us attacked the lungs with such severity that the air sacs filled with fluid, and the lining of the lungs turned black as the virus ate away the healthy tissues and destroyed the healthy lungs to the point that the person was unable to breath.

The family members reported that it started as a mild cough. Then shortness of breath. Finally, full-on respiratory failure. The village had no doctors, hospitals, or medical equipment, and those infected died within a few days of the first cough. What was more chilling to Dr. Woo was that ninety percent of the people in the village contracted the virus without ever eating the pigs, and a third of them died.

That meant it could be transmitted from human to human. Probably through air particles. Even more concerning was that a third were asymptomatic, meaning no one knew they were even sick and could infect others.

The .000015 percent, even as low as it was, had come to pass.

Fortunately, the village was small enough that it could be contained. After fourteen days, the flu-us died out and was confined to that one region.

Dr. Woo brought a team to the area and began researching it to find the source. That's when they discovered the bats in the caves. The virus was dormant in the bats but could be transmitted by a bite. The pigs had their own dormant virus which was common in swine.

The conclusion was that a bat bit a pig, infected him with a virus, the two strains combined their cellular structures, mutated, and then formed the super flu-us modified strain which could be transmitted to humans by eating the pigs or by human transmission such as air particles or touching someone with the virus by shaking hands or just being around them.

Dr. Woo brought the deadly strain back to the GLOVID lab and studied its genetic sequencing. He determined that the odds of it happening again weren't likely. However, with five mutations, it could eventually be transmitted to humans. Five days ago, he injected the mutated strain into two monkeys to see if he was right. So far, neither had shown any signs of symptoms. He wasn't sure quite what to make of that. Maybe what happened to the villagers was an aberration.

He rubbed his eyes and decided to call it a day when the cleaning man arrived. A cleaning boy, really. Dr. Woo surmised he couldn't be more than eighteen or nineteen years old.

"How are you tonight?" Dr. Woo said to the young man who was with the cleaning company.

"I'm doing good," he said.

Dr. Woo wished the boy was older and more experienced to be given a job at such a sensitive site. But after the disappearance of so many people a little over a year ago, most companies were having a hard time finding people to work the manual labor jobs. There simply were more jobs than people willing to do them.

A quick check of the lab satisfied Dr. Woo that everything was in order and nothing infectious was anywhere in the lab. Strict protocols were in place to keep the lethal virus strain confined to the facility. It would be a disaster if a virus somehow escaped from the lab. That thought kept Dr. Woo up at night. He didn't want to be responsible for a world-wide pandemic.

"What am I supposed to clean?" the boy asked.

Dr. Woo gave him a tour of the facility with specific instructions on what to clean. No need to tell him to stay out of the infectious area with the monkeys. It was locked anyway. Dr. Woo pointed to the door that led to the monkeys. "They might make some noise. Just ignore them."

"Okay," the boy said nervously.

Dr. Woo exited the lab and got into his vehicle and left. He was hungry and tired. Suddenly, a chill ran through his spine as a thought ran through his mind.

Did I remember to lock the door to the monkeys?

I did, he decided, even though he couldn't remember doing it.

Are you sure?

Dr. Woo slowed down the mobile and considered returning to the lab. He ran through in his mind everything he did while he was leaving. There was a protocol, a checklist, but he never followed it. It was so ingrained in his mind; he didn't think it possible to forget anything. Could he have missed something? A nagging feeling was overwhelming his emotions.

I'm just being paranoid.

It doesn't matter. The cleaning boy would be the only person there for the rest of the night, and he didn't clean that area anyway. There was no reason to go back. Besides, the monkeys weren't symptomatic.

Satisfied, he continued on home. After a shower and a quick meal, he went to bed and decided to quit worrying about it.

***

Tranquility III, Cruise Liner
The Great Salt Sea

"Can we buy you ladies a drink?" one of the two men said as they unexpectedly walked up to the table occupied by Mrs. Pinkerton and Naomi.

Naomi was shocked when Mrs. Pinkerton said, "Sure," without hesitation.

Her mouth flew wide open when she added, "Have a seat and join us."

The two men sat down, one next to her and one next to Mrs. Pinkerton.

"What are you ladies drinking?" he asked as he signaled for the waitress. Naomi wasn't sure how to answer.

Not that the ladies hadn't imbibed on an occasional glass of wine with dinner. It's just that the last thing Naomi expected was for the two older ladies to be approached by a couple men on the cruise. Plus, they'd already had a glass of wine at dinner. One was her limit.

This was supposed to be a girl's time away. The thought had never occurred to her that there would be single men on the trip. Having been married for more than forty years to her husband, Carl, the thought of another man had never crossed her mind. She still wore her wedding ring.

Mrs. Pinkerton seemed to be enjoying the attention.

"I'll have a gin with tonic," Mrs. Pinkerton said.

"Just a glass of white wine," Naomi said, figuring the men wouldn't stay long, and she'd just have a few sips of it.

"My name is Clarence," the one sitting next to Naomi said. "That's Arthur. He's my brother."

Mrs. Pinkerton smiled broadly. "I'm Mrs. Pinkerton." Naomi knew her first name was Mamie. She was probably one of the few people who knew that.

"Oh, you're married?" Arthur asked.

"Goodness no," Mrs. Pinkerton said. "I haven't been married for years."

"Divorced?"

"No. My husband died many years ago."

"Oh, I'm sorry," Arthur said.

"I'm not," Mrs. Pinkerton said, giggling like a schoolgirl. "My husband was a bore. He did leave me with an obscene amount of jupes, though."

"My wife died last year," Arthur said. "We were married for forty-two years.

"Divorced," Clarence added, waving his naked finger, sans any rings or jewelry on any part of his body that Naomi could see.

"Twice, divorced, actually. Are you married?" he asked Naomi.

The question stumped her so much she had no idea what to say. How did she answer that? Was Carl really dead? Was she cheating on him by just having a drink with another man? Why did this feel wrong?

"Yes. I'm married," Naomi blurted out.

"My loss," Clarence said in a flirting manner.

Naomi didn't respond.

"Is he here on the cruise?" he asked.

"No. He's away," she answered.

Mrs. Pinkerton glared at her. Naomi fidgeted in her chair. She felt very uncomfortable.

The waitress sat the drinks on the table in front of them.

"Well, what happens on a cruise stays on a cruise," Clarence said, raising his glass.

Nothing's going to happen, Mister, Naomi wanted to say but raised her glass, trying not to be rude.

Mrs. Pinkerton took a big gulp, and her laugh turned giddier almost immediately. She was clearly enjoying the attention. Maybe that wasn't a bad thing. Mrs. Pinkerton needed to loosen up a little.

Back home, most thought she was too uptight. It would be good if it didn't take alcohol to do it, but what was the harm? Mrs. Pinkerton was single. She wasn't doing anything wrong. The information about her dead husband was new. Naomi had no idea she felt that way about him.

Naomi took a big sip of her wine. Maybe she was the one who needed to loosen up a little.

The lights dimmed in the restaurant, and a band started playing.

"Would you like to dance?" Mrs. Pinkerton asked Arthur.

"Sure," he said as Mrs. Pinkerton took his hand and practically pulled him onto the dance floor. Arthur was seventy plus years old, considerably overweight, balding, and clearly out of shape. If they hadn't said so, Naomi would never have believed that Clarence and Arthur were brothers. Clarence was tall and thin. In good shape. Sharply dressed. A smooth talker.

"How about you? Do you want to dance?" Clarence asked.

I'm not loosening up that much.

"I'd better not," Naomi said. "I'm happily married." After thinking about it, she was still married. If she believed the Bible, Carl was coming back in less than six years. They would live together for a thousand years in the millennium if she somehow managed to survive the tribulation. She was determined to remain faithful to him.

Clarence had a hurt look on his face but backed off. The conversation came to a screeching and awkward halt. Naomi wanted to go back to her stateroom.

At first, she stayed because she wanted to watch out for her friend and make sure she didn't drink too much or do something foolish. After a while, she wanted to stay to simply watch her on the dance floor. Her arms flailing, her hips gyrating, she was moving like a woman half her age. Naomi wished she had a camera with her. No one back home would believe what was unfolding before her eyes.

She figured eventually Mrs. Pinkerton would tire and want to go back to the room. As it approached midnight, that wasn't happening. By that time, Clarence was ignoring her as they had run out of things to talk about it. When Naomi brought up a discussion about God and Jesus, Clarence shut it down right away. Before long, he just went back to his own table.

Naomi got Mrs. Pinkerton's attention and motioned for her to come over.

"Let's go back to the room," Naomi said.

"I'm having fun. Let's stay a little while longer."

"You can stay if you want," Naomi said. "I'm going to bed."

Mrs. Pinkerton gave her a wave as she abruptly turned and started walking back to the dance floor. Arthur was clearly worn out and stood on the side watching her. Mrs. Pinkerton blew Naomi a kiss and mouthed "I love you," to her. With that, Naomi got her things and went back to the room.

She tried to stay awake, but her eyes were heavy, and the two glasses of wine had relaxed her to the point that she couldn't stay awake any longer. The last time she looked at the clock it was after one.

* * *

The next morning the sunlight burst through the cruise cabin window and into Naomi's eyes. They had a large suite with two bedrooms. Naomi got out of bed and slipped on a robe and walked out into the common area. Mrs. Pinkerton wasn't there.

She went into her bedroom. The bed was made. Mints were still on the pillows. The bed was just like the maid left it the day before.

Naomi called out her name.

No answer. Naomi couldn't believe what was happening.

Mrs. Pinkerton didn't come home last night!

30

GLOVID Lab
Anih C Province

Rou Shing-Ming was nervous. To be expected, considering this was his first night on the job, and he was cleaning in a building with the words "infectious diseases" on the sign out front.

The man who'd been there when he arrived, Director Yuan Woo, was nice and had taken the time to give him specific instructions on what to clean and what was expected of him. Dr. Woo assured him things would be fine. He was in no danger of getting infected from a virus. They had strict protocols protecting all their workers, the Director had said.

His own boss said as much as well. The company had been cleaning the lab for more than ten years without incident. The viruses were securely locked in a separate area. He was only working in the office and administrative part of the building anyway.

He started by lightly dusting the workstations. The only noise he heard was the occasional howl of two monkeys locked in a separate room just off of where he was cleaning. Dr. Woo told him to expect to hear them yell, although the first time they did, he almost jumped out of his shoes.

Really, it was easy work. The only things he had to do was basically empty the trash and clean the floors. A job he was happy to have. Jobs were scarce in Anih C, ever since the disappearance. He lived in one of the hardest hit areas, a poorer section of Jupiter, and things were just starting to pick back up and jobs were becoming more available. With limited education, this was the best work he could expect until he gained more experience.

His life was looking up. He had a new job and a new girlfriend. Wenling was her name. One who kept sending messages to his caller, interrupting his work. He didn't mind, but it was distracting.

Hi, Wenling said. She liked to be called Wendy for short. He had started calling her Wen.

Hey there, he replied.

A caller was something new for him. He got it the same day he got the new job. It was the first thing he bought, and Rou was the first person in his family to ever own one. As messages from a pretty girl streamed into his caller, he beamed with pride at his good fortune.

Wendy sent him a smiley face with a heart that sent a wave of desire through him. Sending Moji Genie characters was something he didn't know how to do yet. She'd have to show him.

What ya doing? he asked.

NMU

Rou stared at the three letters trying to figure out what they meant.

?

Not much You

Oh… Then he figured out she was asking him what he was doing. There was no punctuation or question mark in her message, so it took him a few seconds to figure it out.

I'm working.

Cool

PCML, Wendy said. He didn't know what that meant either.

?

Please call me later LGH

The message brought a smile to his face. She wanted him to call her. He knew LGH meant "laughing." She was making fun of him. That's okay. The main thing was that she wanted him to call, which he'd do as soon as he got off work. The sooner the better. He started working faster, until another message interrupted his work a few minutes later.

WTCO.

Wendy had sent him another message with teenager speak. Wendy had said everybody does it, so parents don't know what the kids are talking about. That made sense, although they were both over age, and his parents didn't care what he did.

Still, he didn't know what it meant. He stared at it, not wanting to send another question mark. Apparently, sensing his struggle, Wendy sent him the interpretation a minute later.

Want to come over?

A sudden burst of happiness flooded through his entire body. Wendy lived in her own apartment. She'd never asked him to come over before. Of course, he did.

It might be late. I have a couple more hours of work to do.

LMK I have KFU

He knew LMK meant "let me know." He didn't know what the rest of it meant other than the u.

I have a kiss for you. KFU

IDCOFS, he responded.

?

He laughed out loud. She didn't know what he meant.

I'll definitely come over for sure.

LGH. You're funny.

"She thinks I'm funny," he said to himself. He could feel the huge smile on his face. "The sooner I get these floors done, the sooner I can go over to Wendy's house," he said aloud.

Rou started scrubbing the floor harder and faster.

Suddenly, out of nowhere, he heard a blood curdling scream.

The monkeys.

Then silence. Eerie silence. Sending chills through his body.

He dropped the handle to the mop and inched his way over to the window at the door to look into the area where the monkeys were located in their cages. He peered in. One monkey was at the edge of the cage, agitated, his hands firmly gripped the metal bars. A panicked look was on his face.

The monkey coughed.

Then their eyes met.

The animal went berserk. He started violently shaking the cage, screaming at the top of his lungs. That caused the other monkey to react. Between them, the sound of their screaming was deafening even through the closed door.

The only break from the noise was when the monkey would stop to cough. A horrible sound in and of itself. Deep. Like something was lodged in his lungs that he couldn't get out.

The monkey would alternate between coughing and screaming. He'd shake the cage. Hysterically. The effort would cause him to cough again. Harder, each time.

The creature suddenly stiffened and started gasping for air, like he was having a hard time catching his breath. This caused him to shake the cage harder. He would violently shake the bars, then stop, grab his throat, and gasp for air. Cough. Then start screaming again. The scene shook Rou to his core.

I have to help him. But how?

The monkey looked like he might die if something wasn't done. But there was nothing Rou could do! The doctor said the door was locked. He didn't know who to call. Rou put his hand on the door-knob more out of reflex than anything else. The handle turned. It wasn't locked after all.

Was it safe to go in?

The large red letters on the door said, "Authorized Personnel Only. You are entering an area with hazardous materials."

It's too dangerous.

But I can't sit here and watch him die.

The argument raged in his head. It became settled when the monkey twisted and contorted his body. The chain became wrapped around his neck. The monkey clasped the chain with both hands trying to wrestle it off him. The effort wasn't working.

I'm going in.

He opened the door slowly. The monkey looked in the direction of the noise and began thrashing around, back and forth, tugging at the chain, then looking at Rou. The monkey in the cage next to him leapt to the front of his cage when Rou entered the room. He acted like he wanted to attack Rou and would've if the cage hadn't been locked. He started screaming at the top of his lungs. The shrill sounds were reverberating through the hallway. Rou's ears were ringing.

The cage was locked.

Rou reacted by running back out of the room to get his mop handle. When he got back, he could tell the monkey was losing consciousness. He slipped the handle through the cage openings and put it under the chain, but it wouldn't budge. It was too tight around the monkey's neck.

Almost without thinking, he put the handle of the mop under the monkey's back. The ape started thrashing back and forth again. With one strong push, Rou was able to push the monkey in the opposite direction of the chain. The monkey rolled over, releasing the chain from around his neck. The animal took several deep breaths. Gasps of life-saving air.

Rou took one of his own. He hadn't realized he'd been holding his breath for several seconds. Before he knew it, the monkey lunged at him. He reached through the bar and grabbed Rou's shirt, but he was able to pull away.

"You ungrateful, little snot," Rou said angrily.

An unusual name for him to call the beast, and he did so only because the animal had snot coming out of his nose and running down his face in large quantities. Both monkeys were shaking their cages back and forth, desperately trying to get at Rou.

Rou backed away. Just as he did, the sick monkey started coughing, even harder this time. His saliva flew out of the cage and right into Rou's face into his mouth and nose with a cascade of saliva and snot.

Some got in Rou's mouth. It was the foulest taste he'd ever known. Rou let out his own scream.

He ran out of the room and back into the safety of the office area, slamming the door behind him. His heart raced. Rou struggled to catch his own breath. The smell of the monkey and his saliva and bodily fluids were nearly making him sick. He could taste the monkey's nasty saliva in his mouth and the stench permeated his nose. He instinctively wiped it on his hands.

He rushed to the restroom, coughing, trying to get the vile smell and taste out of his nose as he turned on the water and frantically splashed it on his face. The cool, refreshing liquid felt good on his face as he kept roughly splashing the water on him, alternating between his nose and mouth. Some had gotten in his eyes. They burned. Stung like acid. He tried to wash it out. So hard, his eyes were turning red.

When he was satisfied that he got most of it off him, he allowed himself a chance to calm down. A few quick breaths slowed his heartbeat. That was the most traumatic thing he'd ever experienced in his entire life.

After his racing heart calmed a few beats, he thought about the situation. What should he do now? Surely, he didn't do anything wrong. Maybe he did. He went into an unauthorized area. *Yeah, but I saved the monkey's life.* What else was I supposed to do? Would he get in trouble? Would he lose the job? He almost didn't care. He didn't want to ever see this place again in his life.

He decided to call his supervisor. The caller was on one of the desks where had set it down when he first heard the commotion. When he came out of the restroom, the office area was eerily quiet. Rather than getting his caller, he slowly crept back over to the door and looked in the window, not sure what he expected to see.

The monkey was on his back, feet and hands up. He didn't appear to be breathing. He looked like he was dead. The animal in the next cage was on the ground, whimpering, trying to reach for his friend.

A tear formed in Rou's eyes. Maybe he didn't save him after all. He thought about going in again and checking on the monkey but thought better of it.

I just want to get out of here.

Rou got his things, walked out the door, locked it from behind, and vowed never to step foot in that place again. He went back to his company office, turned in his ID and credentials and left a note for the supervisor telling him he quit.

He arrived at his girlfriend's apartment a few minutes later, still shaken.

"What's wrong?" Wendy asked.

He decided not to tell her.

"Nothing. I just need to take a shower. Can I crash here tonight?"

"Sure," she said. "I would like that. Tomorrow, can we go to the wet markets?"

"Definitely," he said.

She reached over and gave him a kiss. Abruptly pulling back.

"You do need a shower. You stink," she said, laughing and pushing him toward her bathroom.

As hard as he tried, he couldn't get the stench out of his mind. They made love for the first time. He could hardly enjoy it and barely slept that night.

The monkey's face was still seared into his mind.

31

The next morning, 9:00 a.m.
Anih C, Province

Dr. Woo was almost always the first person in the office each morning. Today was no exception. Today was day five of the experiment with the monkeys. The villagers in the remote region of Ardic D, infected by eating the pigs, began showing symptoms on day five. If the monkeys were going to start showing symptoms, today would be the day.

That's strange.

No noises were coming from the room that housed the monkeys. Usually they made a sound when they heard him open the door. Nothing. He dropped off his briefcase in his office and grabbed his keys to open the door to the room.

He first went to the dressing area and donned his PPG, Personal Protective Gear. From what he learned from the Ardic D village, the virus was highly infectious. If a person came in contact with the virus, he became infected one hundred percent of the time. A third of the time, he showed no symptoms, or they were mild. A third of the time, the virus caused severe respiratory symptoms along with fatigue and fever. Another third of the time, the person died.

Fully protected, he walked over to the door. Looking through the window, he could see that one of the monkeys was dead. Rigor mortis had already set in. The animal's eyes were open, and he had a blank stare on his face.

A wave of panic came over him when he inserted the key in the lock. The door wasn't locked.

* * *

Noon

Still no sign of Mrs. Pinkerton.

When Naomi woke up that morning, Mrs. Pinkerton's bed was untouched. She clearly hadn't slept in it. Naomi went to breakfast, but neither Mrs. Pinkerton nor the two brothers were there. She went to the restaurant bar area where they'd met the two brothers. It was closed.

Her emotions went between concern and anger. She doubted Mrs. Pinkerton was in any real danger. The men didn't seem like serial killers or anything like that, but Mrs. Pinkerton should've shown up by now. She'd heard of people falling off the side of the ship in a drunken stupor, never to be seen or heard from again. Mrs. Pinkerton clearly had too much to drink the night before and wasn't thinking clearly.

To make matters worse, the cruise liner had docked at the Anih C province. Everyone was going to go ashore at 2:00 to visit the wet markets, a major tourist attraction in the area.

Naomi decided to call the ship steward. "I'm concerned about my friend. She didn't come back to the room last night."

"What is your friend's name?"

"Mrs. Pinkerton. Mamie Pinkerton. We're in suite 247."

"When did you last see Mrs. Pinkerton?"

"Last night at the bar. We met a couple of men. I left and went back to our room, but she never showed up."

"A couple of men," he said with a thick accent. "She's probably with one of them." He chuckled. "Maybe both of them. I'm sure she'll show up. People like to have a good time on our cruises. We don't like to bother them."

"Can you give me the men's room number?" Naomi asked, getting annoyed with the steward's lackadaisical attitude.

"I can't give out that information."

"It's two brothers. Clarence and Arthur. I'm sorry. I don't know their last name. Can you at least see if you can find them in your system? Maybe you can call their room. I just want to make sure she's okay. She might have fallen overboard or something."

"That's highly unlikely. I'll check. It'll be awhile though. We are preparing for the passenger's trip to the markets. Call me back later if you don't find your friend. I'm sure she's just having a good time, which is what we want for our customers."

"Thanks for nothing," Naomi said, slamming the caller down.

Now she was mad.

* * *

Just after noon.

Rou woke up to the smell of breakfast cooking. A welcomed scent compared to the smell of the monkey he was still trying to forget.

He looked at his caller, and there were two messages from his supervisor at work. He decided to ignore them. Today was going to be spent with Wendy.

"Hello sleepy head," she said as he walked into the kitchen and sat down at the table. He rubbed his eyes. They still stung from the substance the monkey had sprayed into them the night before.

"I'm sorry," Rou said. "I didn't sleep that good."

"Last night was fun," she said.

He managed a smile. Last night was a night of extremes. The best and worst times of his life, all in one night.

"It was," Rou said. "I'm looking forward to today. Do you still want to go to the wet markets?"

"I do," Wendy said, as she sat a plate of cooked bacon, two fried eggs, and some toast in front of him.

"You can cook too," he said. "Aren't you the perfect girlfriend?"

"Is that what I am? Your girlfriend?" she asked with a wide smile on her face.

He took a huge bite of food. He was starving. The terror of last night suddenly faded into a distant memory.

I hope that lasts.

For the first time in his life, he was actually happy.

* * *

1:35 in the afternoon

"I had so much fun," Mrs. Pinkerton said as she burst into the room, a huge smile on her face, as if nothing at all had happened.

"Where were you?" Naomi asked, while breathing a sigh of relief, which immediately turned to anger.

"What time is it?" Mrs. Pinkerton asked, looking at her wrist. "I don't have my watch. I seemed to have misplaced it."

What could Naomi say? Mrs. Pinkerton was a grown woman. It wasn't like she owed her an explanation. Actually, she did. But Naomi decided not to press the issue. At least she was okay and not floating in the ocean somewhere.

"It's two o'clock," Naomi said, changing the subject. "We have to go. The whole ship is disembarking. We're going to the wet markets today."

Mrs. Pinkerton ran her hand through her hair. Her clothes were disheveled. This was the first time Naomi had seen Mrs. Pinkerton not perfectly kept. Mrs. Pinkerton seemed surprised as well when she stepped in front of a mirror.

"Dear me!" she said. "I look a sight!"

"Hurry up and get a shower and get dressed."

Mrs. Pinkerton had already disappeared into her bedroom. Naomi sat patiently on the living room couch.

When Mrs. Pinkerton emerged from her bedroom forty-five minutes later, she looked like her old self. A patterned dress, extending below her knees. Her hair perfectly formed into a beehive look, like the gray hairs of old used to call it. Naomi grinned and tried to relax a little. The time waiting had helped her to let the anger subside to the point it was nearly gone.

"We're going to have fun today," Naomi said.

"Yes, we are. I called Arthur. He and Clarence are going to meet us at the dock and spend the day with us. You don't mind, do you dear?"

The anger returned with a fury.

* * *

Dr. Woo called the cleaning service again.

"Have you heard from the boy?" he asked the boy's supervisor.

"I haven't. I've left him two messages."

"Call him again. It's very important that I talk to him."

Dr. Woo was concerned that the cleaning boy might've come in contact with the monkey. The door was unlocked overnight. It was unlikely that the kid went into the room, but Dr. Woo wasn't going to take any chances. If the boy somehow entered that room, even if just out of curiosity, he could be infected. If he was carrying the flu-us he could infect others.

Dr. Woo hadn't been concerned until he learned that the boy suddenly quit last night after his shift. Other employees in the office said he seemed upset by something. The boy might've seen the monkey die and tried to help him or opened the door by mistake. The chain was in a strange position when Dr. Woo opened the cage and took the monkey out to examine him.

It could be nothing. However, if that boy somehow took the virus into the community, it could spread into a world-wide pandemic. He would get the blame. No one could ever know about the unlocked door.

I have to talk to that boy.

If nothing else, just to ease his own mind. His imagination was probably getting the best of him. But he was a scientist. Protocols were everything in his lab. He stressed them to his staff almost every day. They had to be followed perfectly. Any breach had to be investigated for any possible contamination.

"Did you send somebody by his house?" he asked the supervisor.

"We did. His mother said he didn't come home last night."

Dr. Woo had a bad feeling about this.

"Is something wrong?" the man asked Dr. Woo. "Did the boy steal something?"

"No. It's nothing like that. I just need to talk to him."

Dr. Woo considered calling the authorities. Having the boy found and questioned and possibly quarantined was the most prudent thing to do. But he didn't want to draw attention to the lab or the virus unnecessarily. No one in the outside world knew about the experiments.

He might be overreacting, but that's what he was paid to do.

If the boy did come in contact with the animal, there was no such thing as an overreaction. It would be a disaster in the making.

32

Five days later

String of Pearls, Province A

Rou and Wendy were having the time of their lives, relishing in their newfound riches. Came upon with a bit of luck, and Rou's pickpocketing skills.

Five days ago, while exploring the wet markets, Wendy had noticed an older woman, a tourist, clearly from the Red Spot region, flashing her jupes around, buying all kinds of expensive things. Each time she'd buy something, she'd pull out her wallet, pay the clerk, and then stick the wallet back in her bag without zipping it shut.

Wendy pointed it out to Rou. Not for any reason other than she thought it was funny how careless the woman was being.

"Someone's going to steal that woman's wallet," Wendy said. "I should tell her."

Rou's response, "Watch this."

Before she could object, he walked right up to the lady, bumped against her, and in one motion reached into her bag, pulled out the wallet, and slipped it in his coat pocket without her having any idea that he'd done so. She stumbled so he grabbed the lady's hand to keep her from falling.

"Sorry," he said.

Before the lady could respond, he grabbed Wendy by the arm and quickly led her away from the area. Almost dragging her along, while she kept looking back at the lady. When they got to a safe place, Rou opened the wallet and started looking through it.

"Give it back," Wendy said.

"I can't. It's too late. I already took it. I'll get arrested if I give it back."

Wendy started to voice another objection but Rou cut her off mid-sentence.

"There's more than three thousand jupes in here," Rou said. "Wow! Look at all the credit cards." He pulled them out and flashed them in the air.

"This is wrong," Wendy said. "We have to return it." She snatched the wallet out of Rou's hand.

"She's a rich woman," he said with a sneer. "She'll never miss it. I don't have a job. I could use the jupe."

"I don't care. It's not your jupes. It's still wrong, even if she is rich. That doesn't make it right." Wendy searched the wallet and found a cruise ID card. Mamie Pinkerton. "I'm giving it back," Wendy said.

Before Rou could voice another objection, Wendy walked back the direction from which they came. Rou ran to catch up with her.

"What are you going to tell her?" Rou said.

"I'll tell her we found it on the ground."

"Good idea. Maybe she'll give us a reward."

They searched everywhere, but the lady was gone.

Rou convinced Wendy that they should keep the jupes but tear up the credit cards and ID and throw away the wallet. They thought about taking it to the cruise ship, but Rou was right. They'd both probably be arrested on the spot. She didn't want a record. Wendy was trying to get into college next fall.

The decision was made, they were now having a fun-filled vacation at Mrs. Pinkerton's expense.

The Pearl Province was just south of the equator. A tropical paradise, it was several hours by airmobile from Anih C. Named the String of Pearls because from the air, the five majestic lakes in the valley looked like a string of pearls. Rather than blue or green, the waters looked creamy—an off-white color like a pearl. An optical illusion. The sandy beaches reflected onto the water, making it look white.

They checked into the fancy hotel under the name of Rou and Wendy Shing-Ming, pretending to be married and on their honeymoon. They spared no expense as they ate at the finest restaurants, shopped in the stores, went hiking, boating, kayaking on Pearl Lake, and got a couple's massage in the hotel spa.

They agreed to use half of the jupes and set aside the rest. The first half would run out tomorrow, and they left enough to get back home. They'd spend tonight enjoying one last night together in the hotel room, dining on a room-service meal complete with beef steak, potatoes, various greens, and a bottle of wine. Dessert was a chocolate mousse souffle.

"I'm stuffed," Wendy said as she lay down in front of the fire, burning in the corner fireplace.

Rou joined her with the last glass of wine from the bottle. "I could get used to this lifestyle," he said. "Thank you, Mrs. Pinkerton." He raised the glass for a toast.

Wendy pushed him in the chest and said, "It was still wrong! Promise me you'll never do that again."

Rou just grinned.

"Promise me," Wendy said in a stronger tone.

"I promise," he said, laughing, setting down the wine on a table, and then pulling her closer to him. They started kissing passionately. "You are so beautiful," Rou said sitting back and looking lovingly into her eyes.

Wendy smiled and stroked his hair as she pulled him back toward her as they laid on the floor increasing the intensity.

Wendy suddenly sat up and pushed him away. She put her hand to her face and coughed into it. "Sorry about that," she said as she let out another slight cough. "I don't know what's wrong with me."

Suddenly. Without warning, the coughing came upon her like a wave. She grasped her throat. Gasping for air, her lungs burned like a searing iron was being branded against her chest.

Rou stood to his feet and backed away. Wendy lay writhing on the floor.

"What's wrong?" Rou said, his voice raised.

Wendy couldn't answer. It took all of her energy to catch her breath. The last thing she heard was Rou shouting, "You sound just like the monkey."

Then everything went dark.

**

Tranquility III
Middle of the ocean

"Bango!" Mrs. Pinkerton shouted for the second time in a row and the third time that night. Several women glared at her as Mrs. Pinkerton filled one row of her Bango card again to the chagrin of the more than thirty patrons sitting in the gaming area of the cruise ship.

"It's just my lucky night," Mrs. Pinkerton said aloud.

Naomi was glad to see her in better spirits. Mrs. Pinkerton had been depressed for the last five days. Since they left Anih C province. Clarence had a personal emergency back home, so Arthur and Clarence caught the next flight out of the province and had to leave the cruise. Naomi was glad to see them go.

To top it off, Mrs. Pinkerton lost her wallet with all her jupes in it. Wiring jupes to her would be easy enough on the ship, but she would have to call each credit card company and get new cards issued. To make matters worse, the cruise ship attendant gave her a hard time when she tried to reboard the ship without her cruise ID.

They were tired and hot from the long day and had several heavy bags to carry from the shopping. The situation was escalating as Mrs. Pinkerton was losing patience. "Here's my room key, you imbecile," she had said to the gating clerk, waving the key in her face.

"Calling her names is not going to help," Naomi whispered. "Try being nice to her."

"She's a moron," Mrs. Pinkerton said loud enough for the girl to hear.

Naomi felt sorry for the young kid. She was only doing her job. Barely out of high school, this was probably a summer job for her. At the same time, Mrs. Pinkerton did have a point. How did she have a room key?

"I can vouch for her," Naomi said. "We're sharing a room."

"I'm sorry, Ma'am. I'm not supposed to let anyone on without their ID. Only the supervisor can do that."

"Well go get your supervisor."

"I can't leave my post. He'll be back in a few minutes. Please step aside. There are other people in line who need to get on."

That really set Mrs. Pinkerton off, and she began yelling at the girl, letting a few too many expletives fly in the process. Enough so that security was alerted and came over to calm the situation, threatening to arrest Mrs. Pinkerton if she didn't calm down. The thought of incarceration was enough to get her to shut up, but not before she made things much worse.

Naomi was hot and tired as well. The only consolation to the day's events was that Clarence and Arthur were gone out of her life for good. Clarence had flirted with her incessantly. Arthur doted on Mrs. Pinkerton like a silly schoolboy in love for the first time. What was cute at first was becoming sickening.

Naomi didn't enjoy the hot and sticky markets at all. They were called 'wet markets" because the floors were continually wet from the melting ice used to keep the seafood fresh. Naomi was throwing away her shoes as soon as they got back to the room. No telling what was on the bottom of them.

The sights in the market were appalling. Dead animals were strung up at booths. The markets sold marmots, snakes, chickens, goats, monkeys, and even dogs and cats. Naomi wasn't a vegetarian, but the sight of the animals in such deplorable conditions, broke her heart.

Even live animals were sold. Some killed and butchered on the spot. She had to turn her head away several times as a store clerk took an animal and slaughtered it in plain sight.

"The fresher the better," some of the locals insisted.

The dry area, which consisted of fresh fruits and vegetables was the only tolerable section as far as Naomi was concerned. And the shopping. The markets did have great prices on quality clothing and accessories. But Naomi couldn't help but think those items were made in some sweat shop by slave labor, kids even, forced to work under horrendous conditions for barely a living wage. Just so rich people like them who could afford to pay whatever it cost and could have the pleasure of buying something they didn't need for a bargain-basement price.

The whole experience disgusted her. Naomi wasn't enjoying the Bango games much either. She hadn't won anything. At least it was air conditioned in the gaming room. Truthfully, she just wanted to get home. The cruise would've been so much better if she'd been with Carl.

The thought brought a tear to her eye.

Naomi was surprised when Mrs. Pinkerton suddenly said she wanted to go back to the room.

"I don't feel well," she said.

When they got back to the room, Mrs. Pinkerton went straight to the couch and lay down.

"Why am I so tired?" she said.

"It's been a long week. You're probably as ready to get home as I am."

"Can you open the sliding door? It's so hot in here."

The air conditioning was actually blaring. Naomi was cold, but she walked over and opened the sliding door anyway.

"Are you sick?" Naomi asked. When Mrs. Pinkerton didn't respond, Naomi walked over to her and put her hand on her forehead.

"You're burning up," Naomi said. She went into the bathroom and got a wet towel.

When she came back into the room, Mrs. Pinkerton started coughing.

33

GLOVID Lab, Anih C Province
Six days after the monkey died of the fluus.

"Why did one monkey die and the other showed no symptoms at all?" Dr. Yuan Woo asked himself aloud.

The Assistant Director of the GLOVID Lab had struggled with that question for six days, ever since the monkey died. Also where was the cleaning boy? Another question he couldn't get out of his mind after the boy left the lab the night the monkey died, quit his job, and then disappeared off the face of Jupiter, having not been heard from since.

The two monkeys were given every test possible, and the results were inconclusive. The monkey who died had lung damage, the extent to which Dr. Woo had never seen before. In one night, the flu-us ravaged the monkey's lungs and ate away at the lining until every tissue was black and scarred.

The monkey literally drowned to death. His immune system became so active trying to kill the virus that it flooded the lungs with fluid, filling the air sacs and closing them off to much needed oxygen. A ventilator might've saved the monkey, had it happened during the day when Dr. Woo was nearby, but even that was questionable.

The other monkey was perfectly healthy. She tested positive for the flu-us but showed no symptoms. There was no logical explanation. The only difference between the monkeys was their sex. The dead monkey was male. But in the village, more women died than men, so the evidence was contradictory.

Dr. Woo was so relieved that the virus hadn't escaped the lab. It had been six days, and he hadn't gotten the call he dreaded most.

A local hospital or doctor reporting a patient with strange symptoms and lab results was his worst fear.

Dr. Woo went back to his notes. He would be meeting with the Director of the lab, Dr. Gao, later that day and would report his findings on the experiment. They had already discussed it. He told the director that he didn't think the flu-us could be spread by human transmission. It was a deadly virus, but an outbreak like what happened in the peasant village with the infected pigs was unlikely to happen again.

No mention was made of the unlocked door or the possible breach in protocol. Unnecessary, since the cleaning boy had obviously not been exposed to the flu-us. The kid was probably off somewhere with a girl, having a good time. He took all his notes about Rou Shing-Ming, the cleaning boy, out of the file and shredded them, just to cover his bases.

"You have a call on line one," his assistant said, interrupting his work.

"Who is it?"

"Dr. MacKenzie."

"Okay. Put him through."

Dr. MacKenzie was the Chief Physician at String of Pearls Regional Hospital. A wave of panic briefly pulsed through his veins. He quickly tamped it down. The hospital was six-thousand miles away. No chance of his virus getting that far that fast. He was just being paranoid.

"Hello Mac," Dr. Woo said. "Are you finally calling to pay me that jupes you owe me?" The two went to college together, lived in the same dorm, and traveled to continuing-education conventions together. Dr. Woo had won ten jupes in a bet, although neither could remember the nature of the wager.

"If I remember right, Woo, I won that bet," Dr. Mackenzie retorted.

"You always say that," Dr. Woo responded with a friendly laugh. "How's your wife and family?"

"Everybody's good," he said as his tone turned more serious. He clearly didn't call to chit chat. "I've got a patient here who has shown symptoms, honestly, I've never seen before."

Dr. Woo's heart did several somersaults.

"Tell me about the patient and the symptoms," Woo said, trying to keep his voice from cracking. His hand was shaking as he gripped the caller. He took the call off speaker so no one else could hear the conversation.

Was his worst nightmare about to come to pass? Surely not. The flu-us couldn't have gotten that far around the world that fast. Of course, it could. The Pearl Province was only a ten-hour airmobile ride. In this global society, a pandemic could spread through the whole planet in just days.

Don't overreact.

He took a deep breath to calm himself as he waited for the answer to his question.

"Nineteen-year-old girl. Perfectly healthy. Came to our Emergency Room with respiratory symptoms. Difficulty breathing. High fever."

That could be caused by a normal virus or flu.

"She's from your area," Dr. Mackenzie added.

Dr. Woo's heart sank.

"She came here with her boyfriend from Anih C Province."

The cleaning boy.

Surely not. That would be too big a coincidence.

"Do you know the boy's name?" Dr. Woo asked nervously.

He heard papers rustling in the background.

"The boy who admitted her to the hospital... his name is Rou Shing-Wing."

No!

Dr. Woo wanted to throw the caller across the room. He tried to stay calm.

"Did you do blood work?" Dr. Woo asked.

"Of course."

"What did it show?"

"A new strain of virus. One I've never seen before."

Don't panic. Stay calm.

"Can you send the results of the blood work to my email? Also, the genetic code of the virus?"

"I'm sending it right now."

"How's the girl?" Dr. Woo asked.

"She died a few minutes ago."

* * *

Dr. Woo sat the caller down in the cradle, slowly, his body suddenly numb. His mind was unable to process what was happening other than the words, *she died a few minutes ago* which kept playing over and over again in his head. The girl was the cleaning boy's girlfriend. She got it from him.

I don't know that.

What if it wasn't the same Rou Shing-Wing? Why would a poor cleaning boy be in the Pearl Province? On vacation. That's where rich people went. But what were the chances it wasn't him. Slim to none. It was too big a coincidence.

He wouldn't take the final leap until he saw the blood work and the genetic code of the virus that killed the girl. If it was the flu-us, he had bigger problems on his hands. The boy had been exposed, gave it to his girlfriend, and they went on an airmobile, potentially exposing hundreds to the virus. The flu-us circulates through the filtration system. Thousands could be infected just from contact with someone exposed. Flu-us can live on surfaces.

Multiplication.

One infects five; five infect twenty-five; twenty-five infect scores of others. In no time, millions are infected. In the village, a third of the people died. In his lab, fifty percent of the monkeys died. A smaller sample size, but the point was that the death rate was unknown. Somewhere between a third and fifty percent. An unscientific conclusion but also confirmed by the fact that Dr. MacKenzie didn't mention anything about the boy showing symptoms.

How could the boy get it, give it to his girlfriend, but not get it himself? Why would she die, but he was fine? Dr. Woo didn't even know how the boy was exposed. Did he open the door to the room? That wouldn't be enough. He had to come into contact with the monkey's bodily fluids somehow. How did that happen? There were too many unanswered questions.

His computer dinged, signifying an email.

Dr. Woo glanced at the bloodwork in the attachment of the email. It didn't tell him what he wanted to know. He scrolled down to the genetic sequence. Every virus has a code. He was dying to know this one's code.

A single, positive-stranded RNA.

29,811 nucleotides long.

Same as flu-us. The virus in the monkey.

Broken down as follows: (32.82%) adenosines, (17.65%) cystosines, (43.77%) guanines.

Strange. Only (5.76%) thymines.

The virus mutated.

So, a human could become a host.

So, it could kill a human.

Not technically. A virus doesn't want to kill its host. Otherwise, it dies as well. It just wants a place to live. It mutates to adapt to its environment. To give itself the best possible chance to survive. Unfortunately, it's not smart enough to know it can kill its host.

The numbers weren't the exact same as the monkey virus, but it didn't matter. This was his flu-us. The one he created in the lab so it could be injected into the monkey. He didn't even have to look at his notes. The numbers were etched in his memory.

His handiwork. A lethal weapon was unknowingly created in his lab. That's not true. Dr. Woo knew the virus was lethal. A young girl was dead because of him. Now billions could be.

From a scientific standpoint, the numbers were fascinating. The original virus in the village had a higher level of thymines, which could only be transmitted to humans by ingesting it in foods. Once in a human, it could be transmitted by air particles from bodily fluids. In early experiments Dr. Woo could not duplicate the same result. So, he mutated the virus. Lowered the thymines. That allowed it to be injected into the monkey and transmitted to others by airborne particles.

A huge mistake. But how could he know it would escape his lab?

The flu-us mutated one more time once the air particles entered the cleaning boy. So, it became more contagious. This virus had mutated into a deadly form. One that could kill a human within one day of showing symptoms.

He called his assistant into the room. "Get Dr. Mackenzie back on the caller."

Less than a minute later, she had him on the line.

"Mac, how many people were exposed to that girl?"

"Several. Her boyfriend, of course. Three or four nurses. A couple of doctors. The lab technician who took the X rays. And the admitting nurse. Why?"

"I think you should quarantine all of them."

"You're making me nervous."

"It's just a precaution. Like you said, I've never seen anything like this before." Not exactly true, but Dr. Woo certainly wasn't going to discuss the details with a practicing physician. No one could ever know what happened in the lab. He wondered if the cleaning boy would keep quiet.

"I'm on it," Dr. Mackenzie said.

"Let's keep it quiet for now. I don't want to alarm anyone. Let me know if you get any more cases like this."

"I will. Did you look at the X-rays on the email?" Dr. Mackenzie asked.

"I did."

"That poor girl. That virus or whatever it was, ravaged her lungs. It must've been really painful for her.

As if Dr. Woo didn't feel bad enough already.

34

10:02 a.m.
Global Office
Red Spot

Dr. Hunter Mertz, the head of Health Services for the Wolf administration, requested a meeting with the Prescom.

"Is it important?" Wade Wilson, the Prescom's Staff Chief had asked.

"Extremely," Dr. Mertz responded. "The sooner the better."

Wilson reluctantly agreed to give him ten minutes, at ten o'clock sharp. Dr. Mertz knew Wilson ran a tight ship and wouldn't want the meeting to go one minute over. Once Wolf knew the topic, though, Mertz would have as much time as he wanted.

The Prescom was two minutes late. Dr. Mertz knew the exact time because he kept looking at his watch every ten to twenty seconds. Not that he was nervous about meeting the Prescom. He'd been in the Global Office more times than he could remember. Three Prescoms had appointed him to the position. It was his for as long as he wanted.

The urgent cable he received earlier that morning was the reason for his angst. The Prescom made his entrance at exactly four minutes after the top of the hour, Wilson right behind him.

"What can I do for you, Hunter?" the Prescom asked, apparently wanting to get right to the point.

That was fine with him. "I'm sorry to bother you," Hunter said. "It may be nothing or may be something."

"Well... That's clear as mud," Wolf joked.

"I'm sorry, sir," Hunter said. No matter how many times he was in the Global Office, he was the consummate professional and always treated the Prescom with the dignity the office warranted, even if the Prescom was setting a tone of informality. Hunter hesitated, trying to formulate his words.

"What is it, Hunter?" the Prescom asked.

"There's a cruise ship just outside of the Red Spot port that is reporting four deaths."

Prescom Wolf raised his eyebrow.

"Do they know what caused the deaths?"

"No. The patients died of respiratory failure. From some sort of virus, probably. But the doctor on board isn't equipped to do extensive testing to find the source of the virus. At least enough to find the exact cause."

"What do you want me to do?"

"The cruise ship wants to dock and let all the passengers off."

"Sounds like a good idea to me. If there are dead people on the ship, we need to get everyone off, including the crew. We need to autopsy those bodies."

"I suggest we quarantine the passengers until we know the source of the virus."

"That's a pretty drastic measure," Wolf said as he stood from his chair and walked behind his desk. Rather than sit down, he remained standing and fiddled with some papers. Wolf often said he thought better when he was moving around.

"There are four dead people, sir."

Prescom Wolf waved his hand dismissively. "They probably caught something at one of the ports."

"This cruise went to the Anih C Province. They spent the day at the wet markets." Everyone, including the Prescom knew the markets were breeding ground for pathogens. Every deadly pandemic had originated in the Anih C Province.

"Any other passengers showing symptoms?"

"Not that we know of, sir."

"Good. That means it's not contagious. Or everyone would have it."

"Sometimes these viruses take several days before people show symptoms. It's also possible that some people are asymptomatic but are carriers. They may be infected and not know it. They could spread it to others."

Wade Wilson, the Prescom's Staff Chief, had been surprisingly quiet.

"This isn't the first time someone died on a cruise, and it won't be the last," the Prescom said callously.

Dr. Mertz didn't not usually get this much pushback. For the most part, Prescoms have followed his instincts. There must be more to it. Wolf must have another reason for not wanting to quarantine the ship.

"I'm just being cautious, sir. That's what you pay me to do. My professional opinion is that we should quarantine the passengers and autopsy the bodies, like you suggested. Let's find out what's going on before we release four thousand people back in their communities to possibly infect others."

"If we close it down and quarantine the passengers, we'll set off a panic," Wade Wilson said, finally interjecting himself into the conversation. "The news media will run with it. That will hurt the cruise line business."

"We shouldn't put economics over people's lives," Dr. Mertz said.

"Wade's right. The cruise business lost a lot of jupes on the days after D-Day. They lost a third of their customers. They're just now rebounding from it. I own stock in most of them. I bought low, after the big sell off," he said smugly.

Dr. Mertz now knew the real reason for the pushback. "We don't have to let the media know," Dr. Mertz retorted. "I instructed that all communications from the ship be halted. No one can call in or out. The internet was shut down. I didn't want anyone panicking their friends and family members unnecessarily."

"That was good thinking," Wolf affirmed.

"Just keep the ship out of port," Dr. Mertz continued. "I'll fly out there on a helicopter and do some tests. It'll only take a day or two, tops... sir."

"Have you talked to Dr. Woo?"

"No, sir. But I talked to his boss, Dr. Gao."

"He's worthless. Dr. Woo is the real expert."

Gao wasn't worthless, but Woo was the real expert, Mertz agreed. A classic case of the student surpassing the teacher, even though the teacher still had the title and superior position.

"I don't disagree. But he wasn't available. Dr. Gao said there haven't been any reports of anything unusual."

"No outbreaks, anywhere?" the Prescom asked.

"No sir. Not since the village with the pigs."

"That was several months ago. And that is contained as far as I understand."

"I think we should let the ship dock," Wilson said.

"With all due respect, I disagree," Dr. Mertz retorted. "I've lived through a major pandemic, and I don't want another."

"Whoa! Who's talking about a pandemic?" Wilson said, raising his voice. "There are only four people dead. There are probably four deaths a day on cruise lines from any number of causes."

Actually, 1.4 deaths per thousand. Mostly heart attacks, natural causes, etc. The people were already sick when they boarded. Dr. Mertz knew his statistics but didn't want to correct the Staff Chief in front of the Prescom.

Before he could give any response to Wilson's outburst, the Prescom said, "Let the ship dock and let the passengers off. If there's an infection on board, the longer they're on the ship, the more risk they're in to get infected. Examine the dead bodies, see what you find, and get back to me."

Dr. Mertz knew the conversation was over. When Prescom Wolf made a decision, no one could talk him out of it. A good quality to have when he was right; dangerous when he was wrong. From Dr. Mertzs' experience, the Prescom was right more often than he was wrong. Either way, he was the Prescom, and Mertz had his orders.

"Thank you for your time, Mr. Prescom."

Wolf was already sitting at his desk, caller in hand as Dr. Mertz stood and exited the room.

I hope this is one time when the Prescom gets it right.

* * *

Dr. Mertz still had an uneasy feeling as he left the Prescom's office, got in his mobile, and drove to his office. When he arrived, he took out his caller and called Dr. Woo. It went to voicemail.

"Dr. Woo, this is Dr. Mertz, hope all is well. Give me a call if you get this message in the next few minutes. I have a situation I want to discuss with you."

He waited an hour. With no return call, Dr. Mertz notified the cruise ship that it could dock and unload the passengers. He instructed that the four dead bodies be brought to his laboratory. The final call was to the coroner to let him know his office wasn't trying to circumvent his authority. The bodies were being brought to his office first, then they would be released to him after testing.

With still no returned call from Dr. Woo, he left the office and turned off his caller for the night.

* * *

GLOVID Lab
Anih C Province
The next morning.

Dr. Woo listened to the message from Dr. Mertz for the fourth time. What was the situation he wanted to talk to him about?

Could word of the girl's death have traveled to him so fast? Not likely. It could be anything. He had to wait to call because Anih C Province was four hours ahead of the Red Spot time zone. Dr. Mertz was an early riser but not that early. Dr. Woo had only slept a couple of hours on his couch in his office. He hadn't even gone home that night.

He'd poured over the dead girl's blood work and genetic coding of the virus, searching for anything that might help him understand the virus better. His eyes hurt from staring at the computer, and his body ached from sleeping on the uncomfortable couch. Whatever pain he was going through was far less than the pain he'd subjected the girl to.

A debate raged in his mind all night long. Was it really his fault? It was an accident, he concluded. It could've happened to anyone. The kid should've never opened the door and then none of this would've happened. Of course, if the door was locked, it never would've happened. He finally called a truce to the blame game. That wasn't going to help the situation.

He needed to focus on solving the problem. He'd even started thinking about a potential vaccine.

That would take twelve to eighteen months. Every day mattered, he concluded. When he was satisfied that Dr. Mertz would be in his office, he picked up the caller and dialed the number. As tired as he was, the anxiety level still elevated to an almost intolerable level. It was likely this call had nothing to do with the girl. Probably something totally unrelated to the flu-us.

He'd feel better once he knew.

"This is Dr. Mertz," the man answered in his familiar deep voice.

"Dr. Mertz, this is Dr. Woo. I got your message."

"Thanks for calling back. Although the situation is handled, I think."

A wave of relief came over Dr. Woo. He felt his heartbeat slow and tension leave his body.

"What was the situation out of curiosity?" he asked.

"We had four deaths on a cruise ship."

The anxiety returned with a fury. Dr. Woo's heart started racing again.

"What was the cause of death?" He was afraid to ask but had to.

"Respiratory failure. The symptoms came on the patients suddenly."

Dr. Woo began to shake. Fear was rising inside of him.

Pull yourself together. You're a doctor. You need a clear head. Let's work on the problem. We have to mitigate this situation.

"Did the cruise ship come to this region?" Woo asked.

"Yes. The wet markets were part of their itinerary."

The fear went up another notch.

"You need to quarantine that ship at once," Dr. Woo said, his voice cracking.

"That's what I was inclined to do, but the Prescom overruled me and said to instruct the ship to let the passengers off. I'm having the deceased brought to my lab."

"Do not let the passengers off that ship for any reason!" Dr. Woo said with urgency.

"Why? What's wrong?"

"I got word yesterday of a young girl in the Pearl Province who died from an unknown virus. I've just started investigating it. She also died of respiratory failure."

"It could just be a bad case of the flu."

"I don't think so. Trust me on this. I think this is a super flu-us. We can't take any chances."

"Hold on," Dr. Mertz said. There was silence on the line for a good minute.

"I can see the cruise ship from my office," Dr. Mertz said when he came back on the line.

Dr. Woo remembered that office. He'd been there twice. It was on the seventeenth floor of a high rise overlooking the ocean.

"We're too late," Dr. Mertz said. "Everyone is already off the ship. I can see the last passengers gathering their bags and going to their mobiles."

Dr. Woo buried his head in his hands.

35

Danni and Liz left the Pinkerton Estate early to pick up Naomi and Mrs. Pinkerton from their three-week cruise.

They stood on the dock awaiting the ship's arrival along with hundreds of other friends and family members who'd come to greet their loved ones. A cheer went up when the massive ship came into view. At first just a small dot on the horizon, now the Tranquility III, in all its magnificent splendor, was close enough to see the passengers. At least those who were standing at the railings on the deck, yelling and waving to the throng of people who were matching their cheers.

"There's Mrs. Pinkerton," Liz said, pointing.

Danni's eyes followed the direction of Liz's hand. Mrs. Pinkerton was standing on a third-floor balcony, leaning over the rail, waving a streamer back and forth, looking their way. She had seen them before they saw her.

"Where's Naomi?" Danni wondered out loud.

"I don't know. She's probably still in the room. Packing maybe," Liz responded.

The intensity of the crowd increased as the ship drew closer to the port. Most people's attention was on the front deck where the majority of the passengers were congregated. Mrs. Pinkerton was still on the balcony. Still no sign of Naomi.

"I'm going over there so I can see better," Liz said as she walked away.

"I'll wait here." Danni noted where Liz went. It would be easy to get lost in the crowd.

Mrs. Pinkerton was waving wildly at Danni, obviously trying to get her attention, close now but not close enough for Danni to hear her over the other cheers. Danni gave her a friendly wave and a smile.

Suddenly, the cruise ship lurched. Slightly. Barely noticeable to the people on the front deck. But Mrs. Pinkerton was leaning over the railings of the balcony at just the moment the ship took the awkward wobble. Danni watched in horror as Mrs. Pinkerton lost her balance. She tried to regain it, but it was too late.

The ship threw Mrs. Pinkerton violently over the side.

Danni let out a scream as Mrs. Pinkerton fell feet first, three stories into the water. Amazingly, no one else seemed to notice.

Danni pushed herself through the crowd to get a closer view. Mrs. Pinkerton was in the water, her arms flailing as she was struggling to tread water. The look on her face was one of utter disbelief as she was clearly stunned from the fall and the icy cold water. The cruise ship slowly pulled away from her as the current was taking her out away from the shore.

Danni tried to get someone's attention. Anyone who could help her. "There's a lady in the water," she shouted at the top of her lungs. No one responded. Everyone's attention was on the front deck as the crowd was pressing in closer.

Danni frantically searched for any authorities. They were all up on the dock, preparing for the ship's arrival. She tried to run that way, but the crowd was too thick to get through.

Her shouts were falling on deaf ears. "Mrs. Pinkerton is not on the ship," she kept repeating, but no one was listening.

Mrs. Pinkerton was drifting further and further away. Danni could hear her yelling, "Help me." Finally, she was out of sight altogether. Whether she went under or just drifted away, Danni wasn't sure.

"Why isn't anyone doing something?" Danni yelled. But no one could hear her. The whole world seemed oblivious to her cries.

Danni grabbed the arm of a man and turned him toward her. "Mrs. Pinkerton is not on the ship!" Danni shouted to the man. He just stood there, staring. No response. No emotion. As if he couldn't hear her.

Then Danni woke up.

She rubbed her eyes. The clock said 3:00. Why did God always speak to her at 3:00 a.m.? The Bible called it the fourth watch. It's when Jesus came to the disciples on the lake in the middle of the storm. Jesus was in anguish in the garden during the fourth watch. God often spoke to people in the Bible at that time. It's just that most people weren't awake then to hear from God.

Calmly, emotionless, Danni got out of bed and walked over to the desk and flicked on the light. Her Dream Journal lay in the center of the desk along with a pen.

Danni opened it to a blank page. She recorded the date and wrote something down.

Mrs. Pinkerton is not on the ship.

Then she went back to bed.

* * *

Three hours later Danni woke up again. The sunlight crept through the blinds casting eerie shadows on the wall. Almost like images of fairies dancing. This time she wasn't calm. A wave of anxiety had come upon her.

The journal caught her eye, sitting on the desk. *Did I imagine it?*

She bolted out of bed and flipped open the journal to the last page that had writing on it.

Mrs. Pinkerton is not on the ship.

She remembered. *I wrote that.*

The dream was real.

But what did it mean?

* * *

"You're being awfully quiet this morning," Liz said to Danni.

They were sitting on the back deck drinking a cup of coffee. Something Danni and Mrs. Pinkerton did on most mornings.

Danni was deep in thought. Her dreams were like prophecies. They almost always came true. Why wouldn't Mrs. Pinkerton be on the ship?

"Don't you think it's strange that we haven't heard from Naomi or Mrs. Pinkerton?" Danni said soberly as she took a big sip.

Liz shrugged. "They're probably having so much fun they didn't have the time."

"When they first left, we heard from them every day," Danni said. "Now nothing. I haven't heard anything for three days."

"Maybe they're in a place where there's no caller service."

"I guess."

They both sat silent for several minutes.

"I think something's wrong." Danni said and then told Liz about her dream. Every vivid detail.

"What do you think the dream means?" Liz asked.

"I think it means Mrs. Pinkerton is not on the ship."

* * *

Neither girl said much on the ride over to the cruise port. Danni had begun to second-guess herself.

The visions were a gift and a curse, but why was it always something bad?

When Naomi got off the ship and Mrs. Pinkerton wasn't with her, Danni burst into tears. So did Naomi as soon as she saw them.

"She's gone," Naomi said between sobs, clutching Danni's neck. "Mrs. Pinkerton is dead."

Liz put her arm on her shoulder.

"I know," Danni said, holding Naomi even tighter.

* * *

They collected the bags and loaded them into the mobile. Mrs. Pinkerton's favorite vehicle. It was to be a surprise. Naomi felt weird loading Mrs. Pinkerton's things in the trunk without her being there.

"What happened?" Liz asked Naomi after they were settled in. The two were sitting in the back seat. Danni was driving.

"We were in the room, and Mrs. Pinkerton started coughing," Naomi began to tell the story mournfully. "A horrible sound. I'll never forget it. She was burning up with a fever. I called the front desk, and they sent someone right away. I was so scared for her."

"I can imagine," Liz said.

From Naomi's vantage point she could see Danni's hands were gripping the wheel so hard her knuckles were white. She hadn't said anything for several minutes. As if she was numb.

"A few hours later, she was gone," Naomi said. "Just like that. One minute we were laughing and having fun, playing Bango. Mamie won three times," Naomi felt warm inside as she remembered the good times on the trip. Thoughts of Arthur, Clarence, and the wet markets—the bad times on the trip—were a distant memory. None of that mattered now.

"Mamie?" Danni asked.

"Mrs. Pinkerton. Mamie was her first name," Naomi said.

Danni laughed. "I didn't even know her first name. I don't remember ever asking."

"I think she liked Mrs. Pinkerton better," Liz said.

Naomi touched Danni's shoulder. "There was a rumor that several people on the ship died. Not just Mrs. Pinkerton."

Liz's mouth flew open, "The plague. You were right, Danni," she said excitedly. There is a plague coming. Maybe this is it. I can't believe Mrs. Pinkerton might've died from it."

Danni only nodded.

"Were you with her when she died?" Danni asked.

"Yes. They let me back to see her."

"Did she say anything? I mean... What did she say before she died?"

"She couldn't say a lot because she was attached to a ventilator. Breathing on her own wasn't possible. And she was in and out of consciousness. Sometimes she was coherent, and I could tell she knew what I was saying and other times... I don't know."

Danni brushed back tears off her face as Naomi did the same.

"She told me to tell you she loves you," Naomi said sorrowfully. "You too, Liz. Right at the end..."

Naomi couldn't continue as she was overwhelmed with grief. Liz handed her a tissue. She tried to compose herself. This very conversation had played in her head many times over the last few days of the cruise. Telling the girls would be hard. She had no idea it would be this hard.

"Right at the end," Naomi continued, "I got this overwhelming urge to ask Mrs. Pinkerton about her salvation. I think it was the Holy Spirit. I don't know. I'm new to these things."

"What did you say?" Danni asked with urgency in her tone while glancing in the mirror to the back seat, then back to the road. Back and forth, trying to keep her eyes on the road but also trying to see Naomi when she was speaking.

"I leaned in real close to her. My mouth was by her ear. 'Mrs. Pinkerton' I said. 'Can you hear me?' She nodded yes."

The girls were captivated by every word. Liz clutched Naomi's hand. Naomi cleared her throat. A frog had settled in and made it difficult to get the words out without completely falling apart.

"'Mrs. Pinkerton,' I said, 'the doctor told me you are dying. Do you know for certain that you're going to be with Jesus?'"

Danni pulled off to the side of the road, put the vehicle in park, and turned and faced Naomi.

"What did she say?" Danni asked.

"It was weird. Suddenly, she was very awake. I wondered if she wasn't going to die after all. Like maybe she was healed or something." Naomi paused, trying to process her thoughts.

"Go on," Danni said.

"She said, 'I'm good. I was baptized as a little girl. I've been saved all my life.'"

Silence again as they were all processing what Mrs. Pinkerton had said and what it meant.

"Is that all?" Danni asked.

"That's it. Those were her last words. Mrs. Pinkerton closed her eyes and then she died."

* * *

The rest of the trip home Naomi told them about the fun things they did. The better memories. The three took turns telling funny stories about old Lady Pinkerton as Danni had called her before she really got to know her.

Naomi left out the part about Arthur and Clarence. *What happens on a cruise ship stays on a cruise ship*, Naomi remembered Clarence saying. That seemed reasonable at that moment. No reason to besmirch Mrs. Pinkerton's reputation with the two girls.

They pulled into the gate and down the long driveway to Mrs. Pinkerton's house. Dr. Tom's mobile was in the driveway.

"Oh yeah. There was something I've been meaning to tell you," Liz whispered to Naomi with a sly grin.

"What?"

"You'll see," Liz said secretively.

Danni pulled in next to Tom's mobile. Tom came out of the house to greet them. Danni flew out of the mobile, ran the short distance to him, and threw her arms around Tom's neck. He kissed her on the forehead, affectionately, almost romantically.

Naomi didn't know her mouth was wide open until she touched her face to close it.

She looked at Liz. Liz looked back at her with a wide grin.

"Yep. Dr. Tom and Danni are a couple. They're in love," Liz said, drawing out the "o's" for effect.

"When did that happen?"

"While you were gone. I think they're going to get married."

"No!"

"I wouldn't be surprised," Liz said.

Tom and Danni walked toward the mobile, arm in arm.

"I'm shocked," Naomi said as she got out and walked toward them.

36

The Red Spot Christian Church was filled to capacity and overflowing as hundreds came out to pay their last respects to Mrs. Pinkerton. Dr. Tom officiated the service, and Danni and Naomi gave eulogies. Danni looked out over the sea of people when Ruth Williams, Naomi's daughter-in-law, sang a beautiful rendition of the hymn, *Sweet Grace*, a song Danni remembered Mrs. Pinkerton saying was her favorite. There probably wasn't a dry eye in the house, Danni surmised, including her own.

After the service, an older man, dressed in a black suit and red tie, came up to Danni and introduced himself as Mrs. Pinkerton's attorney and financial advisor. "Dave Adcock is my name. It was a wonderful service," he said. "I think Mrs. Pinkerton would have been very pleased."

"Thank you," Danni responded. Mrs. Pinkerton often spoke of her "jupes man," but Danni never knew who it was until now.

"She thought a lot of you," Mr. Adcock said. "I can see why."

"Have you known Mrs. Pinkerton for very long?"

"Goodness!" he said with a chuckle. "I've been her attorney for close to thirty years. So, I would say so, yes. I'm also the executor of her estate. Can you come to my office tomorrow morning?"

"I'm sure I can. What for?"

"For the reading of Mrs. Pinkerton's will. I think you will want to be there."

"Of course," Danni said.

The man handed her a card.

"My office address is on the card," he said. "I hope you don't mind, but I'm not going to the graveside service."

"That's okay," Danni said. "It's going to be a small gathering. Of course, you're welcome to come, but I understand if you don't."

"Have a good service. It was a pleasure to meet you. I'll see you in the morning. Nine o'clock, if that works for you," he said, and then walked away.

* * *

Mrs. Pinkerton wanted to be buried on her property. A spot on the top of the hill had already been picked out. Danni didn't know that Naomi and Mrs. Pinkerton had talked at length about each other's funerals. Danni was glad because she didn't have to do hardly anything. All the arrangements had already been made and paid for and taken care of by the funeral home and by Naomi, who knew all the details.

Mrs. Pinkerton only wanted a few people to attend the graveside service. Naomi even had a list written out in Mrs. Pinkerton's handwriting. Those invited were the elders of the church, Liz, and the pallbearers who consisted of church members who were special to her. She wanted Tom and Danni to say a few words. Other than that, "Keep it short and sweet," she'd instructed.

The casket was already in the ground and covered with dirt and flowers per Mrs. Pinkerton's instructions. Danni stepped to the front, faced the group, and spoke first.

"If you had told me a year and half ago that Mrs. Pinkerton and I would be such close friends, I would've said you were crazy."

A laugh trickled through the group.

"But I can say that I grew to love Mrs. Pinkerton over the last year. God sent her to me as a lifeline when my parents were taken in the Seizure."

Danni dabbed at her eyes.

"I didn't know what I was going to do. And there she was. She knocked on my door, and the most unlikely friendship blossomed. I think I would've died if she hadn't come along. Mrs. Pinkerton was like a mother to me. She took me in and let me live here in her house. Drive her mobiles. Eat her food. I'm so very thankful to her for her kindness and generosity. Even though, sometimes she was infuriating. And I could never beat her at any of the games we played."

Everyone laughed.

Danni started to continue but paused as she choked back the tears.

"Yeah. Sometimes she made me mad. I'm sure I made her mad too. But most of the time, we laughed and had fun. I'll always remember her laugh."

Tom gave Danni a reassuring smile.

She'd thought about her last words. How would she phrase them? She wasn't sure until that moment.

"I'll miss her," Danni said. "I really hope she's with Jesus right now."

Tom came and stood next to Danni and took her hand. Then he said, "We commit Mrs. Pinkerton's spirit to eternal rest and into God's hands."

He reached down and grabbed a handful of dirt. "The Bible says that God formed us from the dust of the earth, and to dust all of us will return." He slowly dropped the dirt on the grave. Each person was then invited to do the same thing.

As they were doing so, Danni saw out of the corner of her eye an older, beat-up looking mobile come up the driveway to the house. A woman got out and walked toward them.

Tom asked everyone to bow their heads in prayer. Danni closed one eye but kept the other on the woman.

When Tom finished, the woman was halfway to the gravesite. Danni released Tom's hand and walked over to her.

"Can I help you?" Danni asked.

"I'm looking for Danni Howell." The gum in her mouth smacked seemingly in sync with her words. Her accent was a heavy eastern brogue which could only be described as whiny.

"That's me."

The woman was slightly overweight but wearing extremely tight clothes. Early fifties, although trying to dress like a twenty-year old. Her bulging breasts were almost coming out of the low-cut blouse. It looked like she had put make-up on three times. Like a cake with too much icing.

"What can I help you with?" Danni asked.

"My name is Priscilla. Most people call me Prissy. I'm Mrs. Pinkerton's daughter. Pleased to meet you," she said, holding out her hand. "My attorney, Dave Adcock, said I could find you here."

Your attorney? I thought he was Mrs. Pinkerton's attorney.

Danni reluctantly shook it, and immediately changed her attitude and words to a friendlier tone since it was Mrs. Pinkerton's daughter.

"I'm glad to meet you," Danni said, suddenly feeling the urge to apologize. "I'm sorry. The funeral is over now. I didn't know how to get in touch with you or I would've let you know about it."

"Don't worry about it, honey. I knew about it. Saw it in the obituary."

Why weren't you here then? Danni wanted to ask. *You didn't even come to your own mom's funeral!*

"Where do I put my stuff?" Priscilla asked.

"I beg your pardon."

"My stuff. I'm moving in. Do you know when you'll be moving out?"

"Oh..." Danni said, trying to assess the situation in her mind. This was Mrs. Pinkerton's daughter. She was the rightful heir. *I guess.* "I don't know. We have a lot of stuff to move. There's four of us."

They would all have to move out. No one had really thought about that possibility. Everyone was focused on getting through the funeral.

Prissy laughed. "I don't mean tonight, silly. I wouldn't kick you out without any notice. You can wait 'til tomorrow. Now... which room should I put my things in, Hon?"

Before Danni could answer, Prissy said, "Never mind, Sweety. I'll pick one out. Is the front door open?"

Danni nodded, at a complete loss for words.

Prissy abruptly turned and started walking briskly toward the house. Danni's feet were frozen in place in disbelief.

Tom walked up about that time. "Who was that?" he asked.

"I'm not sure," Danni responded. "Some lady claiming to be Mrs. Pinkerton's daughter."

"I didn't know Mrs. Pinkerton had a daughter."

"She mentioned her once. But I never knew her daughter's name."

"That woman looks nothing like Mrs. Pinkerton."

"I know. I know. I'd better go to the house and see what she's doing."

Danni took off running after her.

* * *

Danni didn't catch up with Prissy until she reached her mobile. The daughter opened the trunk and pulled out four large suitcases and sat them on the ground. The bags had seen better days.

"Where are the servants?" Prissy asked, looking around the grounds.

"We don't have any servants," Danni answered.

"Oh... Could you be a dear and help me with my bags?"

"I'd be happy to," Danni said, trying to be nice.

Prissy grabbed her purse out of the front seat of the mobile, slung it over her shoulder and abruptly walked away toward the front door, leaving Danni standing by the bags with her mouth agape.

"Of all the nerve!" Danni said under her breath.

I'm not carrying her bags.

Danni took off after her again, leaving the bags sitting on the driveway.

Prissy went from room to room with Danni trying to stay by her side, not willing to let her out of her sight for one second. The insufferable woman was making snarky comments at every turn. "The furniture is so gaudy. So passé. What was Mom thinking when she chose these curtains?"

Danni didn't disagree about the curtains but would never have the audacity to say so in front of someone else she barely knew and certainly not about her own mother. The daughter's words seemed so disrespectful to her. A flash of guilt came over her as she remembered her own harsh words for her mother. She decided not to be so judgmental and to give Prissy a chance.

"This paint color will not do," Prissy whined. "I'm going to have to replace all of the carpeting."

"What do you think? Should I knock out this wall?" she asked Danni the question but didn't wait for an answer. Danni just followed her around, speechless. Anger building inside of her at every turn. She was trying to be nice, but the lady was making it hard.

"What is that?" Prissy asked, upon entering Mrs. Pinkerton's study. On the wall behind the desk was a large portrait of Mrs. Pinkerton commissioned years ago by a famous artist. It dominated the wall, and except for the showy frame, it was a beautiful portrayal of a younger Mrs. Pinkerton.

"That's probably your mom's most prized possession," Danni said. "She loved that painting."

"It's hideous."

"It has special meaning to her. I would think you'd want to keep it in the family."

Prissy ignored the comment and took a sudden turn and headed to the living quarters. Before Danni could stop her, Prissy had opened the door to her room.

"I like this room!" Prissy said excitedly. Mrs. Pinkerton had told Danni to decorate it however she wanted. It was her room. Danni had given it more of a modern look with new curtains and updated furniture. Fortunately, she had remembered to make her bed.

"Thanks," Danni said before realizing that the lady wasn't complimenting her. She would have no way of knowing that Danni decorated it.

"Bring my bags in here," Prissy said. "I'll stay here."

"But... this is my room," Danni objected.

Prissy walked over to the desk and picked up Danni's journal and opened it.

Danni snatched it out of her hands.

"Don't touch my things," Danni said rudely. "I'm going to have to ask you to leave."

"Don't get in such a huff," Prissy said, playfully patting Danni on her cheek, although Danni didn't take it that way. "It's only for one night. You'll be out of here tomorrow."

"About that," Danni said. "There are four of us living here. You can't just throw us out on the street with no notice."

"You can go live with your rich boyfriend," Prissy said sarcastically.

Danni was about to become unglued. "How do you know about my boyfriend? And who are you to tell me where to live?"

"There's a lot of things I know about you," she said rudely. "Yeah. That's right. I did my research. You've been mooching off my mother for more than a year. That's going to stop."

Danni wanted to smack her in the face. "I haven't been mooching off your mother. How dare you insinuate such a thing? Mrs. Pinkerton invited me to live here with her. I loved your mother. I would never take advantage of her generosity and kindness. Something she obviously didn't pass on to you."

"You brainwashed her!" Prissy retorted, angrily. "I know all about your cult. You got you a little commune going here. Well not for long. Technically, the house is not mine until tomorrow. So, I can't kick you out yet." Prissy raised her voice with each word. Danni could see the hate in her eyes and the vitriol for anything and anyone associated with her mother.

"That's true. So, get out of my room. Now! Get out!" Danni shouted.

The woman stomped out of the room, slamming the door behind her.

* * *

When Danni calmed down, she called Tom. "What am I going to do? This woman is intolerable." Just saying the words caused the anger to rise back inside of her.

"How do you know she's even Mrs. Pinkerton's daughter?" Tom asked.

"She said she..." Danni started to answer but stopped mid sentence. "I guess I don't know."

"Hear me out. This woman shows up out of nowhere, claiming to be Mrs. Pinkerton's long-lost daughter. She doesn't look anything like her. What if she made it up?"

"How could she... I mean. How would she even know Mrs. Pinkerton had a daughter."

"Did you read the obituary?"

"No. I didn't have time."

"It mentions a daughter. Priscilla. This lady could've read the obituary in the paper, concocted a story, and is pretending to be her daughter. I've heard about these scams before. I'm not saying she's not her daughter, but you should ask her for identification. A birth certificate or something."

Danni heard the back door slam. She looked out the window and saw Prissy walking out toward the garage. She didn't have her purse on her arm. *It must be somewhere in the house.*

"That's a good idea," Danni said. "I gotta go. I'll call you later."

Danni slipped out of her room and searched the house for Prissy's purse. If she had identification, it would be in there. Driver's license, passport, Social Security card, something that might prove her identity.

She finally found it in Mrs. Pinkerton's bedroom along with the four bags. Danni's disdain for the woman only increased two-fold at the audacity of her to take over her dead mother's room with all her things still in it. Danni couldn't imagine such a thing. The thought never occurred to her. She hadn't even considered what they would've done with Mrs. Pinkerton's things. Probably left them alone until the Millennium in hopes that she came back for them.

The purse was laying on the bed. Danni's heart started racing.

This is wrong. I can't look in her purse.

I have to know.

She had to hurry. The woman could come back at any time. She fumbled with the purse clasp. The bag was off white and oversized. The lock stuck. It either stuck or Danni's hand was shaking so hard she couldn't get it open.

Finally, she worked it free and it fell open. The purse was filled with clutter. She rummaged through it until she found the wallet.

Danni looked up as if somehow someone might be watching her. She listened carefully for any hint that Prissy had come back to the house. Hopefully, she'd be mesmerized by all the mobiles and stay out there for a while.

Danni opened the wallet rifling through it looking for an ID. In one of the slots was a driver's license. She pulled it out and stared at the picture and the name.

Danni couldn't believe what she was seeing. The picture was definitely Prissy.

Priscilla Blanchard.

5 foot five, 125 pounds. Yeah! Right. Danni rolled her eyes.

A noise suddenly reverberated through the house. A door shut. Danni fumbled trying to get the ID back in the wallet. Panic was shooting through her like a firework exploding inside her body.

She heard footsteps on the hardwood floors and wasn't able to put everything back like it was. She walked quickly over to the doorway and into the hallway, not wanting to be discovered in the room.

"What are you doing in my room?" the whiny voice said.

Danni didn't know whether to answer her question or ask one of her own.

Who are you, Priscilla Blanchard, and are you really Mrs. Pinkerton's daughter?

37

Danni returned to her room, leaving the door cracked so she could hear if Prissy was moving around the house. The first thing she did was call Tom.

"You were right." Danni said to Tom in a quiet voice. "Her name is Priscilla Blanchard, not Pinkerton. Should I call the police?"

"I don't know what the police would do," Tom responded. "That doesn't prove she's not Mrs. Pinkerton's daughter. It just makes me even more suspicious."

"She knew about Mr. Adcock and the reading of the will," Danni mused. "How could she know about that if she wasn't Mrs. Pinkerton's daughter?"

"These con artists are very clever. You should raise your concerns to Mr. Adcock tomorrow morning. He's the executor of the estate and has a fiduciary responsibility to make sure the funds are distributed to the right person. It's a big firm. They have investigators and ways of exposing a con artist that we don't have."

"What if she *is* Mrs. Pinkerton's daughter?" Danni asked, never remembering feeling this anxious about something. The stress of the funeral was enough for one day without this bombshell thrust on her out of the blue.

"What will I do? She said we have to be out of *her* house tomorrow."

Tom didn't immediately respond. When he did, his words blindsided Danni. "You can come and live here," he said hesitantly.

"Do you think that's a good idea?"

"I have plenty of room. For everybody. You can all live here."

"We are the pastors of a church. We can't live together without being married. I don't want to give people the wrong impression. And you've been a bachelor for a long time. Do you really want four single ladies taking over your house?"

"I'll put your room on the other end. As far from mine as possible. Or... You can even live in the guest house."

"I don't know."

"Just think about it. You don't have to make a decision until tomorrow. Just know that it's an option."

"Thanks. That's sweet of you to offer. I'll think about it."

"There is one other option," Tom said.

"What's that?"

"We could get married."

Danni almost dropped the caller.

"Married?"

"Sure. Why not? You love me, right?"

"Yes."

"And I love you. We practically spend all of our time together as it is. Days anyway. We're going to get married eventually. The sooner the better."

"We are... are we? You sound pretty sure of yourself."

"I usually get what I want, and I want to marry you."

"We've never been on a real date. Never even kissed."

"I know... You insist that we don't kiss until we get married. Fine. Let's get married tomorrow so we can kiss and so you can move in here without sullying your reputation. I don't want to wait any longer to kiss you."

Danni could feel her face blush.

"That's not a very romantic marriage proposal," she said.

"If you want, I'll come over tonight and get down on one knee. I don't have a ring, though."

"That won't be necessary. Let me think about it overnight."

"What's there to think about? You're going to say yes eventually."

"Thomas Collins! You think you know everything, don't you?" she said playfully. Changing to a more serious tone, Danni said, "I hate to bring it up, but since you started talking about marriage, what about our age difference? You're twenty years older than me."

"I've thought about that."

"You have?" Danni asked sarcastically. "And what did you come up with?"

"The Millennium will be here in less than six years."

"Right. What does that have to do with you being older than me?"

"We're going to live a thousand years with Christ on Jupiter. In the Millennium."

"And your point is...?"

"When I'm five hundred-years old, you'll be four-hundred and eighty. That won't seem like such a big age difference."

Danni laughed out loud and then caught herself. Her door was still cracked. "I see you've thought of everything."

"I told you. Have I also told you lately that I love you?"

"I love you too. Will you be able to do the *Two Witnesses* show tomorrow morning without me?"

Before he could answer, Danni heard a sound at her door. Then footsteps. She jumped out of her bed, tiptoed over to the door, and peaked around it. A shadowy figure that looked like Prissy was at the end of the hall and rounded the corner out of sight.

"What was that?" Tom asked.

"I think Prissy was listening to our call," Danni whispered.

"Did she hear us talking about the two witnesses?"

"I think so."

"Oh well. That girl has probably never even heard of us. I doubt she's ever turned on a Christian program in her life."

"I don't know. We've tried so hard to keep our identities a secret."

"Nothing we can do about it tonight. Call me tomorrow. Let me know how things go with the attorney."

"I will." Danni hung up the caller and went back and sat on her bed.

Did Prissy hear us talking? The thought was eating away at her. Danni felt violated. She got back up, closed the door, and locked it.

I don't trust that lady. Not for one second.

* * *

The firm of Adcock & Associates was on the top floor of a twelve-story high rise. The brochure in the waiting room boasted more than five-hundred attorneys on staff. Dave Adcock was the founding member and the Chairman of the Board. Mrs. Pinkerton must've been an important client for the head man to be handling something as small as the execution of an estate.

Danni arrived early so she could express her concerns about the identity of Priscilla Blanchard. The despicable woman hadn't arrived when the clock struck nine, and Danni was led into a room where Mr. Adcock was sitting at a large conference table with one file folder in front of him.

He rose immediately and extended his hand, greeting her warmly. "Thank you for coming," he said. "One other person will be joining us. Mrs. Pinkerton's daughter, Priscilla."

"Yes. We've met," Danni said a little more sarcastically than she intended.

Her face must've also given away that she was concerned because he said, "Is there something wrong?"

"Are you sure she's really Mrs. Pinkerton's daughter? I think her name's Priscilla Blanchard. Not Pinkerton." Danni didn't want to confess how she knew the woman's name.

"That's her former husband's name. She's been married several times. It really is Mrs. Pinkerton's daughter. I've known Prissy since she was about your age. Although, she hasn't been around much lately."

"Oh... Okay." Danni said, as the realization hit her that she would have to move out of the house today. Her mind raced back to last night's conversation with Tom. Should she move in with him? Should they get married? After sleeping on it, she was convinced it was too soon.

"I don't think Priscilla likes me," Danni said, trying to get the thoughts of marriage out of her head. "She told me I had to be out of the house today. Can she do that?"

"I can't really give you legal advice since I'm not your attorney. But hypothetically, if she owns the house, by law, she can make you leave."

They were interrupted by an intercom sounding. "Ms. Pinkerton is here to see you."

"Send her in," Mr. Adcock said, rising to greet her. Danni remained seated.

As soon as Prissy entered the room, she took one look at Danni and said, "What's *she* doing here?"

"I asked her here," Mr. Adcock said.

"She's not family," Prissy said with her lips contorted and her eyes squinted into a frown.

"She's mentioned in the will. That's why she's here," Mr. Adcock said, motioning to Prissy where to sit. He sat at the end. Danni and Prissy sat in the first seats on opposite sides of the table.

Prissy glared at Danni.

Danni responded with her own snarky look. Immature, she knew, but the girl got under her skin. The woman may be Mrs. Pinkerton's heir, but she didn't have to put up with her attitude for much longer. She didn't even care about the jupes. She never even expected to be mentioned in Mrs. Pinkerton's will. The thought never crossed her mind.

If anything, she pitied Prissy. She might get all the jupes, but

Danni got Mrs. Pinkerton's love and affection, if only for one year. The jupes would probably ruin Prissy's life.

"We're here today to read Mrs. Pinkerton's last will and testament," Mr. Adcock said, taking charge of the proceedings with no informalities. "Mrs. Pinkerton requested that the two of you be present. Rather than me read the contents of the will, she wanted to speak to each of you directly."

Mr. Adcock picked up a remote device and pointed it toward the other end of the room where a video screen was mounted on the wall. The black screen flickered, and suddenly Mrs. Pinkerton's image appeared.

Seeing her brought a smile to Danni's face. The video was fairly recent. Danni had seen Mrs. Pinkerton in that dress just a few weeks before. She was sitting in the same conference room, facing the video camera, with some papers in front of her. Her trademark eyeglasses were resting gently on her nose as she peered over them at the camera. She was smiling and seemed happy, obviously enjoying what she was about to do. Or probably excited about the cruise.

"Hello girls," Mrs. Pinkerton said, speaking slowly and deliberately, clearly so each word was enunciated and couldn't be misconstrued. "If you're watching this video, then Danni, you were right. I shouldn't have gone on that cruise."

Mrs. Pinkerton let out a chuckle. Danni remembered that Mrs. Pinkerton was wearing that dress the day she left. Danni told her she had a bad feeling about the cruise, and they shouldn't go on it. If only she had listened to her.

"This is my last will and testament. I am of sound mind and stable faculties." Mrs. Pinkerton leaned forward and said in almost a whisper. "That means I'm not looney. And I know what I'm doing."

Danni could only smile. Mrs. Pinkerton had a flair for the dramatic. This was just like something she'd do.

"This is my fourth will. The first was after my first husband, Theodore, Teddy, as I called him, passed away. In that will, I left all of my earthly possessions to my daughter, Priscilla."

Priscilla managed a smile as she looked over at Danni who didn't return it.

"But then, I didn't hear from Priscilla for many years. We were estranged. I was angry. What I did hear, I didn't like. Her lifestyle. Living with men. Getting divorced. And so, I changed my will and left all of my possessions to Red Spot Christian Church. My dear friend, Dave Adcock, drafted all of these testaments on my behalf."

Priscilla's smile had turned to a scowl. Danni almost felt sorry for her. Mrs. Pinkerton could be judgmental and cruel. The estrangement probably wasn't all Prissy's fault.

"Don't worry Priscilla, I didn't leave everything to the church," Mrs. Pinkerton said as if she anticipated what Priscilla would be thinking.

"No," she continued. "After the Seizure, I had to rethink things. There really was no church at that point. The day after the Seizure, I came into Dave's office, and we changed the will back to making Priscilla my sole beneficiary of all my assets."

The smile returned, only broader, and wider.

"By the way, you may be wondering where I got all my jupes. And how much I have. It's a lot. According to my trusted advisor, Mr. Adcock tells me that at this moment, I'm worth about five billion jupes. That's liquid assets. Cash. House. Mobiles. Investments. Imagine that. Little ole me with that much jupes."

Mrs. Pinkerton took a big drink of water. Probably for effect, to let that number settle over the room.

Danni didn't think Priscilla's smile could get any bigger, but it had.

"Years ago, when Teddy and I were first married, we didn't have two nickels to our name. Those were the best years of our marriage," Mrs. Pinkerton said reflectively, almost somberly. "The saying is true. Jupe doesn't buy happiness. But neither does poverty," Mrs. Pinkerton said with a hearty laugh.

The tension was building in the room as no one laughed with her.

"Why doesn't she just get on with it?" Prissy said rudely. "Tell me how much I get. All of it probably," she said, glaring again at Danni. "She probably gave you a picture or something. Whatever."

"Like I was saying, Teddy and I didn't have anything but each other. One day Teddy came home from work. He worked at the dime store, as a clerk," she said, flicking her wrist almost dismissively. "Anyway, a friend at the store told Teddy about an investment. In a gold mine. He said it was a sure thing. Teddy said it sounded risky. I wanted to do it, but Teddy didn't."

Priscilla folded her arms. Clearly bored with the whole story.

Danni found it fascinating. Mrs. Pinkerton never talked about her late husband. Danni didn't want this video to end. It felt good to have Mrs. Pinkerton back in her life, if only on a tape, and only for a few, short minutes.

"I was the one who talked him into the investment," Mrs. Pinkerton continued. "We took out a loan on our house and nearly went bankrupt. The investment was a bust. They didn't find any gold. We were about to lose everything. Then one day, we got word that they found a vein. Teddy couldn't believe it. I was skeptical as well. But it was true. They found the largest gold deposit that's ever been found on Jupiter."

Danni clapped her hands together. "I love that story."

"That gold mine brings in... Dave, how much jupe does that mine bring in a year?" Mrs. Pinkerton asked.

"Four-hundred-million jupes," a voice in the background said.

Priscilla gasped.

"Four-hundred-million jupes a year," Mrs. Pinkerton said. "I guess I was right about the investment. Anyway, we've made billions over the years. Someone offered me fifteen billion for the mine a few years ago, but I turned them down."

"I'd take it," Prissy said.

"Anyway, I digress," Mrs. Pinkerton continued. "Back to my will. Today, I'm changing it again. I want to leave something to Danni."

Priscilla sat up in her chair and leaned forward, toward the video screen.

Danni just leaned back and wiped away a tear. This video was priceless to her. She never felt closer to Mrs. Pinkerton. The fact that she wanted to leave her something warmed her heart.

Mrs. Pinkerton picked up a pen and wrote something on the paper in front of her. She raised the paper and shook it to cause the ink to dry.

"I just signed a new will. The old one is null and void and is to be destroyed. This officially changes my will, and it reflects my wishes completely," Mrs. Pinkerton said. "If Danni is wrong, and I survive the cruise, then I still want to change my will to reflect these wishes, although I reserve the right to change it at a later date if I so desire."

"How much do I get?" Priscilla said, exasperated. "Just read the damn will."

As if on cue, Mrs. Pinkerton said, "To my daughter, Priscilla, I leave the sum of one jupe!"

"What?"

"To my dear, Danni, I leave the rest of my possessions to do with as she sees fit."

The screen went dark.

Danni's mouth flew open. If it wasn't connected to the rest of her head, it would've fallen all the way to the floor.

38

"This is an outrage!" Prissy said, standing to her feet and shouting at the top of her lungs.

Mr. Adcock opened his file and pulled out a piece of paper.

"Please, have a seat, Ms. Pinkerton. This is a check for one jupe," he said as he handed it to her. "Normally, the government takes twenty-five percent of an estate, but our firm has covered that amount and we're giving you the full jupe."

"This is ridiculous," Prissy said, spitting her words. "I'm the daughter. I'm the rightful heir. That jupe belongs to me. You're my lawyer. Do something. Let's contest the will."

"I'm not your lawyer," Mr. Adcock said. "I'm the lawyer for the estate. I said I would be the lawyer of the beneficiary. You're not the beneficiary. Ms. Howell is. I'm not her lawyer either. But I will be if that's what she wants."

"Of course," Danni said.

"You won't get away with this!" Prissy screamed, waving the check in the air. "I'll contest this will. Mom was obviously not of sound mind. She wouldn't do this to me if she was."

"I can assure you that Mrs. Pinkerton was as sharp as ever," Mr. Adcock said. "She knew exactly what she was doing. Contesting the will is your prerogative, but I can tell you that our firm will vigorously defend Ms. Howell and Mrs. Pinkerton's wishes. I don't think you want to fight me on this. You won't win."

"This lady killed my mom!" Prissy said pointing her finger at Danni. "You heard my mom say it. Danni told her that if she went on the cruise, she would die, and she did. I don't know how you did it, but you killed her."

"That's ridiculous," Danni said.

Mr. Adcock pushed a button on his caller.

"Could you send security in here, please?"

An armed security guard appeared at the door within seconds.

"Please escort Ms. Pinkerton to the exit and don't let her back in."

The guard grabbed her arm. Prissy pulled away.

"You haven't heard the last of me. I'll get you, Danni."

The guard grabbed her arm again only more firmly this time and removed her from the room. They could still hear her screaming all the way down at the end of the hall.

"Sorry about that," he said.

"It's not your fault."

"Okay. Let's get down to business. I have another video to play. Mrs. Pinkerton recorded it just for you."

Danni took a deep breath. Still in shock from the first video.

Another video. *What could it possibly be about?*

* * *

Mrs. Pinkerton's image reappeared on the screen.

"Hello, Danni. I'm sorry to put you through all of that, but I wanted to make a point to my daughter. Don't feel bad about it."

"I don't," Danni said as if Mrs. Pinkerton was right there in the room. Danni's eyes were fixated to the screen.

"Priscilla got what she deserved," Mrs. Pinkerton said matter-of-factly. "All that jupe would've been wasted if I had given it to her. I trust you to take much better care of it."

I will.

"The last year has been the happiest year of my life. Having you in my life." Danni had never seen Mrs. Pinkerton like this. So introspective. So emotional.

"That's so sweet."

"You are like a daughter to me. Like the daughter I never had."

Danni wiped away the tears with the sleeve of her shirt. Mr. Adcock handed her a box of tissues. She ripped a couple out of the box, but just clutched them in her hand, making no effort to wipe the other tears away. She let them flow. They had built up. With all her responsibilities at the funeral and then with the daughter bursting on the scene, she never had time to fully grieve.

"I want to offer you something," Mrs. Pinkerton continued, "but it's completely up to you."

"What?" Danni asked. She felt like they were having a real conversation.

"The New World Order takes fifty percent of my estate if I leave it to someone who is not my child. They only take twenty-five percent of the estate I leave to my children."

"You just said that," Danni said to Mr. Adcock.

He nodded.

"It would be an honor for me if I could legally adopt you. I know I'm not your mother. I'm not trying to take her place. But it would help me to rest in peace, knowing that you were legally my daughter."

Mrs. Pinkerton wiped away her own tears as she said it. A lot of thought had obviously gone into this video. A lot of emotion.

"Plus, it will save you a lot of jupes," Mrs. Pinkerton said with a laugh, changing the mood as she often did with her humor.

"Anyway. You do whatever you want to do. Mr. Adcock can advise you if you want. You can trust him with your life."

Danni looked at Mr. Adcock who gave her a reassuring smile.

"One other thing," Mrs. Pinkerton said. "Please give Naomi the painting in my office. She always admired it. I want her to have it."

"Of course."

"And give Liz and Ruth one of my mobiles. Let them pick out which one. There are ninety-four of them, so I figured you could get by with ninety-two. Also, if Liz wants to go to college, it will mean a lot to me if you'd help her. I know you will. That's why I left you the jupe."

"Danni. I hope you know that I love you so much." Mrs. Pinkerton was nearly sobbing by this point. Danni had never even seen her cry before today.

"I've made a lot of mistakes in my life. I hope God forgives me for them. I know in my heart that this is not one of them. Thank you for being there for me when I needed you."

"Thank you," Danni said, choking back the tears.

"I'll see you on the other side." Mrs. Pinkerton blew Danni a kiss.

The screen went dark again.

* * *

Mr. Adcock opened his file. Danni could see that he was clearly moved by the video. His voice cracked when he said the first words. Danni was glad he was going to talk first. She didn't think she could.

"This is a document saying that you want to retain me as your attorney," he said, his voice cracking when he said the first words. "If that is the case," he continued, "then please sign it at the place marked."

Danni took a pen and signed it without hesitation.

"If Mrs. Pinkerton trusts you, then so do I."

"Thank you for the opportunity to earn that trust. The second document is adoption papers. Mrs. Pinkerton signed it the same day she signed her will. So, if you sign it, it will be effective on that date."

"How much jupe does that save us?"

"Over a billion jupes."

"Any reason why I shouldn't sign it?"

"My understanding is that your parents are deceased."

"Actually, they disappeared in the Seizure. They're still alive in heaven."

"Right. Sorry. That was a wrong choice of words. Your parents are no longer here on Jupiter. That being the case, I see no reason why you wouldn't want to be legally adopted by Mrs. Pinkerton. You don't have to change your name or birth certificate. Nothing happens except a legal formality. I think it's worth saving all that jupe."

"I do too," Danni said as she picked up a pen and signed the paper. "I guess that makes it official."

Mr. Adcock took what looked to be a check out of his file.

"I took the liberty of assuming you would accept the adoption. This check is made out to you. I paid it out of Mrs. Pinkerton's personal account. All of her debts, burial expenses, which were minimal, taxes, and our fee to prepare these documents were deducted. The balance is made out to you."

Danni stared at the amount on the check with her name on it.

$2,575,557,253.55.

Danni tried to say the amount in her mind. Two billion, five hundred, seventy-five million, five hundred and fifty-seven thousand, two hundred and fifty-three jupes, and fifty-five cents. *Did I get it right?*

Danni was struck by how many fives were in the check. Five was the number of grace in the Bible.

There's another billion or so in investments that have not been liquidated. They await your instructions.

"I don't even know what to do with all this jupe," Danni said.

"With your permission, we can just handle things the way we always did with Mrs. Pinkerton. I can put the jupes in an account in your name. We will invest it for you. Anytime you want to make a withdrawal, just contact me, and I'll make sure it happens. That system has worked well for years."

"That sounds good to me."

"The jupes from the gold mine will come directly into that account as well."

"We'll send you a monthly statement with all of the deposits and disbursements. Everything will be transparent, so you can see what we did. Any questions, just give me a call."

"There is one thing."

"What's that?"

"Are any of my investments in stocks?" Danni felt weird calling it her jupes. She still thought of it as Mrs. Pinkerton's. This would take some getting used to.

"Yes. Why do you ask?"

"There's a plague about to come on Jupiter."

"A plague. Really?" His eyebrow raised as he said it.

"The stock market is about to collapse," Danni said. "I want to take all my jupes out of it."

"Mrs. Pinkerton said your predictions almost always came true. Would you like us to short the market?"

"I don't know what that means."

"That means you sell more stock than you own now and then buy it back when the market drops. A stock market collapse would double the value of your investments in just a few days."

"That's a great idea. Let's do it. Do you think I should sell the gold mine?"

"No way. If you're right about the stock market collapse, then the price of gold is about to skyrocket."

"I'm right about it," Danni said. "I think it's only days away. Mark my words. You should do everything you can to protect you and your family. It's going to be bad."

Danni signed a few more documents. The house and titles to the mobile were put into her name.

"So, it's my house now?" Danni asked, hardly believing it was true.

"Yes. It's yours. And everything in it. Except for the painting and the two mobiles."

"So, I can kick Priscilla out if I want?"

"She's staying there?" he said with his eyes widened in a surprised look.

"She moved in last night and tried to take over the place. Said it would be hers today."

"I wish you had called me. You can certainly kick her out. And I suggest you do."

There were more papers to sign. Danni signed stock certificates for the gold mine. Signature cards for new bank accounts. So much was happening, it was overwhelming her.

Mr. Adcock was a godsend. He patiently led her through the process in meticulous detail answering all of her questions.

When they were finished, he walked her to the elevator. He extended his hand, but she ignored it, giving him a big hug instead.

"Thank you so much," she said.

"You're very welcome. Call me if you need me."

Danni stepped onto the elevator and let out a squeal as soon as the doors closed. She kept saying aloud over and over again, "I can't believe this. I can't believe this."

She pulled the caller out of her pocket. "I have to call Tom."

He's going to be shocked.

But first she called Liz.

"Liz. I don't have time to talk. I need you to do something for me. Right now."

"What's that?"

"Go pack up all of Prissy's things. Put them in her suitcases and sit them just outside the gate. I'll explain later."

Then she hung up and called Tom.

***

Prissy sat in her mobile in the parking lot of the attorney's building, fuming. Rage was building inside of her with each passing minute. Growing like a volcano ready to explode.

She kept saying aloud over and over again, "I can't believe this. I can't believe this."

The jupe was stolen from her as far as she was concerned. She had to get it back somehow. But how? No ideas came to mind. She had a gun in her mobile. For protection. But she wasn't a murderer. Death would be too good for that conniving pathetic girl. She'd think of something else. Something that would really hurt her. A way to get back what was rightfully hers.

Where is that girl? What is taking so long?

Finally, Danni emerged from the building. The girl walked out of the building and got into one of her mother's mobiles which infuriated her further, if that was even possible.

She turned the key to the ignition on her mobile. It wouldn't start. She slammed her hand against the dashboard. Last night she was dreaming of new mobiles and houses, yachts and trips around the world. Now she was destitute. The check for one jupe was ripped up and the remnants were laying on the front seat.

The old jalopy finally started on the third try. She pulled out of the parking lot and began following Danni.

"I'm going to get that Danni Howell, if it's the last thing I do."

39

Tom answered Danni's call on the first ring. Probably as excited to hear from her as she was to tell him what happened at the reading of Mrs. Pinkerton's will.

"I have good news," Danni said.

"I like good news."

"I don't have to move in with you."

"How is that good news?"

"Mrs. Pinkerton left me her house," Danni squealed with delight when she said it.

The other end of the caller was silent.

"And all her jupe!" Danni added as the squeal turned into exuberance. "Can you believe it?"

"Congratulations."

"You don't sound too excited."

"No. I am. That's great. It is good news. I was just hoping we would get married and you'd live here with me; that's all."

"Someday," Danni said, avoiding taking the subject further.

"That means I have to keep waiting to kiss you," Tom said in an annoyed tone.

"What's the saying? 'Good things come to those who wait.' You'll just have to wait a little while longer."

"What about the daughter?" Tom said, clearly wanting to change the subject as well, which was fine with her.

"Are you sitting down?" Danni said.

"No. But tell me anyway," Tom said curtly. Danni could tell he was still a little hurt by her excitement about having her own place and not having to move in with him.

"She left her one jupe," Danni said, barely able to contain the excitement.

Tom burst out laughing. "I wish I could've been there to see that." Tom's mood changed in a millisecond with that news. They would talk about the other stuff later.

"She wasn't happy. Her exact words were... 'I'll get you, Danni!'" mimicking her whiny voice as she said it.

Tom's tone turned serious again. The conversation was going back and forth, up, and down, spanning the range of emotions like a roller coaster. "You better be careful, Danni. You made an enemy today. You should let Carter know."

Carter Hall handled the security at Mrs. Pinkerton and Tom's estates along with stocking the food emergency pantry. A former special operations soldier, he was trained to provide security and protection for them, which he was good at.

"I already have," Danni said. "I think Prissy is the least of our worries."

"Why is that?"

"As soon as this pandemic hits in about five days, Prescom Wolf is going to come after us with a vengeance. He has all the power of the New World Order behind him."

"We have the power of God behind us," Tom said confidently.

"Yes, we do. And we're going to need it. And a lot of jupe that God is going to use for his good."

"How much did she leave you, if I may ask?"

"Billions!" Danni exclaimed.

Danni knew Tom was listed as the third richest man on Jupiter. She wondered if their combined wealth would make them number one when they were married.

When?

Deep down, she must really want to marry Tom.

"The Bible says that wealth is stored up for the righteous," Tom said.

"Yes, it is. We can do a lot of good with our jupes. By the way," Danni said. "Do you own any stocks?"

* * *

Cabinet Room
Two Days Later

"You have to shut everything down," Dr. Mertz, the Director of Health, said to Prescom Wolf.

"Are you crazy?" the Prescom said. "That will destroy the economy."

The majority in the room voiced their agreement. Prescom Wolf had called a meeting of the cabinet, and Dr. Mertz had just briefed the members on the possible pandemic. He knew Mertz would make that suggestion to shut everything down, and that was something he wasn't prepared to do. That meant closing all the businesses and issuing an in-home sheltering order, making it illegal for anyone to leave his home.

"Everyone needs to be quarantined for fourteen days," Dr. Mertz retorted. "If we don't, this super flu-us will spread like a fire in dry grass."

"We're just now recovering from D-Day," J.B. Hader, the Director of Commerce, said. "It's taken over a year. The stock market is at an all-time high. Or at least it was until yesterday."

"That reminds me," Prescom Wolf interrupted him, "did you ever find out who's shorting the stock market?"

Hader had met with the Prescom earlier in the day to alert him to some unusual activity in the stock market—a sudden plunge in stock prices. An investigation found it was caused by a massive amount of short selling.

"Someone is shorting the market?" one of the cabinet members asked. Everyone in the room had large portfolios. Talk of the pandemic had suddenly taken a backseat to a discussion about jupes.

"Yes," Hader said. "We're talking billions of jupes. The selling is coming from shell companies that are shielding the identity of the buyers. We have no idea who they are."

"Why would they do that?" a member asked. "The economy's booming."

"We don't know," Prescom Wolf said. "But someone's betting on the market crashing sometime soon."

Short-term selling pushes stocks down in the short-term and makes the market crash steeper if some event did cause it to suddenly go down. The sellers could make a fortune at the bottom. If the stock market went up and not down, the short seller could lose a lot of jupes.

"Maybe, they know about the pandemic," Dr. Mertz said.

That caused immediate silence in the room as members started looking at each other.

The Prescom was thinking what many of them might've been thinking. He said, "It goes without saying but... if I find out that anyone in this room is shorting stocks, I'll personally destroy you. I'll wring your neck with my bare hands."

A slight chuckle went through the room and gained intensity. They might've thought he was kidding, even though he wasn't.

"I'm serious. All of you should be buying stocks on this downturn. We need to make these short sellers pay for their stupidity. There is no pandemic. If you think you have inside information that's going to make you jupes at our expense, it's not happening on my watch. Is that understood?"

Nods and words of agreement were quickly expressed across the room.

"That's why we can't shut the economy down," Prescom Wolf said. "We need to prove these people wrong."

"With all due respect," Dr. Mertz said, "If this pandemic spreads like I think it will, the stock market will be the least of our worries."

"There are only five people dead," Director Hader said. "Why do we think it's going to become a pandemic?"

"It's not contained," Dr. Mertz responded. "Four of those people died on a cruise ship. More people are infected. We just don't know who they are. And we don't have a test to identify them yet."

"How did this virus start?" one of the members asked.

"Dr. Woo says it started in the wet markets in Anih C Province," Dr. Mertz answered.

"He's lying," Brock Benson, Director of Worldwide Intelligence spoke up. "It started in his lab."

"What proof do you have of that?" Dr. Mertz retorted angrily. That accusation, true or not, reflected poorly on his whole health organization.

"The girl who died in Pearl Province," Benson began, "was there with her boyfriend. She actually lives in Anih C Province. Her boyfriend worked for the cleaning company that cleans Dr. Woo's lab. The boy was infected and gave it to the girl."

"That doesn't prove anything," Dr. Mertz said. "The girl could've gotten it from anywhere. The people on the cruise got it from the wet markets."

"Which the boy and his girlfriend visited before they went on their trip," Benson countered. "The boy probably came into contact with passengers and infected them. It then spread to others on the ship."

"How do you know all this?" Dr. Mertz asked.

"We detained the boy and interrogated him. At first, he denied it, then he broke down and told us this story about a monkey, coughing and going crazy in his cage. He tried to help the beast and got sprayed with saliva and monkey snot! Your boy, Dr. Woo, has been lying. Check it out. Dr. Woo created that virus in his lab and his stupidity caused it to get released to the public."

"Where is the boy now?" Prescom Wolf asked.

"We released him yesterday. He's on his way back home."

"Make him disappear," Wolf said.

"I want to test him," Dr. Mertz retorted.

"We can't let him talk to anyone else," the Prescom said sharply. "If word gets out that this virus was created in a lab, the ramifications to us would be devastating. Kill him. Make it look like an accident. But do it right away. Before he can talk to anyone."

Prescom Wolf looked around the room. No one else said anything. The Prescom was agitated. Things were going well on Jupiter. Too well. Talk of this pandemic and quarantine and short selling was making him nervous.

"Hader, find those short-sellers. Dr. Mertz, I'm holding you personally responsible for containing this virus. You can quarantine the ship passengers if you can find them, but I'm not shutting down the whole economy over five deaths. Also, Dr. Woo has some explaining to do. Make sure that virus in his lab is destroyed and cannot get out again. This meeting is over."

The Prescom stood while the others remained seated as was customary.

As he was leaving the room, he said, "Aria, I want to see you in my office. Come with me. Everyone else get back to work."

* * *

Aria didn't think the Prescom could sink any lower into moral degradation, but he just did. Prescom Wolf had just ordered a young cleaning boy killed to protect his own political interests and power. He ignored the advice of his medical professionals and was risking the lives of billions of Jupiterians because he didn't want to risk his stock portfolio going down. She wondered how low he could actually go.

Aria knew that the plague was upon them. It was only a matter of time. She was at Mrs. Pinkerton's funeral. Naomi told her what the plague did to Mrs. Pinkerton's body. How one minute she was fine and five hours later she was dead. Danni had prophesied that the plague wouldn't end until a third of the people were dead, and Aria believed her. She shuddered to think about that much suffering.

What does the Prescom want with me? He probably wanted to talk about the two witnesses.

She followed him into the Oval Office. He sat in the usual place and motioned for her to take the seat next to him.

He leaned forward with his hands clasped in front of him.

"I blame the two witnesses. They're the ones stirring up trouble and turning the people against me. I want them stopped."

"I haven't been able to find them, sir," Aria said.

"I know. It's not your fault. I've had my people looking for them as well. But someone knows who they are. I've put out a reward. A million jupes."

It took all of Aria's self-control to not let her mouth fly open.

"A million jupes?" Aria said in a way that sounded like a question but was more out of disbelief.

"The networks will be reporting on it tonight. There will be a caller number for people to call with information. If that information leads to their arrest, then the person will get the million jupes."

"What do you intend to do to the two witnesses if you catch them?"

"Kill them!" The words spewed out of his mouth like a cobra's venom. "In the public square. They will be humiliated, and their bodies left hanging in the square for public display. What they're doing is treasonous! They're a threat to the New World Order. I will find them."

Aria left the room stunned. The Prescom had lost all moral compass. At one time, she knew him to be a good and decent man. Not anymore. He'd sunk to depths of depravity.

She had to warn her friends. Only a few people knew their identities. The list ran through her mind. None of them would betray Danni and Tom. She was certain of it.

But did anyone else know their identity? Someone who would betray them.

* * *

When Aria left the room, the Prescom took out his caller and made a call.

"Bud, it's me."

"Yes. Mr. Prescom. What can I do for you?"

"I want you to sell all my stocks and begin short selling the market."

* * *

Prissy sat in a bar, nursing her third strong drink. It had done nothing to take the edge off of her pain. Or anger. The animosity toward Danni Howell and her own mom had turned into hatred. She despised them both, going back and forth in her mind as to who she loathed more.

She was convinced they were in on it together. It was probably Danni's idea to steal her fortune, but her mom was taken in and became a willing accomplice.

Over the last two days, she'd been to half a dozen lawyers, pleading with them to take her case and contest the will. They all said it was a hopeless case. She wasn't a spouse. A married partner had a legal right to a portion of an estate. Children didn't. If Mrs. Pinkerton didn't want to leave her anything, that was her prerogative.

One did say he'd take the case but wanted a hundred-thousand-jupe retainer! Where would she get that kind of jupe? He obviously didn't believe they'd win either. The retainer was his way of ripping her off further. Taking advantage of her to see if she was desperate enough to throw good jupe after bad. When it became obvious to him that she was broke, he actually laughed in her face about the one jupe. Which she didn't even have, since she tore up the check, which made him laugh harder.

To make matters worse, Danni had touched her things. Packed them up in her bags and left them outside the gate, like a pile of trash. A big goon named Carter came to the gate to run her off when she tried to climb over it. The memories of the last two days were driving her deeper into despair.

"Give me another drink," Prissy said roughly to the barkeeper.

"I think you've had enough," he said.

"Give me another drink!" she insisted. "I'll tell you when I've had enough."

She looked around the bar which was barely half-full. Not very many men. She'd have to find one tonight and trade her body for some jupes, otherwise she wouldn't be able to pay her bar bill. Or a hotel room for the night.

She slammed her hand on the bar only making things worse as the pain shot through her arm. How did this happen? This morning she was on top of the world. Now she was in a two-bit dive bar, on the road to being nothing more than a hooker.

The vision set above the bar was annoying her. The Red Spot evening news was on. She started to ask the bartender to change the channel when a scroll caught her eye. Something about two witnesses.

Her senses suddenly came alive.

Where have I heard that?

"Turn it up," she said to the bartender. "Turn up the vision. I want to hear this."

"The Department of Justice is offering a reward in the amount of one million jupes for any information that leads to the arrest of the self-proclaimed prophets who call themselves the 'two witnesses.' Their world-wide radio show caused quite a stir when a woman who is one of the witnesses claimed that a plague would come upon Jupiter. Widely discredited, they are highly popular, their show airing on more than five-thousand stations. If you have any information on their identities or whereabouts call this number."

"Quick! Give me a pen and paper," Prissy said to the barkeep.

She jotted down the number.

The memory came flooding back to her mind. The hallway. Outside of Danni's room. She heard her talk about her radio show. It was called the *Two Witnesses*. Danni was the woman.

About that time a man approached her and said, "Can I buy you a drink?" He looked rich enough to tide her over for a few days. Until she could claim that reward.

Prissy suddenly felt much better.

40

Red Spot Community Hospital for Obstetrics

Dr. Matthew King asked, "So we're full? We really have no more beds?"

The Community Hospital for Obstetrics had room for more than two-thousand babies in its nursery and more than two-thousand beds for moms. According to Maggie, his head nurse, every bed in the hospital was full.

"We have more babies than we can pray over," Maggie said, laughing. She'd recently started attending Red Spot Christian Church at his invitation, and they'd become good friends outside the hospital along with professional colleagues inside it. Having been at the hospital for more than ten years, she was his most trusted employee.

"Is delivery full?" Dr. King asked.

"Yes, and we have women in labor in the waiting rooms."

"How do you ask a pregnant woman to wait to deliver?" Dr. King said facetiously.

"Very politely. Obviously, some can't wait. The baby tells us when he or she is going to be delivered. But those who are going to be induced, or the ones with mild contractions are the ones we ask to wait."

"It's a good problem to have, I guess," Dr. King said.

Better than the problem they had fifteen months ago. In the disappearance, the hospital had more than a thousand babies go missing and a third of the mothers and staff. A riot had broken out and the facility would've burned to the ground if it hadn't been for the sprinkler system.

After the Seizure, it took three months to rebuild the hospital. It was rebuilt, bigger and better, under Dr. King's leadership. Even then, they had little to no business for several months. All the children in wombs were taken to heaven in the Seizure. Many couples were afraid to get pregnant again.

Dr. King and his wife, Olivia, were one of those couples. They lost their son Joshua in the Seizure. Pastor Danni said *lost* was the wrong word. They would see Joshua again. That was comforting to them. Especially to Olivia. If it hadn't been for Red Spot Christian Church and Pastor Danni and Dr. Tom, they might not have made it through the grief.

The assurance gave them the comfort and ultimately the faith to have another child. They had just begun trying. Much of Jupiter felt the same way as things were starting to get back to normal and women were getting pregnant again. So much so that the hospital was starting to get overrun with business.

"Dr. King, come to the nursery, stat." Dr. Sellers only called for Dr. King when it was important. Since the memory of the disappearance was on his mind, the message sounded too much like fifteen months ago when Dr. Seller's called him by the intercom to come to the nursery where he found every baby missing.

"Time to go to work," Dr. King said to Maggie, putting the disappearance out of his mind. Danni had said that was a one-time event that would never happen again. He hoped she was right.

"What do you want me to do about the beds?" Maggie asked.

"Call Sinai Hospital and see if they have room. They probably do."

Most women preferred his hospital because of the reputation, so the others were never as busy as his, even though they didn't have as many beds.

"Dr. King, come to the nursery, stat," the message rang out again with more urgency.

"I'm coming," he shouted, looking to the ceiling. "I'm coming."

* * *

When Dr. King arrived at the nursery, he found Dr. Sellers and a group of nurses congregated around one baby. As Dr. King approached, he could immediately see that the newborn was in respiratory distress.

"What's going on?" Dr. King asked, picking up the chart and looking over it.

Dr. Sellers answered. "The baby is experiencing excessive fluid in his lungs, dropping oxygen levels, abnormal breathing, and unproductive cough. My diagnosis is impaired gas exchange RT with collection of mucus in airways, potentially caused by an unknown virus. We're waiting for the results of the blood test. As you know, the lab is backed up."

"When did you first notice symptoms?" Dr. King asked the nurses.

"About an hour ago," one answered.

"Let's have a listen to your lungs, little guy," Dr. King said, taking his stethoscope from around his neck and placing the tips into his ear and the bell on the baby's chest. He moved it around to several locations. What he heard was alarming.

"This child needs to be intubated," Dr. King said sharply. A nurse rushed away without hesitating. "Let's order a picture."

"Already have. Like I said, they're backed up," Dr. Sellers replied.

"Move this boy to the top of the list," Dr. King said. "Give him supplemental oxygen via nasal cannula with a fraction of inspired oxygen of 0.3 for six hours. Give him a contraselanticsteroid to ease the inflammation. When you get the blood work, start him on whatever medicine it warrants to kill the virus."

Dr. Sellers leaned in so that he was whispering directly into Dr. King's ear. "Did you hear what I heard in the anterior basal lower lobe?"

"I did. There's a lot rattling around in there." Dr. King looked around the room. "What I'm concerned about is how fast he has deteriorated. This baby is near respiratory arrest. How could a virus cause a deterioration of his lungs so quickly? Did he have any abnormalities at birth?"

"None. His lungs were perfectly normal."

Dr. King looked around the nursery. Every bed was filled. "Are any other babies showing symptoms?"

"Not that I'm aware."

He listened for any coughs or signs of labored breathing. "I'd like to isolate this baby, in case he's contagious," Dr. King said. "But I don't see anywhere to put him."

"I'll find him a place."

The nurse returned with a ventilator, and Dr. Sellers took it from her hands and told her to follow him and bring the baby with her. Dr. King began going from bed to bed, listening to the lungs of different children. About a third of them showed abnormalities in their lungs.

Before he could do anything about it a message came over the intercom. "Dr. King. Delivery room, stat. DM."

"What?" DM meant they had a deceased mom in the delivery room. Dr. King started to put his hand to his face to rub his eyes. Stopping himself, he realized that he needed to wash his hands first.

Before he left, he told one of the nurses, "I want everyone in this area to put on personal protective gear around these kids. Something's not right." The nurse bolted into action.

Dr. King washed his hands and then left for the delivery room, hearing his name called again on the way. He was an elder at Red Spot Christian Church and knew about the plague prophecy. He also attended Mrs. Pinkerton's funeral. His mind was already racing to the possibility that the plague was upon them. If so, they'd need ten times the number of beds they had in that hospital.

The thought overwhelmed him as he thought back to the nightmare of the disappearance.

This would make the Seizure look like a day at the beach.

He quickened his steps and threw open the double doors into the delivery area. There was an unusual amount of activity. Maggie was at the nurse's station and rushed to meet him.

"A woman died in delivery," she said.

"From what cause?" Dr. King asked. While deaths happened in his hospital, they were rare and generally the patient had an underlying condition that increased the risk, and they knew about the possibility beforehand. It was rare for a woman to die unexpectedly. He was praying it wasn't from the plague.

"Respiratory failure," Maggie answered.

Dr. King's heart sunk.

"She just started coughing. It came upon her suddenly. They tried to revive her but were unsuccessful."

"How's the baby?"

"The baby's fine."

"Has the family been told?"

"She has no family. Apparently, she's been living on the streets. There's no record of a father. She didn't know who he was. Her parents are dead. Died when she was young. She was in and out of orphanages. A lot of that information is in her file, some of it she told to the nurses."

"We'll have to deal with that later. There's a baby showing respiratory distress in the nursery. I want all of our nurses and doctors to put on PPG throughout the hospital. I'm afraid there may be a contagion in our hospital."

"I'm on it," Maggie said as she rushed off.

"Dr. King. Emergency room. Stat."

This scene was starting to look eerily familiar.

***

Dr. King heard the commotion in the ER before he saw it. Hundreds of women filled the room. A line was beginning to form outside.

He used his pass to buzz himself into the back area.

"What's happening?"

No one answered. They were rushing around with purpose, ignoring him, obviously focusing on patients. The hallway was echoing from loud coughing which was coming from a number of rooms. Every room seemed full.

He went to the nurse's desk. No one was there. A nurse came out of a room, walked to the desk, and grabbed a chart, then turned abruptly to go back to the room.

"What's going on?" Dr. King asked.

The nurse shrugged her shoulders and was gone in a flash. He followed her into the room. A woman was on a hospital bed, clearly in labor, but also in respiratory distress. Her face was contorted from the pain of the contractions, but her face was also turning blue as she gasped for air, trying desperately to find her next breath.

One of the biggest challenges to delivery was when the mom had trouble breathing. Mom and baby needed every bit of oxygen they could get through the stress of delivery.

The same scene was playing out in multiple rooms. Not all ladies were in labor, but most were showing signs of respiratory issues. Dr. King went back to the nurse's station, picked up the caller, and pushed the intercom button.

"Level ID 1 Emergency," he declared throughout the entire hospital. Everyone would know what to do. They had run countless drills in preparation. The hospital would be locked down. All entrances and exits closed. ID meant infectious disease emergency. All nurses and doctors would immediately don protective gear.

Dr. King did the math in his head. Pastor Danni said that a third of Jupiter would die in the plague. Two thousand babies and two thousand mommas were in his hospital at that moment. Four hundred staff.

The calculations weren't hard. A third would be 666 babies and 666 mothers. A chill ran through his spine. He'd heard that number in Pastor Danni's sermons. He didn't know what the numbers meant.

He just knew it was something bad.

41

Global Office

Prescom Wolf was working in his office when Staff Chief Wade Wilson excitedly interrupted him, clearly with some good news to tell him.

"I have a woman here who claims to know the identity of the two witnesses," Wade said.

"Is she credible?" the Prescom asked. Having heard the same claim several times already, he was skeptical. Since he offered the one million-jupes reward, they'd been inundated with calls from people claiming to know the identities. Every lead had been a dead end.

"I think she's credible," Wilson said. "She overheard a conversation. The identity of the two people checks out. We did a voice scan and compared it to the voices of the two witnesses, and it's a match with 99.5 percent certainty."

"Bring her in," the Prescom said, elated that they finally had a lead.

His excitement grew even more as soon as he saw her. She was middle aged, provocatively dressed. Loose. That's how he would describe her, if he was being completely honest. Probably really good in bed. His experience over the years had been that girls like her were the most fun. Older. Experienced. Uninhibited. Willing to try new things.

He immediately rose to meet her, flashing her a seductive smile. She picked up on the cue and flashed back a flirtatious look.

"That'll be all, Wade," the Prescom said. "I'll take it from here."

He offered her a seat on the couch and as soon as she took it, he sat next to her.

"I'm Prissy," she said, extending her hand. She wore strong perfume. He liked that.

"You obviously know who I am," he said smugly, but warmly. "My Staff Chief says you know the identity of the two witnesses."

"You like to get right to business," Prissy said.

"Business before pleasure." Wolf laughed.

She smiled widely. "Ahh. Pleasure," she said. "I hope there's some of that too. That's my motto. Work hard and play harder," she said in a whiny voice. He tried to figure out where she was from by her accent. The east side of Red Spot, he imagined. In more of the lower-middle blue-collar section. She wasn't wearing a ring on her finger. Not that it mattered. He was wearing a ring.

If he got her into bed, he hoped she wasn't a talker. That accent would ruin the mood.

"I heard them talking on the caller," Prissy said.

"Who are they?"

"Danni Howell and her rich boyfriend, Tom."

"Do you know Tom's last name?"

"Collins."

"Dr. Tom Collins? The author? Motivational speaker?" The Prescom knew him well.

"Yeah. That's him."

"I know Tom. I've met him several times."

Wolf could tell right away that Prissy was capable of lying. He didn't sense that she was now. She had really heard something.

"How did you overhear their conversation?"

"She was in my house. Her house." Prissy stumbled with the words. "I was staying at her house, and the door to her bedroom was cracked. Her and Tom were talking about their radio show. She called it the *Two Witnesses*."

A jolt of excitement went through him even more than his desire for her. He wanted nothing more than to capture and torture the two who'd become a threat to his New World Order.

"I heard there was a reward," Prissy continued. "So, I called the number. And here I am."

"I'm glad you did. Who is this Danni lady?"

"She stole a bunch of my mom's jupes."

"Really?"

Prissy related the whole story. The will. The jupes. The Pinkerton estate. Mobiles. Her bags left at the gate. A security guard with guns.

"Sounds like the lady is a con artist. I can have her arrested."

"That would be great!" Prissy said excitedly.

He stood and walked behind his desk and called for Wade Wilson to come back into the room.

"I want this Danni girl and Dr. Tom arrested and brought in for questioning. Send soldiers to their houses. A small army. Sounds like they have security there. Use whatever force is necessary, but I want them alive."

"I'm on it."

"Wade," the Prescom called out to him, right before he left the room. "Is the first lady in the residence today?"

"No, Sir. She's at an elementary school today, promoting her *Children First* initiative."

"When will she be home?"

"Not until tomorrow, sir. It's a two-day conference."

"Excellent. Clear my schedule. I don't want to be disturbed. Unless it's an emergency."

When Wade left, the Prescom turned to Missy and said, "Would you like to have lunch with me? In my private residence."

"What about my reward?" Prissy whined.

He waved his hand dismissively. "What if I told you I could get your mother's estate back for you?"

Prissy's eyes widened. "I wouldn't believe it."

"I can seize all those assets. The jupes. The house, mobiles, everything. If she is one of the two witnesses, I'll get all of it back for you."

"You can do that?" she asked.

"I can do anything. I'm the Prescom."

"I don't know how I can ever thank you."

He sat back down next to her and put his hand on her knee. "I have some ideas about that."

"So, do I," she said, putting her hand on his and stroking it. "I would love to have lunch with you," she said with a broad smile.

"Then let's go."

* * *

The Pinkerton Estate

Danni knew the call was urgent as soon as she heard the frantic voice on the other end.

"It's started!" Olivia said. "The plague has started."

"Slow down, Olivia," Danni implored. "I can't understand you when you're hysterical."

Her voice was shaking as she struggled to get out the words. "Matthew just called me," she said between gasping breaths. "He said the hospital is being overrun by patients with the plague. Dozens of babies and mommas are dead already." Matthew was Olivia's husband. Dr. Matthew King, the Director at the hospital for obstetrics. Danni knew when the plague started, his hospital would be hit hard. The suffering would be almost unimaginable.

"Olivia, you need to pack some clothes and come over here. You can stay with us. Here, you'll be safe."

"I tried to get Matthew to come home, but he wouldn't. He said he had to stay with his patients and staff. I'm so scared."

"God has not given us a spirit of fear, Olivia. The plague can't touch a believer unless they are afraid of it. Do what I say. Pack up your things and get over here as soon as possible."

Danni's shoulders slumped as she hung up the caller. She knew this day would eventually come. The only question was, now that the plague has started, what did last night's dream mean?

* * *

"I believe it's time to reveal to the world that we're the two witnesses," Danni said. Tom and Carter were in Mrs. Pinkerton's study discussing the rapidly changing events.

"The Prescom will kill you," Carter said. "There's already a reward out for your heads."

"Danni's right," Tom said. "We can't hide in the shadows while the world is dying from the plague. We have to give them hope."

"You both will die," Carter said.

"I'm not afraid," Tom countered.

"The Lord will protect us," Danni said with confidence. "I saw it in a dream. Last night."

Carter and Tom were already sitting on the edge of their seats. A sense of awe filled the room.

"Tom and I were standing in the Square," Danni started slowly. She was speaking of the square with all of the Prescomial statues. A sudden calm and peace came over them when she started talking about her dream. She could see it in their faces and in their physical demeanor. "We were prophesying—Tom and I were. I had power over the plague. I could tell it to start or stop anytime I wanted. There were people all around who wanted to kill us. But they couldn't touch us."

"This dream is from God," Tom said. "It's a vision. I feel it in my spirit."

Danni continued. "God said to me, 'If anyone tries to harm you, I will devour them.'"

"Did God say anything else?" Tom asked.

"He said he has given me power to shut up the heavens so that it will not rain. He has given me the power to turn the waters into blood and to strike the earth with every kind of plague as often as I want. Even quakes."

"He's given that power to you?" Carter asked. "Why?"

"I don't know. He wants us to be his messengers during the Tribulation."

"Why don't you just stop the plague *now* then?" Carter said. "Before it kills too many people."

"Because it's not time," Danni said. "We are to prophecy for twelve hundred, sixty days. With the suffering will come a Great Awakening. The last one."

"Without the pain and suffering, men won't turn to God," Tom said, nodding his head.

Danni stood up and started pacing. "I saw the antiChrist in my vision," she said. "The chaos in the world is what allows him to rise to power."

"Prescom Wolf is in power," Carter said.

She decided not to tell them what she saw in the vision about the Prescom. They didn't need to know the rest of the vision at this time. She quit pacing.

"Did you call Taylor and tell her to come to the house?" she asked Carter, changing the subject. Taylor was Carter's wife who he saved from a life of prostitution. She got saved at the church and had been on fire for God ever since.

"Yes. And she's calling everyone else," Carter said. "Naomi, Liz, and Ruth are at the homeless shelter serving lunch."

Mrs. Pinkerton created the shelter and funded it back when she was alive. They fed several thousand men, women, and children every day. Danni intended to keep funding it and even expand it.

"They should all stay here at the house, until the plague is over," Danni said.

"What do we do now?" Tom asked.

"I guess we will go to the Square..." Danni said.

Before she could get the entire sentence out, loud barking erupted in the house. Bruno came running into the room, jumping around, frantically trying to tell them something.

Carter leapt to his feet. A loud noise was coming from outside. He ran to the window and looked out. The window faced the main road.

"Someone's coming!" Carter said.

"Who?" Tom asked.

Danni grabbed Bruno by the collar and attached a leash to it. She was trying to calm him.

Before Carter could answer Tom said, "I'm going to go look at the security cameras."

The estate had a sophisticated security system that was state-of-the-art. More than a hundred cameras captured live images in every direction.

Danni and Tom followed Carter into the security room. Bruno was still barking and with even more intensity. Danni tried her best to get him to calm down.

They could immediately see what had upset Bruno on the security cameras. A convoy of soldiers were coming down the road leading to the entrance of the estate. They could even feel the vibrations as they drove down the road.

Carter became surprisingly calm. This was what he was trained to do. Assess and take charge.

"I count a dozen trucks," Carter said. "Those are government soldiers. I would guess each truck holds about a dozen men. They'll be armed. With machine guns. Each man will carry a couple hundred rounds. That's a hundred and forty-four heavily armed men. I don't have the firepower to hold them off. The two of you should leave through the emergency exit."

"I'm not doing that," Danni said as she abruptly left the room after handing Bruno's leash to Carter. They followed her.

"Where are you going?" Carter said.

Danni walked out the door, down the driveway, and opened the front gate. The trucks were nearing the entrance.

Carter and Tom followed.

Danni walked out of the gate and stood in the middle of the road. The armored convoy came to a halt, and a man got out holding a machine gun. He was obviously the man in charge of the operation.

"Are you Danni Howell?" he said.

"I am."

"You're under arrest," he said.

"On what charge?"

"By orders of Prescom Wolf," the man said.

"Prescom Wolf is an apostate," Danni said.

"That's probably why you're getting arrested," he said, chuckling.

Danni stood emotionless, unafraid.

"Is Tom Collins here?" he asked, looking over at Carter and Tom.

"I'm Tom Collins," Tom said, walking from behind the gate to stand next to Danni.

"You're under arrest, as well," the man said roughly. "You're both coming with me."

"I don't think so," Danni said. "God told us to go to the square. Please move your trucks. You're in our way."

42

The standoff had only lasted for a couple minutes, but it seemed longer to Danni. The leader of the small army standing in front of them, along with a hundred and forty-four armed men with their guns pointed directly at her, probably didn't see it as a stand-off. They believed they were in full control, Danni surmised.

Tom stood next to her confidently, while Carter was off to the side, still inside the gate holding Bruno by the leash. A concerned look was on his face as his eyebrows were furrowed and his mouth formed as if he wanted to say something to her, warn her probably. She had no doubt he would die for her if he had to.

That won't be necessary.

Bruno wasn't afraid. He looked ready to take on the entire army by himself and probably would've attacked already if Carter wasn't holding him back. She smiled at the thought that Bruno would defend her with his life.

"Shut that mutt up," the leader of the army said brusquely.

Danni sobered immediately. *Don't talk to my dog that way.* "Carter! Bring Bruno to me," Danni commanded with authority.

Carter walked through the gate and into the middle of the road where Danni and Tom were standing. The soldiers were twenty-or thirty-feet away. The trucks were lined single file in the road. Danni took the leash from his hand.

Bruno kept his gaze directly on the leader. He wasn't barking, but his teeth were in a vicious gnarl with a low growl coming from behind them.

"Sit, Bruno," Danni said.

The dog immediately obeyed her commands, but his thick, powerful muscles were tense, on full alert, ready to spring into action at her command. Danni was surprisingly calm.

If the soldiers were at a heightened sense of alert, they became more so at the sight of the menacing mastiff. Several planted their feet and raised their guns. Some were pointing them at the dog.

Danni began to speak. "I asked you politely to move your trucks. I'm not going to ask you nicely again. If you don't move them, then you will die."

The soldiers started chuckling, which turned into laughter. They began mocking her.

"Do you think this is a good idea, Danni?" Carter nervously whispered under his breath, low enough that the leader couldn't hear him. "We're not armed. And they have us outnumbered a hundred to one."

"Don't be of such little faith, Carter. We aren't outnumbered. There are more on our side than on theirs."

"I don't understand," Carter said.

Danni began to pray. "O Lord, open Carter's eyes and let him see."

Carter let out a slight cheer, raising his fist in the air. "I see them! They're everywhere!"

"What do you see, Carter?" Danni asked.

"I see a multitude of angels with horses and chariots of fire," Carter said.

"We actually don't need them," Danni said. "Look out in the distance."

Tom and Carter looked at a black cloud forming on the horizon in the direction Danni was pointing. Carter let out a sound of amazement. The leader turned his head to look in the same direction, probably wondering what the commotion was about.

The cloud was moving slowly but steadily toward them, getting bigger as it neared.

"Save yourself, Commander, and leave," Danni warned. "Or repent and bow down and worship the Lord of hosts."

"Never," he said. "I have my orders. Men seize them!"

The soldiers started toward them. Bruno started barking wildly. Danni strained to hold him back.

"Hold your ground," Danni told Tom and Carter.

The sky suddenly grew dark as the cloud descended over them. Without notice, hail began to rain down upon the soldiers like fire. Many of them cried out in pain as they were hit by the fiery pieces of ice. They began retreating, the entire throng ran for the cover of their trucks against the admonitions of their leader who just ducked down putting his hands up over his head to protect it.

But it didn't help. A large piece of hail fell from the sky and struck him in the forehead, as he fell to a heap on the ground.

The hail lasted for less than a minute but did considerable damage to the trucks.

Every windshield was broken, and the bodies of the trucks had huge divots in them. Several of the soldiers lay dead on the ground.

The hail didn't touch Danni, Tom, or Carter. Bruno sat down at Danni's command and they all stood silently and watched the carnage unfold before them.

Danni raised her hands in the air and thanked the Lord for their salvation. As she did, lightning bolts flashed from the sky. The light from the bolts were so bright the three of them had to turn away. When they looked back, the trucks were gone. Incinerated by the heat of the lightning bolts. All that was left of the men and machines were twelve piles of ashes, spaced apart where the trucks once stood. One lone soldier stood to the side of one of the piles.

Carter let out a cheer. Bruno bounced around joyfully.

Danni approached the soldier. He raised his hands instinctively like he was going to fire his weapon, but the gun was gone. It had disintegrated.

"God has spared you, so you could go tell the Prescom what you have seen and heard," Danni said. "Tell him that we will be in the Square, preaching. A similar fate awaits anyone who tries to stop us."

The soldier just stood there, stunned.

"Go!" Carter commanded the man. "Do what she says."

The man took off running, looking back a couple times, until finally, bolting into a full-out sprint.

The three of them and Bruno walked back to the house. Danni gave Carter instructions as they walked.

"Tom and I are going to the Square. We'll be there for forty-eight hours preaching, day and night. Stay here with the others. Don't come to the Square. We'll be fine. Make sure everyone comes back here and waits for us. You watch over them. But do not fear. The Lord will protect you just as he has protected us."

When they reached the house, Danni and Tom got in the mobile and drove away.

* * *

The Prescom's Personal Residence

"You were amazing," Prescom Wolf said to Prissy.

"You weren't so bad yourself," she replied, patting him on his chest.

They were lying in the Prescom's bed for nearly three hours. Ever since he sent Wade Wilson, his Staff Chief, away with orders to capture the two witnesses.

"Do you want to go again?" Prissy said.

"We already did it three times! I need a break." The Prescom got out of bed, walked over to a liquor cabinet, and poured himself a drink. He swigged it down in one gulp.

"Just let me know."

"Okay! I'm ready," he said as he hurried back to bed. He playfully jumped on it as Prissy let out a shriek of delight.

Before anything could happen, Wade Wilson burst into the room.

"Don't you knock?" the Prescom said angrily.

"There's been an incident," Wilson said.

"What kind of incident?" the Prescom responded, sitting up in bed. Prissy pulled the covers over her and was holding them up to her chest.

"The two witnesses attacked our soldiers."

"Attacked them?"

The Prescom got out of the bed and walked over to the chair where his clothes were strewn and started putting them on.

"They have some kind of weapon. They destroyed all the trucks and killed all the soldiers. Right outside Danni Howell's estate."

"All of them?" the Prescom asked, not believing what he was hearing. "How many men did they kill?" he asked as rage was boiling up inside of him like a pot on a hot fire.

"One hundred and forty-three men!" Wade said. "Only one survived. He ran back and told us what happened."

"Kill them!" the Prescom said in a raised and angry voice. "Destroy that house."

"No!" Prissy shouted. "That's my house."

The Prescom glared at her and ignored her comment. Wilson waved his hand dismissively.

"They're not there, anyway," Wilson said.

"Where are they?" the Prescom said. "They probably fled. I want them hunted down like dogs and killed."

"They are in the Square." Wilson walked over to the table and grabbed the remote and flicked on the vision. The news channel was showing a picture of the Square. Throngs of people had gathered around two people who were standing in the center, speaking to the crowd. The headline across the bottom of the screen read, *Two Witnesses Predict the End of the World.*

"That's them!" Prissy shouted. "Danni and her boyfriend."

"Turn up the volume," the Prescom instructed.

One of the two witnesses—the man—was speaking, shouting into the crowd. He didn't have a microphone or any amplification. News reporters were picking up his words on their microphones.

"Listen to me!" the man shouted. "We are in the last days. How terrible it will be for pregnant women and for nursing mothers in these days. There will be greater anguish than at any time since Jupiter began. And it will never be so great again. In fact, unless the time of calamity is shortened, not a single person will survive."

"It will be shortened for the sake of God's chosen ones," the woman said. Prescom Wolf is a hypocrite and a liar, full of every impurity." The crowd was eerily silent. Obviously hanging on her every word. The woman suddenly looked straight into the camera. A chill went down Prescom Wolf's spine as it seemed like she was looking right at him.

"God will strike Prescom Wolf dead!" she said. "This very hour as he lays with a Jezebel!"

"Why haven't you seized them?" the Prescom shouted at Wilson.

"I wanted to update you on the situation, first."

"They have a lot of nerve, showing their faces in the Square after they murdered a hundred and forty-three of my men. They're the ones who are going to die!"

"The crowds are supporting them," Wilson said. "We need to think this through. If we go in and kill them, we'll make martyrs out of them, and the crowd may turn on us."

"I want David Nelson in the situation room, now!" the Prescom said, sternly. David Wilson was the Director of Defense. He was the head of all the armed forces of the New World Order.

"He's already there, sir."

Prescom Wolf wasn't surprised. Those were his men killed at the estate. Nelson would want revenge as much, if not more, than Prescom Wolf. Known for his ruthlessness, David Nelson was probably already planning their demise.

"I'll be in shortly," Prescom Wolf said. "Wade, escort this lady out of here and off the premises."

Prissy got out of bed, keeping the bedspread covering her to the best she could. She quickly gathered her things and rushed into the bathroom. A minute or two later she emerged fully dressed. Wolf was straightening his tie in front of a mirror.

Wade walked over to her and took her by the arm, but she pulled it roughly away.

"When can I see you again?" she asked the Prescom in a sweet tone.

"You won't ever see me again," the Prescom said. "You were fun, but not that much fun."

"What about my reward?"

"There is no reward," the Prescom said. "What do I need you for?" He pointed at the vision set. "The two witnesses are right there in the Square. I don't need anyone to identify them."

"What about my house and the jupes and the mobiles?" Prissy said as Wilson dragged her away.

"I'm going to keep them for myself," the Prescom retorted. "That was a good idea to seize them. Tom Collins is worth billions. Both of their estates will become mine."

Prissy started sobbing. "You can't do this. That estate belongs to me."

"Get this woman out of my sight. I have no more use for her."

A security guard came into the room, probably having heard the commotion. He grabbed Prissy's other arm. Wolf could hear her shouting and spitting obscenities all the way out the door and down the hall until he couldn't hear her anymore.

***

Wade Wilson was right, the Prescom concluded, after thinking about it for several minutes. This situation needed to be handled delicately. He needed a plan. One had already formulated in his mind.

He walked into the closet, sat down on the ottoman, and put on a pair of shoes.

He put his hand to his face and coughed.

43

Red Spot Community Hospital for Obstetrics

Dr. King immediately regretted his decision to shut down the hospital and took steps to reverse it. He found Maggie and told her to open the doors that had been locked when he declared the infectious disease emergency. Maggie was his chief nurse and his most trusted employee.

"We'll be overrun," Maggie said.

"I always regretted closing the hospital during the disappearance," he responded. "We're a hospital. That's what we do. I've had nightmares thinking about what it would've been like to be one of those people in need, locked outside a hospital. I won't do that again. We'll just have to figure out how to help everyone. We can expand our capacity by a few hundred. Somehow."

Maggie didn't resist further; she followed his instructions without further comment, which was one of the things he appreciated most about her.

Within an hour, he regretted his decision. The hospital was overrun, not with hundreds of cases, but thousands.

The first difficult decision followed shortly thereafter.

"Dr. King, we're out of masks. What do you want me to do?" Maggie asked him. The masks were to protect their workers, the doctors, and the nurses. Sending them into a room with patients infected with the plague was like sending them on a suicide mission, or like telling a soldier to storm a hill with no ammunition.

"Tell them to use what they can," Dr. King replied. "Make cloth masks out of anything you can find."

"The cloth won't protect them."

"I know. But it's better than nothing."

Maggie started to leave, but Dr. King stopped her. "Where's your mask?" he asked.

"We ran out before I got one."

"Here. Take mine," Dr. King said, removing his from around his neck and handing it to her.

"I can't take yours."

"Go ahead," he said. "I'll be all right. I insist."

She took it from his hand and left.

An hour later Maggie again came to him. "We have fifty babies and over two-hundred mothers who need ventilators, or they'll die," Maggie said soberly.

"How many ventilators do we have?"

"Ten. And they're already in use."

Dr. King put his hands to his face and covered his eyes. Rubbing them roughly. Tears forced their way through his fingers.

"Dr. King?" Maggie said softly. "What do you want me to do? Who gets the ten ventilators?"

"I don't know! How can I make that decision? I'm not God. How can I decide who lives and dies?"

"You have to decide. I've got to get back to the patients."

"Give them to the babies. The ones most likely to live."

***

Two Days Later

Dr. King underestimated the number of people who would die in his hospital. By a lot.

When Pastor Danni had prophesied the coming plague, she said a third of all Jupiter would die. He based his predictions on that, not taking into an account that he ran a hospital. Only those who were sick came there. The death rate for someone with the virus was close to a hundred percent.

The decisions he made over the last two days were horrifying. Unimaginable.

The basement was filled with thousands of dead bodies. Babies and mothers. Some died in labor, alone on the floor or in the waiting room before ever seeing a doctor or a nurse, their babies dying with them before they could be birthed.

For two stays, his staff fought the plague valiantly. Fighting exhaustion, they worked through the night, barely stopping to get a quick snack or drink, as the river of patients kept coming through their doors. When the deluge subsided, they worked tirelessly to treat the survivors and locate family members. Matching the babies who survived who lost their mothers with surviving family members was an almost impossible challenge.

Dr. King finally sent everyone home. Except Maggie, who was still there helping him with the last patients and refusing to leave until he did. Dr. King made up an excuse and left her in the nursery and walked around until he found an empty room that didn't remind him of the carnage of the last two days.

He sat on the couch in the snack lounge, buried his head in his hands, and sobbed, quietly. Letting the strain of the last two days finally overcome his emotions.

A comforting hand touched his shoulder.

Maggie.

He couldn't look up, and no words made it out of his mouth between the sobs. Maggie rubbed his shoulder and gently spoke soothing and encouraging words. When he finally found the strength to compose himself, he looked up to see her blood-shot eyes from her own tears that stained her cheeks and soaked her shirt.

"Are you okay?" she asked softly.

"I don't think I'll ever be okay again. With what we've been through."

"You did everything you could. And more. Many lives were saved because of you."

"I wish I could've done more. I keep thinking back and second guessing myself. Is there something else I could've done?"

"You're torturing yourself. What happened here was bad enough without you making it worse. We just went through a war together. A lot of people died. But that's what happens in war. You did the best you could. What we did was nothing short of miraculous."

"I couldn't have done it without you," he said sincerely.

Dr. King put his arm around Maggie and pulled her close. Something he never allowed himself to do with one of his female employees. Nothing felt inappropriate about it.

"You should go home, Maggie, and get some rest."

"What are you going to do about the babies?"

"How many do we have left?"

"Four."

Dr. King let out a huge sigh.

He remembered the single mother who was homeless, who came in with no family. She was the first patient he saw in the emergency room. The mother died in labor, but the baby was saved. Family Services said they'd send someone but never did. Eventually, they quit answering their callers.

Three other babies were lying in the nursery in the same situation. No mom or dad. Helpless. As far as they knew, no family members left on Jupiter.

"I'll figure something out," Dr. King said.

"I'll stay here and help you," Maggie insisted.

"It's okay. Go home. I'll manage."

They both stood wearily. It took every ounce of strength to just stand and walk out of the room. One last hug and he sent Maggie on her way and walked back to the nursery.

When he got there, he took one look at the four newborns, sat back down on the floor, and sobbed. Uncontrollably. He did nothing to stop the tears until there were no more left to shed.

* * *

The Pinkerton Estate
Two Hours Later

Dr. Matthew King drove down the long driveway to the house. His wife, Olivia, came running to meet the mobile. Several others followed her out of the house.

Matthew had barely opened the door when Olivia threw her arms around his neck and kissed and hugged him profusely, barely letting him get out and get his footing.

"I've missed you so much. Are you okay?" she said. By the look on her face, he could tell she was struggling with conflicting emotions. Joy, seen through her bright smile, and worry revealed through her wide eyes and eyebrows furrowed with concern.

Naomi and Ruth, Carter and Taylor, and Liz were there as well. He'd called earlier to discuss his plan. Everyone had agreed.

Danni and Tom were still at the square. No one knew when they'd be coming home, or if they even would.

Matthew gave the others a warm greeting. He would've given them a hug, but Olivia was draped on his arm. He walked around to the rear of his vehicle and opened the back hatch.

He took one of the babies out of a makeshift carrier and handed him to Olivia. She took the child out of his arms slowly and carefully and gazed upon him with a look of a mother seeing her newborn for the first time. Dr. King had seen that look hundreds of times.

"Oh... He's so beautiful," Olivia said, adjusting the blanket and wrapping him tighter so he was covered in the night air. The others gathered around to look at him.

Olivia was eight months pregnant when the disappearance happened. The baby was taken from her womb. She said yes immediately when Matthew discussed the possibility of them taking one of the four babies. Preferably the boy.

"Carter and Taylor, here's your baby," Matthew said as he handed them one.

"Is it a boy or a girl?" Carter asked.

"It's a boy," Matthew answered.

"Yes! Honey. We have a boy!" he said excitedly to Taylor, his wife.

Thinking of Carter and Taylor was when the idea had come to Matthew. Sitting in the nursery, on the floor, sobbing, with no idea what to do with the four orphaned babies. Taylor couldn't have children. They tried for several years until they finally gave up. Then they split up, and that was the end of trying. Now they were back together and doing well. It seemed like God was answering their prayers by giving them a child.

"Where's mine?" Ruth said, nervously.

"Right here," Matthew said gently. "It's a girl."

Ruth took the baby in her arms as tears started flowing down her face. Naomi wiped them away as Ruth's arms were firmly under the baby who had started to cry. She lifted the tiny girl toward her face and kissed her softly and began to reassure her.

In the Seizure Ruth's newborn, Kate, had disappeared out of her crib. Olivia had been skeptical as to if Ruth would want another baby. They both knew nothing could ever replace Kate. And her husband, Jake, went to heaven in the Seizure as well. She'd have to raise this baby alone until he came back after the Tribulation.

At first, Ruth was skeptical. When Olivia pleaded with her, she finally agreed. The baby girl had no one else. She was all alone in the world. Now seeing Ruth with the baby, Matthew knew no one could take that baby from her even if they wanted to. Ruth would love that little girl like she was her own. Which she now was.

"There's one more," Matthew said looking around.

"Don't look at me!" Naomi said, backing away. "I'm too old to take a baby."

Matthew looked at Liz, with a sly smile. At first, she didn't get it. When she finally did, she said, "No way! I'm not taking a baby. I'm too young. I'll babysit for you. But that's it!"

Matthew laughed, and everyone joined in, easing the tension in the air. For the first time, Matthew felt some release from inside him.

Olivia patted Matthew on the arm. "Quit joking around," she said. "She's ours. You can't give my baby away." Olivia and Matthew had decided to take two of them. A boy and a girl.

Matthew closed the back of the vehicle and held the baby close to him as they all walked into the house.

He couldn't help but think that maybe some good came out of this after all.

44

Seven Days Later
The Prescomial Square

Danni hadn't questioned her calling as one of the two witnesses, until now. For seven straight days, Danni and Tom preached in the square to multitudes of people. They'd had no food or drink and only slept a few hours each night. The only thing that kept her going was the supernatural power of God.

That's also what protected them. The square was filled with an angry mob. Danni had lost count on how many people had tried to kill them. Government soldiers had stormed the square to arrest them. They met a similar fate as the soldiers on the road.

The more heartbreaking to Danni were the angry men and women who had lost loved ones to the plague. She understood how they felt. She might feel the same way if she were in their shoes. This prophetess had come along and ruined their lives, or so they thought. Danni readily admitted that she had called the plague down on Jupiter, inciting the crowd to even more fervent levels of hatred for them.

There were also thugs wanting to collect a reward. Anyone who tried to harm them was killed. Some were struck down by the angels protecting them. Others were killed by fire that came out of their mouths. One particular hoodlum charged at Tom, ready to plunge a knife in his back. Danni yelled for Tom to look out. Instead of words, a flame of fire like a dragon came out of her mouth and consumed the man.

Why couldn't she just incapacitate these people? Why did she have to kill them? She felt compassion for them, even though they were trying to kill them. The whole scene in the square was tragic. It wasn't the lack of food or the danger that made her question her calling. It was the message.

From Danni's vantage point in the square, she could look over the city. Many times, Danni and Tom simply wept out of sorrow for the lost who were like sheep without a shepherd. Not unlike when Jesus wept over Red Spot when he was brought there to be killed somewhere near where they were standing.

She often thought this must be what it had been like for Jesus. He went forty days and forty nights without food or water. Danni didn't think that was possible. Nor would it be necessary. God told her the night before in a dream that the fast would be over today. Today was also the day that the plague would come to an end.

Danni stood in the square and quieted the crowd. The Jupiter News Network covered them nonstop, and she could see the cameramen angling for a closeup. They'd been there since Tom and Danni made their first appearance in the square. They cut away for a period of time after the death of the Prescom, but when people lost interest after that, they quickly resumed coverage of the two witnesses.

"Thus, sayeth the Lord," Danni cried out in a loud voice, "the plague on Jupiter has ended. No one else will die from it." There was no official death count, although Danni already knew the number. A third of Jupiter had died. That was the prophecy given to her. The plague ended the moment that exactly one third were dead. The Great Plague was a tragedy of epic proportions.

A cheer went up among the throng, although not from everyone. Some still mocked her. Others were angry and wanted to exact revenge.

The words she was about to say next was another reason why she questioned this calling. Life and death were really in her tongue. What she spoke came to pass. The burden of her words was almost too much to bear.

"People of Jupiter listen to me," Danni continued. "As the Lord God of all creation lives, there will neither be dew nor rain on Jupiter except at my word. And a great famine will sweep the land. You will sow much seed in the field, but you will harvest little because locusts will devour it. You will plant vineyards and cultivate them, but you won't drink the wine or gather the grapes, because worms will eat them. You'll have olive trees throughout the world, but you won't use the oil. Swarms of locusts will take over all your trees and the crops of your land. The water will turn to blood."

Danni could feel the rage in the crowd. Many wanted to attack and kill them for those words but were obviously afraid. They'd seen the mighty hand of God strike down armed soldiers and professional bounty hunters. They didn't dare lift a hand against them.

Tom began to prophesy. "The Lord will strike you with severe heat and drought and with blight and mildew and will not end until a third have perished."

Danni cringed. The words were sharper than a two-edged sword. But they had to be spoken by someone. This was their bane to carry.

"Is there anything we can do to stop it from happening?" someone cried out.

"You will not fear the terror of night, nor the arrow that flies by day," Danni said. "Nor the pestilence that stalks in the darkness, nor the plague that destroys at midday."

Tom shouted, "A thousand may fall at your side, ten thousand at your right hand, but it will not come near you."

"Call on him and he will answer you," Danni said.

"What must I do to be saved?" another man shouted, falling to his knees in front of Tom.

"Confess with your mouth Jesus is Lord and believe in your heart God raised him from the dead, and you will be saved," Tom implored.

God added to their numbers three thousand people that day in the square.

Danni suddenly felt better. That was why she had to fulfill her calling. The world needed a witness. For whatever reason, God had chosen her and Tom. In a small way, she understood what Jesus went through in the garden the night before his death.

He had said, "Father, if it be your will, let this cup pass by me."

She had prayed that same prayer several times over the last seven days. Jesus understood what he was going to do was a horrendous sacrifice. But it was for the good of mankind.

God called the two witnesses to such a time as this. It was a tremendous burden to command the death of billions of people. To cause so much human suffering just from the words of her mouth. But from that same mouth would come hope to the masses. It wasn't for her to question God or his plan for her life.

"We must go now," Tom said, taking Danni by the hand. Darkness was beginning to descend on Jupiter.

"Where are we going?" Danni asked as many of the crowd followed them. The camera crews scrambled to become mobile to capture whatever happened next.

Tom answered. "We're to go throughout all of Jupiter proclaiming the good news that Jesus is coming again and will set up a thousand-year reign. God has sent us to tell everyone about the kingdom of God and to heal the sick."

"Are we going to the estate to get a mobile or the airmobile?" Danni asked.

"No. God spoke to me and said we are to take nothing for the journey, not even a walking stick, a traveler's bag, food or jupes, or even a change of clothes."

Danni laughed. "I own ninety-four mobiles and you own more than a hundred. You're telling me we have to walk all over Jupiter?"

"That's what it means."

"You know what else it means, don't you?" Danni said with a sly grin.

"What?" Tom retorted.

"It means it's going to be a long time before you get that kiss."

* * *

The End of the 1260 Days

The Antichrist rose to power halfway through Danni and Tom's journey to the ends of Jupiter. He pursued them all along the way, sending enemies to kill them, but to no avail. God protected them so that no weapon formed against them could prosper. That didn't mean there weren't hardships.

The Antichrist established himself as the sole ruler of Jupiter. Bastion was his name. He instilled a process for buying and selling called a currency mark. The Bible called it the *mark of the beast*. No one could buy or sell without that mark. Tom and Danni refused it.

Collectively, they were worth close to a hundred billion jupes. The short selling of the market had been a windfall, increasing their assets by a hundred-fold. Yet they refused to transfer their wealth into the world's system, leaving their billions worthless. So, they had to constantly trust in the Lord.

In almost every city, town, and village someone took them in, fed them, and gave them a place to sleep. At the places that didn't, they went to the edge of the town and shook the dust off their feet, symbolically and literally bringing a curse on the town.

For more than three years, they traveled the far reaches of the planet, preaching the good news of the coming of Christ. God was adding to their numbers daily.

One day Tom came to Danni and said, "It's time to go back to Red Spot."

"I know," she said. "The time of prophesying is coming to an end. I have mixed emotions. On the one hand, I love being with the people. But I'm also tired and ready to go home."

"The Antichrist will be waiting for us," Tom said. The Prince of Darkness had established his rule at the center seat of Jupiter in Red Spot. He controlled the entire world, except those who were Christians who refused to bow down and serve him. They were being put to death and persecuted by the thousands as he ruthlessly sought to kill all who opposed him.

"God showed me in a dream that the square was the exact spot where Jesus was killed for the sins of the world," Danni said.

Tom was amazed. No one knew exactly where that spot was.

"When the 1260 days are over," Danni said, "God will no longer protect us. We may die as well."

"I'm not afraid," Tom said. "We'll walk right into the square and face Bastion. God's will be done.

"I'm not afraid either. But I want to go home first."

"Is there a home left to go to?" Tom asked. "Our homes may have been destroyed and our friends... killed." They did not carry their mobiles with them. They'd had no contact with anyone in Red Spot since they left.

"Let's go find out."

45

They walked up to the Pinkerton Estate gate exactly 1260 days after God first called them to preach in the square. From the entrance, the home looked the same. However, they didn't see any activity at the house.

"I wonder if anyone will recognize us," Tom said laughing.

He was right. They both looked twenty-years older. Their clothes were tattered and worn. He needed a shave. His once perfectly dyed and sculpted hair, for years cared for by one of the top hairdressers in the world, was now mussed, graying, and down to his shoulders.

"We do look pitiful," Danni joked. "I can't wait to get in the shower and sleep in my own bed."

"Do you remember the gate code?" Tom asked.

"I do. But it's probably been changed." Danni entered the four-digit code and the gate opened. "It worked!" Danni exclaimed. "Is it safe to go in?"

"I don't know. Bastion may have seized the house."

Danni knew that God's protection ended when the time of prophesying ended on the 1260th day. But she didn't know if it lasted until midnight or if it had already left them.

"There's only one way to find out," Danni said as she walked through the gate and up the driveway toward the house in full stride. God's miraculous protection may have run out, but that didn't mean God would forsake them. At any rate, she wasn't afraid of the Antichrist. The only thing he could do was take her life which meant she would go to be with Jesus and her family sooner. Today would be fine with her if that were to happen.

They made it thirty feet down the driveway, when Bruno came around the corner of the house. When he saw them, he bolted toward them and jumped on Danni at full speed, knocking her to the ground. He licked her face profusely, hovering over her and not letting her stand up. Her face was wet from his kisses.

"I'm happy to see you, too, Bruno!" Danni said, wiping her face on her sleeve only to have him lick her again. She finally managed to get to her feet, but that didn't calm him. His tail was wagging, and he bounced back and forth between Danni and Tom.

"Where is everybody?" Danni asked Bruno.

As if on cue, a young woman appeared at the front door of the house. Tall and blonde with sea blue eyes. Three years older but easily recognizable.

Liz.

Liz's eyes widened when she saw them and recognized who they were. She held a toddler on her hip. Probably about two-or three-years old.

Danni's mouth flew open when three more appeared in the doorway and grabbed hold of her leg, shyly, obviously looking for her to protect them from the strangers. They were all the same age.

"Who are those kids?" Danni asked Tom incredibly.

"Let's go find out."

***

One by one, everyone started arriving home a few hours later, giving Danni and Tom enough time to shower and change and get a good meal. For the first time in three years, Danni felt normal.

They sat around the living room as Liz explained about the kids and talked nonstop about everything that had happened since they'd been gone. If possible, the house and estate looked better than when they left it. Liz said it was because of Carter. He did everything. Provided security, maintenance to the house, and kept the food pantry stocked. They couldn't have survived the famine without him.

Carter and Taylor were the first to arrive. Before they could greet Tom and Danni properly, their little one, Rave, demanded all of their attention, which they freely lavished on him. Danni couldn't help but notice how good Taylor looked and how happy the couple seemed. Considering where they'd been, the survival of their marriage was nothing short of miraculous. The transformation was unbelievable. Something only God could do.

"Bastion controls everything," Carter explained, when they had a chance to really sit down and talk. "He killed everyone in the Prescom's administration and now runs everything from a throne he established in the government building."

"He killed everyone?" Danni asked. "Including Aria?" Aria was the Director of Human Relations for the Prescom. She was saved at the first meeting at the Red Spot Christian Church. Her position in the government was invaluable in helping them build the church and run their two witnesses radio show.

"No. Aria is alive," Carter said. "She's hiding over at Tom's house."

"Thank the Lord," Tom said, which Danni echoed.

Carter explained his intricate security plan to protect everyone. It was brilliantly conceived, and the Antichrist had left them alone, for the most part. No soldiers were willing to come down the road after what happened to the men and trucks who were disintegrated by the storm cloud three years before.

"Bastion did cut off the water and electricity to the property," Carter said.

"What did you do?"

"I constructed a generator," he said proudly. "It powers the entire house. I purchased enough gasoline to keep it running. I took the supply out of the storage tank." Mrs. Pinkerton had built a couple large storage tanks to supply gas to her ninety-four mobiles. That's what Carter was referring to.

"I replenished it, though. They're full right now. I go and get the gas whenever there's supply. They never turned off the power to your house," Carter said, looking at Tom.

"What about water? There's been a drought," Tom asked.

"I drilled wells," Carter answered. "Here and over at your house. We dug deep enough to get under the water table, even though it's been going down."

"How much food do you have left?" Danni asked.

"We have enough for at least seven more years."

Danni let out a gasp of amazement.

"We're using the excess for the poor and needy," Carter said.

Before the mark of the beast was instituted, Carter explained that he had taken some of the billions left behind by Tom and Danni and set up a vast distribution network to stock food pantries all across Red Spot in anticipation of the effects of the drought and famine.

"I hope you don't mind," Carter said. "I used some of your jupes. But there were a lot of people in need. I didn't know if you would come back or not."

"We don't mind at all," Tom said, looking at Danni before answering for her.

Naomi and Kate arrived next and were stunned to see them. Liz had said they were at the homeless shelter serving a meal. They had somehow managed to keep the shelter open and provided meals every day for thousands of men, women and children from the food supplied by Carter. The group of them had become a well-organized team.

"God is so good," Naomi said. "Every day we make two pots of soup or some kind of stew served with two loaves of bread. We have two tables set up. I stand at one and Kate at the other."

Danni and Tom were listening intently. Danni's heart warmed to see that the work of the Lord was continuing without them.

"What's amazing," Ruth added, "is that the soup and bread never run out. We always have leftovers."

"What do you mean?" Danni asked.

"We keep scooping out the soup, but the pot never runs dry until the people have had enough to eat," Ruth said. "The Lord just keeps miraculously filling it until everyone is full."

"The bread, too!" Naomi said. "We break the bread, and it multiplies. Like when Jesus fed the five thousand. Every day we have enough food to feed more than five thousand people with just two pots of stew and two loaves of bread."

They heard the door open and close, and Dr. King and Olivia came in with Aria. They had swung by Tom's place to pick her up after Liz called to let her know that Danni and Tom were back. She said she had to see them.

Matthew and Olivia King's little girl, Donna, threw herself into her mother's arms as soon as she walked in and didn't leave her for one second. They had been at the hospital. Dr. King had used some of their jupes to reopen the hospital after the plague and now provided free community health care at the facility. It started small, but they now delivered twenty to thirty babies a day and provided healthcare to hundreds of women.

"How does it feel being a mother?" Danni asked Ruth, Taylor, and Olivia.

"I can't even describe it." Ruth said. Tears formed in her eyes as she said it.

"I know," Danni said. "You miss Jake and Kate." Jake was Ruth's husband and Kate her newborn who were taken in the disappearance, now almost four years ago.

Ruth nodded. As did everyone in the room. They had all lost someone. Danni included—her mother, father, brother, and sister were all taken.

"Tom and I want to talk to you about that," Danni said. "We don't have any reason to grieve. They are with Jesus. And we will see them soon."

"When will we see them?" Taylor asked.

"I'm glad you asked. Last night I had a dream. I want to tell you about it."

46

Word must have traveled fast that the two witnesses were back in the Prescomial Square because it had already begun to fill up with people. Both supporters of Danni and Tom and their enemies. The networks were scrambling to get cameras set up in the location with the best view possible.

Danni still thought of it as the Prescomial Square even though all of the statues of Prescom Wolf were gone. Replaced by various graven idols of Bastion, the Antichrist, the Prince of Darkness who had moved from the shadows of the spiritual where he unleashed his havoc on mankind for centuries, into the physical where he now ruled the world in a human form.

Danni knew from Scripture that Bastion's reign would be coming to an end, soon. In the meantime, he had the power to rule the world, basically unrestrained.

Today was the last day of prophesying. As was their divine protection, that would run out at the same time as the assignment. There were no regrets. She had dutifully carried out to the best of her ability. As had Tom, who looked over at her with a faint smile. He knew what was about to unfold as well.

The protection was still in place, though. A couple of bounty hunters arrived shortly after they did. The two of them hid behind a makeshift barrier just a few yards away and aimed weapons at them. Danni saw them first and yelled a warning to Tom. When they fired the guns, the weapons exploded in their faces, blinding them. As they lay writhing on the ground, the spirit of the Lord slayed them with the sword of his mouth.

Their bodies were dragged away. The crowd was murmuring, warning others not to try the same thing.

"How much longer will that protection last?" Danni wondered and asked Tom who had no idea either.

"I hope it continues a little longer," he said nervously pointing to the hundreds of soldiers who came out of the government building and were heading to the square. They were clearly Antichrist soldiers, heavily armed, and were moving with a purpose.

Bastion obviously knew they were there. He would make an appearance soon as well, Danni figured. But when?

She looked out on the square and at the clocktower that dominated it.

5:45 p.m.

It suddenly occurred to her. Observances in the Bible ended at 6:00 p.m. or sundown, not midnight. That must be when their protection would run out. It's also when her power to prophecy would end as well.

Was she right? If so, she had to hurry. But the cameras weren't set up yet. She wanted the world to hear the message of her dream.

A panic swept through her. Would she have enough time? For 1260 days, time never seemed to be an issue. It seemed like a lifetime. Now that Danni was nearing the end and had an important message to relay to the people, time suddenly became her enemy.

I need more time.

That must be what it was like for most people when they near death, Danni mused. How many people wished they had more time? Those who were seized were fortunate. It happened in the blink of an eye. So fast, they had no time to consider time. Danni laughed at that thought and the play on words.

The people seized were also blessed that they did not die. Danni shuddered at a thought that suddenly dominated her mind.

Am I about to die?

5:50 p.m.

Was ten minutes enough time? She wanted to yell at the camera crews to hurry up.

Tom came and stood right next to her. He must have sensed her angst. Maybe he realized time was running out as well. He gave her a nod as if to say it was time to begin. After all the days spent together, they could almost read each other's minds.

5:53 p.m.

She had to start the prophecy. Otherwise, it would be too late. Just as she began to speak, the green light on the top of one camera flickered on. At least one network was live and would capture her words. She suddenly felt the power of the Holy Spirit come upon her as he had many times over the last 1260 days.

"Men and women of Jupiter listen to my words," Danni began with authority. A hush went over the crowd. "The time of desolation is near. You see all of the buildings, statues, and adornments before you in the square. A time is coming when it will all be destroyed. Every stone in this square will be toppled upon itself by a large quake. One tenth of all buildings in Red Spot will be destroyed in three days."

A collective groan filled the square. The suffering on Jupiter had already been devastating. Before the Seizure, eighty billion people lived on the planet. Now it was less than ten.

5:58 p.m.

Many in the crowd began to revile them with angry words. One of Bastion's armed men took his spear and hurled it toward Danni. Tom yelled a warning, but the spear was already in the air. An angel of the Lord intercepted it as it fell harmlessly to the ground. The man who threw it was struck down and died. The crowd let out a loud gasp. Some reporters with handheld cameras rushed to get a close up of the scene.

They were still protected.

But for how long?

Tom tried to quiet the crowd. Danni noticed that all the cameras were live. That was good. They would capture their last words. The most important ones.

"Let her speak," Tom implored. Others in the crowd shouted down the mob as well.

When the din subsided, Danni began to speak again. Slowly. Deliberately. Her words were measured but strong.

"Immediately after the quake, twelve volcanoes will erupt all across Jupiter," Danni said. "So that the sun will be darkened, and the moons will no longer give off their light. Darkness will cover the world and two-thirds of the inhabitants of Jupiter will perish. Only a third will be left."

5:59 p.m.

Bastion arrived with a flare. He was tall, muscular, and good looking by worldly standards. His eyes were like coals of fire, filled with hate. He was within ten feet of them in seconds.

"Bastion is the prince of the power of the air, who seeks only to kill, steal, and destroy each of you," Tom said pointing an accusing finger at him.

"Do not listen to them," Bastion cried out. "They are the ones who destroy you. They prophesy death and destruction. I bring you life and hope, peace and prosperity."

"Lies," Tom shouted at the top of his lungs. "Even though we prophesy the plagues, quakes, locusts, famines, and droughts, Satan is the one who brings them upon you. He wants to kill every person on Jupiter."

The clock tower began to toll drawing everyone's attention to it.

6:00 p.m.

"Do not fear," Danni said, knowing that her protection was gone. She felt it in her spirit.

"Listen to my words, those of you who love Jesus," Danni cried out as tears were filling her eyes. Her hands shook, and her voice was quivering.

At the mention of the name of Jesus, Bastion suddenly cowered. He quickly recovered his strength, and Danni could see that every muscle in his body was tense. Danni assumed that Bastion didn't know that their protection was gone. That was what restrained him.

Danni was emboldened as she realized they had more time. At least until Bastion figured it out or became so overwhelmed with rage that he threw all caution to the wind and attacked anyway. Danni was determined to fan those flames even if it provoked him to wrath.

"Bastion and his minions will lay hands on you and persecute you," Danni said as a smile came over her face as she remembered who she was and where she had come from. Only a few short years ago, she was a rebellious teenager, breaking her parent's rules, skipping school, dreading having to go to church. Now she was a prophetess, having led tens of millions of people into a relationship with the Lord.

Now... she was face to face with Satan himself.

"They will deliver you up to prisons and some even to death," Danni said in a loud voice. "You will be brought before the Antichrist and his rulers for his name sake. It will be an opportunity for testimony." These words were coming from her heart not from the prophecies.

She could see the anger building in Bastion. His fists were clenched, his eyes were filled with fury.

Tom stepped closer to Danni as Bastion's soldiers began to surround them. Bastion was only a couple of steps away now.

"Therefore, settle it in your hearts not to meditate beforehand on what you will say or how you will answer their charges," Danni said, unafraid. "For the Lord, your God will give you a mouth and wisdom which all of your adversaries will not be able to contradict or resist."

The tension in the square was rising like a volcano about to explode. Danni thought of the volcanoes that were at that very moment building to an eruption. She could feel that all of Jupiter was straining under the physical and spiritual battle that was taking place.

Tom began to speak. "You will be betrayed by parents and brothers, relatives and friends. And many of you will be put to death."

Then peace enveloped her, slicing through the chaos and fear.

Danni imagined that millions of people who had come to the Lord through their journey were listening to their words right now. She thought of Taylor and Carter, Matthew and Olivia, Liz, Naomi and Ruth, Aria, their friends who stood by them until the end. They would be watching right now. She almost wished they weren't.

I must encourage them.

"Seize them!" Bastion said to his soldiers. But none would attack. They just stood there paralyzed in fear. Some were even shaking. They had no doubt seen the many who were struck down when they dared to try to kill the two witnesses. How could they know that Danni and Tom were no longer under the protection of the angels?

"But not a hair on your head will be lost," Danni shouted, sensing their hesitation. She was no longer speaking to Jupiter warning them of the plagues. That time had passed. She wanted to spend her last moments encouraging those who believed.

Bastion let out a loud, eerie, blood curdling scream. He grabbed one of the soldier's swords and pushed him aside lunging at Tom thrusting the sword at him. Instinctively, Tom turned to the side and put his arm out to block the attack.

Danni screamed.

The sword struck a glancing blow on his arm, but the blade was at just the right angle to cause a gash down the side of it. Blood squirted out like spray out of a bottle. Tom's wounded arm went limp, hanging by his side.

Bastion turned his attention on Danni. He lifted his arms high above his head, both hands clutching the sword. Danni stood her ground and braced for the blow that never came.

Even with a bad arm, Tom put himself between Bastion and her. As the sword came down, it hit him and not her, slashing through his head, splitting it open. He fell to the ground in a heap.

The whole scene played out in slow motion. Tom's body landed in a thud. His skull cracked against the concrete. Danni knew he was dead. She bent down next to him and took Tom in her arms. Tears were flowing down her cheeks, his blood covered her clothes and hands as she pulled him close, into her chest.

Bastion was laughing hysterically. The soldiers seemed emboldened that one of the witnesses was killed. They seized Danni and tried to drag her away, but she wouldn't release her hands that were still clutching Tom tightly.

Finally, they were able to pry her away from him. They dragged her by the hair to the center of the square. Blood was oozing from the cuts and scrapes from her arms and legs that were scraped across the concrete.

They stood her to her feet and displayed her to the crowd. They held her arms as she struggled to free them. A wave of fear hit her like a sledgehammer. She fought it away. They would not see her afraid.

The urge to flee or pull away from her captors was overwhelming. She resisted it. Not that there was no fight in her or that she knew the situation was hopeless. The world was watching. She had just told the followers of Christ to not be afraid and that not one hair on their heads would be lost. Her actions needed to match her words.

She quit fighting and let them control her.

They might take my life, but they can't take my faith.

"Father forgive them for they know not what they do," Danni said as she bowed her head to pray.

Danni put her shoulders back and her head toward heaven as they dragged her over to a lamppost and tied her to it.

Tom's lifeless body was strapped to a post nearby.

Danni knew that death would not come for her as quickly as it had for Tom.

47

Three days later

Carter had watched in horror from the living room of the Pinkerton Estate as Bastion overpowered Tom and killed him in the public square and then tortured Danni unmercifully for more than six hours. Everyone else in the house refused to watch. Even Dr. Matthew King said that he'd seen enough death at his hospital to last him for two lifetimes and couldn't bear to watch what the Antichrist might do to his beloved Pastors, Danni and Tom.

The brutality was worse than Carter could have ever imagined. As a special operations soldier, he'd seen the ravages of war. Nothing compared to what unfolded on the screen.

After Danni finally gave up her spirit and died, Carter went to the square to try and get their bodies for burial, but the authorities refused. They intended to keep the bodies on display indefinitely. When Carter protested, he was detained and feared for his own life. With his training, he was able to free himself from the guards and disappear into the crowd and return home.

He realized it was a foolish thing to do. His wife and new son needed him, and everyone living at the Pinkerton Estate were counting on him to get them through the coming two years that would be the worst days of the Tribulation according to Danni.

So, he just continued to watch helplessly from his living room, his anger building with each passing day.

* * *

For three and a half days, people from all over Jupiter traveled to the square to gaze upon the bodies. Many came to ridicule and gloat over Danni and Tom because they had tormented them and caused so much destruction on Jupiter.

Others came to mourn. The Christians whose lives had been touched by their ministry, risked their own lives to bring flowers and gifts and lay them at their lampposts. Some were arrested and taken away, maybe even to their death. Still, thousands of believers made the journey to honor the two witnesses while taking a risk of possibly facing the same brutality.

Tom and Danni taught that there was a martyr's reward in heaven and that they were not to be afraid of Bastion.

That's why Carter was back at the square. He came with the blessing of Taylor, his wife. No one in the house could stand to see what the Antichrist was doing to Danni and Tom, and he had vowed to put a stop to it. He stood away at a distance, surveying the scene, creating a tactical plan. Armed, he was determined to use force if necessary, to seize the bodies and take them back for a proper burial.

His resolve became even stronger when he saw the abhorrent conditions of the bodies. Danni and Tom were still strapped to the lampposts. Danni's appearance was so marred, she was beyond any appearance of human likeness. Tom was unrecognizable if Carter hadn't known it was him.

The righteous fire of indignation raged inside of him. He touched the gun he'd concealed in his coat and considered a full-on frontal assault but thought better of it. While the soldiers weren't really guarding the bodies, they were close enough that he would be gunned down before he got to them.

He needed a distraction.

Then he got one.

* * *

At first, it was a slight movement of the arm. Carter blinked his eyes hard, twice, and stared at Danni, thinking he'd imagined it.

Then a woman screamed and fainted. Carter scanned the square. Several were pointing at Danni. Her eyes blinked. Several times. Then opened. Carter knew that bodies on the battlefield sometimes did that, so he didn't immediately process what was happening. Muscle memory often caused twitches and unusual movements from people who had been dead for several days.

He realized it was more than muscle twitches when Danni raised her head and was looking around like she was trying to get her bearings. The straps holding her to the lampposts suddenly fell to the ground. Carter instinctively ran toward her to catch her fall.

Danni didn't fall. She was suspended in the air where she hovered for several seconds and then was slowly lowered to the ground. How, Carter had no idea? A supernatural force was controlling her movements.

Angels?

At that moment, Tom began to shake his head violently from side to side. He let out a cough.

Terror filled the square as people ran away.

The straps that bound Tom fell away as well. He was lowered to the ground like he was attached to wires from above him like what Carter had seen at a circus and like what happened to Danni.

Carter rushed to them. They recognized him immediately. He wanted to grab them in a tight embrace but was concerned about their wounds. To his amazement, there were no wounds. Their faces were no longer marred. The only evidence of the brutal treatment were the stains on their clothes. While he hesitated to touch them, they didn't, as they took him in their arms and hugged him tightly.

Carter touched their hair and faces, trying to convince himself what he was seeing was real. "I thought I was seeing a ghost!" Carter said, excitedly.

"We aren't ghosts," Danni said. "We are very much alive."

"It's a miracle." Those who were believers in the square hadn't run away. They were collectively praising God with their hands raised and their voices lifted in mutual worship.

Carter's training kicked in, and he looked around to see if there were any threats. There were none. Everyone else had fled. The soldiers were all running back to the government building next to the square. Even the camera crews scattered, dropping their equipment, and leaving it. One lone man stood his ground and continued filming.

"Hurry," Carter said. "Let's go back to the house where you'll be safe."

"We can't go to the house," Danni replied.

"If you stay here, it's only a matter of time until Bastion comes after you," Carter retorted. "At the house, I can protect you. I can't here."

"Listen very carefully," Danni said as she began to give Carter instructions.

∗∗

A few minutes later, as expected, Bastion came storming out of the government building and started sprinting toward the square. Hundreds of armed soldiers followed him.

"You have to go," Tom said to Carter.

"They'll kill you," Carter said.

"Go!" Danni yelled, pushing Carter away.

He hesitated. Bastion had already entered the square. It was too late for Carter to escape. They'd gun him down before he could get ten feet.

Less than a hundred feet from them, Bastion came to a stop and motioned for his soldiers to take aim. The soldiers lifted their rifles and prepared to fire.

"Give yourselves up," Bastion said. "I killed you once, I'll kill you again. This time it won't be so quickly."

Carter drew his gun even though he was outmanned by insurmountable odds. Danni screamed for him not to. Carter ignored her. As he took aim to fire, the ground suddenly began to shake. A slight tremor at first, then it was like an ocean wave that started at one end of the square and carried to the other. Carter almost lost his footing. Some of the soldiers did.

Bastion yelled for them to fire. When they did, their shots were erratic. Some went in the air. Other volleys of bullets fell harmlessly away from them. The soldiers couldn't take direct aim with all the vibrations that were growing in intensity. This was an opportunity for Carter to run, but he couldn't make himself leave Tom and Danni.

Then a loud voice came down from heaven. "Come up here," the voice said. They all looked up to the sky, including Bastion and the soldiers.

Danni grabbed Carter's hand, getting his attention. She smiled at him reassuringly. "Go!" she said.

Danni let go of his hand as Tom reached out and grabbed hers. Tom and Danni suddenly rose in the air. Slowly at first, then rapidly. They went up into heaven in a cloud while their enemies looked on.

Carter was already moving. Running away. Using the distraction to make his escape. Bastion saw him and shouted to his men to open fire. Carter could feel the rounds bouncing off of the concrete around his feet with a loud crack of fire and sound. His path was serpentine, not by design, but by the moving ground that kept swaying him back and forth, almost causing him to lose his balance and fall. Also making him a harder target to hit.

Out of the corner of his eye, he could see several soldiers sprinting from the square at an angle, trying to cut him off. He heard another rapid volley of pops, explosions that sounded like fireworks going off. The sound was familiar to him. He'd heard it many times in battle.

Generally, there's a fog of war in a firefight, but in this case, Carter's senses were heightened, and he could see everything clearly. He evaluated his options. If he stayed on his current path, he'd intersect with the soldiers near the south exit. So, he changed direction. The path was longer to his mobile, but if he sprinted fast enough, he could get to the parking lot through the north exit before the soldiers knew where he went.

His pursuers changed their direction as well, taking a more direct path to him. That forced Carter to go further to the north of the exit than he wanted to. He came to a big embankment. The quake was gaining intensity. The ground shook, and he lost his footing on the hill and he tumbled down it. The jolt to his shoulder sent a searing pain through his body.

The fall cost him valuable time. The soldiers were able to take the lower sidewalk avoiding the steep embankment. They were closing in. He couldn't make it to the exit. His only option was to traverse a wall nearly ten-feet tall. He wasn't sure he could do it with the throbbing in his shoulder.

He didn't have to.

The ground jerked violently. And then in the distance, he saw it. The volcano just to the north of Red Spot erupted. A fire cloud rose in the air like a bomb going off, brightening the sky even that far away. Carter stopped in his tracks to see the wondrous sight. The soldiers did the same.

The ground shook so hard that Carter was thrown to the ground again. The soldiers began running the other direction as the massive cloud started building over the volcano. Carter followed them with his weapon drawn. They never looked back. While they headed back to the building for safety, Carter veered to the left, through the south exit, and out to the parking lot where he got into his mobile and sped away.

* * *

He pulled into the driveway of the Pinkerton Estate just as the plume of ash and lava rock began to rain down on Red Spot. He could see Taylor at the window.

Taylor looked out the window and then burst out of the door and was at the mobile before he could get out.

"I was so worried about you," Taylor said, grabbing his arm and pulling him out. She threw her arms around him as soon as he was standing next to her.

"Let's get inside," Carter said. "I'll tell you all about it."

Once in the house, Carter stripped off his shirt. Olivia wiped off the black ash from his hair and face. Dr. King examined his shoulder and determined it was just a strain. He treated the small burns on his arms and face. When the ash fell and landed on his skin, it acted like acid and caused small burns.

Everyone gathered in the living room. They'd watched everything on the vision set, including the resurrection of Danni and Tom. They saw Carter in the square talking to them and were anxious to know what happened and what they said.

Carter said. "I still wouldn't believe it if I hadn't seen it with my own eyes."

"What happened to Tom and Danni?" Naomi asked. "On the vision screen, they just disappeared."

"A voice from heaven called for them. I saw them rise through the air and into a cloud. I think they're in heaven."

"Did they say anything?" Ruth asked.

"They did. They told me what we're supposed to do," Carter answered.

"What did they say?"

"Don't go out of the house except for food or water."

"For how long?"

"Until we hear a trumpet sound."

48

September 11, 2068

3:30 p.m.

Seven Years After the Seizure

Everyone heard the sound of the trumpet, even the kids, who came running into the family room, along with the adults who were startled by the loud and vibrant blast.

Carter went to the windows and opened the blinds which had been closed since the volcanoes erupted. Rays of sunshine burst through the windows and flooded the room with light. Several people began to cry as the reality of what was happening settled in.

They all knew the promises. The Bible said Jesus would come back to Jupiter after the seven-year tribulation was over. They all believed it by faith. That didn't make the wait any easier or the doubts any harder to overcome. The house was large and massive but after a while their nerves became frayed and tempers were short.

When the trumpet finally sounded and sunshine returned, they were overwhelmed with tears all around the room. They'd been quarantined in that house for more than two years. Not even able to go outside for longer than a few minutes, and that was with their faces covered with masks. The volcanoes had darkened the skies and filled the air with all kinds of toxins and deadly materials.

Now Carter felt like they were finally free, and a huge relief came over him. He carried the burden of protecting, feeding, and providing them with shelter for several years. Their long nightmare was finally coming to an end.

"Let's go outside," someone said.

They ran out of the house and into the backyard where everyone danced around and hugged each other effusively.

Eventually, they fell into the chairs on the patio, exhausted, but happy.

"You seem different," Taylor said to Carter a few minutes later.

They were sitting around in a circle—Dr. King and Olivia, Naomi and Ruth, and Liz.

The kids were playing in the yard. Bruno was bounding around with them.

"I feel different," Carter said.

"So, do I," Olivia added as did her husband Matthew.

"I don't feel any anxiety," Ruth said.

"Me either," Naomi agreed. "Come to think of it, my arthritis is gone."

Naomi had developed severe joint pain over the two years of isolation. The medicines stockpiled in the emergency storage weren't powerful enough to blunt the pain.

She raised her arm above her head and circled it in an arc in every direction. "I couldn't do that yesterday," Naomi said, smiling.

"It's like all my burdens are lifted," Olivia said.

"That's to be expected," Carter replied. "We've been cooped up in the house for two years."

"It's more than that," Taylor said. "I can't quite put my finger on it."

The night before, Carter and Taylor had an argument. They'd gone to bed angry with each other. The animosity had carried over into today. Now, all animosity was gone. All the past hurts and future worries had disappeared when the sunshine returned.

"Doesn't the Bible say that the thousand-year reign starts when the trumpet sounds?" Matthew asked.

"It does," Naomi answered. "It also says that Satan is restrained. There's no more evil in the world."

"That's what it is!" Olivia said exuberantly. "That's what we're all feeling."

Carter felt it too. It was an overwhelming love and joy. Everyone was at peace. He could see it on their faces as the tension had left their countenances.

"Look at the kids," Ruth said, pointing out to the yard.

Everyone turned and looked. The kids had a ball and were kicking it around. Taking turns sharing it.

"They're all so happy," Ruth continued. "Look how well they're playing together. I haven't heard one of them fuss or start crying yet. By now, they'd be fighting over the ball."

"You're right," Taylor said. Her son, Rave, was one of the biggest instigators. The tallest of the group, he often tried to dominate them. He was out there playing with everyone else, kicking the ball, chasing it down, giving it to the others, and doing it with a huge smile on his face.

They played for two hours. Not one parent had to say one word to any of the kids.

"I'm going to like the Millennium," Carter said.

They all nodded in agreement.

* * *

Bruno heard the honking horn first. He took off running around the house and everyone followed. A mobile was coming up the driveway. Carter recognized it as a vehicle from Tom's garage. The mobile came to a stop. The doors opened, and the occupants started filing out.

Danni!

She was the first out of the mobile. Then an older man, a woman, a boy, and a teenage girl. When Danni saw her friends, she ran right to where they were congregated and threw herself into the first available arms.

After lots of hugs and kisses and brushing aside tears, she introduced everyone. "This is my father, Lindsey, my mother Nancy, my brother Todd, and my sister Avery."

"This is Carter and Taylor," Danni said. "Ruth and Naomi," she continued. "Dr. Matthew King and his wife Olivia. And you know Liz."

"We've heard a lot about all of you," Nancy said, taking Liz in her arms and giving her a gentle, but affectionate squeeze.

They all had to hug each other, which took some time, since it was a big group.

The parents introduced their kids.

"This must be Bruno!" Danni's father said, bending down so he was face-to-face with the massive dog. "You're bigger than I even imagined you to be," he said. Bruno lavished the attention and treated Lindsey like he was his long-lost owner. Carter noticed a change in Bruno as well. All of his mean streak was gone. He seemed as gentle as a lamb.

Everyone looked toward the entrance to the driveway as another mobile pulled in, blaring its horn like the one before it.

Before it could come to a stop, Ruth ran full speed toward it.

"Jake!" she cried out. Jake was her husband taken during the Seizure. She hadn't seen him for seven years.

His door flew open before the vehicle came to a complete stop, and he got out and met her as she took a big leap into his arms and wrapped her legs around him. She kissed him profusely. Tears streamed down her face. His as well.

"I've missed you, so much," she said. "I can't tell you how much I've missed you. I can't believe you're here."

The crowd of people came down the driveway and surrounded them.

"There's someone else here who desperately wants to see you," Jake said as he released his hold on Ruth.

Ruth turned to look back at the mobile. Kate had just emerged from it. Though six months old when she was seized, she had a spiritual adult-like body while still maintaining her child-like features in her face. She could walk, talk, and function as well as the rest of them.

"Mom!" she cried out.

"Oh, my baby!" Ruth said, holding her arms out and erupting in tears. Kate ran into her mother's embrace.

"Let me look at you," Ruth said, pushing her back so Kate was at arms-length but close enough to where she could still hold her.

Naomi wiped away the tears from her eyes with her arm still around Jake. Ruth got her attention. "Kate, this is your Nana," she said, introducing Naomi to her.

"I know," Kate said in a sweet voice as Naomi took Kate into her arms.

Naomi was so focused on her son and granddaughter that she didn't see the man coming up behind her. He'd been in the back seat on the passenger side and had gotten out of the mobile last.

Carter figured it was her husband, Carl, who'd also been seized.

"Do you remember me?" Carl said, tapping Naomi on the shoulder.

Her mouth flew open into a wide smile as she wrapped her arms around his neck.

"I do remember you," Naomi said between sobs. "Although I'm still mad at you. You left without saying goodbye," she said as she patted him playfully on the chest.

Carter knew Naomi was joking, but he also knew that things were different. He didn't think they could get mad at each other in the Millennium like they did before.

Before they could go back to the house, a steady stream of mobiles pulled into the driveway with horns blaring.

Aria was in the next mobile to arrive. Then Tom and his parents, Randy, and Carol.

A third mobile carried Joshua, Dr. King and Olivia's newborn, who was taken from her womb. Somehow, his parents knew him as soon as they saw him, even though they'd never met in person before the Seizure.

After their own tearful reunion, they introduced Joshua to his brother.

No one wanted to rush this moment. They spent several minutes on the driveway, barely able to contain their excitement. Eventually, the kids took off running into the backyard to play.

Everyone else went to the back patio and spent the next few hours talking and laughing. That night they had a huge feast. Before today, Carter had rationed food. He was always so careful to make sure nothing was wasted. That night, no one cared. Everyone ate and drank all they wanted until they were full.

The conversation continued non-stop. Those who'd been behind on Jupiter recounted the trials and tribulations of the last seven years. Those from heaven fascinated the others with descriptions of heaven, the pearly gates, the marriage supper of the lamb, and life with Jesus.

They described the Seizure and how they were caught up into heaven. Then they related how Jesus brought them back that afternoon. The whole throng of them. The trumpet sounded, the clouds opened, and they descended back onto Jupiter.

"What was that like?" Matthew King asked.

"It's hard to describe," Tom said. "It only took a blink of the eye, and we were back on Jupiter. All of us returned to my house. That's where we got the mobiles and then came over here."

"Where is Jesus?" Carter asked.

"He's at the square," Danni answered. "When he returned, he waged war with Bastion and destroyed all of the strongholds he'd set up on Jupiter. All the graven images and idols have been demolished."

Everyone was silent for a couple minutes to let that sink in.

"Carter, you did an amazing job taking care of everything around here," Danni said.

The whole group clapped and nodded in agreement.

"She's right," Dr. King said. "If we didn't have that food storage, I don't know what we would've done."

Carter suddenly sat up in his chair in such a way that startled the others.

"Where's Mrs. Pinkerton?"

The group from heaven quieted and became somber.

"She didn't go to heaven," Danni finally said. "She was never saved."

That put a damper on the evening. There would be no sorrow in heaven, but there was still sorrow in the Millennium. They just didn't have the evil working against them.

Pastor Lindsey Howell, Danni's father tried to explain it to them. "I always found that people like Mrs. Pinkerton were the most difficult to reach. They think they're saved but aren't. Believing something that's a lie is the biggest obstacle there was to finding salvation. Other gods. Other religions. jupes. People put those before the one true God."

"That's why Jesus said it was hard for a rich person to get saved," Tom said.

"I think it was more than that with Mrs. Pinkerton," Lindsey explained. "It is hard for a rich person, but Mrs. Pinkerton's problem was that she relied on her own good works. That's a mistake a lot of people make. It's not about how good we think we are."

"I think she knew deep down that something was missing," Danni said. "That's why she was so judgmental. To cover up for her own shortcomings. It's easy to look at the splinter in another person's eye and not deal with the log in your own."

"That's such a good point," Lindsey said. "It's all about Christ. What he did on the cross. The thing is that Mrs. Pinkerton knew the

Bible backward and forward. Belief was not the problem. Accepting God's grace was. She relied more on her own works."

Lindsey related that when Mrs. Pinkerton died, she went to the judgment seat, and her name was blotted out of the Book of Life. She was cast into the lake of fire set aside for the demons and for Satan himself. There she perished. Her soul was destroyed for an eternity.

"I do appreciate what she did for our daughter," Nancy said thoughtfully, referring to Danni.

"She gave me this beautiful house," Danni said tearfully.

"It was like an ark for all of us," Carter said. "It saved our lives."

No one talked for several minutes as if out of respect for Mrs. Pinkerton. Danni finally changed the subject and the mood. "By the way, don't plan anything for this weekend."

"Why?" Ruth asked. "What's going on?"

"There's going to be a wedding," Tom said, taking Danni by the hand.

"That's right!" Danni said. "We're getting married. And you're all invited."

The celebration returned in no time.

49

The day was like any other since the start of the Millennium. Sunny and a balmy seventy-two degrees. A gentle breeze blew from the south. Hundreds of people had gathered on the Pinkerton Estate to watch Danni and Tom become husband and wife. Millions more were watching by vision. The day was filled with great anticipation.

Danni thought that she and Tom were the unlikeliest of couples. Yet, their love was rooted in hardship and adventure unmatched by any couple who'd ever lived on Jupiter. Tom had commented the night before that if their commitment could survive what they'd been through, it could survive anything. She was sure he was right. This wedding was something she'd wanted for years. More than anything else she had ever wanted in her life.

Danni was in a room just off the back deck, preparing to walk out into the sunshine and down the aisle arm-in-arm with her dad. She was so glad her dad was there and that they'd waited to be married. Tom's dad was officiating the wedding. His grandparents were attending. All of those people had been in heaven and wouldn't have been able to be there if they hadn't waited. It seemed like God's timing had worked out perfectly.

"You are stunningly beautiful," Danni's dad said. "You look like your mother."

Danni wore an understated but delicate chiffon wedding dress, with beaded laced bodice and a sheer veil. Her long, flowing honey-colored hair was accented by her porcelain-white skin, courtesy of three years in heaven. Her bright green eyes were radiating, and her soft features didn't reflect the hardships she'd suffered during the tribulation. Again, three years in heaven had worked wonders on her complexion and what used to be her hard, determined de-meanor.

It had only been four days but living life with no evil influences to battle every day was beyond what she could even describe to someone who'd never experienced it. Unmatched only by the glory of heaven. There was no marriage in heaven, so in some ways, this was better. The thought of living a thousand years as Tom's wife warmed her heart to where it overflowed with joy.

The wedding procession had started several minutes before. It took so much longer to get to her, because everyone wanted to be a part of it. The four kids rescued from the hospital, and Kate and Joshua, led the way as flower bearers, junior bridesmaids, and groomsmen, and Bruno was the ring bearer, which was a risk in and of itself. Danni wished she'd been outside to see the spectacle of Bruno bounding down the aisle, with the rings around his neck. There was no telling what he did or who he stopped to see along the way.

Liz was her maid of honor, and Taylor, Olivia, and Ruth her bridesmaids. They were already in line outside. Naomi coordinated the wedding and flitted around, making sure everything went smoothly, which was what she was best at.

Naomi finally stuck her head in the door and said it was time.

Danni stepped out of the house as the music began playing her song. She took her dad's arm as she exited the door and Tom came into view, immediately. Her heart began to flutter. Or maybe it was the butterflies in her stomach. She wasn't sure. All she knew was that this was the happiest day of her life.

* * *

"Tom, do you take Danni, to be your wedded wife in the eyes of God? Do you promise to honor and cherish her for as long as you both shall live?" Tom's father asked.

"I do." Tom said, his voice cracking. Tom's hands were shaking when he put the ring on her finger a few seconds before.

She'd never seen him so nervous.

"Danni, do you take Tom to be your wedded husband in the eyes of God? Do you promise to honor and cherish him for as long as you both shall live?"

"Absolutely, yes," she said. "I do!" The crowd laughed at her exuberant response.

"Tom and Danni," he said, "It's my pleasure to pronounce you husband and wife. What God has joined together, let no man put asunder. You may now kiss your bride!"

"Finally," Tom said in a louder than normal voice. He lifted Danni's veil and looked deeply in her eyes. Danni started to giggle.

"I told you good things come to those who wait," Danni said to him with a wide smile.

Then she made sure it had been worth the wait.

THE EDEN STORIES

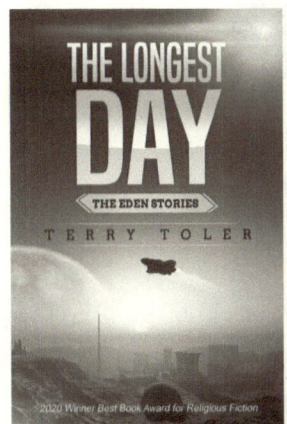

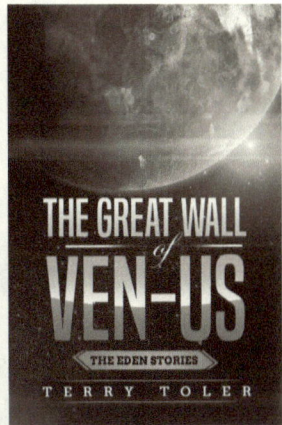

About the Author

TERRY TOLER is the author of *The Eden Stories* series, along with the Alex Halee and Jamie Austen book series. He is a minister, public speaker, counselor, and retired entrepreneur. Impacting the lives of people worldwide through storytelling has become one of his passions in life. He can be followed at terrytoler.com.

www.ingramcontent.com/pod-product-compliance
Lightning Source LLC
Chambersburg PA
CBHW051529250626
47156CB00001B/291